Qu...

A collection ... the world's le...

Three novels ... ...ernational bestselling author

CAROLINE ANDERSON

PRAISE FOR CAROLINE ANDERSON:

"*The Baby Bonding* by Caroline Anderson has an interesting story." — *Romantic Times BOOKReview*

"*The Pregnant Tycoon* is nicely grounded in an entertaining idea – businesswoman meets Mr Mom." —*Romantic Times BOOKReview*

"Caroline Anderson writes a deeply emotional exploration." —*Romantic Times BOOKReview* on *The Chemical Reaction*

"Caroline Anderson pens a charming romance between two emotionally deep characters in *With This Baby…*"—*Romantic Times BOOKReview*

MILLS & BOON
100 YEARS
of pure reading pleasure

100 Reasons to Celebrate

We invite you to join us in celebrating
Mills & Boon's centenary. Gerald Mills and
Charles Boon founded Mills & Boon Limited
in 1908 and opened offices in London's Covent
Garden. Since then, Mills & Boon has become
a hallmark for romantic fiction, recognised
around the world.

We're proud of our 100 years of publishing
excellence, which wouldn't have been achieved
without the loyalty and enthusiasm of our
authors and readers.

Thank you!

Each month throughout the year there will
be something new and exciting to mark the
centenary, so watch for your favourite authors,
captivating new stories, special limited
edition collections...and more!

CAROLINE ANDERSON

Baby Bonds

Containing

The Baby Bonding,
The Pregnant Tycoon
& The Baby from Nowhere

All the characters in this book have no existence outside the
imagination of the author, and have no relation whatsoever to anyone
bearing the same name or names. They are not even distantly inspired
by any individual known or unknown to the author, and all the
incidents are pure invention.

BABY BONDS © by Harlequin Books S.A. 2008

The Baby Bonding, The Pregnant Tycoon and The Baby from
Nowhere were first published in Great Britain by Harlequin Mills
& Boon Limited in separate, single volumes.

The Baby Bonding © Caroline Anderson 2003
The Pregnant Tycoon © Caroline Anderson 2004
The Baby from Nowhere © Caroline Anderson 2004

ISBN: 978 0 263 86719 0

025-1108

Printed and bound in Spain
by Litografía Rosés S.A., Barcelona

The Baby Bonding

CAROLINE ANDERSON

The
Queens of Romance
Collection

Dear Reader,

I can't begin to tell you how excited I was to discover that three of my very favourite books were going to be put together in this celebration collection for the Mills & Boon Centenary – and the fact that I'm apparently a Queen of Romance is astonishing! The books were all, in their own way, very unusual and interesting to write, and all of them had a very definite tug on my heartstrings.

The Pregnant Tycoon is different in that the heroine and not the hero is the tycoon, and it starts at a time in her life when she, like many tycoons, wonders what it's all about. She's reunited with Will, an old flame, and when the fire rekindles, her life takes a dramatic and very different turn for the better!

The Baby from Nowhere was a little more daring, and is one of my all-time favourite books. The title gives a little hint, but I won't spoil the surprise for you! Suffice to say that James is there for her through thick and thin…

Different again is *The Baby Bonding*. Molly is a strong, courageous and warm-hearted woman who has acted as a surrogate mother for Sam and his wife – she's not related to the baby, but when Sam comes back into her life with little Jack in tow, she falls hard and fast. So did I. Of all my heroes, Sam Gregory is probably the one I love the most.

Although that's so hard to say…! It's a huge anniversary for me too, this year, as my seventy-fifth book comes out, and of all those heroes, choosing only one would be just too hard. Luckily I don't have to. I can have them all, and I give you these three, Will, James and Sam, with my love. I hope you love them, too.

Caroline

PS Talking of lovers reunited, I've been asked to write a new book for the Romance line, with a couple whose marriage has fallen apart, and it will be on the shelves in the UK in February. It promises to be a real sizzler…

Caroline Anderson has the mind of a butterfly. She's been a nurse, a secretary, a teacher, run her own soft-furnishing business and now she's settled on writing. She says, "I was looking for that elusive something. I finally realised it was variety, and now I have it in abundance. Every book brings new horizons and new friends, and in between books I have learned to be a juggler. My teacher husband John and I have two beautiful and talented daughters, Sarah and Hannah, umpteen pets and several acres of Suffolk that nature tries to reclaim every time we turn our backs!" Caroline writes for the Mills & Boon® Romance and Medical™ series.

Look out for an exciting new Medical novel from Caroline in December 2008.

CHAPTER ONE

IT COULDN'T be him.

Not now, surely, when she'd got over him at last, stopped thinking about him every minute of the day, finally stopped caring if he was alive or dead.

No. She hadn't stopped caring. She'd never stop caring about that, but she'd stopped obsessing about it.

More or less.

And now here he was in front of her, as large as life and handsome as the devil, his face creased with laughter as always, and the sound of his deep chuckle sent shivers running through her. His long, rangy body was propped up against a pillar by the desk, and his pale blue theatre scrubs hung on his frame.

He'd lost weight, she thought with shock. He'd never been heavy, but now he was lean, and amongst the laughter lines there were others that hadn't been there before. Deeper ones that owed nothing to humour.

He's older, she reminded herself—three years. He must be nearly thirty-five. He was a little less than two years older than her, and she'd be thirty-three soon. How time passed. Gracious, she'd only been twenty-eight when they'd met, thirty the year Jack had been born.

Jack.

She swallowed the lump. Some things you never got over.

He shrugged away from the pillar and turned towards her, and for a moment he froze.

Then an incredulous smile split his face and he strode

down the ward towards her, arms outstretched, and she found herself wrapped hard against the solid warmth of his chest.

'Molly!'

The word was muffled in her hair, but after a second he released her, grasping her shoulders in his big, strong hands and holding her at arm's length, studying her with those amazing blue eyes.

'My God, it really is you!' he exclaimed, and hugged her again, then stood back once more as if he couldn't quite believe his eyes.

Her defences trashed by the spontaneous warmth of his welcome, she smiled up at him. 'Hello, Sam,' she said softly. She could hardly hear her voice over the pounding of her heart, and she felt her smile falter with the strength of her tumbling emotions. She pulled herself together with an effort. 'How are you?'

So polite, so formal, but then they always had been, really. It had been that sort of relationship, of necessity.

His mouth kicked up in a crooked grin that didn't quite reach his eyes, and her heart stuttered for a second. Was something wrong? Something with Jack?

'OK, I suppose,' he said lightly. Too lightly. Something *was* wrong. 'Busy,' he added, 'but, then, I'm always busy. Goes with the territory.'

'And—Jack?' she asked, hardly daring to say the words.

The grin softened, his eyes mellowing, and she felt the tension ease.

'Jack's great,' he said. 'He's at school now. Well, nursery, really. He's not old enough for school yet. And you? How are you? And why are you here?'

She smiled a little unsteadily, the relief making her light-headed. 'I work here—I'm a midwife, remember?'

He looked at her then, registering her uniform as if for

the first time, and a puzzled frown pleated his brow. 'I thought you worked as a community midwife?'

'I did, but not now. I only ever wanted to work part time, and it's easier to do that in a hospital, so when this job came up, I applied for it. But what about you? I didn't know you worked here—how did you keep that a secret?'

He laughed, his eyes crinkling again. 'No secret. I wasn't here until a few days ago, and I had no idea you were here, either. You used to live the other side of Ipswich, so you must have moved, too, unless you're commuting.'

'No, I'm not commuting, we've moved. We live in Audley now—near Mick's parents, so they can see Libby. I've been working here for six months.'

He shook his head, his eyes bemused. 'Amazing—but I suppose I shouldn't be surprised. There aren't that many hospitals, and it's not the first time I've run into someone I know.' He glanced up and checked the clock on the wall. 'Look—are you busy now?'

She gave a tired laugh. 'I'm always busy—it goes with the territory,' she said, quoting his words back at him. 'What did you have in mind?'

'Coffee? Lunch? I don't know—just a chance to catch up.'

Her heart hitched against her ribs. She wasn't sure she wanted to catch up. She'd worked so hard to put Sam and Crystal behind her, and she'd battened down her heart around her memories of Jack. 'Catching up' sounded like the perfect way of ripping it all open again, exposing the wound and prodding it just for the hell of it.

'I don't know,' she said honestly, not wanting to hurt him, but not willing to hurt herself again, either. 'I'm not sure I want to, Sam. It was a long time ago—a lot of water under the bridge.'

His face became shuttered, and she could feel him withdrawing, all that glorious warmth pulling away from her and leaving her cold and lonely and aching.

'Of course. I'm sorry, I didn't mean to be so thoughtless. Well, it's lovely to see you looking so well. No doubt I'll see you again.'

And turning on his heel, he strode away, leaving her standing there in a daze.

Idiot, she chastised herself. You fool! You should have talked to him. You're going to have to work together, how can it help you to have this cold and awkward distance between you? And there's Jack...

Jack's not your son, she told herself. Let it go.

She dragged in a deep breath and stared blindly out of the window. Count to ten, she told herself. Or twenty.

Or ten zillion.

Or you could just go after him.

She went, freeing her feet from the floor with a superhuman effort and then, once she'd started to move, almost running after him down the corridor.

She reached the lobby just as the lift doors were sliding shut, and called his name.

A hand came out, blocking the doors, and they hissed open and he stepped out, his expression still guarded.

He didn't say anything, just stood there waiting, watching her. The lift doors slid shut again behind him, but still he stood there. Oh, lord. She looked down, unsure what to say, then abandoned subterfuge and pretence. She'd never been any good at it, anyway. She let her breath go on a little whoosh.

'I'm sorry,' she said softly. 'I didn't mean to sound so cold. I'd love to have coffee with you.'

He was silent for a second, then nodded slowly. 'Now? Or later?'

She shrugged. 'Now would be fine for me. I was going to take a break now anyway, and nobody's doing anything exciting at the moment. If things change they'll page me. How about you?'

'I'm fine. I've finished in Theatre. I only had a short list this morning, and we're all done. I was just going to change and do a bit of admin. You'll be doing me a huge favour if you take me away from it.'

She laughed, as she was meant to, and, instead of calling the lift again, he ushered her towards the stairs. They went down to the little coffee-shop at the back of the hospital, the one, she told him, that members of the public hadn't really discovered, and he bought them coffee and sticky gingerbread slices and carried them over to a sofa. It was by the window, tucked in a corner overlooking a courtyard, and it was the closest thing they'd get to privacy.

For a moment neither of them said anything, and Molly wondered what on earth she was doing here with him. She must be mad.

He'd leant forward, his elbows on his knees, his fingers interlinked and apparently requiring his full attention, and she wondered what he was thinking. Then he looked across at her, catching her with her guard down, and his eyes seemed to spear right through to her soul.

'So—how are you?' he said, his voice low. 'Honestly?'

She shrugged, suddenly swallowing tears. 'I'm all right. Still the merry widow.' Her laugh was hollow and humourless, and he searched her face with those piercing blue eyes that missed nothing.

'Ah, Molly,' he said gruffly, and, reaching out, he gave her fingers a quick squeeze. 'I had hoped you'd be married again by now, settled down with someone worthy of your love.'

'I am with someone. I've got Libby.'

'A man, I meant.'

'We don't all need to be in a relationship, Sam,' she pointed out softly. 'Sometimes it's better not to be.'

She looked away, not wanting him to read her eyes, but he was looking down at his hands again anyway, staring fixedly at his fingers as they threaded and unthreaded through each other. When he spoke, his voice was gruff.

'I'm sorry I reacted like that—assuming you'd be as pleased to see me as I am to see you. It was crass of me. I apologise. I should have realised you'd moved on.'

'I *am* pleased to see you,' she told him, unable to lie, unable to let him believe anything less than the truth. 'It's just—I found it so hard, three years ago. I didn't think I would, but it's been really difficult, and I didn't want to stir it all up, but now it is, anyway, and—well, I've longed to know how he is.'

He looked up and she met his eyes, and she saw sorrow and compassion in them, and an amazing tenderness. 'He's wonderful, Molly. Beautiful. Jack's the best thing that's ever happened to me. He's brought me more joy than I could ever have imagined—and I owe it all to you.'

She swallowed again, shocked at how readily the tears seemed to form. She was always so grounded, so sensible, so dispassionate.

But not about Jack.

'I'd love to see a photo,' she said, wondering if she was just opening herself up to heartache but unable to deny herself this one small thing.

'A photo?' He laughed softly. 'I've got hundreds—and videos going back to his birth. You're welcome to them. Why don't you come round? Then you can meet him, too.'

An ache so large it threatened to destroy her built in her chest. 'But Crystal didn't want us to stay in contact.'

'And I never did agree with her. Besides, it's irrelevant,'

he added, his voice curiously flat. 'Crystal's dead, Molly. She died two years ago.'

Molly felt shock drain the blood from her face. 'Dead?' she echoed silently. 'Oh, dear God, Sam, I'm so sorry.'

His face tightened. 'It was a long time ago,' he said, but she could feel his pain, could remember her own when Mick had died, and she ached for him.

She reached out, her hand covering those interlinked fingers, and he turned his hands and caught hers between them, renewing the bond that had been forged three years ago in blood and sweat and tears.

'So—how do you manage?' she asked, her voice surprisingly steady. 'About Jack, I mean? Who looks after him?' Oh, lord, she thought, tell me you're not married again. Tell me someone else isn't bringing him up.

'I have a couple who live in the house—Mark's disabled after an accident and can only do very light work, and Debbie needs to be around to look after him, but between them they look after the house and the garden and take Jack to and from nursery. They do it in return for their accommodation and a small salary, and because they live on the premises it gives me cover when I'm on call for the night or the weekend or whatever, and it's much better than having an au pair. Been there, done that, and this is streets better.'

'Gosh. You were lucky to find them. Do you think they'll be all right? Does Jack like them, or is it too soon to tell?'

He smiled. 'Jack loves them and, yes, I was lucky, but it's not a new arrangement. They've been with me for a year now, and so far it's been brilliant. Mark's a tapestry designer—he's a great big guy, an ex-biker with multiple piercings and the most unlikely looking person with a needle and thread, but he's amazingly gifted, really successful, and Debbie's just a miniature powerhouse. She makes me tired just watching her.'

'Didn't they mind moving up from London?'

'Didn't seem to, but it's early days. We only moved three weeks ago, and I've only been in this job three days.'

While she'd been on her days off, of course, which was why she hadn't known he was here.

A pity. It might have given her a chance to prepare.

Or run.

His bleeper summoned him and, standing up, he drained his coffee and shot her an apologetic smile.

'Later—we'll talk some more. Perhaps over dinner.'

She smiled and gave a noncommittal nod. 'Perhaps,' she said silently to his retreating back, and wondered what hand fate, with her twisted sense of humour, would deal them this time.

It wasn't too late to run...

So many memories.

Crystal, determined and focused, her gimlet mind fastened on this one idea to the exclusion of all others, one last attempt to rescue the tatters of their marriage.

'I want a child,' she'd said. 'What about a surrogate mother? You're in the business—can't you find one?'

And then he had, by a miracle, by sheer coincidence, because a patient of his had had a baby for someone else, and he'd talked to her, told her about Crystal's idea.

'You need to talk to my friend Molly,' she'd said, and then Molly had been there, coming through the door behind him, warm and generous and full of life and laughter, filling the room with sunshine and making him glad to be alive. His first impression of her had been that he'd could trust her with his life and with that of his child, and nothing she'd ever done had taken that away.

They'd become friends over the next few weeks and months, and she'd been a rock during the endless procedures, the meetings, the conversations, the dealings with the solicitors. He remembered how calm she'd been, how in control, how understanding and gentle with Crystal.

The pregnancy had seemed to last for ever, such a long wait until the phone call came to say she was in labour, and he could remember every moment of the drive to the hospital, the waiting again, and then being there, holding Molly, supporting her while she'd given birth to Jack— the son he and Crystal had thought they'd never have.

Their son, carried for them by Molly, who'd generously agreed to act as a host mother to their embryo. A tummy mummy, she'd called herself, and their son had been loved and nurtured and protected by her body until the time had been right to hand him over to them.

And then Jack—tiny, screaming, enraged by the insult of birth, only calming when the midwife had taken him from the panic-striken Crystal and given him to Sam.

Then Molly had let out a long, ragged breath and smiled tearfully at him and nodded, and it had been all right.

Or so he'd thought, for the last three years.

And now he'd seen her again, and she'd admitted she'd had problems, and the doubts had come back to plague him. Had it been the right thing to do, to ask another woman to make such stupendous sacrifices for them, so Crystal could have what she wanted?

He nearly laughed out loud. What she'd *thought* she wanted, anyway. What was that saying? Be careful what you wish for, you might get it?

'So—is it possible?'

Matt Jordan, the A and E consultant, stood beside Sam with his hands thrust into the pockets of his white coat, watching as he examined their patient. It was the first time

he'd met the big Canadian, and he liked him instinctively—not least for calling him so quickly on this somewhat puzzling case.

'She could be pregnant, yes. Certainly looks possible.'
Sam gently palpated the distended abdomen of the unconscious woman in Resus and shook his head thoughtfully.
'I think you're right, I think she is pregnant, but I can't be
sure without a scan or a pregnancy test. It could be all
sorts of things—a tumour, an ovarian cyst, fibroids—without a heartbeat it's anybody's guess, and I can't pick one
up on the foetal stethoscope. It could just be fluid, but it
doesn't really feel right for that. What do you know about
her?' he asked Matt.

'Very little,' he was told. 'She was brought in a few
minutes ago after collapsing at the wheel of her car. The
police are working on it, but it doesn't seem to be registered to a woman, so they don't know who she is. They're
checking with the car's owner.'

He nodded.

'Well, the first thing we need is an ultrasound to check
if there's a live baby, and we'll go from there. In the meantime do nothing that would compromise the baby if you
can avoid it. Once we know if she's carrying a live foetus,
we can get a proper scan to work out its gestational age
and decide if it's viable if we need to do an emergency
section for any reason. I don't suppose you can hazard a
guess as to what's wrong with her?'

'No. Not diabetes, we've checked that, and her heart
seems fine. Pupils are a bit iffy, so it could be drugs or a
bang on the head. Could it be anything obstetric?'

Sam frowned and shook his head. 'Don't think so. It's
hard to tell without more information. I want that scan,
fast. If she's twenty-eight weeks or more and remains stable and unconscious, we can remove the baby to give her

more chance, if necessary, but the baby's chances will decrease with every week less than that. And, of course, there are other complications. She's a smoker, for a start, so it might be small for dates, and starting from a disadvantage. Still, there's no point in speculating till we get the scan and know if she is pregnant and the baby's still alive. If she is pregnant, we'll take her down to the big scanner and have a better look if you think she's stable enough.'

The young nurse beside him frowned in puzzlement. 'How do you know she's a smoker?'

He shrugged. 'She smells of smoke—and her teeth are stained.'

His eyes met Matt's. 'She's a heavy smoker, I'd say, so watch her lungs, too, with the added stress of pregnancy. She might have breathing difficulties—and if she shows signs of respiratory distress or hypovolaemia, call me. She might get an amniotic fluid embolus or an antepartum haemorrhage as a result of the impact.'

'We'll watch for that. She's got a wedge under her left hip to take the pressure off her aorta and vena cava. Anything else specific we should be doing?'

He shook his head. 'Not really. Some answers would be good. Bleep me again if you need me, and when you get the results of the ultrasound. I'll be in my office.'

Sam walked back up there, unable to do any more without further information, and at the moment at least she seemed stable. He'd worry about her once he knew a little more but, in the meantime, other thoughts were clamouring for his attention.

With each step, the young woman faded further from his mind, crowded out by an image of Molly that blanked his thoughts to anything else.

She hadn't changed at all—well, not enough to notice. She'd got her pre-pregnancy figure back, of course, but apart from that she seemed no different. Her eyes were still that same warm, gentle shade of brown, her hair a few tones darker and shot through with gold, and her smile...

He felt choked, just thinking about her smile. She smiled with her whole face, not just that gorgeous, mobile mouth that was so amazingly expressive.

He growled under his breath. So she was an attractive woman. So what? So were lots of women. Hell, he worked with young, attractive women all day, both staff and patients, and he managed to cope. So why had he picked on Molly, of all people, to be so acutely aware of? She was the last woman in the world he could entertain those sorts of thoughts about.

His relationship with her was hugely complex because of Jack, and absolutely the last thing it needed was any further layers added to it!

'Keep breathing, nice light breaths—that's it, that's lovely. You're doing really well.'

Liz, her young patient, sobbed and shook her head. 'I can't do this...'

'Yes, you can,' Molly told her calmly, recognising her panic for what it was, a sign that she was moving into the transitional phase between the first and second stages of labour. 'You'll be fine.'

'I bet you've never had any babies, midwives never have,' she said with no real venom.

Molly gave a soft laugh. 'Sorry—I've had three.'

'You're mad. I'm never having another,' the girl moaned, leaning against her partner and biting her lip. 'God, I hate you! How could you do this to me, you bastard? I never want to speak to you again.'

He met Molly's eyes over her shoulder, panic flaring in

them, and she squeezed his hand as it lay on the girl's shoulder and smiled reassuringly at him.

'She's getting closer. Tempers often fray and it's usually the father who gets it. She'll be fine.'

'Going to be sick,' Liz said, and promptly was, all down his front.

To his credit he didn't even wince, just led her back to the bed and wiped her mouth, then looked at Molly. 'I could do with cleaning up,' he said softly, and she nodded.

'We'll get you some theatre pyjamas to wear. Just sit with her for a second.'

She slipped out, grabbed the scrubs from the linen store and was about to mop up when Liz's waters broke.

'OK, let's get you back on the bed and check you. I reckon it'll soon be over now,' she said encouragingly. When she examined her patient, though, she found that the cord had prolapsed down beside the baby's head, and when she checked the foetal heart rate, it was dipping alarmingly.

It would be over soon, but not for the reason she'd thought!

'Liz, I want you to turn on your side for me,' she said, pressing the crash button by the head of the bed and dropping the backrest simultaneously. 'We've got a bit of a problem with the baby's cord, and I want to get your head down and hips up a bit, to take the pressure off. It's nothing to worry about, but we need to move fast, and I'm going to get some help.'

'Need a hand here?'

Sam's deep, reassuring voice was the most wonderful sound in Molly's world at that moment.

'Prolapsed cord,' she said quietly. 'Her waters went a moment ago, and she had quite a lot of fluid. Watch where you walk, by the way. Liz, this is Mr Gregory.'

'Hello, Liz,' he said, moving in beside her and throwing her a quick, reassuring smile before he lifted her hips effortlessly and slid a pillow under them. He met Molly's eyes. 'What's the previous history?'

She shook her head. 'None. First baby, full term—'

'And the last,' Liz groaned. 'What's happening?'

'The cord's got squashed between your cervix and the baby's head,' Sam told her calmly. 'We've got a choice under these conditions. We can deliver the baby as quickly as possible the normal way, with the help of forceps, or give you a Caesarian section. I just need to take a quick look at you to help me decide which is the best option, OK? Gloves, Molly.'

She handed him the box, and he snapped them on and quickly checked the baby's presentation and the extent of the prolapse of the cord. As he straightened, he met Molly's eyes again, his own unreadable. 'What do you think?' he asked. 'Want to try?'

She shrugged, not wanting to argue with him on their first shared case, but deeply concerned because it was a first baby and it was still a little high for comfort. If she had problems...

'We can try, I suppose, if you want to—but we haven't got long.'

He nodded agreement, and approval flickered in his eyes. 'I know. Let's go for a section. Push that head back, Molly, until the cord's pulsating again, and hold it there until she's in Theatre. I don't think we can get the cord back up, there's too big a loop, so we just have to keep the pressure off. I'm going to scrub.'

The room had been filling up while they talked, people responding to the crash call, and he turned to his SHO. 'Get a line in, please, and give her oxygen, and terbutaline to slow the contractions if we can. Cross-match for two

units as well, please. I'll see you in Theatre, Liz. Don't
worry, we'll soon have your baby out.'

He squeezed her partner's shoulder on the way out, and
Molly thought how like him that was, sparing a thought
for the shocked young man standing paralysed on the sidelines, even in such a chaotic moment. He'd always seemed
to have time for things others often overlooked.

Within a very few minutes Liz was on her way to
Theatre, Molly's gloved hand firmly pushing the baby's
head back away from her cervix, keeping the pressure off
the cord to prevent the baby dying from lack of oxygen.

They didn't have much time, but as long as she could
keep that cord pulsating, the baby stood a good chance of
coming through this unharmed.

Sam was waiting, and he wasted no time in opening Liz
up once she was under the anaesthetic. Her partner, David,
was hovering outside Theatre and had looked scared to
death, but Molly didn't really have time to worry about
him.

All her attention was on holding that baby's head back,
during the shift across to the operating table, positioning
Liz ready for surgery with the head of the table tilted
downwards, and trying desperately to ignore the cramp in
her arm and back from the awkward position she was in.

Finally she felt the pressure ease, and looked up to meet
Sam's eyes as he lifted the baby clear and handed it to the
waiting nurse.

'It's a boy,' he told Molly, throwing a quick smile in
her direction before returning his attention to Liz. 'Time
of birth fifteen twenty-seven. He's all yours, Molly.'

She straightened and flexed her shoulders, then, after
clamping and cutting the cord, she took the baby immediately over to the waiting crib and sucked out his airways.
His cry, weak and intermittent until that point, changed

pitch with indignation and turned into a full-blown bellow, and she felt the tension in the room ease.

'Apgar score nine at one minute,' she said, and glanced up at the clock on the wall. She'd check again at fifteen thirty-two, by which time she was sure the slight blueness of his skin would have gone and he would score a perfect ten.

Relief made her almost light-headed, and she smiled down at the screaming baby, his colour improving and turning pink as she watched. His heartbeat was strong, his cry once he'd got going was good and loud, and his muscle tone and response to suction had been excellent.

It was a pity things had gone wrong so Liz had missed his birth, she thought, wrapping him up in heated towels and taking him out of the Theatre to David, but trying for a normal delivery would have been too risky. She'd known doctors who would have taken the risk, others who would have gone for the section without a second thought regardless of the circumstances.

Sam, thank God, didn't seem to fall into either of those categories. He'd rapidly weighed up both options in the light of his examination, and had made what she felt had been the right decision. She felt able to trust his judgement—and that was a relief, as she was going to have to work with him.

She pictured his eyes again over the mask when he'd smiled, his eyes crinkling at the corners. She'd always loved that about him, the way he smiled with his eyes...

'Is everything all right?' David asked, and she nodded, putting the baby in his slightly tense arms.

'So far, so good. I've done a quick check and all the obvious bits are present and correct, and Liz is doing really well.' She smiled up at David, but he didn't notice. He was staring down in frank amazement at his son.

'We've got a baby,' he said, his voice faintly incredulous. Lifting his free hand, he stroked one finger gently down the baby's translucent, downy cheek, still streaked with blood and vernix. The little head turned towards the finger, his rosebud mouth pursing, and Molly smiled, an all-too-familiar lump in her throat.

'He's hungry. She can feed him just as soon as she comes round, but in the meantime he just needs a cuddle from his dad. Just hold him and talk to him for a minute. He'd recognise your voice, he will have heard it from the womb. He's a bit messy, but we won't wash him until Liz has woken up and seen him, or it could be anybody's baby.'

He nodded, and she took him through to Recovery to wait for Liz while she herself went back into Theatre to check on her.

'Apgar up to ten?' Sam asked, checking on the baby's progress even as he worked on Liz.

'Yes—he's fine now. His colour was a bit off, but it's not surprising.'

'You did a good job,' Sam said softly to her, and she felt her skin warm.

'You aren't making too big a fist of it yourself,' she said with a smile, and he chuckled quietly under his breath.

'You're too kind. The placenta's there, by the way.'

She studied it carefully, making sure no parts of it were missing and likely to cause the mother future problems, and nodded. 'It's OK.'

'Good. Now, could you do me a favour, Molly, if you're happy with the baby? Can you phone down to A and E and ask about the young woman who was brought in a couple of hours ago—query pregnant, no ID, unconscious in the car?'

'Sure.'

She used the theatre phone, and discovered that the woman had regained consciousness and discharged herself.

Sam frowned, his brows drawing together in disapproval. 'Did they scan her?'

She shook her head. 'Not that they said. She came round just after you left her, and wouldn't stay another minute. The police think she'd stolen the car, apparently.'

'How bizarre. Oh, well.' He shrugged and carried on with closing Liz while Molly checked the baby again. He was snuggled in his father's arms, blissfully asleep now, and, judging by the look on David's face, he wasn't the only one feeling blissful.

Through the glass she saw Sam straighten up and flex his shoulders. He said something and the anaesthetist nodded, and he stepped back, handing Liz over to the anaesthetic team. Stripping off his gloves and mask, he came out to join them.

'All done, and she's fine. She'll be with us in a minute.' Looking down at the baby, he ran a finger lightly over the back of his tiny hand.

'Hello, little fellow,' he said softly. 'Has he got a name?'

'I don't know. Lucy.'

Sam met David's eyes and smiled. 'That may not be appropriate, under the circumstances.'

David chuckled, his shoulders dropping with the easing of tension. 'Perhaps we'd better think again. I don't know, we were sure she was having a girl. Something about the heartbeat, Liz said. Probably an old wives' tale.' He pulled a face and swallowed hard. 'Um—thanks, by the way. I'm really grateful to you all for getting him out safely. Liz would have been gutted—'

He broke off, and Sam laid a comforting hand on his shoulder.

'Any time,' he said. 'They'll bring her through to Recovery now, and she can hold him and feed him, then Molly will take you all back to the ward once they're happy she's stable. This little fellow seems to be fine, but a paediatrician will come and check him in due course, just as a matter of routine. In the meantime, I'll leave you with Molly. She'll look after you both.'

He threw Molly a smile and went to change, and it was as if the lights had gone out.

Oh, damn. And she'd really, really thought she was over him...

CHAPTER TWO

'HE's been such a good boy today, haven't you, Jack?'

The little dark head bobbed vigorously, a smile lighting up his face like a beacon. 'I did painting, Daddy—see!'

There was a slightly tattered piece of grey sugar paper held to the fridge door with magnets, and Sam studied the wild, multicoloured handprints on it and felt his heart contract with pride. He grinned a little off-key and ruffled his son's hair.

'So you did. Well done. What else did you do?'

'Um—singing, and played in the sandpit. We had fish fingers for lunch—I'm hungry,' he added, tipping his head back and looking hopefully up at Debbie.

She laughed softly. 'You're always hungry. Come on, sit down at the table and you can have your tea while you tell your dad all about your day, and I'll make him a nice drink. Cuppa, Sam? Mark and I are just having one.'

'Thank you, Debbie, that would be lovely.' He shrugged out of his jacket and glanced across at Debbie's husband. 'Hello, Mark.'

'Hi. You good?'

He smiled tiredly. 'I'll do. Yourself?'

The big man nodded from his seat by the window. 'Good. The latest effort's coming along—what do you think?'

He held up a large square of canvas, and even from across the room Sam could see the wonderfully subtle colours and almost three-dimensional quality of the tapestry Mark was creating. It was a study of leaves, but close up and personal. There was nothing pretty-pretty about it, but there was a vigour in the composition that was the trade mark of all his designs, and this one was no exception.

'You're getting a bit good at this,' Sam said, genuine admiration in his voice, and Mark lifted a shoulder, awkward with the praise.

'I thought I'd do apples and pears next—you know, a sort of orchard theme. Maybe some plums, or autumn leaves. The country's really inspired me—let something loose inside. I just hope they sell.'

'Of course they'll sell. They always sell. The shops love your designs,' Debbie said pragmatically, sliding a mug of tea across the table. 'Sam, take the weight off. You look done in.'

'Busy day,' he said. Busy, and emotionally exhausting. He sat down at the big, scrubbed pine kitchen table that filled the centre of the kitchen and leant back in his chair with a sigh. His mind was whirling with thoughts of Molly, and all he could see was her face. He wished he'd got her number, but he hadn't, so he couldn't ring her—unless she was in the book?

He reached for it, conveniently at arm's length on the dresser behind him, and flicked through the pages. Hammond. There. He ran his finger down the list, and found only a few, none of them Molly.

Unless her initials didn't start with an M. Chewing his lip thoughtfully, he ran his finger down again, and paused. A.M.?

Yes, of course. Annabel Mary, she'd been christened. He remembered now. He remembered a lot of things...

He shut the book. Perhaps he'd ring her later.

But then Jack would be in bed.

Now, then?

He needed to sort out the videos, dig out the photos.

Heaven only knows what's happened to them, he thought. They were probably in the boxes in the loft and they'd take him ages to find.

But Jack was here, now, and Molly's eyes, when he'd talked about the boy...

Picking up his mug, he got up and went into his study and closed the door behind him with a soft click.

Molly stared at the phone warily, hope warring with common sense.

Of course it wouldn't be Sam. He hadn't got her number, unless he'd looked her up in the book, but her first initial wasn't M., so he probably wouldn't find her automatically.

Then again, he'd known her full name all those years ago, seen it enough times on the endless paperwork, so maybe...

'Oh, just answer it,' she muttered to herself, and lifted the receiver. 'Hello?'

'Molly?'

Her heart lurched and steadied again, and she closed her eyes briefly. 'Sam.'

'Hi. I hope you don't mind me ringing. Um, about you seeing Jack—I meant to say something earlier, but I didn't get round to it. Are you busy this evening? I mean, it's not very much notice, but I thought, if you'd like...'

Her heart lurched again, and she threw a quick glance at the door. Libby was on the other side of it, scraping on her violin, trying to get to grips with a difficult passage. She'd done her homework, and now she was grappling with this. She'd been at it for nearly half an hour, but she wouldn't give up until she'd got this bit right, at least. Molly just hoped it was sooner rather than later, for all their sakes.

'What did you have in mind?' she asked cautiously.

'I wondered if you'd like to come over. I mean, don't worry if you've got other plans, or you'd rather not, but I just thought—'

'I haven't got plans,' she said quickly—too quickly. Slow down, she told herself, and drew a deep, steadying breath. 'Tonight would be fine,' she went on, deliberately calming her voice despite the clamouring of her heart. 'I need to check with Libby, of course, but I'm sure there won't be a problem. She'd like to see him, too, I'm sure.'

'Fine. Whenever you're ready—the sooner the better, really, because he goes to bed at about half-seven.'

'That late?' she said, and could have bitten her tongue for the implied criticism. It was none of her business...

'He has a nap when he gets home from nursery, and Debbie lets him sleep as long as he wants. That way I get to see him when I get in,' he told her, and she wasn't sure if she'd imagined a mild note of reproof in his voice. 'Whatever. I think in any case we could make an exception tonight—apart from which, he's as bright as a button to-day, so I don't suppose he'll be in any hurry to go to bed. He's full of it.'

She closed her eyes against the image, the ache of longing growing with every word. 'We'll come now,' she said. 'If that's OK? It was the first day of the new term today, and Libby goes to bed at eight on school nights. I try and stick to it if I can,' she added, trying not to sound so pathetically eager and ending up sounding like a school matron instead. Oh, grief, he was going to think she was obsessive about bedtimes...

'Now's fine. I'll give you directions.'

She scrabbled around for a piece of paper on the table and found an old envelope. 'Fire away,' she said, jotting down the address—surprisingly in the country, not in the town as she'd first thought. 'I didn't realise you lived out of town,' she said, studying the directions and trying to place the road in her mind. 'Will it take long to get there?'

'No. It's easy to find, and it's not far out. Ten minutes from the hospital, tops. I'll see you soon—and, Molly?'

'Yes?'

'He doesn't know—about you carrying him for us. I haven't told him. I'm still trying to work out how, but in the meantime I'd be grateful if you and Libby could be careful what you say.'

'Sure. Don't worry, we won't say anything. I'll see you soon.'

She cradled the phone, then sat for a moment gathering her ragged emotions. The scraping had finished, a sweet, pure sound now pouring through the door—well, mostly, she thought with a motherly smile as another tiny screech set her teeth on edge. Still, Libby wasn't quite ten yet. There was plenty of time.

The door opened and Libby bounced in, the image of her father, blonde hair bobbing round her shoulders, her pale blue eyes sparkling with achievement.

'Did you hear me?' she said. 'I did it!'

'I heard,' Molly said, her heart swelling with pride. 'Well done, your father would have been proud of you. And talking of fathers, I meant to tell you, I saw Jack's father today. He's working at the hospital.'

Libby's head tipped on one side. 'Jack's father? Your baby Jack?'

She nodded. 'Well, not mine, but yes.'

The girl's eyes sparkled even brighter. 'Cool! Can we see him? I only saw him that once when he was born, and it was ages ago.'

'Three years—and, yes, we can see him. Tonight—in fact now. If you're OK with it?'

'Sure. Can we go?'

Molly laughed and stood up. 'Yes. Brush your hair, it's a mess, and make sure you've put your violin away properly.'

'Yes, Mother,' she teased, but she bounced out and reappeared a moment later, her hair sort of brushed and the violin case in hand. 'I'm ready.'

Molly picked up the directions, read them through again and put them in her pocket. 'OK. But, remember, he doesn't know anything about me being his tummy-mummy, so don't say anything.'

Libby's eyes widened. 'He doesn't know? How weird. Laura knows, she talks about it all the time.'

Molly thought of her other surrogate child, with whom she had an affectionate and loving relationship, and smiled gently. 'Yes, I know—but Jack doesn't, and it isn't really our place to tell him.'

'It's OK, I won't say anything,' Libby promised.

'There's another thing you ought to know—his mum died.'

Libby's face fell. 'Oh, poor baby,' she said, her soft heart so typically responding to his loss. 'Still, he can have you now,' she suggested, her face brightening again.

If only, Molly thought, the ache returning. Libby would love to put the world to rights, but unfortunately it just wasn't that easy.

The drive, however, was easy, his house simple to find and really not at all far from the hospital, as he'd promised. It was a lovely house, a simple, red-brick cottage-style farmhouse, with a porch in the middle and windows all around. A rambling rose, intertwined with a late-flowering honeysuckle, scrambled over the porch, and tacked on one end of the house under a lower section of roof was what looked like another little cottage, with its own white front door, and she guessed this was where Debbie and Mark lived.

Bathed in the sunshine of a late summer evening, it looked homely and welcoming, and just the sort of place she could imagine him living in. Nothing like their London house, but she'd never felt that had been him.

The garden was bursting with colour and scent, a real cottage garden, and as they walked up the path she bent to smell the last of the roses, just as Sam opened the door.

She straightened and laughed. 'Sorry. I can't resist roses.'

'Nor can I. They're why I bought the house.' His gaze dropped and he gave her daughter a friendly smile. 'Hello, Libby, nice to see you again. How are you?'

'OK. I like your garden, it smells lovely.'

'It does, doesn't it? I can't take any credit for it. It was like this when we moved, and Debbie does all the gardening anyway. Come in, Jack's in the kitchen, ''washing up'' with her.' He held up his hands and drew speech marks in the air with his fingers as he spoke, and his face said it all.

'Oh, dear,' Molly said, biting her lip at the laughter in his eyes, and they exchanged a smile that made her knees go weak. Oh, lord, this was such a bad idea. She was going to get herself in such a mess.

She followed him down the hall, Libby at his side, and as he ushered her into the kitchen she came to an abrupt halt, her hand coming up to cover her mouth, her eyes filling.

No. She wasn't going to cry, she wasn't.

'Jack, come and say hello to some friends of mine,' Sam was saying, but she couldn't move, she just stood there and devoured the little boy with her eyes as he climbed down off the chair and ran over to them.

He was so tall! So tall and straight, and the image of his father, with those same astonishing blue eyes filled with laughter, and a mop of soft, dark hair that fell over his forehead, just like Sam's.

He tipped his head back and looked up at her, examining her unselfconsciously. 'Hello. I'm Jack,' he said unnecessarily, and she crouched down to his level and dredged up an unsteady smile.

'Hi. I'm Molly, and this is Libby, my daughter.' She looked at his sodden front and resisted the urge to gather him to her chest and squeeze him tightly. 'I hear you're helping with the washing-up.'

He nodded, his little head flying up and down, grinning from ear to ear. 'I do spoons, and we make bubbles.'

'We've got a dishwasher, but it's not as much fun, and this way the floor gets washed, too,' Sam said, laughter in his voice.

She chuckled at the words and straightened up, her gaze finally going past Sam and meeting the clear, assessing eyes of a woman in her late twenties. Her hair was spiky and an improbable shade of pink, and she was dressed in faded old jeans and an orange T-shirt that clashed violently with her hair. She looked like a tiny and brightly coloured elf, but, despite being so small, she radiated energy.

'You must be Debbie,' Molly said.

The woman nodded, and tipped her head towards the window. 'This is my husband, Mark.'

She turned her head and saw him for the first time, sitting quietly in a chair in front of the long, low window, one leg propped up on a stool and a cat curled up on a riotous heap of wool in his lap. The sun glinted on an armoury of piercings, and there was an elaborate tattoo running up one arm and disappearing under his sleeve.

The unlikely tapestry designer, of course.

She smiled across at him. 'Hi, there. Nice to meet you. Sam's told me a lot about you both.'

'Oh, dear, sounds ominous,' Debbie said, laughing and scooping Jack up to sit him on the table and strip off his soggy T-shirt. 'I think you'd better put something dry on, don't you? You'll catch a cold—and don't tell me it's an old wives' tale,' she said, levelling a finger at Sam.

He threw up his hands in mock surrender and pulled out a chair. 'Molly, have a seat,' he said, and she sat, quickly, before her suddenly rubbery legs gave way.

'Thanks,' she said, shooting him a grateful glance, and he smiled down at her understandingly.

'Any time. Can I get you a drink?'

'Only tea or coffee, as I'm driving,' she said, her eyes fixed on Jack's small body, taking in the strong, straight limbs, the sticky-out ribs so typical of little boys who didn't sit still long enough to gather any fat. The need to hug him close was an overwhelming ache, and she had to fold her arms and lock them to her sides to stop herself.

'I'll make coffee,' Sam was saying. 'Mark? Debbie?'

'Not for me. I'll have one when I've finished in here,' Debbie said, tugging a clean T-shirt over Jack's head, and Mark shook his head, too.

'Another ten minutes and I get my pint,' he said with a grin. 'I think I'll hold on for that.'

So Sam made coffee for Molly and himself, and poured juice for the children, and then, because it was such a lovely evening, they went out into the garden and sat amongst the scent of the roses and honeysuckle and listened to the droning of the bees while the children played in the sandpit a few feet away.

'What a gorgeous spot,' Molly said, delighted to know that Jack was living in such a lovely place. She and Libby lived in a very pleasant house with a pretty garden, in a tree-lined street convenient for the hospital and Libby's school, but it was nothing like this. Sam's house was only ten minutes from the hospital, fifteen from the town centre, and yet the peace and quiet were astonishing. They could have been miles from anywhere, she thought with a trace of envy, and then quickly dismissed it.

It wouldn't have been nearly so convenient for them, particularly not for Libby, and Molly didn't want to spend her life driving her daughter backwards and forwards every time she wanted to see a friend or visit her grandparents. It was hard enough fitting in Libby's schedule around her own work timetable without having to factor in being a taxi service.

No, living in the town suited them, but she was still glad for Jack that he would grow up with the song of the birds drowning out the faint hum of the bypass in the distance.

'So, what do you think of him?' Sam asked softly, and she dragged her eyes from the little boy who wasn't her son and smiled unsteadily across at him.

'He's gorgeous. Bright and lovely and...'

She broke off, unable to continue, and she looked away quickly before she disgraced herself.

'It's OK, Molly. I feel the same about him, so I do understand you.'

'Do you?' she said quietly. 'I'm not sure I do. He's not my son. Why do I feel like this for him?'

'Because you gave him life?'

'No. You and Crystal gave him life. I just incubated him until he was big enough to cope alone.'

'Don't underestimate your part in it. Without you he wouldn't be here. I think that gives you the right to feel emotional the first time you see him in three years.'

She closed her eyes against the welling tears. 'I've thought about him so much,' she confessed softly.

'You should have seen him,' Sam said, his voice gruff. 'I should have kept in touch, no matter what Crystal said. I wasn't happy with it. I always felt she was wrong, and I should have done something about it. I'm sorry.'

Molly shook her head slowly. 'She was his mother. She had the right to make that choice,' she pointed out, determined to defend the dead woman's decision even though it had torn her apart, but Sam made a low sound of disgust in his throat.

'She didn't want to be his mother,' he said, his voice tight and dangerously quiet. 'She went back to work when he was four months old, because she was bored at home. Seven months later she went off with her boss on a business trip to the Mediterranean, and she never came back. Her son wasn't even a year old, and already she'd turned her back on him.

'She wanted a life in the fast lane, and that was how she died—with her lover, on a jet-ski, late one night. They smacked into the side of a floating gin palace that was just coming into the harbour at Antibes and they were killed instantly. They'd both been drinking.'

Molly stared at him, shocked at the raw emotion in his voice, the anger and pain that had come through loud and clear even though his voice had been little more than a murmur. Without thinking, she reached out to him, laying her hand on his arm in an unconscious gesture of comfort.

'Oh, Sam, I'm so sorry.'

He looked down at her hand, then covered it with his and gave her a sad, crooked smile before releasing her hand and pulling his arm away, retreating from her sympathy. 'So was I. It was a hell of a way to find out my wife was being unfaithful to me.'

'Didn't you know?'

He shifted slightly, moving away as if even that small distance made him less vulnerable. 'That they were lovers? I suppose I should have done. The signs were clear enough, although she'd never told me in as many words, but, no, I didn't know. She'd been itching to get back to work from the moment Jack was born, apparently, but she'd never really said so. Like everything else, she just let me find out.'

'But—why?' Molly asked, stunned that anyone could keep secrets in a marriage. It wouldn't have occurred to her to keep anything from Mick.

'Just her way.' He pursed his lips thoughtfully. 'I suppose the first hint I had that things weren't all sweetness and light was when I came home one day and found an au pair installed—so we'd have a resident babysitter, she told me. She wanted to go out at night to glitzy restaurants where you pay a small ransom for a miserable little morsel of something unpronounceable, when I was coming home exhausted from work and just wanted to fall asleep in front of the television with my son in my arms.'

'So who won?'

He gave a sad, bitter little laugh. 'Who do you think? Crystal wanted to go out—and what Crystal wanted, Crystal got. She said she had cabin fever—said she could understand how women got postnatal depression.'

'And did it make any difference?'

Again the low, bitter laugh. 'No, of course not. Then a few days later I opened a letter addressed to her by mistake. It was a credit-card bill, and in three weeks she'd run up thousands—and I mean thousands, literally. I went upstairs and looked in her wardrobe, and tucked in amongst the clothes she already had were loads of new things I'd never seen—sexy little dresses, trouser suits, skirts, tops,

all designer labels, all from the big Knightsbridge stores—
the sort of thing you'd wear if you wanted to seduce your
boss.'

'And it worked, I take it.'

'Oh, yes. I confronted her about the clothes, and she
cried and said she was miserable at home, and of course
she loved Jack, but she just wanted to get back to work,
she missed it. They were work clothes, she said. She had
to look the part. So I paid the credit-card bill, and she went
back to work, and the rest, as they say, is history.'

She wanted to reach out again, to comfort him again,
but he'd withdrawn from her and she couldn't. Instead she
concentrated on watching the children, wondering how
much this fractured upbringing had affected Jack.

Would she have had him for them if she'd known what
had been in store? She'd had doubts about Crystal, but
only when it had been too late, towards the end of her
pregnancy. Had it been a mistake to hand him over at
birth?

And then she heard Jack laugh, and saw the happy smile
on his face and the love on Sam's as he watched his son
play, and she knew it hadn't been a mistake, any of it.

Mick had died, too, although their stories couldn't have
been more different, but the result was the same and Libby
was now in the same boat as Jack. Molly could never have
said that having her daughter had been a mistake, or regretted her birth for a moment.

No, she had done the right thing for Jack. It was Crystal
who had failed him, not her, and Sam was certainly making a good job of parenting him now, as she'd known he
would.

She looked at her watch. 'It's getting late,' she murmured, and Sam nodded.

'Yes. I suppose they both ought to go to bed soon. Have another coffee before you go—just a quick one.'

And so she did, just because he didn't seem to want her to leave and Libby and Jack were getting on so well, and in any case, given a choice she would have sat there all night watching Jack and absorbing every little detail about him.

She followed Sam back into the kitchen, deserted now that Debbie and Mark had gone to their own rooms in the little cottage on the end of the house, and as Sam made the coffee, she watched the children through the window.

'Penny for them.'

She shook her head. 'Nothing, really. It's just so good to see him. I just want to hug him...'

Molly broke off and turned away, but before she could move far she was turned gently but firmly back and wrapped in a pair of strong, hard arms that gathered her against his chest and cradled her in his warmth.

The sob that had been threatening since she'd arrived broke free, and he shushed her gently and rocked her against his body, and gradually she felt her emotions calming, soothed by the comfort of his arms.

'OK now?' he asked, his voice gruff, and easing back from her he looked down into her eyes.

She nodded, dredging up a watery smile, and Sam lifted his hands and carefully smudged away the tears with his thumbs.

'That's better,' he said, a smile hovering round his eyes, but then something shifted in their clear blue depths, and she felt her heart thump against her ribs. His brows drew together in a little frown of puzzlement and he eased away, releasing her abruptly and stepping back, busying himself with the coffee.

'Um—about the photos. I'm not sure where they are.

I'll ask Debbie to dig them out. They know who you are, by the way, so you don't have to worry about what you say in front of them if Jack's not there.'

She nodded, willing her heart to slow down and her common sense to return.

If she hadn't known better, she could have sworn he'd been about to kiss her and had then thought better of it.

No, not better. She couldn't think of anything better than being kissed by him, but he obviously didn't agree, to her regret.

Still, he was probably right. Their relationship was complicated enough without throwing that particular spanner in the works, however much she might want him to, and of course he had no idea how she felt about him—how she'd felt about him for years.

They went back out to the garden and drank their coffee and talked about the hospital—nice and safe and neutral, but there was a tension between them that could have been cut with a knife, and it was almost a relief when Sam put his mug down and stood up. 'Right, time that young man went to bed, I think,' he said briskly. 'It's nearly eight.'

Molly almost leapt to her feet, quick to follow his lead. 'Good grief. I didn't realise it was so late,' she lied, and hustled Libby off the swing and towards the car.

Sam scooped Jack up, and just as she was about to get into the car, he leant over in Sam's arms and held out his arms to her.

'Kiss!' he demanded.

Swallowing the lump in her throat, she hugged him gently and received his wet little kiss with a joy that brought the emotion surging back.

'Night-night, Jack,' she said unsteadily, and met Sam's eyes. Her own must be speaking volumes, she realised, but he would understand. 'Goodnight, Sam—and thank you.'

'Any time,' he said, his voice gentle, and the concern in his eyes nearly set her off again. She got hastily into the car, fumbled with her seat belt and drove away, eyes fixed on the road.

'Are you OK?' Libby said, seeing straight through her as usual, and with a little shake of her head she pulled over, folded her arms on the steering-wheel and howled.

Libby's little hand came out and squeezed her shoulder, and Molly wrapped her hand firmly over her daughter's and squeezed back.

'Poor Mummy—you've missed him, haven't you?' she said with a wisdom way beyond her years, and Molly laughed unsteadily and nodded.

'Yes. I miss Laura, too, but at least I see her. Still, I'll be able to see Jack now, so it'll be OK. It was just such a lot all at once. I'm sorry, darling. I'm all right now.'

She pulled herself together with an effort, blew her nose and wiped her eyes, and then swapped grins with her darling daughter. She was so like Mick, so sensible, so good at understanding her, hugely generous and loving.

Crazy, but even after all this time, she still missed him. He'd had the best sense of humour, the sharpest wit, the most tremendous sense of honour.

And dignity. Despite the accident that had left him in a wheelchair, and with all the resultant dependence on others for his most intimate bodily functions, Mick had never lost his dignity, and she'd been unfailingly proud of him.

She wondered what he would have made of her decision to be a surrogate mother. She'd always thought he'd have been supportive and understanding, but he would have worried about her. She could never have done it if he'd still been alive, but he wasn't, and it had been something to do to fill the huge void that his sudden and unexpected death had left behind.

In those black months after the pneumonia had claimed him, she'd been lost. She'd cared for him for years, and suddenly there had been only her and Libby, and she'd felt useless.

She'd needed to be needed, and because of a chance remark, she'd been given an opportunity to do something to help others who were unable to have children naturally. Because of Mick's paraplegia they'd only been able to have Libby with the help of IVF, and it was only one step further to imagine the anguish of a fertile mother who, due to a physical anomaly, was unable to carry her own child.

She couldn't have done it except as a host, but neither of the two children she'd carried had been genetically hers. They'd both been implanted embryos, so handing them over hadn't been like handing over her own child. That would have been too big a wrench.

Handing Jack over and knowing she wouldn't see him again had been bad enough. It had taken her years to get over the pain, and she realised now that she had never truly recovered. If he'd been her own child, it would have destroyed her. It had nearly destroyed her anyway, but now, by some miraculous stroke of fate, he was back in her life, and she didn't intend to let him out of it ever again.

The fact that Sam would also, by definition, be part of her life as well was something she would have to deal with—and so would he.

CHAPTER THREE

'YOU'RE needed in A and E, Mr Gregory.'

He frowned. He was covering one of the other firms because the consultant was on holiday and the registrar was off sick, and, frankly, being on take again for the second day running was the last thing Sam and his registrar Robert needed. He hadn't got round to any of that paperwork yesterday afternoon, and he'd hoped to get some done this morning before his afternoon clinic. There were urgent letters...

'Can't Robert do it?' he asked, but the ward clerk shook her head.

'Sorry, he's already in Theatre, and it sounded quite urgent. The girl you saw yesterday—the one in the car who was unconscious and discharged herself?'

He was already on his way to the lift by the time she finished speaking. That girl had been a crisis brewing, and he'd been mulling her case over in his mind all night—in between remembering the look on Molly's face when she'd seen Jack, and when the little tyke had kissed her goodbye. It had haunted him all night, racked him with guilt. He should have contacted her when Crystal died— should have insisted, even earlier, that they kept in touch.

Don't go there, he told himself firmly, striding down the corridor to A and E. He palmed open the door and went through to the work station, where he was directed to Resus.

'So what's the story today?' he asked, going in.

'The same, except this time she was picked up in the

41

street,' Matt Jordan said tersely. 'Drugs, possibly, or some bizarre form of epilepsy, but we're getting some pretty confusing results. Positive pregnancy test, though, and we picked up a heartbeat for the baby, but it was pretty erratic. We're getting a portable ultrasound down here now, and the neurologist is on his way.'

'Still no ID?'

Matt shook his head. 'No, nothing, but the car she was found in yesterday was stolen, and she hasn't washed or changed her clothes since then, so I would guess she lives in a squat. That makes the drugs more likely, but I'm almost certain there's something else as well.'

Sam nodded. That made sense. If only he could know what was making her black out, he could make a better assessment of the baby's needs. Just then the portable ultrasound machine arrived, and within moments the baby's existence was confirmed.

'Well, she's pregnant with a single foetus, and there's a heartbeat, although it's rather weak,' the sonographer said to them. 'I can't tell you any more without the big machine.'

Just then the alarm on the heart monitor went off, and Matt swore softly under his breath.

'Damn, she's arrested.'

The team moved smoothly in to start CPR, but Sam was unhappy. After two minutes of frenzied activity, she was still showing no signs of recovery, and the baby was bound to be suffering from lack of oxygen by now, even with their best attempts to support her circulation.

'How's it looking?' he asked tersely.

'Lousy. I can't worry about the baby, I'm going to have to shock her,' Matt said. 'There's still a chance we can get her back, and if this is drugs, the baby's chances are pretty slight anyway.'

Sam nodded agreement and stood back, watching grimly as they fought—and failed—to save her.

He checked the clock on the wall and sighed. They'd been working on her for nearly half an hour, and there was no way the baby was still viable, he didn't think.

He took the business end of the portable ultrasound and ran it over her abdomen, but the heartbeat they'd detected before was gone, just a shadow remaining to show the position of the heart. The baby itself was motionless.

'Damn,' he said under his breath, then straightened up. 'OK, forget the baby. We've lost it.'

And not only the baby. Despite the continuous external cardiac massage, shocking her, ventilating her, injecting her heart with adrenaline, still they were unable to get her back.

With a muttered oath Matt Jordan stripped off his gloves and looked up at the clock. 'OK, everybody. That's enough. Agreed?'

They nodded. 'Time of death ten thirty-eight,' he said, and scrubbed a tired hand through his hair. 'If only she'd stayed in yesterday, given us a chance to assess her.'

'She didn't. You can't hold people against their will,' Sam pointed out. 'There are too many damned if onlys in this job.'

He stripped off his gloves and gown, and after attending to the necessary paperwork he headed back towards Maternity, sick with the tragic waste of two young lives. Maybe the post-mortem would reveal why she'd died, but in the meantime he needed to get back to the paperwork on his other patients, finish those letters off.

Then maybe he'd have time for coffee with Molly, if she was free.

He growled under his breath. Molly. She was all he

could think about, all he could focus on. It was going to drive him mad, if he wasn't there already.

'Mr Gregory?'

He paused and turned, and there behind him was a man of his own age, the badge on his white coat declaring him to be Mr Nick Baker, Accident and Emergency Consultant. He'd seen him in Resus a few minutes ago, dealing with another patient. Now he'd followed him, for whatever reason.

'Mr Baker—what can I do for you?'

'It's Nick.'

'Sam.' He shook the man's hand, his eyes making a rapid inventory while he waited for him to come to the point. Slightly shorter than Sam, his hair was rumpled as if he'd run his hands through it, and he had laughter lines bracketing extraordinary blue eyes, but there was no laughter in evidence now. His smile was taut, and didn't reach his eyes.

'It's about my wife—she's a patient of yours. She was under Will Parry, but he moved away, so you've inherited her. I don't know if you've seen her notes, but I just wanted to fill you in.'

'Sure—of course. Is there something I should know?'

He nodded. 'She—we—lost a baby eight, nearly nine years ago. She had a congenital heart defect, and she was born at thirty-two weeks. This is our first child since, and—uh—'

'You're worried.'

His smile was wry. 'Yes—just a bit. Sally's thirty-five weeks now, and she's been scanned in London because of the problems the other baby had, and everything seems fine with this baby's heart, but—well, you know what it's like once you've had a setback of any sort, and seeing that girl in there just now...'

Sam laid a reassuring hand on his shoulder and squeezed gently. 'Don't worry. I'll look up her notes, and I'll watch out for her in clinic—when's she due in again?'

'Next week—Thursday, three o'clock.'

'I'll make sure I see her—and come with her, if you can get away. In the meantime I'll make sure that they call me in if she's admitted. In fact, I'll do one better than that. I'll give you my phone numbers—home and mobile—so you can get me at any time. OK?'

Relief flooded Nick's eyes, and he nodded, his mouth tightening. 'Thanks. I hate making such a fuss, but—'

'Forget it. I think you have a right—just as I think there's no need for you to worry either, from what you've said. I'll go and look up her notes, so I'm totally familiar with them.' He patted his pockets and came up empty-handed. 'I'll have to phone you with the numbers, I don't have anything on me to write on, but don't worry, I will do it today.'

'Thanks.'

With one last reassuring smile, Sam turned and headed up to Maternity, his mind returning inevitably to Molly.

He ran up the last flight of stairs to the department just as she emerged through the double doors. She saw him and her face lit up in one of those amazing smiles, and his heart slammed against his ribs.

Dear God, she was lovely—and he wanted her in a way he hadn't wanted a woman for years.

'Hi. I'm just going for coffee,' she said. 'Got time to join me?'

He thought of his paperwork, thought of the young mother lying dead in the hospital mortuary, her poor baby gone with her. The paperwork would still be there later, and there was nothing, sadly, that any of them could do for the girl and her unborn child. He'd ring Nick Baker with his numbers when he went back to his office, but in the meantime...

'Yes, I've got time,' he said, and turning on his heel he went back down the stairs with her at his side.

'What's wrong?'

Sam looked up and she saw a lingering sadness in the depths of his eyes. 'Oh, I've just lost my first patient here—that young woman I asked you to phone about yesterday, the one who discharged herself?'

She nodded. 'What was it?'

'Don't know. Drugs? Something neurological? Whatever, she arrested, and she didn't make it.'

'And the baby?' she asked, knowing the answer, her soft heart reaching out to the poor little thing.

'No chance. Even without all the other strikes against it, the mother was a smoker and obviously had something else going on, either a habit or an illness that affected her health, so even if we'd got it out, the baby was probably doomed. It certainly wasn't very big, so it might not have been viable yet anyway. I don't know, the post-mortem will tell us the rest of the story, hopefully.'

He dragged in a deep breath and sat back, studying her thoughtfully over the top of his mug. 'So, how are you?'

'Me?' Molly laughed a little self-consciously, remembering her rather hasty departure from his house the previous evening. 'OK. Thanks for last night.'

His smile was gentle and understanding—too understanding. 'Any time,' he said, then added softly, 'You did very well. It can't have been easy.'

'Oh, it wasn't,' she confessed with a rueful smile. 'Jack's wet little kiss did me in. I didn't get far down the road before I had to pull over. Libby was wonderful.'

'She is wonderful. She's a lovely girl.'

'She's just like Mick—so many of his best qualities, and none of my failings, thank God.'

He chuckled. 'I'm sure she has failings.'

'Oh, yes—but not mine. Not sloth and disorganisation and paranoia.'

He laughed again. 'Are you paranoid?'

'Only about things that matter,' she admitted. 'Things like safety and being honest and being fair.'

'And bedtime,' he teased, and she felt herself colour.

'I'm not really paranoid about bedtime,' she told him. 'It's just if you don't have rules, you let things stretch further and further and that isn't good for anyone.'

'You're so sensible.'

She laughed a little awkwardly. He wouldn't have said that if he'd been privy to her dreams last night, but that was between her and her maker, and there was no way he was getting an inkling! She changed the subject swiftly.

'I've got something to tell you. Did you know that Liz and David—the prolapsed-cord people—are calling their son Samuel after you? It was apparently on their list, and, since you saved his life yesterday, they thought it was appropriate.'

Sam chuckled. 'It's probably more appropriate than Lucy, anyway.'

Molly laughed. 'Probably.' She glanced at her watch. 'I need to go. I've got a mum hotting up a little—I know I've got my bleeper, but it's her third, and I have an idea that when things start moving, they'll go so fast I won't even get the gloves on before the baby arrives!'

'Well, enjoy it. Nothing like a nice, uncomplicated birth and a healthy baby to set the world to rights.'

She smiled at him gently. 'Feel free to join us if you need a little therapy.'

His answering smile was crooked. 'You know, I might just do that,' he said.

She left him finishing his coffee and went back up to Maternity, arriving just in the nick of time as her patient, Christine, suddenly shifted up a gear or three and went into the second stage, without bothering with transition except to retch quietly and tell her husband she was never speaking to him again.

Ten minutes later they had their baby, a beautiful little girl, the daughter they'd longed for, and in the midst of the tears and laughter Molly turned and found Sam standing by the door, a wistful smile on his lips.

Their eyes met and he pulled a face and grinned.

'Feel better?' she asked softly, and he chuckled.

'Yes, thank you. You obviously don't need me. I'll see you later.'

He went out, leaving her to attend to her patient with a little glow of satisfaction and the warmth of his smile still curled around her heart.

The unknown woman had died of a cocktail of drugs complicated by a massive brain tumour. She'd probably been taking the drugs to dull the pain—either that or she'd been on them anyway. Whatever, the combination had been enough to kill her, and so far, two days later, they were still no nearer knowing who she was.

A photograph of her was put on the television news, but nobody came forward, and Sam couldn't believe that a girl so young could die such a lonely and unmourned death.

The police were running missing persons' checks, using DNA and fingerprints as well as the photograph to try and identify her, and hopefully that would yield some results.

Sam felt for the little boy who would have been her son. At least Jack had a father who loved him, and Debbie and

Mark to care for him, and now Molly was back in his life. That poor baby would have had nobody—no history, nothing to tell him where he'd come from. How would that feel as an adult?

Hideous. Lonely, isolating—unbearably sad. Still, it was all academic, because the baby wouldn't get the chance to find out. One comforting thought was that he'd been too young to be viable, so even doing an emergency section to get him out wouldn't have helped.

Sam sat on the edge of Jack's bed and looked down at the sleeping child, and felt a great welling of love rise up inside him. His son was sometimes the only thing that kept him sane, and although there were other times when Jack nearly drove him to distraction, Sam couldn't imagine life without him.

And it was all thanks to Molly.

With a quiet sigh he stood up and went downstairs, not to the sitting room—so big, so empty—but into the sanctuary of his study. After the kitchen, it was fast becoming his favourite room in the house, and he used it as a bolt-hole when things got too much.

He had a comfortable old sofa in there, and a bookcase full of well-thumbed old favourites, and a pile of his favourite easy-listening CDs next to a little sound system.

There was an Eva Cassidy album in the CD player, and he pressed the 'play' button, dropped into a corner of the sofa and closed his eyes with a grunt of relief. The day was officially over. When he could be bothered he'd get up and go and pour himself a glass of wine, but for now he was content just to sit and listen to Eva's soft, haunting voice filtering through the speakers, and do nothing.

There were lights on in the house—a dim glow from an upstairs window, lights at Debbie's and Mark's end, and a welcoming glow from the room to the left of the front door.

Molly walked slowly up the path, pausing to glance in through that inviting window. There was a cat on the window-sill, and it eyed her with supercilious disinterest for a moment before turning away. Smiling to herself, she looked past it and into the room, and the smile softened.

Sam was lying on the sofa, his feet up on one end, his head propped against the arm at the other, and she could hear music playing softly in the background. He looked utterly relaxed and completely at home, and at first she thought he was asleep, but then she noticed one big toe moving in time to the music.

She stepped closer, reaching out to tap lightly on the glass, and his eyes opened and he turned his head towards her.

'Molly.'

She didn't hear, just saw his mouth form the word, and then the smile of welcome curved his lips and softened the harsh lines bracketing his mouth.

He went out of the room, and they arrived at the front door simultaneously, both speaking at once.

'I'm sorry to come unannounced—'

'It's good to see you—'

They laughed softly, and he drew her in, taking her arm and ushering her through the door and down the hall. 'We'll go in the sitting room,' he suggested, and she glanced at the lit doorway behind him.

'Can't we go in there?' she said wistfully. 'It looked so inviting as I walked up the path.'

'It's a mess,' he warned, but she didn't care.

'It doesn't matter. I'm not here to check on your house-keeping skills.'

He laughed. 'That's a good job. They're slight in the

extreme, and the only thing Debbie's allowed to do in there is vacuum the floor.' He didn't go in there, though, but led her through to the kitchen, put the kettle on and then turned and propped himself against the front of the Aga and tipped his head on one side, eyeing her thoughtfully.

'So—bearing in mind I'm pleased to see you whatever the reason, *was* there a reason for your visit, or is it just a social call?'

'Oh.' Molly coloured slightly, feeling suddenly a little awkward. 'I was at a loose end, and I was passing. I just thought—you said something about videos.'

Sam pulled a face. 'Oh, Molly, I'm sorry. I still haven't found them. I think they might be in a box in the loft, but I still haven't got round to looking, to be honest. We can go and look now, if you like?'

She shook her head and backed towards the door, not wanting to crowd him. 'Don't worry. Any time will do. I was literally passing—I've just dropped Libby off with my parents for the weekend. I'm on a late tomorrow, and I'm working the weekend, so she's with them from tonight. I just thought, as I was so close…'

'Sorry. Still, at least you haven't had a wasted journey over here. I will try and find them, I promise. Can I get you a drink anyway? I've put the kettle on, but I can offer you juice, or wine, or whatever.'

'Coffee?'

'Sure—unless…' He shrugged. 'If you want, we could share a bottle of wine and you could stay the night, if you don't have a pressing reason to get home.'

Her heart crashed against her ribs. Stay? With him?

'I've got two spare rooms,' he went on, 'and I keep them permanently made up. Jack's in bed, Debbie and Mark are off duty and I was about to break open a bottle, but I hate drinking alone. If you aren't on until late tomorrow, we could have a dig around in the loft, settle down for a long and self-indulgent session in front of the television and watch Jack's videos from start to finish.'

Molly was so tempted.

Tempted by Sam, tempted by the company. Above all, tempted by the thought of seeing all those images of her son—no, not her son. Jack.

And Sam's intentions seemed totally honourable.

Unfortunately.

No. She mustn't think like that. Keep it simple.

'Are you sure?' she asked, in no hurry to go home to her empty house and stare in disinterest at the indifferent summer offerings on the television. She could do the ironing or weed the garden, but this—well, this was so much more appealing.

'Of course I'm sure. The evenings get a bit lonely sometimes,' he admitted, and there was a flash of something in his eyes that her soft heart recognised and reached out to.

She smiled, and one heavy brow quirked upwards in enquiry.

'So—was that a yes, then?'

She laughed. 'Yes—please, if you don't mind. I won't stay, but I can have one glass of wine, and I'd love to sit and wallow in the videos. I know there are a million things I should be doing instead, but…'

She broke off with a shrug, and he shot her a crooked grin and shrugged away from the Aga, sliding the kettle off the hob and putting the lid down. 'Tell me about it,' he said drily. 'Right—first stop the loft, then back to the kitchen for the bottle of wine, then wall-to-wall baby videos.'

*   *   *

She should have expected to feel emotional watching it, but somehow the video of Jack's birth brought back so many deeply buried feelings that she was utterly unprepared.

Crystal was wielding the camera, and there were some candid shots that she could have lived without, but it was the expression on Sam's face in the recording as he encouraged and supported her through her labour that she found most revealing.

She'd been a little preoccupied at the time and so she hadn't really noticed how he'd reacted, although she'd been hugely reliant on his presence throughout. And when Jack had been born, he'd made no attempt to hide his very evident emotion.

She hadn't realised that. She'd been too busy trying to hide her own to worry about anyone else's, and, anyway, her attention by then had all been on the baby.

And he, of course, had been handed to her initially, and then once the cord had been cut, to Crystal.

Sam had taken over filming at that point, until Jack's screams had got to them all and the midwife had taken him from his uneasy mother and handed him to Sam. He'd given Crystal back the camera, and she'd caught the moment when Sam had taken his son in his arms for the first time.

The screams had stopped, settling to soft, unhappy hiccups and then to silence, and Molly had met Sam's proud and tear-filled eyes and had slowly nodded her approval.

That, she realised, was the moment when she'd relinquished the child who wasn't her son—the child she'd nurtured and supported from the moment he'd been implanted into her womb, the child she'd felt kick and squirm inside her for all those long months until the moment of his birth.

She'd handed him over, as agreed—but not to his

mother, she acknowledged now in a moment of astonishing clarity. She'd given him to his father, instinctively realising that he was the one she could trust with this precious gift.

Was that why Jack had stopped crying? Because he, too, had instinctively trusted his father? Or was it because Sam was used to handling babies and was more confident with him?

She didn't know, and it didn't really matter now, she supposed. Not after so many other things had happened in his short life.

Molly felt something splash on her hand, then again, and she realised in surprise that she was crying. Not sobbing, just—crying, tears streaming down her cheeks as she watched the fractured images and remembered.

'Here,' Sam said gruffly, and she felt him press a tissue into her hand.

He didn't touch her—didn't hug her or offer any words of comfort, and for that she was grateful, because she would simply have fallen apart. Instead he crouched down in front of the video machine and swapped tapes while she scraped her ragged emotions together and mopped herself up.

Then he sat down again beside her, put her glass of wine in her hand and settled back.

'Do you want to stop?'

She shook her head. 'No. No, I'm fine. It was just—it brought it all back.'

He nodded slowly. 'I know. I haven't seen it before. Crystal put it away.'

His voice sounded rough, unused, and it dawned on her that he might have left her alone in order to be alone himself—that maybe crouching down in front of the television had been to give himself time to recover, as much as her.

Had the images of Crystal hurt him? Did he still love her, despite the way she'd behaved before her death?

She didn't know, and it didn't seem appropriate to ask, but her heart reached out to him. She'd been devastated when Mick had died, and nothing but time had taken away the pain.

Time, and doing what she'd done, loaning her body to bear someone else's child, so they too could experience the happiness she and Mick had shared when Libby had been born.

Except, of course, she hadn't been detached enough, even just as a host mother. She'd allowed herself to care too much about each of those babies, and although she'd stayed in touch with Laura, being denied access to Jack had torn her apart.

Or was it really Jack? Had it been Sam she'd missed, in fact, Sam she'd wanted to see so that every day had become a wasteland without his smile?

She remembered the first time she'd seen his smile, when she'd visited her friend Lynn in London after she'd given birth to her first surrogate baby. Sam had been standing beside her bed, and Lynn had looked up and said something to him, and he'd turned to her, and their eyes had met and locked.

In that moment, before she'd known what he'd want from her, before she'd had any idea of what lay ahead, some bond had been forged between them. And over the months their friendship had grown and deepened, forming a bond so deep she would have trusted him with her life. Under other circumstances, she thought—but there had been no other circumstances.

Until now.

But now was no different. Nothing had changed, he still

wasn't available. He was still in love with Crystal, she realised, and so she was destined to be hurt all over again.

'This bit's snippets of the next few weeks,' he told her, and pressed the 'play' button on the remote control. The images flickered to life on the screen, Jack in the bath, Jack having a bottle, Jack with Crystal's parents—and as the video played, Sam watched Molly out of the corner of his eye.

She seemed all right now, more composed, laughing at the funny bits when Jack was older and his character started to show.

There was a chronological jump from when he was a little under a year to almost eighteen months, the time just after Crystal had died. She'd done most of the filming up till then, something that had hardly dawned on him, and it had all been staged.

Once things had settled down after her death and he'd started filming again, it had been more spontaneous. He would grab the camera if something funny happened when he was around, and the result was predictably less tidy but warmer, somehow. Strangely, their life felt like that now— less tidy, but warmer, more spontaneous, more genuine.

What a sad indictment of Crystal's contribution to their family life.

The tape came to an end, and for a moment Molly said nothing, then she turned to him with that understanding look in her eyes that seemed to see straight through him, and said, 'You really love him, don't you?'

Sam's smile felt a little off-kilter. 'It would be hard not to,' he said, remembering even so that Crystal had seemed to manage. The thought brought a familiar pang of sadness, but he ignored it, looking instead at Molly's glass and raising an eyebrow.

'Are you sure I can't talk you into having another one and staying? You're very welcome.'

'Are you trying to get me drunk?' she asked laughingly, and then their eyes met, and need, hot and urgent and totally unexpected, ripped through him.

He dragged his eyes away. 'As if I would,' he said lightly—or tried, but his voice sounded raw and unused, and he stood up and walked over to the television, gathering together the videos and his thoughts before he disgraced himself.

'I really ought to go,' she said softly. 'Thank you so much for showing me all of them.'

'There are more—here, borrow them and watch them in your own time, there's no hurry to have them back,' he said, rising and turning towards her with two more tapes in his hand. He thrust them at her, and she took them, her eyes scanning him warily. He didn't need her looking at him that closely. God only knows what she'd see.

He went past her and opened the door, and she gathered up her things and followed him, pausing in the confines of the entrance hall to look up at him one last time.

'Thanks again,' she murmured, and before he could move, she came up on tiptoe and brushed a feather-soft kiss against his cheek.

Then she was gone, leaving nothing behind but a lingering trace of her scent and a raging desire that would taunt him for the rest of the night.

CHAPTER FOUR

MOLLY was glad she hadn't stayed the night.

Even though she found the house empty and lonely without Libby, she needed to be alone to wallow in a totally self-indulgent howl. She watched the other videos, alternately laughing and crying, and as she watched she built up an image of Jack's life.

He seemed to integrate well with other children. Birthday parties and events at his nursery in London showed him happy and well adjusted, and she realised it was largely due to Sam and his enormous warmth.

Debbie and Mark had also taken turns filming over the last year, and so there were lots of scenes with Sam himself—scenes in which Molly found herself taking a very close interest for an entirely different reason.

'You're an idiot,' she told herself, after watching one scene three times on the trot. Stabbing the 'rewind' button, she went into the kitchen and made herself a hot drink, then turned off the television and video player and went to bed.

That didn't help. She could still see him laughing helplessly at something Jack had done, and closer to home, she could feel the rough scrape of stubble against her lips as she'd kissed him goodbye.

It would have been so easy to linger, to go back for more, to kiss him on those mobile, sculpted lips that her own were crying out to touch...

With a groan of frustration she set down her cup, flicked off the light and resolutely lay down on her side, one hand under her cheek, and forced herself to relax. She knew how to do it—she spent all day showing women in labour how to let go of tension to ease their contractions.

It just wasn't working for her tonight, that was all.

Relax your jaw, she told herself, and as her teeth lost contact with each other, she felt the tension drain away. Not for long, though. Not long enough to fall asleep and escape the memory of those laughing eyes and the rasp of stubble against her cheek...

It was one of those labours.

Typical, Molly thought. It's just because I've had practically no sleep and all I want to do is crawl into a corner and hide.

'Come on, let's go for another walk around and see if we can't move things on,' she suggested to the weary mother, and helped her off the edge of the bed. They walked slowly out of the delivery room and down the ward, round the nursing station and back to the delivery room, pausing on the threshold while Kate had another contraction.

'Oh, Molly, I can't do this,' the exhausted woman said when it had passed, and Molly was beginning to wonder if she wasn't right.

The baby's presentation had been fine initially, but it was a few days overdue and from her examination Molly had felt that it was a large baby. Not that it was always possible to tell, but she had a good feel for these things and her instincts were suddenly screaming that something had changed.

It wasn't Kate's first baby. If it had been, Molly would have called Sam in before now, just to be sure there wasn't a problem with her pelvis that had been missed.

Her last baby had been born normally, without any undue fuss by all accounts, and this was her third. It should have been easy, and it wasn't. It wasn't made any easier, either, by the fact that Kate's naval husband was on a tour of duty abroad and she was having to do this alone.

'Come on, let's have another look at you,' she said. 'I've got a feeling your baby's managed to get itself jammed in your pelvis, but I can't tell without a look.'

Molly helped her back onto the bed, and the briefest examination confirmed her fears. The baby's head was crowning, ready for delivery, but it was a posterior lie, with the baby facing the front, not the back, and the baby's shoulder was jammed over the top of the pubic bone, so the poor little thing was wedged and unable to descend any further.

'OK,' she said, stripping off her gloves. 'Your baby's got itself stuck. We just need to increase the diameter of your pelvis, and to do that I need you to rock on all fours, or go up and down steps, squat sharply, rock with one foot on a stool—anything like that which will stretch out that pelvis and give it a bit more room for that shoulder to come down.'

'Will it be enough?' Kate asked doubtfully. 'I thought they broke things when that happened, or is that just a myth?'

Rats. Molly paused, then went for the truth. Kate was an educated woman and there was no point in insulting her intelligence. 'No, it isn't a myth. It might mean that the baby's collar-bone has to bend to free it, so it could end up with a little greenstick fracture, but it won't be a problem for it, and we'll immobilise it if it happens so it won't feel pain afterwards, and they heal very quickly.'

Kate closed her eyes and swallowed. 'Oh, damn,' she said unsteadily. 'How dare Pete be away when I need him?'

Molly sat on the edge of the bed and gave Kate a re-assuring hug. 'Come on, we can do this. The sooner your baby's born, the better, really, and once that shoulder slips past the pelvis, it'll be out in no time, I promise, and there's a good chance it'll be absolutely fine.'

'Right.' Kate pulled herself together and gave Molly a brave smile. 'What do you want me to do?'

Molly helped her struggle awkwardly off the bed. 'Here—we've got some big hard foam blocks we can use.'

That was how Sam found them a few minutes later, with one of Kate's feet on the edge of a block, rocking back and forth.

He arched a brow in enquiry, and Molly sent him a silent plea for help.

'Kate's baby's shoulder's managed to get stuck, and it's a posterior lie,' she said calmly. 'We're just trying to free it, but we haven't had any luck yet.'

'Have you tried a squat?'

She shook her head. 'Not yet. We were just about to.'

'Try it—here, Kate, hang on the end of the bed and squat down quickly. Molly'll steady you, and I just want to see if I can give the baby's shoulder a little help with my hand to drop it off that bone,' he suggested, and Kate obediently changed position and tried again, with Sam crouching almost under her.

He placed the heel of his hand on the baby's shoulder, just above Kate's pelvic arch, and as she squatted he pushed firmly backwards.

'Oh,' she said, and looked up, alarmed. 'I can feel some-thing—oh, my God. It's moving— Ow!'

She sagged towards the floor, but Sam was there first, catching her before she hit the deck.

'OK, Kate, I've got you. Molly, check her while I sup-port her here.'

'She's there, it's free. And you shouldn't be holding her like that, the health and safety executive will have your guts for garters,' she muttered under her breath, but he just grinned.

'They have to catch me first. It's OK, Kate, we'll soon have you sorted.'

He took the big inflatable gym ball Molly shoved in his direction and helped Kate drape herself over it, then knelt down behind her as Molly quickly covered the floor mats with clean sheets in the nick of time.

'Kate, pant for me, don't push,' Molly instructed, but Kate wasn't having any of it. With a feral growl, she strained down and delivered her baby without further ado.

Sam didn't have gloves on, neither did Molly. There simply wasn't time, but neither of them cared. Kate and the baby came first, and just then their concern was for the little boy who was born screaming furiously and flailing one arm and both legs.

'Clavicle,' Sam said, lifting the tiny arm and holding it in place on his chest to relieve the stress on the fractured collar-bone.

'It's a boy, Kate, and he's fine,' Molly told her, hugging her gently. 'He's lovely. Let's just sit you down and you can hold him.'

She helped Kate roll over and lean against a backrest, then Sam pulled up her gown and laid the baby against her abdomen, skin to skin.

'I'm afraid his collar-bone's cracked, but he's going to be fine,' Sam told her. 'Just hold him like that for a moment, and we'll get the paediatrician to come and look at him and strap it so he'll be more comfortable, OK? In the meantime—well done. You did well—he's a heck of a size.'

'That's my husband,' she said, staring down at her baby

with a mixture of joy and concern in her eyes. 'He's six foot four, and every inch of it solid bone and muscle. The other two were big, but not like this. Oh, well, at least his lungs are all right!'

The baby's screams had subsided the moment he was put on Kate's now soft abdomen. Following her instincts, she shifted the baby carefully towards her breast and brushed the nipple against his cheek.

Immediately he turned, taking the nipple in his mouth and sucking vigorously, and Kate looked up with tears in her eyes.

'Well, there's nothing wrong with his jaws, either,' she said laughingly, and they all chuckled, the tension in the room dissipating as the baby's loud sucking replaced the sound of his whimpers.

'What about the placenta?' Sam asked quietly, but Molly just smiled and shook her head.

'I let nature take its course in the third stage, unless I'm worried. I don't believe in using Syntocinon unless I have to. If a mum's managed everything else herself, I reckon she can usually manage that, and there's no contraindication in her previous history.'

Sam nodded, a slow smile of approval appearing in his eyes. 'Good. Well, since you don't seem to need my muscles any more, I'll leave you to it.'

'You couldn't see if you could rustle up a cup of tea for Kate, could you?' she asked with a grin, and he rolled his eyes.

'I don't know—porter, kitchen assistant. You'll have me swabbing the floors next.'

Molly looked at the trail of amniotic fluid leading from the bed to the mats, and laughed. 'Since you mention it…!'

His snort floated on the air behind him, leaving both women chuckling.

'Do you think I'll get tea?' Kate asked, a smile lingering on her lips.

'I wouldn't be surprised,' Molly told her, and, true enough, a few minutes later he reappeared with a tray, three cups of tea and a plate of biscuits.

'Oh, top man,' Molly said with a smile of thanks, and he bowed and clicked his heels.

'We aim to please. Any progress?'

'Yes, we have one placenta, all present and correct, and everything's fine.'

'Excellent.' He passed Kate her cup once Molly had shifted her onto one side so the hot liquid wouldn't be above the baby, and settled down with one hip hitched on the edge of the delivery bed and his foot dangling, swinging idly in time to some inner beat.

He looked utterly relaxed, and yet Molly knew he was watching Kate for the slightest hint of trouble.

There was none, of course. She drank her tea, her eyes never leaving the now sleeping baby, and then, while Sam cuddled him, Molly helped Kate onto the bed, checked her and did the two little sutures that were necessary.

'Right, that's you fixed and sorted,' Molly said with satisfaction, and stripped off her gloves.

The paediatrician, Josh Lancaster, appeared at that moment and grinned at them.

'Hi, there. Got a baby for me to look at?'

'Wow, we get the boss man,' Molly joked, and Josh laughed.

'I was up in SCBU and my registrar's off sick, so I thought I'd call in on the way down. Hi, I'm Josh Lancaster, one of the consultant paediatricians,' he said to Kate, then looked at her more closely. 'Don't I know you?' he asked, and she smiled.

'Yes, possibly. My oldest, Nicky, had meningitis last year.'

'Of course. Doyle, isn't it? Kate and…Peter?'

She laughed, amazement in her voice. 'That's right. I'm surprised you remembered.'

'I never forget a parent, they're my greatest asset,' he said with a grin, and perched beside her. 'So, what happened?'

'He got stuck,' Kate said in disgust. 'Poor little scrap.'

'Little?' Sam said with a gust of laughter. 'Tell it to the fairies! Have you weighed him yet, Molly?'

'Oh, yes. He's a fraction under five kilos—that's almost eleven pounds.'

Kate's eyes widened. 'Good grief,' she said faintly. 'I thought he felt big when I was holding him, but I had no idea he was that big. He feels tiny compared to the others now, but I suppose he is huge.'

Josh chuckled. 'He must take after your husband—I seem to remember he towered head and shoulders over everyone in Paediatrics.'

He stood up and took the baby carefully from Sam. Laying him on the bed at his mother's feet where she could watch his examination, he carefully assessed the baby and nodded.

'Well, everything's fine. All his reflexes are good and he's all quite normal, except for the size and this clavicle which should heal very quickly—within days, really. I'll strap it to his chest to immobilise it—Molly, could you clean him up a bit for me first?'

She didn't attempt to bath him, not with the injury, just wiped him carefully with warm, damp swabs and patted his fragile skin dry.

Minutes later his arm was secured against his chest to stop any unnecessary movement, and Josh had shown Kate how to handle the baby so as to not put any pressure on the healing bone.

By this time Sam had been bleeped and had disappeared to another patient, and when Josh went, Kate looked up at Molly and gave her a shaky smile.

'OK?' Molly asked her gently, and without warning Kate burst into tears. 'Oh, sweetheart, he'll be all right,' she crooned comfortingly, rocking both of them against her chest. 'Don't be sad. He's OK.'

'It's just a shock,' Kate said, sniffing and easing away. 'I want to see Pete...'

And she started to cry again. Molly sat back and rubbed her hip gently and let her cry. After a few minutes Kate sniffed to a halt and gave Molly a watery smile.

'I'm sorry. I feel such an idiot.'

'Don't be daft. Your husband's thousands of miles away, you've just had a difficult and traumatic delivery, and you're only human. Here.' She plonked a handful of tissues in Kate's fingers and stood up. 'Let's move you back into the other room and get you settled. You'll be more comfortable there. Can I ring anyone for you, or get you the phone so you can contact anyone?'

Kate nodded. 'The phone would be good. I can get a message to Pete—he knew I was in labour this morning, and he'll be on tenterhooks by now.'

'I'll bet,' Molly said with a laugh. 'Come on, then, let's get you settled down and you can ring him and have a nice long chat.'

Molly was exhausted. She hadn't finished work until nine, and by the time she got home it was after half past and her lack of sleep the night before was telling on her.

She was just about to fall into a chair when the phone rang, and she sighed and picked it up. 'Hello?'

'Molly? It's Sam,' he said unnecessarily. 'Are you OK?'

She gave a short laugh. 'Knackered, but fine. Why?'

She could almost hear the shrug. 'Just wondered. Have you eaten?'

'Eaten? As in food? Not that I remember,' she said with a wry smile. 'To be honest, I don't think I can be bothered to cook.'

'That's what I thought, and Debbie doesn't cook for me on Friday nights because they go out to the pub for a meal at six, so I haven't eaten either. How do you fancy a take-away?'

Frankly, all she really fancied was crawling into bed, but then her stomach rumbled and reminded her just how hungry she was—and anyway, an excuse to spend time with Sam couldn't be bad.

'Sounds good,' she said, a little bit of her wondering how she'd find the energy. 'Shall I pick one up on the way over?'

'I'll come to yours, it was my idea,' he said promptly. 'And I've found the baby photos. I'll bring them. You need to give me your address.'

'One forty-seven Rushbrook Road,' she said. 'It's—'

'I know where it is. I looked at a house there when I was buying. Is your car on the drive?'

'Yes. The house is on the left as you head out of town, and the number's on the gate.'

'OK. Give me fifteen minutes. Chinese or Indian?'

'Don't care,' she said, placing her hand flat over her howling stomach to suppress it. 'Whatever's nearest to you—Chinese, probably. There's one on the roundabout near the hospital. Why don't you call them in advance? I can give you the number.'

'I tell you what, why don't you call them and order

whatever you fancy, and I'll pick it up? Get lots, I'm starving, and there's nothing I don't like.'

Lots, he said? Molly ordered a set meal for two with other bits and pieces, her stomach causing a ruckus through the entire procedure, and then to pass the time until he arrived she threw her breakfast things into the dishwasher, put some plates to warm and went round the sitting room like a whirling dervish, patting cushions and clearing up Libby's scattered possessions.

Not that it mattered what he thought of her house, of course, but she was suddenly and belatedly afflicted with an attack of house-pride, and of course she'd been saving the housework to do this weekend while Libby was away.

Sam arrived just as she was realising how bad the house was, and with a sigh of resignation she went to the door and opened it.

He was standing there with a white plastic carrier bag and a lazy, sexy grin. 'I take it you're hungry, too,' he said, brandishing the carrier bag, and stepped over the threshold, stooping to brush her cheek with his lips in passing.

Her heart stopped, then started again with a crash.

Food, she thought. Talk about the food.

'Well, you said lots,' she reasoned, trying to ignore the thrashing pulse in her throat and the jiggling in her stomach caused by his very presence. He'd shaved this evening, she noticed. His chin, as it had grazed her cheek, was smoother than his jaw had been the other night—gracious, last night.

Had it been only last night she'd sat up with him and watched the videos?

She led him through to the kitchen and pulled out a chair at her kitchen table—much smaller than his, and altogether less lovely, but all that would fit in her house—and waved him towards it.

'Here, sit down, the kitchen's not big enough for two people standing up,' she told him, and pulled the plates out of the oven, putting them down in front of him. He was unpacking the carrier bag, lifting out carton after carton of wonderful-smelling food, and her stomach rumbled loudly.

He laughed. 'Well, that answers that question,' he said with a grin, and pulled a bottle out of his pocket. 'Here— wine. I can only have one glass, but I'm sure you can finish it up on your own at some point.'

Molly would have drunk it all there and then in one swallow if she'd thought it would settle her gyrating heart. Instead she settled for handing him two glasses and the corkscrew while she opened the cartons and found some cutlery and the soy sauce.

For a while there was silence. Not an uncomfortable silence, but the dedicated and companionable silence of two hungry people sharing a meal together. Finally Sam laid down his fork and threw his hands in the air in defeat.

'I submit,' he said, laughing. 'I'll die if I eat any more.'

'Me, too,' she agreed, pushing away the remains of her third plateful. 'More wine?'

He shook his head. 'No, I mustn't, I'm driving. Don't let that stop you, though.'

Was it the wine, or his presence? Whatever, her guard was down. She made him coffee and poured herself another glass of wine, and they went through to the sitting room. He settled down on one end of the sofa and patted the cushion beside him, his face impassive.

'Photos,' he said, and she sat next to him and tried to maintain a distance, but it was impossible. She had to lean over to see the photos, and within a minute or two she'd ended up with her shoulder resting against his arm and her head so close to his their hair was touching.

She could feel the warmth of his body seeping into her, and she ached to snuggle up against him and absorb his warmth and companionship.

More than that, of course—much more than that, but more would be greedy, and frankly she'd settle for this…

'Molly? Are you asleep?'

She shook her head and straightened up. 'No. Just tired.'

'Here.'

Sam lifted his arm and tucked her into the hollow of his shoulder, wrapping his arm around her and snuggling her close, and then he carried on sifting through the photos and telling her about them, his voice warm and low, lulling her…

Sam looked down at the sleeping woman curled against his side and swallowed hard. She looked exhausted, but peaceful. Too peaceful to move, he thought, and, stretching out his legs, he shifted down the sofa a little and drew her closer to his chest.

Molly snuggled down, and he took the opportunity to study the room. It was very comfortably furnished, full of little homely touches that made him feel like an intruder— like the picture on the mantelpiece of her standing with a young man on a windy clifftop, laughing up at him while her hair streamed out behind her. The same man appeared in two other photos, one a wedding photo with Molly at his side, the other with Molly and a baby. In the last two photos, he was in a wheelchair.

Mick.

His arm tightened involuntarily, and she made a tiny, sleepy noise that nearly finished him and wriggled closer still. He looked down at her, soft and warm and inviting, and all the blood in his brain migrated south in aid of a more needy cause.

He closed his eyes and dropped his head back. Down, boy, he told himself. Too complicated. Too messy. Too hot to handle.

Oh, rats, he was going to get so seriously burned!

Molly woke some time later with a crick in her neck and the imprint of Sam's shirt buttons on her cheek. She knew that, because she could feel the dents in her skin when she rubbed it.

Great. She must look wonderful, with her hair all mussed and her skin flushed and creased and her eyes half-closed and bloodshot...

His arm tightened around her, drawing her back against him. 'Where are you going?' he asked, his voice low and gravelly in her ear.

'Nowhere. I was just sitting up.'

He released her, and she straightened and stretched a little, easing out the kinks. 'I'm sorry,' she said, embarrassment dawning as she woke up more and realised just how comprehensively she'd been asleep. 'I must have been more tired than I thought. Um—what's the time?'

He glanced at his watch and blinked to clear his eyes. 'Twelve-thirty.'

'Really? Oh, I'm so sorry.'

'Don't be.'

He caught her hand and she turned to look at him, her heart suddenly clamouring again.

'I need a drink,' she said hastily, pulling away from him. 'It's the Chinese. It always makes me thirsty. All that salt.'

She stood up and went quickly out to the kitchen, hoping he wouldn't follow her, but it was too much to expect. He was there at her elbow, taking her glass after she'd finished with it and filling it again, his throat working rhythmically as he drained it.

He was close to her—too close, so she could see every pore of his skin, every short, dark hair that stubbled his jaw.

He set the glass down and sighed.

'I must go. I'll leave the photos for you—you can go through them again at your leisure. They're all on disc, so I can print you copies of the lot, if you like.'

Molly swallowed. 'Thanks. I'll look at them tomorrow. And thank you for the meal and the wine, they were lovely.'

'Put the leftovers in the fridge. You'll have enough for tomorrow—today, even.'

'And the next day—if I can ever eat again,' she said with a hollow laugh. 'I still feel full.'

'You'll live.'

Sam paused just inside the front door and turned towards her. 'Thank you for your company this evening. It was fun. Eating alone is just refuelling, really, and—well, it was nice to have someone to share it with, make it more of an occasion for a change.'

He bent to kiss her cheek, just as she moved her head to shake the hair back from her face, and their lips collided. For a second they froze, then with a ragged sigh Sam drew her into his arms, tunnelled the fingers of one hand through her hair and anchored her head as his mouth came down on hers.

She'd never really understood the word hungry before, she thought dimly. Or urgent.

Sam was both, and his hunger fuelled hers. A cry rose in her throat, trapped by his lips, and she lifted her arms and threaded her fingers through the dark, silky strands of his hair, pulling him down again when he would have re-treated.

With a groan he shifted, pressing her body against the wall, his thigh hard and insistent between hers, rocking against her until she whimpered with need.

Then he lifted his head and stared down at her, swal-lowing convulsively and stepping back, ramming shaking fingers through his hair and leaving it rumpled and even more tempting.

'Hell, Molly, I'm sorry—I don't know what I was think-ing about. Dear God, I'm so sorry...'

She pressed her fingers against his lips and shook her head. 'Don't. Don't apologise. It was as much me as you.'

He gave a snort of disbelief and shook his head to clear it. 'Molly, I—I don't know what to say.'

She smiled somehow. 'Goodnight might be sensible,' she offered pragmatically, and he laughed and drew her back into his arms, hugging her gently before releasing her and stepping back.

'You're right, of course. Goodnight, Molly. I'll see you on Monday.'

And with that he was gone, leaving her in a welter of heated emotions and cold fried rice.

She laughed, because otherwise she would have cried, and because she couldn't bear to come down and sort it out in the morning, she cleared up the kitchen, loaded the dishwasher and went up to bed.

It was going to be another restless night, she thought, but she was wrong.

Even her overindulgence couldn't disturb the peaceful slumber she fell into, and she slept dreamlessly until nine the following morning, waking refreshed, if thirsty, and ready for the day.

She attacked the house and laundry until the place was

sparkling, and then settled down with a cup of tea and a Danish pastry, courtesy of the bakery round the corner, and looked through the photos again. She just had time to flick through them before she had to go to work at three.

The ones of Jack were lovely, of course, but it was the ones of Sam that drew her again and again. One in particular, of him with his son, made her heart swell just looking at it. And in another he was grinning cheekily, and the camera had caught a sexy dimple in his cheek that made her long for things she couldn't have.

Or could she? What was there to prevent her having a relationship with Sam?

Nothing. Mick was dead, and so was Crystal. They were both free, both apparently willing, and, heaven knows, it would be wonderful to be with him and Jack. Libby would love having a father, especially one as caring and warm as Sam, and Jack needed a mother.

If not his own, then who better than the woman who'd carried him?

No. That was going too far into the future, aiming for the moon and the stars, but down here, realistically within reach, surely there was something for them? There hadn't been before, and indeed it had never even been suggested, but now—who knows? She'd loved him before, with nothing between them and no hope of anything in the future that she'd been aware of. Now, with no reason why not, she realised her love had grown.

Molly stared sightlessly at the photo of Sam. She might not be the woman he'd put top of his list, but Crystal was gone, and there was something there between them, she knew that. Did they have a chance at happiness? And if so, didn't they owe it to themselves—and the children— to take it?

She focused on the picture, taking in again the planes

and angles of his face, the crease in his cheek, the deep laughter lines around his eyes and mouth, and she thought of his face after he'd kissed her, taut with desire.

The heat in his eyes had nearly brought her to her knees, and it gave her hope. If he wanted her that much—and it seemed certain that he did—perhaps that was the way to start.

An affair—nothing more, nothing complicated, just good old-fashioned chemistry given free rein.

She laughed softly. Oh, yes. That would be good—and it was about darned time.

All she had to do now was persuade Sam...

CHAPTER FIVE

SAM could have kicked himself all the way home. Why had he kissed her?

Idiot, he growled to himself. Stupid, stupid idiot. They had to be friends, for Jack's sake, and he had no business screwing around with Molly's emotions and messing her up. She'd had enough trauma in her personal life to date without him contributing to it in a fit of adolescent hormones!

He pulled up on his drive and dropped his head back against the headrest with a heavy sigh. Lord, she'd felt so good in his arms. Soft and ripe—and willing. Oh, yes, she'd been willing—but that wasn't the point.

The fact that they were attracted to each other was irrelevant under the circumstances. Jack was the only one who mattered here, and he'd do well to remember that.

Even if it meant he never got to lose himself in her arms, to bury himself in her body and find that glorious oblivion he knew was waiting for him there...

Damn!

He slammed his hand on the steering-wheel and winced, shaking it ruefully and rubbing it to ease the inevitable bruise. He wanted her. He'd wanted her for years, ever since he'd first set eyes on her, if he was honest, although he'd never acknowledged it before, and now that they were both free it was going to be even harder to walk away.

He'd do it, though. He'd do it for Jack.

He locked the car and went inside, closing the communicating door on the landing so Debbie and Mark would know he was home. Going into Jack's room, he stared down at him for an age, just to remind himself how important his son was.

Not that he needed reminding.

Jack was lying on his back, one arm outflung, and he looked so young, so vulnerable. He was only three years old, and he'd already lost his mother. Both his mothers, in fact.

First, he'd been separated from Molly, the woman who'd borne him. Had the baby he'd been then missed her? There was no way to tell, but Sam wouldn't have been surprised. Then Crystal, his real mother, hadn't wanted to be, and had escaped her responsibilities whenever possible. Had that damaged him? Sam had done everything in his power to minimise that damage—but then, with her death, their young son had suffered the ultimate loss.

Sam couldn't expose him to any further hurt, and he wouldn't, even if it meant denying himself a relationship with Molly. He'd sooner die than hurt his child any more.

Kissing Jack lightly on the forehead, he tucked the covers round his skinny little shoulders and went to bed, only to lie there till dawn tormented by a need that went soul-deep, a need he refused to acknowledge as anything but physical.

It was just frustration. It had been over two years, after all. More than that, probably. He'd hardly touched Crystal after Jack was born because she'd withdrawn from him, and, naïve fool that he was, he hadn't realised why until it was too late.

There'd been no one since. He'd been too busy making sure that Jack's life was as smooth and happy as possible, and there'd been no time to think about what he was missing.

He was only thirty-four, though—thirty-five in November. Still young enough to burn for a woman.

And, dear God, he was burning for Molly. He closed his eyes against the morning light and rolled to his side, pulling the quilt up over his eyes. It didn't help. He could still see her, her mouth soft and swollen from his kiss, her eyes wide and vulnerable, their beautiful golden brown trusting and confused.

He swallowed hard. She'd been his for the asking. He could have been with her even now, this terrible ache burned away by the fire that would have consumed them—

'Daddy?'

He pulled the quilt down from his eyes and raised himself on one elbow, stifling a groan. 'Hello, Jack. You OK, son?'

Jack nodded, clambering up onto the bed and squirming down under the covers against his chest.

'Do you need the loo?' Sam asked him automatically, but Jack shook his head.

'Done a wee by myself. Want a cuddle,' he said, thrusting his skinny bottom towards Sam's stomach. His cold little feet settled on Sam's thighs, and the steady rise and fall of his chest slowed into sleep.

Sam's heart contracted. This was what it was all about—this was all that mattered.

Tears filled his eyes and, closing them, Sam snuggled the little body closer to his own and finally, comforted by his son's presence, he drifted off.

It was a busy week, and there weren't any chances to talk.

At least, not to say what Molly had to say to Sam, and she was beginning to wonder if there would ever be an opportunity. And gradually, as the days went by, it dawned on her that he was avoiding her.

Oh, he was perfectly polite, but instead of seeking her out for coffee, as he had done the previous week, he seemed to be permanently tied up.

So, if she wanted to talk to him, she was going to have to make it happen.

She collared him on Thursday afternoon just as he was leaving the ward, and if she'd had any doubts before, the way his eyes avoided hers laid them to rest.

'Have I done something wrong?' she asked quietly, and his eyes met hers briefly and slid away, their expression shuttered and unreadable.

'Wrong? Of course not.'

'So why are you avoiding me?'

'I'm not—'

'Don't lie to me, Sam,' she said softly. 'You owe me more than that.'

'Oh, hell.' He stabbed a hand through his hair and sighed. 'I just— Last Friday night—'

'Sam, it was just a kiss.'

He said something short and to the point, and his eyes met hers then, their expression far from shuttered this time. She felt a warm tide of colour sweep her skin, starting at her feet and working up steadily to her hairline, and it was her turn to look away.

She didn't let herself, though, not for more than a second. 'I wanted to talk to you,' she said, taking her courage in both hands. 'When can we meet? Alone?'

'I'm not sure that's a good idea.'

She sighed. 'Sam, we're both adults.'

'That's the trouble,' he admitted, and this time when their eyes met they held. After a moment he let his breath out on a gusty sigh and rammed a hand through his hair again, defeat showing in every line of his body. 'OK. Whenever. I've got the resident babysitter, you tell me.'

'Saturday afternoon? Libby's got a birthday party from two in the afternoon. I don't have to pick her up until ten on Sunday morning.'

Something—heat or panic—flared in his eyes, and he looked away. 'OK. I'll come to you—say, three o'clock?'

She nodded. 'Fine. I'll make a cake.'

He made a strangled sound that could have been disbelieving laughter, and backed away, heading for the door. 'I have to go—I'm meeting a patient and her husband, and they're waiting for me. I'll see you later.'

'I'm off duty now until Monday. I'll see you on Saturday.'

He nodded, turned and strode away from her, and Molly got the unsettling feeling that if he could have outrun his thoughts, he would have done exactly that.

They make a good-looking couple, Sam thought as he walked down through the antenatal clinic to his office. He wondered why they'd waited eight years before trying for another child, but there was nothing in the notes to indicate they'd had trouble conceiving.

Was it just anxiety that had made them hold back?

They saw him coming and got to their feet, and he held out his hand in greeting, a smile coming readily to his lips. 'Sally, it's good to meet you. Glad you could make it, Nick. Come on into my office.'

He ushered them in, closed the door and waved at the chairs in front of his desk. 'Please, take a seat, make yourselves comfortable.' He settled himself behind the desk, opening the notes which lay in front of him but scarcely giving them a glance. He knew about the notes. It was

Sally he wanted to look at, and she looked well, he was pleased to see.

'Can I say something before you start?' Nick said, and he nodded.

'Of course.'

'It's about the other day. I hope you didn't think I was pulling rank or trying to get preferential treatment—'

Sam waved him aside. 'Don't be silly. I'm glad you came and found me, Nick. I always try to see staff myself if I possibly can, just as a matter of professional courtesy, but with the change-over from Will Parry you could easily have slipped through the net, so I'm glad you brought it to my attention. And anyway, if you can't help your colleagues, it's a pretty lousy system.'

He glanced down at the notes, checked the EDD, or estimated date of delivery, and looked up again at his patient. 'OK, Sally, you're thirty-six weeks this week, is that right?'

Sally nodded. 'Yes—thirty-seven weeks on Sunday. I've been monitored every fortnight, and it's down to weekly now—and I had the scans in London at twenty and twenty-eight weeks to check for congenital heart abnormalities.'

'And they were clear.'

'Yes.'

Sam ran his eye over the notes again, checking them for the umpteenth time, but he knew the contents by heart except for the new weight, blood pressure and urine test results which had been added today. All of them were fine. He shut the folder and sat back.

'OK, now, obviously I can't make you any guarantees, but your check a fortnight ago with Will Parry seems to have been fine, as were all the previous ones, and so far everything looks OK today. We're as certain as we can be from the ultrasound scans that the baby's heart is normal, and, from looking at your notes from that time, it seems highly likely that your little girl's heart defect was a tragic one-off developmental anomaly, and it's most unlikely to be repeated.'

Sally nodded, but there was a lingering worry in the back of her eyes that only the safe delivery of a normal, healthy baby would take away.

'Is there anything you want to ask me?' he prompted, but she shook her head.

'Nothing you can tell me without lying,' she said with a brave smile. 'I'll just have to wait and see, but it's getting harder. I mean, I know the baby's heart is probably fine, but—well, there are other things that can go wrong, and I can't help worrying about them. I just feel…' Her eyes filled. 'I don't know—threatened, somehow.'

Sam nodded slowly. 'I'm sure. It's understandable. Just hop up on the couch and let me have a look at you.'

He rubbed his hands together to warm them, then laid them gently on the firm swell of her pregnant abdomen. He could feel the curve of a little bottom hard up under her ribs, and as he pressed down on it, he could feel the head descending neatly into the pelvis.

The baby wriggled in protest, and he could feel its solid little heels tracking over the inside of Sally's uterus under his hand.

'It's going to be a footballer, we reckon,' Nick said, watching from the sidelines, and Sam threw him a smile.

'Certainly active and reactive. It's a good size for your dates, not too much fluid—everything feels absolutely text-book normal. Having many Braxton-Hick's contractions?'

She nodded. 'Constantly. I didn't really have them before, it was too early on.'

He felt the tightening of her uterus then, under his hands, and then after a few seconds it relaxed again. 'Is that typical?'

'Yes—they're like that all the time. Is that OK?'

'Fine. It's what I'd expect. The head isn't engaged yet, but it's going to drop soon, and that should ease the discomfort under your ribs—give you a bit more room to breathe.'

He helped her sit up, and went back behind his desk, jotting down a few remarks in her notes while she straightened her clothes and sorted herself out. Then he capped his pen and sat back.

'Right, go home, do nothing abnormal. Don't over-exert yourself, don't treat yourself like an invalid, just be sensible. If it feels OK, it probably is. You've got my numbers. Call me at any time, day or night—and I really mean that. I'll see you next week unless you decide to go into labour. If you do, I'll see you before—but don't worry. As I said, everything looks textbook normal, and there's no reason why it shouldn't be. The baby's perfectly big enough now to be viable, and I'm sure it'll come when it's ready.'

She nodded and stood up awkwardly, Nick helping her to her feet with gentle concern.

Sam looked away, suddenly stupidly jealous of this devoted couple on the threshold of a miracle. To make a baby in the normal way, to watch it grow, to see it born, to raise it—this was everyone's birthright, and yet it had eluded him and Crystal and countless others. It had eluded these two before as well, of course, and that made this time all the more special.

And it wasn't only the baby, he realised. It was the love they shared, this couple, the tenderness between them, the gentle banter as she rearranged her clothes and Nick put her shoes back on because, as she said, her feet seemed to have got further away.

'You go and relax now,' he said, conjuring up a smile and holding the door for them. 'I'll see you soon. Take care of each other.'

He watched them go, then closed the door of his office and slumped down at the desk, suddenly acutely aware of how lonely his life was, how devoid of any meaningful adult relationship.

It didn't have to be, of course, but that was even more terrifying than the loneliness.

Molly wanted to see him, to talk about last Friday, and he didn't know what the hell she was going to say. He just felt he wasn't going to like hearing it, and he didn't want to open that particular can of worms again in a hurry. It had taken him the entire weekend to get the lid back on, and now nearly a week later he wasn't sure how successful he'd been.

He still wasn't sleeping properly, and when he did, his dreams were full-on Technicolor and definitely X-rated. They were getting worse, the worms thrashing away against that insecure lid and doing their damnedest to escape.

And Molly, for sure, was going to rip the lid off again and, unless he was very much mistaken, tip the whole wretched mess out all over his carefully orchestrated life.

* * *

'Angie?'

'Molly, how lovely to hear from you! How are you?'

Molly laughed wryly. 'Confused. Are you around? I'd love to talk to you if you're not busy.'

Angie chuckled. 'I'm always busy, but I'm always ready for an excuse to stop. Want to meet for coffee? Or lunch?'

'Coffee would be good. I need to get back for Libby.'

'And I've got to pick Laura up at three-thirty, so why don't we do a light early lunch? We'll meet halfway—in Norwich?'

'That would be wonderful.'

They chose a venue with a car park, and an hour later Molly walked into the café and Angie's open arms.

Her friend hugged her and stood back, searching her face. 'You look good,' she announced, and Molly laughed.

'I don't know why. I'm not sleeping properly.'

'Man trouble?'

Trust Angie to cut right to the chase. 'Not exactly,' she said evasively, but that wasn't good enough.

Angie's eyes lit up with curiosity, and she steered Molly towards the counter. 'Come on, we'll get coffee and then you can tell me all.'

All? Molly wasn't sure about that, but Angie, as the mother of Molly's other surrogate child, was the one person in the world who would understand Sam's feelings as well as Molly's, and she wanted a bit of inside information before confronting him tomorrow. If that meant spilling her guts, well, she'd just have to do it.

They found an empty table by the window and Angie set the tray down, slid into the seat and leant forwards, her eyes still alive with curiosity.

'So—tell me all.'

Molly laughed again. 'You really go for the jugular, don't you?' she said ruefully, chasing froth round on her coffee with a spoon.

Angie's face was immediately contrite. 'I'm sorry, but you know me. I can't do small talk—not when there's big talk lurking in the wings, and this is big, isn't it?'

Molly nodded slowly. She took a sip of her coffee and propped her elbows on the table, nursing the cup while she groped for words. 'How much does it matter to Laura, having me in her life?'

Angie blinked, and sat back a little, her face puzzled. 'A lot—a huge amount.'

'Because she knows who I am.'

'Yes—but she would have to. Mothers talk to their daughters about their obstetric history. I can't do that—I'd have to lie to her or refuse to answer her questions, and I won't do that, so she had to know.'

'But would it matter if I wasn't here?' Molly persisted. 'If she'd never met me, or didn't know who I was? Would it matter to her?'

Angie stared at Molly thoughtfully. 'I really don't know,' she said slowly. 'Yes, I'm sure it would. She feels comfortable with you—safe. It's like the circle's completed. She has three parents—me, Doug and you. Of course you matter.'

Her brows drew together into a puzzled frown. 'Molly, why are you asking me this? What's it about?'

For a moment she didn't answer, then she took a steadying breath and prepared to open her heart. 'Jack,' she replied slowly, 'it's about Jack.'

Angie leant forward, her face suddenly concerned. 'Your other surrogate baby?'

Molly nodded again. 'I've met up with him—and his father. His mother's dead, and his father's working at the hospital.'

'Good grief. And I take it from what you've been asking me that Jack doesn't know anything about you?'

'No, not yet. That's nothing to do with me, really, and he's only just three. I'm just trying to come to terms with seeing him when I thought I never would, and I wondered if you'd ever wished I wasn't around in Laura's life.'

'Never,' Angie said firmly, and so emphatically that Molly knew it was from the heart. Her eyes filled, and she nodded.

'Thank you. I needed to know that.'

'So—have you seen Jack? Is he all right? And what about his father? Is that really awkward? I mean, is he difficult about you and Jack? I thought they didn't want you to see him.'

'Sam didn't mind, it was Crystal,' Molly explained. 'And Sam hasn't been awkward—just the opposite. He's been wonderful.' She hesitated. 'That's the trouble. There's this attraction...'

Angie's mouth rounded in a silent O. 'Does he want to have an affair with you?' she asked, the curiosity back in her eyes at this new turn.

Molly shrugged. 'I don't know. I hope so. I want one with him.'

Angie studied her thoughtfully for a moment. 'Are you sure?'

'Sure?'

'That it's not just about Jack? About getting closer to him?'

She shook her head. 'No. Absolutely not. This is about

us, me and Sam, nothing to do with Jack. My relationship with Jack is just a complication, and I don't want to compromise it. That's why I wanted your advice.'

Angie nodded slowly. 'OK. Well, I would say if it's what you want, then go for it. It just doesn't seem like you—but, still, it's about time. When did you last have an affair? Yonks ago, I'll bet—either that or you're dead discreet.'

Molly gave her coffee an unwarranted amount of attention. 'Angie, I don't do affairs. That's why I needed to talk to you.'

'Well, *I* don't do affairs!' Angie said in amazement, and then leant forwards and lowered her voice, belatedly conscious of all the other diners. 'So, anyway, how can I help you?' she murmured. 'I'm not sure I'm qualified to give advice.'

'Oh, you are, because it's Jack I'm worried about.'

'Jack?'

Molly nodded. 'I've never had an affair—Mick was my first and only love, so I don't know what it's like when things go wrong. I just feel—I need to stay friends with Sam, no matter what happens, to keep the lines of communication open between me and Jack. If he needs me, he should be able to see me, and I don't want our relationship compromised because his father and I have history.'

Angie eyed her assessingly. 'You realise, of course, that you've already condemned this relationship before it's even started?'

Molly gave a humourless laugh. 'I have, haven't I? I think he's still in love with Crystal.'

'And yet you think he'd have an affair with you?'

She nodded.

'Why?'

Her cheeks burned, and she looked down into the cold, unappealing froth on her coffee. The chocolate sprinkle was drying round the rim, and she dipped her finger in the liquid and rubbed it, loosening the residue.

'Molly? Why do you think you could end up having an affair?'

She sat back, rubbing the tip of her finger on her napkin and reluctantly meeting Angie's all-too-seeing eyes.

'He kissed me.'

'Just once?'

Just? Molly laughed softly under her breath. 'Just once,' she agreed. 'I thought the hall would catch fire.'

'Spontaneous human combustion,' Angie said thoughtfully, and smiled. 'Sounds interesting. I should go for it.'

'And Jack?'

'You'll work it out. All sorts of people have relationships in compartments in their lives. You don't have to be all things to each other and, anyway, if it goes wrong it shouldn't stop you seeing Jack. After all, divorced couples manage to sort out custody arrangements.'

'But they have rights. I have no rights.'

'So don't let the affair end if you don't want it to,' Angie said, and she made it sound so simple that Molly believed her.

'I have to let it start first,' she pointed out, but Angie just laughed.

'It doesn't sound as though that's going to be a problem—and if you want me to babysit, just ask.'

Molly met her eyes and smiled slowly. Excitement and anticipation were bubbling inside her. 'I might just do that,' she vowed.

*   *   *

'Can you babysit for me tomorrow afternoon?'

Debbie shoved the door of the dishwasher shut with her hip and nodded, rubbing her hands on a teatowel to dry them.

'Sure. Have you got to go to the hospital?'

Sam contemplated lying, then thought better of it. 'No. I'm meeting Molly,' he said, and then immediately regretted his honest streak as Debbie's face became a window on her curious and warm-hearted soul.

'It's just to sort out some things to do with Jack,' he said lamely, trying to distract her, but she wasn't that stupid.

'Yeah, right,' she said, and, dropping the teatowel into the washing-machine, she propped herself on the front of the Aga and gave him a searching, level look. 'It's time, you know.'

'What's time?' he asked, kicking himself for encouraging her and not telling her to go to hell.

'Time you had a woman in your life. You're lonely, Sam. You shouldn't be. You've got so much to offer, and Molly's lovely. You should go for it.'

'There is no "it",' he said, lying to himself now as well as Debbie, but she saw straight through him and snorted softly.

'If you say so. Your supper's in the bottom of the Aga— it's some leftover cottage pie from last night. Mark and I are off now to the pub, we'll see you later. Oh, what time tomorrow, by the way?'

'I said I'd be there at three.'

'OK.' She headed for the communicating door, pausing as she went through it. 'Just think about it, Sam. Don't close the door on it—not till you've seen what's on the other side.'

And she closed her door, the real door, leaving him alone on his side.

Was that what he'd do if he turned away from Molly? Shut himself in alone on his side? But what lay through that door?

He swallowed hard, fear wrestling with eager anticipation. Damn. Too many feelings, too much emotion.

Jack wandered through from the sitting room, Mark's and Debbie's cat draped over his shoulder like a limp rag, and looked up at his father.

'Want a video,' he said.

Sam nodded, too distracted to insist on the 'please'. 'OK. Let me get my supper and I'll come.'

He spent the evening with Jack, watching children's movies and contemplating the can of worms that lay in wait for him on the other side of that door, and wished he could see into the future.

If he could, of course, if he'd been able to, he wouldn't be here now with Jack.

Maybe it was just as well that some things remained unknown—but just now, he would have given almost anything for a glimpse into the future…

CHAPTER SIX

IT WAS three o'clock on Saturday afternoon, and Molly felt sick. Her palms were damp, and her heart was thrashing against her ribs.

What if Sam laughed at her? What if he just said a flat-out no?

What if he didn't?

Her heart lurched into her throat, and she closed her eyes and sat down abruptly at the kitchen table. She was being silly. She was thirty-three and, as Angie had said, it was about time.

The cake was cooling on a wire rack on the side, and the kitchen was fragrant with the smell of baking. The kettle had boiled, the pot was warming, and all she needed now was Sam.

She glanced up at the clock. Three-ten. He was late.

Or else he wasn't coming.

Disappointment coursed through her, and with wry honesty she laughed at herself.

'Either you want him or you don't,' she said out loud, just as a car swept onto her drive and pulled up under the kitchen window.

Their eyes met through the two sheets of glass, and for a moment they both sat there. Then, drawing a steadying breath, Molly got to her feet and went to the door, her legs like jelly.

He was there by the time she reached it, flowers in his hand, and his face was unusually serious.

He's nervous, she realised with sudden insight, and felt instantly better.

'Come in,' she said, and he stepped past her with a quick flicker of a smile that didn't reach his eyes.

She led him to the kitchen, then looked down at the white-knuckled grip he had on the flowers and smiled.

'Are they for me, or did you just want something to strangle?' she asked softly, and he gave a short huff of laughter and held them out to her.

'I'm sorry. My social skills are a bit rusty. That's just to say I'm sorry about last week. I was a pig.'

'No, you weren't. You were just...' Running scared? She shrugged, leaving the end of the sentence hanging in mid-air for him to finish how he would. 'And thank you for the flowers, they're lovely.'

She took them from his hand and put them in the sink in the utility room, filling it with water to give them a chance to recover before she arranged them.

'Sit down,' she said, waving at the table as she turned the kettle on again and emptied the now lukewarm water out of the teapot.

'Cake smells good,' he said, to fill the silence, and she threw him a smile over her shoulder.

'It's date and walnut.'

One eyebrow shot up. 'Really? That's a bit risky, lots of people hate it.'

'But you don't. It's your favourite.'

The eyebrow came down, joining the other in the centre in a puzzled pleat. 'Lord. You remembered.'

Sam looked astonished, and she busied herself with the teapot. She remembered everything about him—every word, every gesture, every look he'd ever given her. It was all engraved on her heart, next to the bit that said, Molly loves Sam, but he didn't need to know that.

'It wasn't hard to remember, it's my favourite, too,' she said, dismissing it lightly and scooping up the laden tray. 'Could you open the door for me?'

She took him through to the sitting room, tidied within an inch of its life in his honour, and, setting the tray down on the coffee-table, she positioned herself firmly in an arm-chair and waved at the sofa. 'Sit down and make yourself useful. You can cut the cake.'

They ate, they drank, and then finally the pot was drained and there was nothing left to do, nothing to hide behind, and Sam's patience seemed to come to an end.

He put his cup back on the tray, leant back and eyed her warily.

'Molly, what's this about?'

Oh, lord. The palms of her hands prickled and she scrubbed them discreetly against her jeans. There was no way to do this subtly. She wasn't into seduction and sub-terfuge, it wasn't her way—at least, not that she was aware of. She looked up and met his eyes, dredging up the last ounce of her courage.

'How do you feel about having an affair?'

Sam thought he was going to choke.

His eyes widened, and he let his breath out on a shocked huff of surprised laughter.

'Pardon?' he said, convinced he hadn't heard her right, but apparently he had, because Molly said it again, slowly and carefully, avoiding his eyes this time and with hot colour scalding her cheeks.

He was glad she wasn't looking at him, because his face was bound to be transparent. His feelings were so confused he couldn't work them out, and he sure as hell couldn't explain them to her. He couldn't explain them to himself—

but gradually, as the seconds ticked by, one emotion fought its way to the top.

Need.

Raw, naked and unashamed, it ripped through him, leaving him gasping.

'Molly, I—'

'I don't want an answer now,' she said quickly, cutting him off. 'Just think about it. It seems logical, really,' she went on in a reasonable voice totally at odds with the screaming of his body. 'I mean, we're both free, we're both lonely, and we get on well, don't we? I thought having someone to do things with—silly things, like going for a walk and not having to feed the ducks, and going to the theatre and seeing a real play instead of a pantomime—all sorts of things, well, it would be fun. Wouldn't it?'

His body was still screaming, but his mind was following her words, and there was something missing from them—something his body was going to be sorely disappointed in, if he was right.

'You said—affair?' he said carefully, not wanting to leave any room for doubt on that one.

Her eyes flew up and met his, wary and—good grief, shy?

'Yes.'

'Is that what you meant?' he asked, pursuing it relentlessly. 'A sexual relationship? As well as the theatre and walks and other stuff?'

Her cheeks coloured again softly, but she held his eyes, her chin coming up a fraction. 'Yes. If you want. We don't have to, obviously—I don't want you to feel under any pressure if you don't want to change things—but, yes, that's what I meant.'

'Right.'

Hell's teeth. He had to admire her courage. Any fool

could allow a situation to develop and run out of control. It took real guts to take that first deliberate step that could change a relationship so fundamentally.

And that worried him, when he thought beyond his first immediate physical reaction, because their relationship was already complicated.

'So—where does Jack fit in all this?' he asked, his common sense finally fighting free from the tentacles of lust to reassert itself in the nick of time.

'He doesn't,' she said emphatically. 'Jack's something totally separate. I want to see him, off and on, for the rest of my life, and ultimately I think I'd like him to know who I am, as Laura does—but that's nothing to do with this. This is about us—you and me, two adults struggling alone to bring up our children, sharing adult...'

She floundered to a halt, clearly casting around for the right word, and Sam was content to wait for her to find it. It saved him having to think of anything to say, and as the only thing that came to mind was '*Yes!*', procrastination seemed like a good idea.

'Things,' she said eventually.

Sam still didn't speak—not until he could trust himself not to be hasty. Instead he stared down the garden, watching as a bluetit pecked at the fruit on a crab-apple tree, quite unaware of a cat on the fence just feet away watching it intently.

Finally the bird flew away, and he looked up at Molly again, searching her face for any hidden motive, any private agenda she wasn't revealing.

Not that it would be hard to guess at. It was obvious that if she had any other motive, it would be connected with Jack, but for some reason he didn't really understand he believed her when she said it was nothing to do with his son.

He thought of the kiss they'd shared in the hall just feet away, and heat surged through him. It would be so easy to take her up on her offer—too easy. And what then?

Would she demand commitment? She deserved it, God knows, but he didn't do commitment, not any more. Not since Crystal.

'What's the catch?' he asked, without thinking, and pain flashed in her eyes, quickly concealed.

'There is no catch,' she said softly, and she sounded hurt that he could even think it. 'No strings, Sam. Just you and me, for as long as either of us want, having a bit of fun when it's mutually convenient.'

Perversely, he felt disappointed that she'd settle for so little, but it was all he'd want for himself, and maybe she was still in love with Mick's memory and just being realistic. After all, why shouldn't they have some fun? They both worked hard, and they deserved a break.

'Can I think about it?'

She nodded slowly. 'Of course. I want you to. I want it to be a reasoned decision, nothing hasty or ill-considered that either of us will regret later.'

Sam nearly laughed. Oh, he'd regret it—he'd regret it whatever his answer was, one way or another.

'More tea?' she was saying, but he needed to get away from her before he lost his head and said or did something else he'd regret.

'I don't think so. I ought to go. It's Debbie's day off, really, and I don't like to take advantage.'

'OK.'

She looked relieved, he thought, as she ushered him out to the hall. He hesitated at the door, wondering if he dared to kiss her goodbye, but before he could move she came up on tiptoe and brushed his cheek with her lips, taking the decision out of his hands.

'Go on. Go and think. I'll see you next week.'

She stepped back, carefully placing herself out of reach, and with a wry smile he let himself out and drove away without looking back.

Well, she'd asked him.

Molly slithered down the wall onto the hall floor, her heart pounding, her legs finally giving way. Heaven only knows what he'd thought, but at least he hadn't laughed at her. He'd probably gone away to work out how to say no without hurting her feelings, knowing him.

Or did she know him? She'd thought she did, at least a little, but now she wasn't sure. She was horribly afraid she'd made a mistake and screwed up their future relationship—in fact, he'd probably gone to take legal advice about keeping her away from Jack!

Phrases like 'unfit mother' and the like sprang to mind, and she had to tell herself not to be ridiculous.

She wasn't Jack's mother, anyway, so it was irrelevant.

She got up, dusted herself off and went into the sitting room, clearing away the debris of their tea and cake and needlessly eating another thick slice just to settle her nerves.

It didn't. It sat on them like a lead weight, and she spent the entire evening with horrendous heartburn. Go and think, she'd told him, and now she wondered how long he'd think.

Too long, whatever.

The thought did nothing for her indigestion.

Molly went in on Monday morning wondering if Sam would have an answer for her, but within minutes she was too busy to worry about her own personal life.

She took over the management of a labour from the

midwife who'd been on all night. Her patient was exhausted, and the midwife, Karen, handed over the notes with a tired sigh.

'She's making heavy weather of it. She's just ground to a halt, really, poor girl. I've been trying to get her to eat and drink to keep her blood sugar up, but she's been refusing everything but water for the last couple of hours and I'm frankly glad to hand her over to someone else. I'm bushed, and so's her poor husband. I wish you luck.'

Great, Molly thought. Just what she needed to start the week off—but perhaps it was. She glanced at the notes. It was Alice's first baby, and she had been in labour since the early hours of Sunday morning. Now she was fully dilated but her contractions were going off, and she was too tired to care.

Molly went in and introduced herself to the couple, and even a quick glance revealed how worn out Alice was.

'Come on, darling, have a little apple juice,' her husband was saying, but she just turned her head away.

'Tony, I can't. I just want to go home. Can't I go home? I'll come back tomorrow, I promise, but I'm just so tired...'

Molly rubbed Alice's hand comfortingly and perched on the edge of the bed.

'You need to drink something with sugar in it to boost your blood-sugar levels. You probably need to eat, really, but at this stage it's probably better if you don't.'

'This stage? What stage? I've been like this for hours!'

'That's what I mean,' Molly said gently. 'You're nearly there, but you aren't making any progress, and your baby's exhausted, too. We need to move things on for both your sakes so that we don't have to intervene.'

'Intervene?'

'I think she means do a Caesarian section,' Tony said, obviously a couple of steps ahead of his wife.

She rolled her eyes. 'So you're saying drink up, like a good girl, and I'll feel like pushing? I don't think so. Not in this lifetime.' Her laugh was wry and bitter, and Molly felt for her.

'You'll be surprised how much better you'll cope with a bit more energy.'

'I could eat chocolate,' she said after a moment.

Her husband laughed. 'You can always eat chocolate. I've never known a time when you couldn't manage chocolate.'

'Well, she can have some. That's fine. It'll boost her blood sugar.'

'Except I haven't got any.'

'Go down to the shop in the entrance,' Molly suggested, and he went, leaving her alone with Alice. She met the woman's tired eyes and smiled reassuringly. 'Rest for a little while, and when Tony gets back you can eat some of the chocolate, and then we'll see if we can get you going again.'

'And if not?'

Molly shrugged. 'I don't know. I'll talk to Mr Gregory, the consultant in charge of your care, and see what he thinks. He might just let you carry on, or he might want to use suction.'

'Suction? That's like forceps, isn't it? Does that hurt the baby?'

Molly shook her head. 'No, I don't think so. Not like the old forceps did, or the early suction cups. The cups now are silicone, and they're lovely and soft. They fit neatly over the top of the baby's head and just help to guide it and give a bit of added traction. It'll just give you a hand if you can't manage the last bit on your own, and it's better for you than a section, if we can avoid it.'

Alice nodded. 'OK. I'll try without, first, if the chocolate works—but I really am so tired...'

Tears filled her eyes, and Molly hugged her gently and settled her down against the pillows, tucking the covers round her shoulders to keep her warm. Poor thing.

Still, hopefully the chocolate would help, and if she could get Alice to wash it down with a bit of apple juice, they might be in business.

It was a vain hope. Molly kept a close eye on the labouring woman's temperature and blood pressure, and monitored the baby's heartbeat every contraction, but the contractions were getting so weak now it hardly registered with the baby.

Then, miraculously, they seemed to pick up, but Alice was too tired to help, and the baby's heartbeat began to dip.

Molly didn't like it. She'd given her long enough, and Alice's husband had half walked, half carried her round the ward a couple of times to see if gravity could assist, but to no avail.

She called Sam, and then, of course, she realised she'd have to see him, and she didn't feel in the least bit prepared for it. What if he was funny with her?

He wasn't. He walked onto the ward moments after she bleeped him and beckoned to her, and she slipped out of the delivery room and was confronted by the calm, quiet professional she'd grown to respect.

'Morning, Molly. What have you got for me?'

She looked up into his eyes, wondering if she'd see an answer there, but there was nothing. No clue, but nothing to fear, either. Just Sam. Relief flooded through her, and she got straight to the point.

'Ineffective labour—she's a primigravida, and she's really struggling. She's been wonderful, but she's been in labour since yesterday morning and she's exhausted. She's fully dilated and still having contractions, but they're losing strength and she needs help, Sam. She's never going to do this on her own.'

'Have you catheterised her?'

She shook her head. 'Not yet. I was waiting for you, but it was my next trick, to see if we can buy her a little more room. I think she's just got so tired she can't do the last bit. She's had a bit of a sugar boost and that's helped the strength of her contractions, but she's too far gone to do much. Anyway, the baby's struggling now—the last leak of amniotic fluid was stained with meconium and the heartbeat's fluctuating now with every contraction. I think she's run out of time.'

He nodded. 'OK, let's have a look, and if it's that straightforward, I'll do a little lift with the suction. Has she had an epidural?'

Molly shook her head. 'No. She's refused all pain relief, I gather. I certainly haven't given her any.'

Sam arched a brow. 'Could be tricky. What if she needs an episiotomy?'

'She doesn't want one.'

'Nobody ever does, but I take it she wants the baby?'

'Of course. She's too tired to be sensible. We'll just have to look after her, Sam. She hasn't had any sleep. I've been putting warm compresses on her perineum to relax it and encourage her contractions, so she might not need it.'

He nodded. 'OK. We'll do what we can. We may not need to interfere too much, if we can just use the vacuum to give her enough help so she can do it herself. Let's have a look.'

While Sam examined Alice and explained what they

were going to do, Molly prepared the catheter and then inserted it, draining Alice's bladder and removing a potential obstacle to the passage of the baby. It wasn't always easy to empty the bladder completely when in labour, and when the mother was as exhausted as Alice, every little bit of pelvic capacity they could buy her helped.

'Right, let's just watch her through a contraction and see how she gets on. Alice, I'd like you to sit up on your heels for me, and when you have a contraction, just rock forwards onto the headboard so you're on all fours but a bit upright, OK? That'll give you the help of gravity and should make it easier.'

With Molly supporting her on one side and her husband on the other, they held her in position, but her contraction was weak, and even pushing as hard as she could, the baby made virtually no progress.

'OK, this isn't going to work, I agree. There just isn't enough maternal impulsion,' Sam said, stepping back so they could ease Alice down onto her side. 'If you can prop her up a little, she can stay like that if someone can support that top leg. Alice, I'm going to help you get the baby out, OK? I'm going to use a suction cup on the baby's head, and when you push, I'm going to give a little pull, and see if we can't do this together, OK? But you're going to need to help me as much as you can, all right?'

Alice nodded, tears filling her eyes. 'I wanted to do it properly. I wanted to do it myself, without help.'

'Darling, you can't, you're knackered,' her husband said tiredly. 'Let them help you.'

She nodded again, all fight going out of her, and Molly and Sam exchanged glances. If she gave up completely, she'd need a Caesarian, and Molly didn't want that for her.

'Come on, Alice, have some more apple juice,' she coaxed. 'Just a little bit. Tony, see if you can get her to take a bit more. She's going to need more strength to do this, we can't do it all.'

Leaving him coaxing, pleading and exhorting his wife to take chocolate and apple juice, Molly helped Sam set up the vacuum extractor.

'I don't like doing this without at least a local and an episiotomy—'

'I'm not having an episiotomy,' Alice said drowsily, and Sam sighed under his breath.

'OK, Alice, but you're going to have to help me as much as you can. I'll leave it for now, but if I feel the baby's suffering, I may have to do it anyway. Can I give you a local anaesthetic in readiness, just in case?'

She shrugged. 'If you must.'

'I must,' he muttered, and, taking the syringe Molly handed him, he infiltrated the tissues carefully with the anaesthetic. 'Right,' he said, and without any further delay he slipped the soft suction cup over the baby's head, his face creasing in concentration as he struggled to position it blind.

'OK, that feels good. Let's give it a go. Next contraction, Alice, I want a real effort from you, please, if you can.'

She nodded, and with her husband and Molly cheerleading and encouraging her, and Molly holding her leg, she pushed down as Sam gently pulled, and the baby slid down a little, the crown of its head appearing. With the next contraction the head was born, and with one final push the little body slipped out into Sam's waiting hands.

There was a second of breathless silence, then a sorry little wail came from the baby and they all started to breathe again. It wasn't a lusty cry, but it was a cry for all that, and the baby's colour improved immediately.

They laid her on Alice's now soft tummy, and Molly took Alice's hand and rested it on her daughter's back.

'You've got a beautiful little girl,' she told them with a smile, and Tony's face crumpled.

'Well done,' Sam said with feeling. 'That was a terrific effort, Alice. You're a clever girl.'

He stripped off his gloves, squeezed Molly's shoulder and backed towards the door. 'I have to go, I'm in the middle of a clinic. I'll be back later. Bleep me if there are any complications, but I don't think there will be. She did it herself in the end.'

Molly nodded and watched him go, and it was only as the door swung shut she realised she still didn't have an answer to that burning question...

Sam changed his white coat for a clean one, tossed the other one into a laundry basket in the clinic and headed back to his office. He had patients to see, backing up into the hereafter, and he really didn't have time to think about Molly, but he just couldn't get her out of his mind.

Her proposition had been on his mind since Saturday afternoon, and he was no nearer a sensible conclusion now than he had been then.

A patient came in when he called her, leaving her companion in the waiting room.

'Is that your partner? He's welcome to come in, too.'

She smiled and shook her head. 'No, he's not my partner, or the baby's father. He's just a friend. We're both single parents, and he gives me a hand. We do stuff together as well, go to the cinema, the pub—it's nice to have a companion sometimes, without having the strings of a relationship.'

Sam made some noncommittal reply, but it gave him food for thought. He missed adult company, even though he had Debbie and Mark around, but they were a couple, and watching them together made him feel, if anything, even more alone.

Maybe he should take Molly up on her suggestion, but with qualifications. He'd talk to her later, he resolved, and turned his attention back to his patient.

It was much later, after Jack was in bed and he'd procrastinated even further, before Sam had time to talk to her.

He didn't want to do it over the phone, but asking Debbie and Mark to listen out for Jack yet again seemed unfair and, anyway, they might have gone out.

He went to make himself a drink and found them both still in the kitchen, however, with paperwork spread out over the kitchen table and deep in conversation.

'Hi,' he said as he walked in, and Debbie looked up and smiled distractedly.

'Hi. Sorry, did you want the table? Only we were looking at this business plan, and it needs a big space, but we'll move if you like.'

'No, that's fine,' he said, waving dismissively. 'Help yourself.' He tipped his head on one side and eyed Debbie thoughtfully. 'Does this business plan mean I'm going to lose you?' he asked, and she laughed and straightened up.

'I doubt it. It's for Mark's tapestries. We just thought there must be a better way than selling designs to shops.'

Mark looked up and shrugged diffidently. 'I dunno—we thought about marketing kits. Advertising in the Sundays, home magazines, that sort of thing. What do you think?'

Sam walked over to them. 'May I?'

They nodded, and he ran his eye over the plan, noting the careful costings, the projected time span before profitability—they seemed to have taken it very logically and without excessive optimism, and for their sakes he hoped it worked. It deserved to. Mark was extraordinarily talented, and Debbie was highly organised. It could be a winning combination.

'Looks good. I hope it works for you. Before you get too busy with the marketing, though, you couldn't do me a favour, could you?'

They looked wary, and he grinned. 'I'd like to pop out for a while—will you be in if I leave Jack?'

Their faces eased, and Mark's eyebrow went up, the ring in it catching the light and giving him a faintly piratical air. 'Molly?' he asked, and Sam felt the colour rise on the back of his neck. Was nothing private round here?

'Just one or two things of Jack's I wanted to show her— from the early days. I forgot to take them the other day.'

'You don't have to make excuses, mate,' Mark said, a grin spreading over his face. 'You go for it—she's a real cracker.'

Et tu, Brute? They all seemed in a hell of a hurry to get him involved with a woman again—to free them to develop the business? Who could tell?

He didn't pause to ring her. She might have been out, but it was a risk he was prepared to take. And, of course, when he arrived there was another car on the drive, and she had visitors.

Damn. He'd turned into her drive, of course, and his headlights had swung across and caught her attention, and she was standing at the kitchen window now, looking out at him. He could hardly drive off without talking to her, and yet this conversation wasn't one he wanted to have in a hurried way or on the doorstep, with strangers hanging on their every word.

She'd left the window and he contemplated running, but then the front door opened and she came out, hugging her upper arms against the chill of the evening, and he was trapped.

He turned off the engine and got out, walking over to her, still not knowing quite what to say.

'Come on in,' she invited. 'Mick's parents are here. Come and meet them.'

The Hammonds were the last people in the world he wanted to meet, bearing in mind what he was going to say to their daughter-in-law, but he went anyway, and they were lovely—friendly, interested in Jack's progress. And when Molly turned to them and asked if they'd mind keeping an eye on Libby for an hour while she slipped out, they didn't turn a hair.

Good grief, he thought, don't tell me they're in on it. But that was stretching his imagination a little too far.

She shrugged into a light jacket, picked up her bag and smiled her thanks at them. 'You've got my mobile number. We won't be far away—we'll just go for a quick drink.'

'You take your time. It's nice to see you getting out a bit,' Mick's father said, and Sam wondered if he'd be quite so magnanimous if he knew what his daughter-in-law had proposed—and what Sam's response was going to be!

They took his car and drove out into the nearest village, finding themselves a quiet table in the corner of the bar. Neither of them were drinking, and Sam regretted his scruples about drink driving. A hefty slug or two of whisky would help this conversation along a treat, he thought.

'I'm sorry to break up your evening,' he began, but she laughed.

'Don't be silly. I'd much rather be with you. They're dear, sweet people, but we're not exactly on the same wavelength.'

Well, that allayed his fears about what she might have told them, anyway!

'So,' she said, finally breaking the silence that was stretching between them like over-stressed elastic, 'I take it you wanted to talk to me?'

He set down his glass with needless precision, centring it exactly on the beer mat, lining up the edge of the mat with the table—anything to avoid taking that next, terrifying step.

Her voice cut into his whirling thoughts. 'Is it no? I can take it, Sam. Just tell me.'

Leave it to Molly to make it easier. He looked up and smiled wryly. 'No, it's not no. It's not yes, either—not exactly. I mean—can we try the theatre thing first? We can't turn the clock back, and I don't want us to do anything hasty that might turn out to be wrong for either of us.'

Sam fiddled with the mat again, pushing it so it was diagonally across the corner, adjusting it by microns. Finally he started speaking again, the carefully rehearsed words sounding stiff and awkward in his head. He abandoned them, going instead with his feelings, letting his heart talk.

'I know you don't do this sort of thing lightly, and the fact that you asked me—well, I was going to use words like privileged and honoured, but they just sound patronising, and I don't mean to. I don't want you to think I don't want you, Molly—you must know I do. Hell, I make it obvious enough. It's just—can we take it one step at a time? See how it goes? It would be too easy just to go to bed with you and take what you're offering, and I don't want to do that. You're too important to me, and I respect you far too much to do that.'

She smiled, her eyes filling. 'You are silly. I wouldn't think you didn't respect me.'

'I just don't want to rush it.'

'Fine. We won't. We'll start now, with a drink, and we'll go from there. OK?'

He felt the tension seep out of him like a perished balloon, and he laughed softly and lifted his glass to her. 'Good idea—except I have to get back. I'm intruding on Mark and Debbie's time again.'

Molly withdrew a fraction, her smile becoming fixed. 'Oh, well. Another time.'

'Thursday? There's a new film out I'd like to see. I thought maybe we could have a meal as well—if you can get a sitter. I'm sorry it's midweek, but Debbie and Mark have the weekend off, and Friday's sacrosanct for them.'

Her eyes softened, and he realised she'd thought he was brushing her off, letting her down gently.

Like hell.

'That would be lovely,' she said, the smile lighting her eyes, and Sam wondered how he was going to keep his hands off her until then.

He didn't, in fact. He drove her home, and just before they reached the streetlights in her road, while they were still in the rich velvet darkness of the countryside, he pulled in to the side of the road and drew her into his arms.

'This is just a goodnight kiss, in private,' he said, his voice threaded with tension again. As she melted against him, he lowered his mouth to hers.

She tasted glorious. He wanted to lose himself in her, and it took all the strength he had to release her and ease away, sitting up with his arms wrapped round the top of the steering-wheel and his forehead resting against his white knuckles.

'Sam?'

Turning the key, he lifted his head and turned towards

her, studying her in the dim light of the instrument panel.
'Yes?'

'Thank you.'

His laugh was harsh and cynical. 'Don't thank me. I
was this close—'

'Me, too. That's why I'm thanking you.'

One step at a time, he reminded himself. Pulling out
onto the road again, he took her home.

CHAPTER SEVEN

WELL, Molly thought.

It was a start—and what a start, if that goodnight kiss was anything to go by. Sam might be taking it one step at a time, but he had a long stride! Humming softly to herself, she went upstairs, checked on Libby and ran herself a bath.

The Hammonds had gone home, gently curious but not pushy—never pushy. Unlike Mick, they were prepared to give things time. He'd always been impatient—a bit like Sam, really.

How interesting. She'd never thought of them like that before, but she supposed in many ways they were alike.

She eased herself into the hot water, her brow pleating into a little furrow as she considered that extraordinary fact. Sam and Mick, as different as chalk and cheese and yet with the same essential qualities of decency and loyalty and human-kindness.

Not to mention impatience and a terrible tendency not to talk about things. Mick had been reluctant to talk to her at first, but then they'd reached a turning point in their relationship, and he'd opened up to her and given her everything.

Would Sam ever do the same—and if he did, would he say what she wanted to hear?

She was rather afraid not.

Oh, rats. She must give up this stupid habit of trying to second-guess everything, and just give events time to work themselves out. Refusing to think any more about that kiss or the possible consequences of it, she slid under the water, coming up gasping with her hair streaming in wet ribbons over her shoulders.

Sam would keep. Just for now she had to get bathed, dry her hair and get to bed, because she was on an early tomorrow and time was pressing on.

And in the afternoon, she'd go and see her GP and get herself put on the Pill.

Just to be on the safe side.

Thursday came before he was ready for it. Sam had spent the entire week alternately regretting the kiss and looking forward to the next one, and suddenly it was Thursday evening and he was taking Molly to the cinema.

He'd seen Nick and Sally Baker in his clinic that afternoon, and unless he was mistaken Sally was about to go into labour—which was all very well, but he really, *really* didn't want them to ring him tonight!

He put his phone on silent and slid it into his trouser pocket, so he'd feel it vibrate if they called him, and pulled up on Molly's drive five minutes early.

Looking keen, he thought in disgust, and decided it was better than looking indifferent and being rude.

Whatever, she was ready and came straight out, looking better than a woman of thirty-three with three kids under her belt had any right to look, and he was suddenly glad they were going to the cinema and it would be dark.

The film he'd wanted to see, however, was full when they arrived, and he kicked himself for not booking in advance. Lord, he really was losing his grip. Molly, however, didn't seem to mind at all.

'I didn't really fancy it that much anyway,' she confessed, wrinkling her nose and filling him with an overwhelming urge to kiss the tip. Idiot. She was pointing at the display behind the cashier. 'How about that?' she suggested instead.

'That' turned out to be a romantic comedy, and its silly tenderness made him want to laugh and cry and hug her—preferably while he had her in his arms in a great big bed somewhere miles from anywhere. Much less thought-provoking than the film he'd intended them to see, and with quite the opposite effect, of course. Once again he was grateful for the darkness.

They'd decided not to do dinner, because Debbie and Mark were both feeling a little off colour, so when he turned into her drive after the film it was still quite early.

'Would you like to come in?' she asked, and he nearly agreed, but Libby was staying with her grandparents and so their chaperone was missing. Not a good idea, he decided. The likelihood of him disgracing himself was so high it didn't bear thinking about, especially after that silly, tender film—and, anyway, he couldn't get out of the car or she'd be only too aware of his feelings.

'I shouldn't,' he said. 'I've got work to do, really.'

Not a lie, but not the truth, either. Oh, hell. A shadow fell over Molly's face, and he wasn't sure if it was a trick of the light or if she was disappointed. Damn. Maybe he should go in and to hell with the consequences...

'Right,' she said quietly. 'Well, thanks for a lovely night. I really enjoyed the film. I'll see you tomorrow?'

'Sure.'

She opened the door and got out, and on impulse Sam leant over and looked up at her as she was about to close it again.

'Molly? What are you doing on Sunday morning? I know you said you'd like to go for a walk without feeding the ducks, but you also want to see Jack. The trouble is, if we go anywhere near the park Jack will insist on feeding the ducks, but I would guess Libby's much too old and sophisticated to do that now.'

She laughed, a lovely sound that rippled over his nerve-endings, and he saw the light come back into her eyes. 'Libby loves the ducks. If I contrive a whole loaf of stale bread as an excuse, I'm sure she'll manage to deal with her pride.'

'Fine. Do you want to meet us there, or shall I pick you up?'

'We'll meet you there—unless it's raining. If it's raining we'll have to think of something dry to do.'

'I'll work on it. I'll see you tomorrow morning—are you on early?'

'Yes, for my sins. That's why the Hammonds have got Libby.'

'Look out for Sally Baker—Nick's wife—A and E consultant?'

'Yes, I know them both. Sally's a nurse. Heavens, is she due already?'

'Just about. She's around thirty-eight weeks. I don't know if you're aware of it, but she lost a baby some years ago with a heart condition, and she's fretting, even though this one seems absolutely spot on. She'll need TLC—and I want to know if she turns up. I saw her earlier today and I have a feeling she's imminent.'

'OK. I'll look out for her. I'll see you tomorrow—and thanks again. I really enjoyed it.'

'Me, too. Take care. Sleep well.'

'You, too.' She smiled, her face softening, and closed the door, and the moment she was inside the house he put the car into reverse and turned it round, shooting off down the road in a squeal of tyres and growling with frustration.

Why had he had to tell her to sleep well? The last thing he needed to think about was her lying in bed, those soft brown curls spread out on her pillow, her body warm and relaxed in sleep.

Until he touched her...

Sam gave a low growl and slowed for a roundabout, gunning away from it with another immature display of testosterone.

Despite his parting remark, Molly didn't sleep well. That silly film had left her even more aware of her loneliness and the yawning void in her emotions that only Sam could fill. If he'd come in...

If he'd come in, she told herself sternly as she showered for work, she would have thrown herself at him, and made a complete fool of herself. He clearly wasn't interested in taking their relationship that far, even if he did respond to her. It was just automatic. He was a man. It was like breathing to them—woman equals sexual reaction.

Oh, rats.

She arrived on the ward to find that Sally Baker had been admitted at five a.m. She went into the labour room and met Sue in the doorway.

'Oh, hi. I was just coming to look for you before you got embroiled somewhere else. Mr Gregory wants you to look after Sally.'

'I know, that's fine. How are things?'

'Fine. Great. Good, steady progress. She was four centimetres dilated at six—I haven't checked her since but I would think she's about five or six now. Good, strong contractions every five minutes, but I think the interval's closing now and she's going to hot up.'

'Pain relief?'

Sue shook her head and lowered her voice. 'She doesn't want anything that might affect the baby—she's got history. You need to look at the notes.'

'Sam filled me in briefly.'

'OK. She's managing well—she's got a good coach. Do you know Nick?'

Molly nodded, smiling at him over Sue's shoulder. 'We've met, down in A and E. Hello, Sally.'

'Molly? Hi. Are you going to look after me?'

'For my sins,' she said with a smile.

'They're both in the profession, of course, so they'll keep you on your toes,' Sue said, loud enough for them all to hear, then turned back to Sally and Nick with a grin. 'Right, Sally, I'm going to leave you in Molly's capable hands. I hope you have a really great day, and I'll come and see you and the baby tonight, OK?'

'OK.' Sally's smile was faint, just a polite social smile, and Molly could see the fear behind it. Poor girl. Still, from what Sam had said she had no need to worry, but that wouldn't stop her, and to reassure her Molly would be monitoring her very closely.

She smiled at them, going over to Sally and rubbing her shoulder gently. 'Hello, my love. How are you doing? I gather from Sue that you've got a really good coach here.'

Sally gave another faint smile that didn't reach her eyes. 'Yes, he's great. It's OK so far—or it was. Oh, rats. Nick?'

He moved closer, rubbing her back gently through the contraction, his attention focused totally on his wife. When it was over he straightened up and met Sally's eyes and smiled.

'OK now?'

She nodded.

Molly checked her watch again, timing the length of the contraction and making a mental note. 'Right, the first thing I want to do is check your obs, then I'll examine you and see how much progress you've made in the last hour and a half, and we'll go from there. Are you feeling more comfortable now?'

'I'm all right.'

'Have you had breakfast?' she asked as she took Sally's temperature, but she shook her head.

'She won't eat,' Nick said gruffly.

'What about you?' Molly asked him, checking Sally's pulse, her eyes flicking across to take in his strained eyes and rumpled hair. He didn't look a lot better than his wife, she thought.

'No, I haven't had anything.'

'Well, I think you both should—especially you, Nick. We don't want you keeling over, you're much too big to catch. Why don't you go and—'

'I don't want him leaving me,' Sally said, reaching out to him.

'I'm not going anywhere, darling.'

'Yes, you are. You're going to stick your head out of the door and ask a passing HCA to rustle up some tea and toast, some apple juice and a pot of honey.'

Nick's face relaxed a little. 'OK. Now you've started talking about it, I'm absolutely starving.'

'And you, young lady, are going to eat something too,' Molly said firmly but kindly. 'Right, your obs are fine. Let's have a listen to this baby.'

'Can't I have a foetal heart monitor on?' she asked, and Molly looked at the fear in her eyes and hugged her.

'Of course you can, if you want, but I'm sure there's really no need, and they're quite restricting. Let's just listen with the Sonicaid for now.'

She picked up the baby's heartbeat instantly, strong and regular and as steady as a rock, and Sally's whole body relaxed.

Not for long. She had another contraction, the second

since Molly had come in, and checking her watch Sally saw that it was just over three minutes since the last. Sue was right, Sally was hotting up.

Molly washed her hands, snapped on a pair of gloves and checked the progress of Sally's cervix with deft, gentle fingers.

'You're doing well,' she said with a smile as Sally relaxed again after yet another contraction. 'Six to seven centimetres. Right, I think we need to get a little food into you if you think you can eat, but certainly apple juice for the sugar boost.'

Sally nodded. 'So—how long will it be?' she asked, and for the first time Molly saw a thread of hope and excitement in amongst the fear.

'I don't know. One to three hours, at a guess, but I can't tell. It might be less.'

She chewed her lip for a moment, then looked up at Nick who was hovering in the doorway, still waiting to catch someone's attention to ask for the food.

'Nick, go and find someone. I'll be all right if you're on the ward.'

'You sure?'

'Of course I'm sure.'

With one last backward glance Nick left them alone, and Sally looked up at Molly with worried eyes. 'I'm so scared,' she confessed. 'I really wanted this baby, but my whole pregnancy's been a nightmare of worry. They keep telling me everything's all right, but I don't dare to believe it. Do you think I'm mad?'

Molly shook her head. 'No. I think it's perfectly understandable. You've had a terrible experience and it's been very damaging. Of course you're frightened, but everything looks wonderful so far, and the best thing you can do for this baby is relax as much as possible. It'll soon be over.'

'Not soon enough.'

'It really won't be long,' Molly said gently. 'When you're holding your baby in your arms, this will all seem like a bad dream.'

'I know the heart's all right,' Sally said, twisting her hands together. 'It's all the other things that can go wrong. Sometimes I wish I wasn't a nurse. Have you had any children?'

'Three.'

'I bet they're a real handful.'

Molly smiled wistfully. 'Well, Libby can be, but the other two aren't mine—I was a host surrogate mother for them, so other people have the joy of struggling with them.'

Sally's eyes widened. 'How on earth could you go through all this and give them away?' she asked, stunned.

Molly shrugged. 'I wanted to help other people. Libby gave us so much joy. I wanted to share that.'

'And doesn't it hurt you?'

She shrugged again. 'Sometimes, of course, but not really. I see them both, they're lovely, happy children—I've got no regrets.'

'Good lord, I think you're amazing. It took Nick nearly a year to talk me into this, but he wasn't there when I lost the other one. We—weren't together at the time. We'd lost touch, and I didn't see him again for seven years. He didn't really know what it was like—or, at least, I didn't think he did, but I think now he's more worried than I am.'

Molly squeezed her hand. 'I wish I could reassure you. You know the statistics, though, I'm sure. The chances of anything going wrong at this stage in a normal, healthy pregnancy are very slight, and I'm watching you like a hawk, anyway. But you just won't believe me, will you, till you're holding your baby?'

Sally gave a hollow laugh. 'Sorry. I know you're right. It's just—'

'Hey, presto! Breakfast!'

Nick came in brandishing a tray, and Sally took one look at the contents, sniffed the air slightly and went green.

'Oh, no, I'm going to be sick,' she said, and promptly followed through, leaving Nick looking shocked and riddled with guilt.

'Just take the tray out,' Molly advised with a smile, cleaning Sally up with practised hands. 'Eat something while you're out there. You can come back in with the apple juice in a minute.'

'I'm having a contraction,' Sally said, her eyes widening and searching frantically for Nick.

'It's OK, I'm here. Roll on your side towards me,' Molly said firmly. 'Now just flop. Let all the tension go, and breathe nice and light up here, in the top of your chest—that's lovely. Well done. Good girl. That's brilliant.'

Her hand was rubbing gently over Sally's back as she spoke, and she could feel the tension drain out of her as the contraction passed. 'Good girl. Well done. It's all over.'

'For a minute.'

'They are getting closer. I think you're moving into transition.'

'I'm not moving anywhere,' Sally said, a trace of truculence in her voice.

Molly chuckled. 'That's fine. You can have your baby here, there's no problem with that. I'll just get Sam Gregory, though. He'll be cross with me if he misses it.'

Had he been listening outside? Whatever, as she voiced

the thought he came in with Nick at his side, and his eyes flicked to Molly for a quick update, one eyebrow arched in enquiry.

'I think she's in transition.'

He nodded briefly, and smiled at Sally. 'Hi, there. You're doing well, I gather. Molly, have you checked her cervix recently?'

'Not since seven-thirty.'

Sam checked the clock on the wall. It was nearly nine. 'Time to do it again?'

'Want to do the honours?' she offered, but he laughed softly and shook his head.

'I'm not a midwife. You'll do it better.'

She chuckled in surprise. 'Such high praise—or are you saving yourself for the dramatic stuff?' she teased as she examined Sally. 'If so, I'm going to have to disappoint you. She's fully dilated and ready to go, and everything's hunky-dory.'

'That's fine, I'll sit back and watch the proceedings. I could do with a lazy morning, having been dragged out of bed at something after four because someone decided to go into labour in the middle of the night.'

Molly looked at him in surprise. 'Have you been here since then?'

'Yes—why? You sound shocked.'

She laughed. 'Well, not shocked, exactly, but I would have thought you'd be in here making your presence felt before now.'

'What—annoying the midwife?' he ribbed. 'More than my life's worth. I know my place, I come when I'm called.'

'I'm glad someone does,' Sally offered with a pointed look at her husband. 'Most consultants make it their job to interfere with the nursing staff.'

'And vice versa—which, of course, is how you got yourself in this mess,' Nick teased, and Sally laughed weakly.

'I didn't mean that kind of interference,' she said, and then the smile vanished from her face and a look of intense concentration came over it. 'Oh, help, I want to push. I want to get up. Nick? I want to kneel. I want—'

'Want, want, want,' Nick said, but despite the teasing note in his voice his eyes were troubled. The end was close, and any minute now they'd know if their baby was all right.

'Sally, pant for me,' Molly instructed a few minutes later, crouching down behind her as she hung on to the head of the bed with Nick supporting her. 'Don't push any more, you're nearly there, just let it come slowly—that's lovely. Well done, the head's here—and the rest. Well done!'

The baby's cry was strong and immediate, and Sally turned round and collapsed down onto the pillows, tears streaming down her cheeks.

'Oh, he's lovely. It's a boy, he's gorgeous! Oh, hello, baby,' she said softly, reaching out to hold him as Molly laid him on her now soft tummy. 'Oh, Nick...'

Nick couldn't speak. The tears were flooding his eyes, and he sat down beside her, wrapped her and the baby in his arms and just held them.

Molly turned away, giving them a moment of privacy, and met Sam's bleak eyes. He smiled, but the smile was strained and he turned away.

'Well, that's excellent. I'll check him in a minute. Apgar score?'

'Ten, from what I can tell. He's lovely—he reminds me of Jack.' Her voice cracked, and she stripped off her gloves and washed her hands, then checked the baby again, covering him once more in a warmed towel and helping Sally to put him to the breast.

'He is OK, isn't he?' Sally said worriedly, and Molly smiled and nodded.

'He seems fine—gorgeous. We'll get a paediatrician down to check him now, though, just to set your minds at rest. Apgar ten at five minutes,' she murmured to Sam, turning her head, but he wasn't there. He'd slipped silently from the room while she'd been busy, and she wanted to go after him, but she couldn't leave them, not at this stage.

But those bleak eyes haunted her, even after Sam came back in a few minutes later with some excuse about calling the paediatrician, and his eyes were just his eyes again, filled with gentle smiles and teasing humour and reassurance for the blissful family in his care.

So what had put that look there?

Jealousy? Was Sam jealous of Nick and Sally and their happiness? She could understand that. There were times— like this—when other people's happiness just underlined the emptiness of her life. Did Sam feel like that, too?

And if so, would he turn to her in the end to fill that void in his life? She could only hope.

Sam smiled and chatted and cuddled little baby Baker dutifully, and all the time he just wanted to get the hell out of there, away from so much love and happiness.

Molly was giving him strange, assessing looks, and he was glad when Josh Lancaster came down and he could leave them all with the paediatrician and make his escape, promising to come back and see them all later.

It was getting a little crowded in there, anyway, with a continuous stream of visitors from A and E, and they hardly noticed he'd gone.

All except Molly, of course. She caught his eye as he

slipped out, and the searching look she gave him was the last straw. He left the department, going down to the clinic and apologising to his registrar for abandoning him with all the patients. Within minutes he was up to his eyes again, and the Bakers, for the time being, were pushed to the back of his mind.

Sunday was a gorgeous day. The autumn tints were just starting to touch some of the trees in the park, and Molly found herself racing Libby down a grassy hill towards the duck pond. She tripped at the bottom, Libby cannoning into her, and they ended up in a tangled, giggling heap at the edge of the path.

'Such unseemly behaviour.'

Suddenly conscious of what an idiot she must look, she tipped her head back and looked up into Sam's laughing eyes.

'Well, hello there,' she said, still breathless, and scrambled to her feet, brushing grass and leaves off her clothes and helping Libby up with the other hand. 'Hello, Jack. Fancy seeing you here.'

Jack looked at her as if she'd come from outer space. 'Hello, Molly,' he said, and looked up the hill. 'Me run like Libby.'

'I don't think that's a good idea,' Sam said. 'And anyway, the ducks are waiting. They'll want their breakfast.'

'We're going to feed the ducks, too,' Libby said, looking pleased that they'd got company. 'Mum forgot we'd got fresh bread and took a loaf out of the freezer yesterday, so we've got tons. We haven't fed the ducks for ages. Shall we go and find them, Jack?'

She took his hand in hers and set off with him along the path, Sam staring worriedly after them.

'It's fine, she knows where to go, she's fed the duck here for years with Mick's parents.'

He threw her a rueful smile. 'Sorry. There are just so many nasty people about.'

'I don't think there are, we just hear about them now but I know what you mean. Don't worry, we'll soon catch them up.'

They followed them down the path, keeping them easily in sight, and as they started walking Molly winced a little.

'Are you OK?'

She laughed. 'Just too old to throw myself down hills,' she confessed. 'It seemed like a good idea at the time.'

'You looked as if you were having fun.'

'We were.' She shot him a searching look. 'Sam, are you OK?'

His stride faltered for a second. 'Of course. Why?' He managed to sound puzzled, but Molly wasn't fooled.

'Oh, the other day,' she said calmly. 'With the Bakers. You seemed a bit—I don't know. Unhappy.'

'Just thoughtful. I'd come from the clinic. There was another couple there who aren't going to have such a happy outcome. It just brought it home a bit.'

How plausible. Funny that she didn't believe a word of it, but if he didn't want to tell her the truth, she could hardly make him. She held up her bag, changing the subject. 'I've got the bread—we'd better catch them up,' she said, and hurried after the children, leaving Sam to follow in his own time.

They'd just reached the fenced edge of the pond when Molly caught up with them. She handed Libby the bag of bread and watched as her daughter tore up the bread and handed it to Jack, a piece at a time, and helped him throw it to the waiting ducks.

'You shouldn't really give them bread,' Sam murmured

n her ear, and she turned to reply and found him just
inches away.

They froze, and his eyes tracked to her mouth and then
slowly, feature by feature, traced her face and returned to
her eyes. Heat blazed in his eyes and, swallowing hard, he
stepped back a fraction and the tension eased.

'Yes,' she said inanely. 'I know. It pollutes the water.'

'And gives them too much refined grain and salt. They
don't need salt.'

I can't believe we're talking about the ducks, she
thought almost hysterically. He was *that* close to kissing
me...

'Jack, no, don't put your fingers through the bars, that's
a good boy.'

The spell was broken, and Molly moved away from
Sam, giving him room to get to his son while she took the
bread bag from Libby and ripped up some of the slices.
Anything to vent her frustration!

'Feel sick,' Jack said suddenly, and there was a retching,
splashing noise and Libby leapt out of the way with a
shriek.

'Oh, Mummy, my shoes!' she wailed, and Jack started
to cry.

So much for that little outing, she thought, and sighed.
'Go and wipe them on the grass, darling. Sam, is he OK?'

Sam was crouching down, wiping Jack's mouth with a
tissue and scanning his face worriedly.

'I don't know. He feels a bit clammy. I think I'll take
him home. Is Libby all right? I'm sorry about her shoes.'

'Don't worry, they'll be fine. They'll wash. Ring me
later, let me know how he is.'

'Will do.'

She watched him go, then went over to Libby and
helped her clean up her shoes.

'Oh, Mummy, they stink. I don't know how you can be a nurse.'

'I'm not a nurse, I'm a midwife, but you just get used to it. Shall we go home and change your shoes and do something else?'

Libby nodded, and they returned to the car, putting the offending shoes in the boot for the journey home, arriving back in the nick of time before a sudden squally rainstorm. It was the end of the nice weather that day, and they spent the rest of the day pottering about in the kitchen and making cookies, and then Molly cleared up while Libby did her violin practice.

She was getting better, Molly thought with pride, and wondered what her father would have made of her. He would have adored her, she knew. She'd been the apple of his eye, and he would have given anything to watch her grow up.

Sudden foolish tears stung Molly's eyes, and she brushed them away angrily. This was all because of Nick and Sally Baker and their lovely baby. All that abundant joy was a bit much to take, and knowing how richly they deserved it did nothing to stop the emptiness inside.

She made some sandwiches, put the cookies on a plate and made a pot of tea, then went through to the sitting room.

'Time to stop,' she told Libby. 'The cookies are cool enough to eat now—although I notice there weren't quite as many as I thought we'd made.'

Libby giggled guiltily and put her violin down, kneeling on the floor on the other side of the coffee-table and taking a sandwich, peering inside it inquisitively.

'Tuna,' Molly told her, and Libby sank her teeth into it and sighed.

'Yum. I was hungry. Lunch seems hours ago.'

'Lunch *was* hours ago. You've been practising for an hour, and it took us ages to make the cookies.'

'Can I have one?'

'No. Sandwiches first,' she said, 'and then, if you're very lucky and I leave you any, you can have one.'

'One?' Libby wailed, and Molly laughed and relented.

'All right, more than one,' she conceded, and, curling her feet up under her bottom, she settled back in the corner of the sofa and watched her daughter.

CHAPTER EIGHT

THEY watched television together that evening, and then Libby went to bed, leaving Molly alone with the rest of the evening stretching away ahead of her like a prison sentence. She curled up with a book, but neither it nor the television could hold her attention, and in the end she went to bed at half past nine.

The phone rang at ten to ten, just as she put her light out, and it was Sam.

'Jack's a bit better,' he said. 'I'm sorry I'm ringing you so late, but he's been really grotty all day. He's just gone to sleep now. He hasn't been sick for hours, but Debbie tells me there was a bug at playgroup. How are Libby's shoes?'

Oh, lord. 'Still in the car,' she said, contemplating getting up and going outside in the rain to fetch them and clean them up ready for the morning. Oh, well, Libby could wear her others. 'I hope you get a decent night's sleep.'

'I think I will now,' he said, and he sounded weary enough. Molly could empathise. She'd been through it with Libby several times, and knew just how wearing a sick preschooler could be.

By the morning, she had a fair idea of what a nearly-ten-year-old could be like. At six-thirty she phoned the hospital to say she couldn't come in until later, and at eight she called the Hammonds and asked them if they could help.

They came over immediately, and she arrived on the ward just as Sam came down from Theatre.

'Hi—you look harassed. Is everything all right?' he asked, and she laughed.

'Sort of. It seems to be catching. Libby's been up most of the night.'

'So've I,' he said, and she noticed the lines around his mouth. 'You'd better go home. You're bound to get it, and we don't really need it on the ward. It's short and sharp and vile, but at least it's over quickly.'

He wasn't wrong. It only took five hours to work its way through her system, but in that time she could quite cheerfully have died.

Molly went back to work the following day feeling almost one hundred per cent, and found several of her colleagues had been struck down with the bug. She was rushed off her feet for the next two days, and hardly saw Sam.

When she did it was Thursday morning, and he caught up with her just outside the ward.

'Molly.'

She went over to him, wondering what he wanted, but one look in his eyes proved it was nothing to do with work.

'Tomorrow night—it's really short notice, but is there any chance you could get a babysitter? Mark and Debbie are away for the weekend and they're taking Jack down with them and leaving him with Crystal's parents for a few days—I'm picking him up on Wednesday. I just thought, if you could get someone to look after Libby...'

She tried not to grin inanely. 'Libby's with my parents for the weekend,' she told him. 'I'm working on Saturday morning, so they're coming to pick her up tomorrow afternoon after school and keeping her until Sunday night.'

Something flared in Sam's eyes and was quickly controlled, but an answering flame shot through her. 'What did you have in mind?' she asked as casually as she could.

'I thought I might cook for you.'

'You, cook?' she said, somehow surprised.

'I'm a good cook,' he said a little stiffly, and she relented and smiled.

'I'm sure you are. That sounds lovely. What time?'

'Whenever. Six? Seven?'

'Make it seven. I'll look forward to it. Oh, and I don't like kidney beans.'

'Good. Something else we've got in common,' he said, and with a farewell wink that made her knees go weak, he headed for the lift and left her to it.

Molly didn't know what to wear. Casual, of course, because he was cooking for her at his house and that didn't call for anything dressy, but on the other hand she didn't want to be too casual and offend him.

Whatever, nothing fitted, nothing looked good, nothing seemed to suit her.

She ended up with almost the entire contents of her wardrobe on her bed and a huge crisis of confidence, and in the midst of it the phone rang.

'Hello?' she said, and was greeted with Angie's voice bubbling with curiosity.

'Hi, sweets. How are you?'

'I'm fine.'

'How's the plan going?' she asked, cutting straight to the chase as ever, and Molly laughed.

'I'm not sure. I'm having dinner with him in half an hour—he's cooking for me, and I've got my entire wardrobe on my bed and I just look awful in everything. I'm going to end up going in my uniform at this rate.'

'Rubbish. Have you got that blue thing?'

'The jersey dress?'

'Yes—the straight one with the floppy neck that makes you look like a stick insect with boobs. Wear that.'

'Really?' Molly said, staring at it doubtfully. 'It's a bit—'

'Sexy is what it is,' Angie told her bluntly. 'Wear it—and ring me after the weekend and tell me what's happened.'

'You're just nosy.'

'No, I just care. I love you. Have fun.'

The line went dead, and Molly cradled the phone, smiling wryly. Have fun.

OK. In the blue dress.

Oh, yipes.

She put it on, eyeing herself critically in the mirror and sucking in her stomach. Hmm. There was nothing she could do about it, she'd had three children—and one of them was his. That was one of the key things about stress management—change the things you could, and learn to live with the things you couldn't. Her stomach she'd learned to live with.

She turned round and peered over her shoulder, and decided the back view was OK, and it did make her bust look good. 'All right, I'll wear it,' she said to the absent Angie. Slipping on her shoes, she went downstairs, shrugged into her jacket and let herself out.

She'd picked up a bottle of wine at the supermarket last night, but no doubt it was the wrong colour for what Sam was planning. Never mind, it was the thought that counted and she couldn't really take him flowers.

And then she started wondering what, exactly, he was planning for that evening, and her heart went into overdrive.

*   *   *

Sam was wondering if he'd gone crazy. He'd bought steak and salad and baby new potatoes, nothing complicated, and a frozen chocolate dessert that couldn't possibly go wrong, and yet he was nervous.

It took him a moment to work out that it had nothing to do with the food. Food like that he could cook with his eyes shut.

No, it was Molly—or, more precisely, Molly's proposition.

It was the Bakers' fault, of course. All that happy families stuff this time last week had got to him, and after a week of reasoning he'd distilled it down to one significant fact.

He was alone, and he hated it. Some people thrived on it, but he didn't. He needed company, needed companionship, needed—hell, yes, he needed sex. There was nothing wrong with that, and Molly was offering, for heaven's sake! Only a saint would turn her down.

So here he was, trying to cook her a meal tonight with his mind quite definitely on other things! If it wasn't a charred disaster, it deserved to be.

He uncorked the wine, sniffed it and left it to breathe near the Aga. The potatoes were boiled and keeping warm in the bottom oven, smothered in butter and olive oil, the salad was in the bowl ready to dress, the steaks were in the fridge where the cat wouldn't get them, and all he needed now was Molly.

Right on cue, the doorbell rang and he went to let her in.

It was still daylight, sort of, and the last rays of the sun were gilding her skin and touching her hair with fire. She smiled and held up a bottle of wine, and as he took it his hand touched hers and heat shot through him.

'Thanks. Come in,' he said gruffly, and stepped back so

she could pass him. The light fragrance of her skin lingered in the air, and he felt his gut contract. 'I'm pottering in the kitchen,' he told her. 'Go on through.'

He followed her, unable to take his eyes off her ankles under the hem of that dress. Was it a dress? He thought so, and then she slipped the jacket off and he got a closer look at it, and heat slammed into him all over again.

He put the bottle down with a little thunk and took her jacket, hanging it over the back of a chair to give himself time to get his composure back. Then he turned to her and dredged up a smile.

'You look lovely tonight,' he said, and soft colour brushed her cheeks.

'It's ancient.'

'I wasn't looking at the dress,' he said, and her colour rose again, her eyes widening and darkening, her lips parting softly.

'Are you flirting with me?' she said after a moment, and he gave a wry grin.

'No. I was just talking without thinking. I do that sometimes. My mouth moves without bothering to engage my brain.'

'I'm not complaining,' she said, and he realised she was smiling.

He felt the tension going out of his body. Good grief. At this rate, he might almost enjoy the evening. He poured her a glass of wine—just a small one, she said, because she was driving later, but not if the gods were on his side—and put the cast-iron skillet on the hob to heat.

'How do you like your steak?' he asked her over his shoulder, and she turned away from Jack's latest offering on the front of the fridge and came over to him, threatening his sanity with that delicate fragrance and the nearness of her body.

'Slightly rare,' she murmured, peering at the pan. 'What's the Aga like to cook with?'

He gave a slightly strained laugh. He was dying here, and she wanted to talk about the Aga? 'I'm still getting used to it,' he confessed, and held the first steak suspended over the skillet. 'I should mind yourself, this might splatter a bit.'

She stepped back, giving his sanity a little elbow-room, and he dropped the meat into the hot pan and pulled the plates and the potatoes out of the bottom oven.

'You could dress the salad,' he said over his shoulder, and watched out of the corner of his eye as she drizzled olive oil and balsamic vinegar over the leaves, crunched pepper and salt over the top then tossed it all together.

She was a joy to watch, he thought, staring at her, and then remembered the steaks in the nick of time.

'That was gorgeous,' she said, sitting back and smiling at him over the top of their empty plates.

'Good. More wine?'

Molly shook her head. 'No. I'm driving, remember? I could kill a coffee, though.'

Sam laughed and stood up, putting on the kettle and rinsing out the cafetière with hot water. Moments later it was ready, and he picked up the tray, complete with after-dinner mints, and headed for the door.

'Come on, we'll go in the study, since you seem to like it so much.'

She followed him through and made herself comfortable on the sofa, sitting with her feet curled under her bottom and looking totally relaxed. No. Not totally. There was an inner tension there, he noticed, and he felt his own tension rise a notch in response.

He handed her her coffee and sat down at the other end

of the sofa, the chocolates on the cushion between them, and for a moment neither of them said anything.

Then, without engaging his brain again, his mouth said, 'That affair you were talking about—is the offer still open?'

She went utterly still, and then, setting her coffee down with great deliberation, she looked across at him. 'Why?'

He put his own coffee down, safely out of the way, and met the warm caramel caress of her eyes. 'Because, if it is, I'd like to take you up on it.'

She stared at him unblinkingly for a moment, then she swallowed, revealing that tension again. 'OK—but before we do, there's something you ought to know.'

He nodded slowly, his heart racing out of control. Stay calm, he thought. 'OK. Tell me.'

She took a deep, steadying breath and closed her eyes, then opened them again, staring down at her fingers. They were knotted together, he noticed, and he wondered what on earth she had to say.

'I'm thirty-three,' she announced eventually.

He blinked and stared at her. 'I'd already worked that one out, being reasonably good at maths,' he teased gently.

'And I've had three children.'

Oh, lord, the silly woman was worried that he wouldn't find her attractive! 'I know. I was responsible for the last one—remember?'

'And I'm a widow.'

He didn't come back quite so quick on that one, because suddenly the conversation was taking a different tack and he wasn't sure any longer where it was headed. 'I know,' he said finally, his voice gentle. 'Is that a problem?'

She looked up at him then, her eyes wide and wary. 'I don't know. You see, it's a bit silly. I'm thirty-three, the mother of three children, and a widow—and I've never done this before. I don't know what to do.'

So that was it. He gave a little huff of laughter in relief. 'Is that all? I'm sure the principle hasn't changed that much in ten years. It's like riding a bike—you don't forget how.'

She shook her head. 'No. You don't understand. I mean, I've *never* done it before, Sam. I don't know how. I'm a virgin.'

He felt his jaw sag, and snapped it shut. A virgin? But...

'You were married—you had Libby.'

'By IVF. You do know Mick was a paraplegic, surely?'

'Yes, but—not when you met him? There's a picture of you on your mantelpiece, standing with your arms round each other.'

'That was before the accident. Before we fell in love and got married. Libby was conceived by ICSI—intra-cytoplasmic sperm injection—using sperm harvested from Mick by syringe. Mick never made love to me, Sam, he couldn't—and there's been no one else.'

Sam felt strangled. He went to loosen his tie and realised he wasn't wearing one. He looked at her again, and the full impact of what she'd just said hit him like a sledge-hammer.

'Why me?' he asked, his voice rough with shock.

She shrugged. 'Why not? You're a good friend, a reasonably attractive specimen...'

He nearly choked. 'Well, thanks for that,' he muttered, and she laughed softly.

'My pleasure. I'm pretty sure I'm not going to get any nasty diseases from you—and anyway, I've had your child,' she added softly, 'so why not you? You're the obvious choice.'

He dragged his eyes away from her and picked up his

coffee, giving it very much more attention than it deserved. Or maybe not. Perhaps it was just what he needed—a bit of caffeine to clear his head after all that wine.

It was nothing to do with the wine, of course. He'd only had one glass, and he felt stone cold sober. Still, he drank the coffee for something safe to do and, reaching for the jug, he topped up his mug.

'More?'

'I haven't drunk this yet,' she pointed out.

'No. Well—um—chocolate?'

'Sam, talk to me.'

He shook his head to clear it. 'Molly, I can't. I need to think.'

'Why? Don't tell me you're going to change your mind!'

'Maybe.' He looked at her solemnly. 'Molly, this changes things, you must see that.'

'Why? I'm an adult, Sam, and so are you. We're both free. It doesn't change anything—unless the idea of making love to a virgin turns you off.'

'Turns me off?' he exclaimed, jackknifing up and pacing to the window. 'Hell, Molly, don't be silly.'

'So what's the problem, then?'

He shrugged. 'It should be something special.'

'So make it special,' she said softly. 'Please, Sam. I've waited such a long time. I'm thirty-three—don't you think it's about time?'

He turned, and she was behind him, so close he nearly fell over her. For a moment he stood there, then with a ragged groan he drew her into his arms, tucked her head under his chin and hugged her, hideously aware of her warmth and softness, the firm press of her breasts against his chest, the gentle swell of her hips...

'OK,' he sighed, too weak to turn her down, 'but not

now. Not like this—please. Your first time should be special.'

'It will be.'

'Yes—but not tonight. Tomorrow. Give me time to prepare things.'

'You'll change your mind.'

'No. No, I won't, I promise. Not a chance. I just have to do it right this time, Molly.'

'This time?' she asked, and he sighed. He might as well tell her.

'When I lost my virginity, I was seventeen, and so was the girl. It was the first time for both of us, and it was messy and uncomfortable and undignified. I didn't even know her name, and I never saw her again, so I never had a chance to apologise. I vowed then that if I ever made love to another virgin, I'd do it properly—and I will. That's a promise. Now go home, there's a good girl, before I lose my resolve. I'll ring you. Go.'

He fetched her jacket, helped her into it and turned her into his arms, lowering his mouth to hers for a teasing, tempting kiss that left them both aching for more.

'Go on,' he whispered, and pushed her gently out of the door. He saw her to her car, closing the driver's door with some regret, and then, as her taillights disappeared through the gate, he closed his eyes and sighed.

His hands were shaking—his whole body was shaking—and he nearly got into his car and followed her. He must have been mad to send her away.

Still, it would be worth it—if he survived the suspense!

Molly went to work the next morning in a daze. She'd spent the night torn between anticipation and the fear of disappointing Sam, and when her alarm went off she was only too relieved. She arrived at work to find the place crawling with newspaper reporters and film crews from the local television stations, and went into the sanctuary of the ward to find out what was going on.

'So who's the celebrity in labour?' she asked, but Sue shook her head.

'No celebrity. A baby girl was found last night left in the loo at a twenty-four-hour supermarket. She was very new—minutes rather than hours old, and the cord was hacked through and not even tied, so she was very lucky to survive. They think she'd been born there, but nobody had noticed anything strange.'

'Really? Must have been a multigravida,' Molly said thoughtfully. 'A first-time mum would have made too much fuss, surely, and been in there too long.'

'Maybe. The worrying thing is, there was no sign of the placenta. She might have flushed it down the loo, but they're a bit big to go willingly.'

'Oh, lord. Oh, poor thing—whatever must she be going through? Where's the baby? Special Care?'

Sue shook her head. 'No—in here. SCBU's full, and she seems to be full term. We've given her milk from the breast-milk bank. Josh Lancaster's been in and checked her over, and he's happy that she hasn't suffered any adverse affects, but she should be with her mum.'

'And her mum,' Molly said, troubled, 'should be in here, being checked over. What if she had a retained placenta? It doesn't bear thinking about. Oh, well.' She shrugged the thought aside. 'So what else is going on? Any labours I should know about?'

'No, it's really quiet. You could cuddle the baby and feed her, if you elbow everyone else out of the way.'

Molly laughed. 'I might just do that. I always seem to be too busy to cuddle the babies.'

She went into the nursery and found the little scrap on

her own. All the other babies were with their mothers, and there were precious few of them anyway. She'd never known it so quiet, she thought, and wished it would hot up a bit, to take her mind off Sam and tonight.

Not until she'd had a cuddle with the baby, though!

She was starting to stir, her little arms flailing from time to time, her mouth working rhythmically. Molly glanced at the notes, saw she was due for a feed and was on her way to get it when a nursery nurse came in with a bottle.

'May I?' Molly asked with a smile, and the girl handed the bottle over reluctantly and left her to it. She scooped the little thing out of her clear Perspex crib and settled into the nursing chair, cuddling the baby against her as she brushed the teat against her mouth. Her rosebud lips fastened hungrily on the teat and she sucked, then coughed.

'Too fast for you, sweetheart? Slow down a little, don't be so impatient.'

The crooning seemed to soothe her, and she settled back to suckle quietly while Molly stared down at her and wondered how anyone could walk away from her child and leave it in a public toilet. What on earth was she going through?

'Molly?'

Her heart skidded to a halt and picked up again, thrashing against her ribs. She looked up as Sam came towards her, hunkering down beside her and stroking the baby's cheek with the back of his finger. The tender gesture nearly undid her. 'Is this our mystery baby?' he asked softly.

Molly nodded. 'Yes—poor little thing. I'm just giving her a feed. What are you doing here? I didn't realise you were in.'

'Oh, I'm on call. I've come in to check a patient with an elevated temperature post-op—probably peritonitis. It was a nasty, messy operation that had been left too late,

so it doesn't surprise me, even with the blockbuster antibiotics she's on. I'm on my way home now, but I wanted
to talk to you about tonight.'

Oh, lord, he's changed his mind, she thought, and disappointment washed over her in a wave. Then she met his
eyes, and realised she was mistaken.

'I'll pick you up at seven,' he said, his voice rough and
low. 'Wear something suitable for dinner and dancing.'

'Dancing?'

'Don't you dance?'

'I didn't realise we were going out.'

He smiled, his eyes smouldering. 'We aren't. I'll see
you later.'

Her heart thumped against her ribs, and she watched him
go in a stunned silence. Dinner and dancing? At home?
Wow. It was just beginning to dawn on her what he'd
meant by 'doing it right', and she wondered what else was
in store for her.

She burped and changed the baby on autopilot, and put
her down to sleep again after a little cuddle to settle her.
There was nothing to do on the ward, so she went into the
empty delivery room and sorted through the equipment and
tried not to guess what Sam was planning.

She blew up the gym balls that were used to support
women in labour if they wanted to hang over something,
and checked that all the necessary delivery packs were
there and nothing was missing—and thought about Sam.

She was just coming out onto the ward again when
someone came through the doors at the other end of the
corridor and stood there, looking round a little wildly.

Even from here Molly could see that she was distressed,
and instinctively she realised that this was the mother of
the abandoned baby. She was looking for the nursery,
Molly guessed, and there was no way she was going to

snatch her baby back and leave without medical attention if Molly had anything to do with it.

'That girl's here. Tell Security to watch out for her, and get Sam—now. He might still be in the building,' she said out of the corner of her mouth as she walked past the ward clerk, and without hesitating she went up to the girl and gave her a casual smile.

'Hi. Have you come to visit someone?' she said, giving her a reason to be there, and the girl nodded, her eyes sliding away from Molly's.

'Well, why don't you come and have a cup of tea while you wait? It isn't visiting for a few more minutes, and I was just having one.' She led the girl into the kitchen, pushed the door shut and turned on the kettle, propping herself in the way so she couldn't escape. The girl was chalk-white and twitchy, and Molly was worried about her. How to proceed, though?

'It's been a bit of a dramatic night,' she said casually, wondering how hard she could push it. 'We've had a baby brought in without her mother. Lovely little thing—I've just fed her. She's really pretty—a bit like you.'

The girl went still. 'So—she's all right?'

'Yes, she's fine—but we're worried about the mother. She probably needs help, and we can't help her unless she'll let us.'

The girl met her eyes then, defeat written in them, and tears spilt over and ran down her cheeks. 'I can't keep her.'

Molly's heart went out to the girl. 'Maybe not,' she said softly, 'but someone ought to look after you in the meantime. Can I have a look at you? I'm a midwife—I deliver babies and look after the mums.'

'I can't be a mum. I'm only seventeen—my parents think I've been at art college, but I left. I told them I'd gone round Europe for the summer—part of my course. They'd kill me.'

'I doubt it. I've got a daughter, and I wouldn't kill her.'

She shook her head. 'Dad's a minister. Mum's a teacher. They'll be so ashamed of me.'

She put her hand over her mouth to hold in the sobs, and the other crept to her still-distended abdomen. 'I feel really ill—I want my mum…'

'Come on, sweetheart, let's sort you out,' Molly said, and, putting her arm round her shoulders, she led the girl across the corridor into one of the little side rooms. As she went in, she caught sight of Sam hurrying towards her, and she shook her head slightly.

He slowed, and she knew he'd hover in earshot, so she left the door open a crack.

'Right, my love, hop up on the bed and let's have a look at you.'

She didn't get any further. With a tiny cry the girl crumpled, and to Molly's horror the floor beneath her turned dark crimson.

'Sam!' she yelled, but he was already there, lifting the girl onto the bed, elevating her legs and pressing firmly into her abdomen to try and halt the haemorrhage.

'I'll have to take her up to Theatre—come with me, we don't have time to wait for the ODA.'

The next few minutes were tense, and Molly worked alongside the theatre team to get lines in and fluids into the girl to support her system until blood supplies arrived. Finally Sam was satisfied that the haemorrhaging had stopped and he'd removed the placental fragment that had been causing it, and her uterus was contracting down well.

'OK, thanks, everyone,' he said. Stripping off his gloves and mask, he threw Molly a grin. 'Thanks for that. She should be down with you in about half an hour. Any idea of the story?'

Molly shrugged. 'She wants her mother, that's all I know.'

'Did you get a number?'

'Nothing. There wasn't time. She is going to make it, Sam, isn't she?'

'Of course she is. I'll get her down to you straight away, and you can reunite her with her baby—if she wants that.'

'I don't know if she does, but she ought to,' Molly said. 'She may not know she wants it yet, but she will, later in life, and it could be too late then. She needs to talk to her mother first before she makes a decision either way.'

Molly went back to the ward, prepared all the paperwork for the girl's admission and went to see the sleeping baby. 'Your mum's here, little one,' she said softly. 'I hope she can love you enough to find a way to stay with you.'

There would be hundreds of couples out there—probably thousands—who would have her if not, Molly knew, but somehow she felt that that poor girl needed her baby, whatever her parents might feel. Surely a minister and a teacher would have enough human-kindness and understanding to support their daughter through this?

Molly could only hope so, for all their sakes.

The girl was called Rosalind, and her parents came instantly when they were phoned. Molly was there, helping her to feed her baby, when the door opened and they came in, and a more tearful and loving reunion it was hard to imagine.

'Silly, silly girl,' her father kept saying, tears streaming down his cheeks, and her mother just held her and the baby and rocked them and sobbed.

'A granddaughter—I can't believe it,' she said, and sobbed again.

'I'll get you some tea,' Molly said, and left them alone together for a few minutes. When she went back in Rosalind was explaining the circumstances of the baby's conception, and it seemed she'd been the victim of a date-rape drug.

'I have no idea who the father is,' she was saying. 'There wasn't anyone in particular, just a whole group of lads at this party, and I don't remember anything about it. I just woke up feeling—really dirty...'

She started to cry again, and Molly took the baby gently from her and tucked her up in her crib by the bed. There would be plenty of time to cuddle her later. Just now, the poor girl needed to talk, and her parents needed to listen.

'Ring the bell if you need anything,' she said, and went out, almost bumping into Sam in the doorway.

'I gather her parents are here,' he murmured.

'Yes. Can you leave them for a few minutes?'

'If I can persuade a pretty young midwife to make me a cup of coffee in the meantime.'

'Sorry, you're out of luck, I'm the only one free,' she said, and he chuckled and followed her into the kitchen, kicking the door shut and turning her into his arms.

'That's a glass door,' she pointed out, but it was only a small glass panel, and he leant against it, obscuring them from view while he kissed her thoroughly and systematically.

'That's just to keep you ticking over till tonight,' he said, and then, without waiting for coffee, he opened the door, backed out into the corridor grinning wickedly and left her there, her body clamouring for more...

CHAPTER NINE

SAM'S car pulled up on her drive at two minutes past seven, and as Molly watched him walk up to the door, her first reaction was relief.

He was wearing a dinner suit. Wear something suitable for dancing, he'd said, and absolutely the only thing in her wardrobe that qualified even slightly was a ballgown she'd bought in a charity shop for a Stoke Mandeville fundraiser two years ago.

So that's what she was wearing, a sleek, slightly A-line skirt with a fishtail pleat in the back, and a boned, fitted basque that fitted her like a glove and did incredible things for her figure. She'd been hovering in her bedroom, waiting to see if she was hopelessly overdressed.

Her immediate problem dealt with, she allowed herself to study him as he strode purposefully towards her door, and her mouth went dry.

What was it about men in dinner suits? No, not men. Sam. He looked stunning. The stark contrast of the white shirt against his skin, the cut of the suit emphasising the breadth of his shoulders and hinting at the lean, powerful muscles of his legs—he looked magnificent, she thought, and she felt suddenly totally out of her depth.

Like a lamb to the slaughter, she picked up her bag, checked her reflection one last time and headed for the stairs, her long coat covering the dress and giving her something to hide behind. Dredging up a smile, she opened the door.

'Hi—you're ready,' he said, sounding surprised, and she smiled faintly.

'Of course I'm ready,' she said, wishing it were true, and stepped outside. The night air was cool, and she shivered with anticipation. He turned up her coat collar, snuggling it closer, and brushed a teasing kiss over her lips.

'Your taxi awaits, ma'am,' he murmured, and, closing the door behind them, he ushered her to the car and settled her in it.

He's treating me like royalty, she thought, and stifled the sudden desperate urge to giggle. He opened the other door and slid in behind the wheel, throwing her a fleeting smile before pulling away. They hardly spoke on the journey to his house, and she got the strangest feeling that he was as nervous as she was.

Sam? Nervous?

They pulled up outside his house, and he ushered her inside and through to the kitchen.

'Sorry it's not very glamorous,' he said with an apologetic grin, 'but I have a choice of leaving you in the sitting room alone, or having you with me in the kitchen, and I've just got a few finishing touches to put to things. Let me take your coat.'

Molly felt her chin come up a notch. Would he approve, or would he think she'd gone totally over the top?

She turned her back to him and allowed him to slide it from her shoulders, and his soft intake of breath gave her confidence. She turned back to him and was gratified to see the warmth of appreciation in his eyes.

'You look beautiful,' he said, his voice gruff, and he draped her coat over the back of a chair and eased a finger round his collar under the bow-tie as if it was strangling him. 'Let me get you a drink.'

He pulled a bottle out of an ice bucket in the sink, and deftly twisted off the wire cage holding the cork.

'Bubbly?'

'Mmm—with a difference,' he said, twisting off the cork inside a teatowel and pouring the smoking liquid into two tall flutes, handing her one. As the bubbles settled, she could see a thin, brown stick bobbing in the glass. She sniffed curiously.

'Vanilla?' she said, and he smiled.

'It's an aphrodisiac,' he murmured, and lifted his glass to hers. 'Here's to tonight—may it be a night to remember.'

She met his smouldering eyes over the top of the glass and wondered why she didn't just catch fire. Her nerves evaporated, driven off by the intensity of his eyes, and she smiled back a little unsteadily. They didn't need an aphrodisiac.

'To tonight,' she concurred, and, without taking her eyes from his, she sipped the wine.

It tasted—interesting. Different. Fragrant and heady— and if she wasn't careful, that's exactly where it would end up, going to her head. She lowered the glass.

'So, what else is on the menu?' she asked, even more curious now.

He smiled and tapped the side of his nose. 'You'll see.'

'I will—I intend to watch you.'

'No. You'll put me off. You look too damn beautiful in that dress, you're distracting me to bits. Go and sit on the other side of the table before I forget all my good intentions and make love to you on it.'

A warm tide of colour ran over her skin, and she retreated to the safety of the far side of what until then had been just a simple piece of furniture. She regarded it warily, then with curiosity.

'No,' he said, his voice gruff, and turned back to the stove, leaving her with a temptress's smile playing around her lips.

She tested the air. Asparagus, and something vaguely seafoody—not fish, but something that teased at her memory. Scallops? He'd just put a tray into the top oven, and he was steaming something on the hob—the asparagus, she'd bet.

He put a little pan on beside the asparagus, then poured the contents into a bowl, lifted out the bright, fresh spears and placed them into a warmed dish and turned to her, clicking his heels and smiling.

'Dinner is served, madam,' he announced.

'Shall I lay the table?' she asked, and he chuckled softly.

'It's done. Bring the champagne.'

She followed him, the two flutes and the bottle in hand, and he led her into a room she'd never seen previously. It was dark, and as her eyes adjusted she heard the flick of a lighter and the soft glow of the candles illuminated the table, casting an intimate pool of light that sparkled on crystal and silver.

Good heavens. Sam really had pulled out all the stops. There were crisply folded linen napkins on the tablemats, and fingerbowls that he filled with hot water from a flask. The scent of citrus filled the air, and he seated her and then took his place at right angles to her, close enough that their knees brushed as he sat down.

He placed the dish of asparagus between them, picked up a spear and dipped it in the butter, then held it to her lips.

Oh, good grief. He was going to feed her...

She opened her mouth and bit into the sweet, juicy stem, butter running onto her lips. He brushed it away with a blunt fingertip, then touched it to his tongue. Heat shot through her. How could eating be so incredibly erotic? she wondered, but this was just the appetiser.

She picked up a spear and fed it to him, absurdly aroused by the sight of his strong, white teeth biting cleanly through the pale green flesh. My goodness, she thought, at this rate we won't get through the first course.

She'd reckoned without Sam. He fed her the last morsel, left her with a murmured command to stay put, and came back moments later with a steaming dish of scallop shells, topped with crisp, golden breadcrumbs and smelling absolutely heavenly.

'Scallops and oysters,' he told her, 'with wild rocket and basil salad.'

'Aphrodisiacs?' she asked, knowing the answer before he smiled acknowledgement.

'I found a very interesting website. Open wide.'

The flavour burst on her tongue, and she picked up her fork and returned the favour. 'Whatever did we do before the internet?' she asked, and he chuckled.

'I don't know. Open.'

Aphrodisiac or not, she thought she'd never tasted anything so delicious in her life. He was right, he was a good cook—and his presentation was faultless.

The dishes were cleared away, and he reappeared with a plate of fresh fruit—strawberries, frosted grapes, slices of pear, apple and banana, juicy triangles of pineapple—and in the centre of the plate was a dish of melted dessert chocolate.

Sam poured her a glass of a dark red wine and she raised her eyebrows.

'Cabernet sauvignon—it's a very good one, very fruity, lots of body. It's stunning with the chocolate.'

She laughed. 'I believe you,' she said. 'You've been right about everything else.'

He dipped a slice of pear into the chocolate and held it to her lips, and the contrast of the bitter chocolate with the sweet, crisp flesh of the pear was astonishing. She sipped the wine, nodded and set it down.

'You're right. Here.'

Molly fed him a strawberry, then some of the pineapple, and as he bit into it a dribble of chocolate ran down his chin.

'You're a messy eater,' she said gently, and, leaning forwards, she stroked it away with her tongue.

A deep groan erupted from his chest and he leant towards her, but she backed away, shaking her head. 'Uh-uh. We haven't finished yet.'

'How do you know that?'

'I'm sure you've got some trick up your sleeve with the coffee,' she said, and he gave a strained laugh.

'How did you guess? Are you ready for it?'

She chuckled. 'The coffee?'

'The coffee.'

'Absolutely.'

He whisked away her chair for her with all the skill of a *maître d'*, and she allowed him to lead her to the sitting room.

Soft music was playing, and on the coffee-table there was an array of petits fours, tiny truffles and marzipan fruits dipped in dark chocolate—not the chemical-flavoured bought variety, she realised, but home-made, sculpted by his own highly skilled and industrious hand.

'When on earth did you find time?' she asked as he came back into the room with a tray and set it down beside the sweets.

'Nothing took long,' he told her, and she realised it was probably true. Everything had been very simple, apart from the scallops and oysters, and even that was probably a quick dish to prepare.

It was the thought that had gone into it which touched her, the care and attention to detail. Her eyes filled with tears and she blinked them away.

'Coffee,' he said, passing her a tiny little cup filled with a black, fragrant brew with a touch of...

'Nutmeg?' she said, puzzled, and then shook her head when he smiled. 'Don't tell me—the website. It's got a lot to answer for.'

He picked up a little marzipan orange and held it to her lips, but he didn't release it. Instead he waited until she bit into it, then put the other half in his mouth.

She swallowed, the sweet almond paste gliding down her throat, fragrant and smooth. She sipped her coffee, hot and strong and strangely refreshing, and then, picking up a truffle, she held it to his lips and copied his actions.

It left her fingers covered in chocolate, and he caught her hand and drew it to his lips, their eyes locked, suckling each fingertip in turn until her body hummed like a bow-string. Heat pooled in her and a tiny moan escaped her lips.

Without releasing her hand, he drew her to her feet and into his arms, his hands resting lightly against her spine. They swayed gently to the music, their bodies scarcely touching, the warmth of his hands, the hard brush of his thighs against hers and the feel of his shoulders under her hands their only points of contact.

Easing back, she reached up and caught one end of his bow-tie and pulled it slowly undone, then slipped the button free and pressed a light, taunting kiss against the hollow of his throat.

His hands slid lower, easing her against him, and she

felt the heat of his arousal burning through the fabric of her dress.

His head dipped, his breath warm against her ear, and she felt the soft graze of his jaw against her throat. He nuzzled closer, his lips burning a trail down over her collar-bone and back up, past her ear, over her cheekbone, her eyes, her chin, then finally settling against her mouth with a ragged sigh.

He tasted of dark, bitter chocolate, fragrant coffee and sweet-scented almonds, and the combination was unbelievably erotic.

His tongue traced her lips, coaxing them apart, and then he deepened the kiss, the moist, hot velvet of his tongue delving into her mouth again and again, challenging her, duelling with her, until she grew bolder and returned the caress.

His groan erupted against her lips, his hands urgent now, trembling against her as they cupped her breasts, and she threaded her fingers through the soft, silken strands of his hair and drew him closer, clinging to him in case she should fall.

He lifted his head, resisting her, and stared down into her face with eyes of fire.

'Molly, I need you,' he said, and the simplicity of the words nearly brought her to her knees.

'I need you, too, Sam—now, please...'

He released her, easing away from her with obvious reluctance. Holding out his hand, he led her through the house without a word, up the stairs, along the landing and into his room.

'Close your eyes,' he murmured, and she heard the scrape of his lighter wheel against the flint. 'You can open them now,' he said, and she did so, knowing what she'd find and yet still touched by the beauty of the flickering flames in every corner of the room.

Big church candles, tiny floating lights drifting in bowls of water, tall, slender tapers in simple glass holders—each was beautiful, but the total effect was incredible, unbelievably romantic—and in the midst of them all was the bed.

It was huge, a beautiful mahogany four-poster just made for loving, and the simple ivory bedspread was scattered with rose petals.

'Oh, Sam,' she whispered, and looked up into those amazing blue eyes that seemed to reflect the flame of every single candle, focusing them all into a fire so bright she thought it would consume her.

'Undress for me,' she whispered, and he gave a gruff, startled laugh.

'I thought that was my line,' he said, but his hands came up and stripped away the bow-tie she'd already undone, his fingers trembling too much to manage the buttons.

'Help me,' he pleaded, and she stepped closer, slipping the buttons free one by one until his chest was revealed to her. She slid her hands inside the fabric, parting it, and pressed her lips to the warm, smooth skin. There was a light scatter of hair in the centre, just enough to tease her lips, and she moved the shirt aside until she found one taut, flat male nipple and took it gently in her teeth.

He groaned and rocked against her, and suddenly her patience was gone. She needed him, and she needed him now. She was done with subtlety and foreplay, and she thought if she didn't feel him against her skin in the next few seconds, she'd surely die. She dragged the shirt aside, whimpering when it caught on his wrists, and he wrenched it free.

His trousers followed, kicked aside with his shoes and socks, leaving him utterly naked and breath-stealingly beautiful.

'How does this come off?' he asked, his chest rising and falling sharply as he stared in frustration at her basque.

'There's a zip—at the back.'

He found it, sliding it down until it parted, and the top fell away, spilling her breasts into his waiting hands.

'Dear God, Molly,' he breathed, and then his lips found them, his breath hot against her skin, then cold as it fanned across the damp trail of his tongue. His fingers found the zip on her skirt and it fell to a pool at her feet, leaving her standing there dressed only in a tiny black lace thong that Angie had sent her for Christmas as a joke.

It didn't seem like a joke now. His eyes flared, and he drew her into his arms and held her there for a moment, his body almost vibrating with the tension running through it.

'Lie on the bed,' he ordered softly, and she climbed up and lay down, suddenly self-conscious in front of him. Molly knew her figure wasn't bad, but three pregnancies had left inevitable consequences.

'You're beautiful,' he said, his voice raw with need. He closed his eyes, as if he was counting to ten, she thought, and then he opened them again and reached out to the bedside table, lifting a foil packet in trembling fingers.

'No,' she said, reaching out and covering his hands with hers. 'You don't need that. I went on the Pill two weeks ago—just in case. I didn't want anything between us.'

His breath left his body in a harsh gust. Dropping the

little wrapper, he knelt at her feet and drew the tiny scrap of lace slowly down her legs. It went the way of their other clothes, and then he came down beside her and drew her into his arms, the heat of the contact making them both gasp.

His mouth found hers, fierce with hunger, and then he lifted his head and stared down into her eyes. 'God help me, Molly, I'm not going to last ten seconds.'

'Neither am I. I want you, Sam—please. Now.'

He moved over her, his hands threading through her hair, fanning it on the pillow, and his eyes locked with hers. Then he was there, inside her, with her every inch of that long, glorious climb to oblivion, and when she reached the top he was there with her still, his harsh cry mingling with her own as she crested the peak and fell headlong in his arms.

Sam was stunned. He'd never known anything like it in his life, and he didn't think it was anything to do with all the preparation or scene-setting. He had a feeling that if he'd just taken her there and then on the kitchen table when she'd arrived, it would have been the same.

He'd have to try it later, he thought, his free hand idly stroking the smooth, satin skin of her back. The other hand was meshed with hers, cradled on his chest, and one slim, silky leg was wedged firmly between his thighs.

Molly was asleep, and he was taking advantage of it to get his emotions in order. He snorted softly. Not a chance. There was no way his emotions would ever be the same again, he realised, and the thought terrified him.

He loved her.

It was that simple, and that complicated. So much for

their no-strings, someone-to-do-things-with affair. His fingers tightened on hers, and she lifted her head and looked deep into his eyes, as if she was searching for something.

'What's wrong?' she murmured.

'Nothing.' He drew her closer. 'Come here.'

He made love to her again, slowly this time, kissing every inch of her until she wept with frustration, then taking her to the peak again and again until he couldn't stand it any more and went with her, tumbling even further into the fathomless abyss of love.

'Can I ask you something incredibly intrusive and personal?'

Molly stopped drawing circles on Sam's chest and looked up at him in the grey morning light. He looked troubled, and she pressed her lips to his rough, stubbled jaw. 'Of course.'

'It's about your marriage. Tell me to go to hell if you like, but last night, whenever I touched you, whatever I did, it was as if it was the first time—for *everything*. I mean, I know he was paraplegic, but so many of the things I did with you, he could have done, and yet you felt so incredibly—I don't know. Untouched?'

'Because I was,' she said honestly. 'We didn't do anything.'

'Never? Why?' Sam asked, sounding astounded. 'If that had been me, I'm sure I would have wanted to touch you, to give you pleasure. It would have been its own reward for me.'

For a moment she didn't reply. She couldn't, because she was dragged back into the past, back to Mick and that awful, heart-rending night.

'Maybe,' she said eventually. 'Or maybe not. He tried once. He said it wasn't fair to me, that I shouldn't be denied a sex life just because he couldn't do anything, and he kissed me and...' She broke off, the words somehow too hard to find. 'We gave up in the end. It just felt all wrong, when I could give nothing back. It didn't seem important enough, and so we just went to sleep.'

She fell silent, hoping Sam would leave it at that, but he didn't, of course.

'There's more, isn't there?' he murmured.

She nodded slowly, reluctantly. 'I woke up later because he'd got out of bed. He did that sometimes, because he didn't sleep well, and he usually pottered about and made a drink, read a book, something like that, and then he'd come back to bed later. I suppose I must have dozed off again, and then a noise woke me—a terrible noise, like a wounded animal.'

Sam's arm tightened around her, his hand splaying out on her back, comforting her, as if he knew what was coming.

'I found him in the kitchen, on the floor in the corner. At first I thought he'd fallen, but he'd dragged himself there as if he was trying to hide from the pain. I thought something terrible had happened to him—which I suppose it had. He told me to go away, to leave him. I wouldn't, I covered him with a blanket and curled up with him to keep him warm, because he was freezing and he couldn't feel it.'

'Couldn't you get him back to bed?'

She shook her head. 'No. He wouldn't move, and he was far too heavy to lift, so I stayed with him. He wouldn't talk to me, he just kept shuddering, and in the end I got angry and yelled at him. I was worried sick, and he wouldn't share it with me, and I couldn't take any more. He told me to leave—said it was over. I knew he didn't mean it, so I made him talk to me. I nagged and bullied until he broke down and let it all out, how he wasn't man enough for me, how I deserved better, a real man, someone who could give me children—rubbish like that. So I told him how much I loved him, and I asked him to marry me.'

'You weren't married?'

Molly shook her head again. 'Not then. It took me a week or so to wear him down, but finally he agreed, after we'd found out that we could have a child by IVF. We could easily afford it, because of the compensation payout after his accident, and it took away his strongest argument.'

'So you got married.'

'Yes. A few weeks later, but he never touched me again, apart from the occasional affectionate kiss. It was like some unwritten agreement, and we both respected it. Two years after that we had Libby, and it changed him completely. He felt like a man again, he said, and he was a wonderful father. She brought him so much happiness and then, when she was eighteen months old, he got pneumonia. I had a call at work to say he was sick, and twelve hours later he was dead.' She gave a little shrug. 'So, that was us, really.'

She blinked away the tears she always cried for Mick's wasted life and, lifting her head, she looked down into Sam's eyes. They were over-bright, and as she watched, a tear slid out of the corner of one and ran down into his hair. His hands gentle, he drew her down into his arms again and cradled her head against his chest.

'Molly, I'm so sorry. I had no idea. I wouldn't have asked.'

'It's a long time ago,' she said, but it didn't seem so long now, talking about it, and she felt the tears welling again for the tragic waste. She should have shared this joy with Mick, too, she thought. It was so unfair—so horribly, horribly unfair.

A sob rose in her throat, and Sam made a tutting noise and rocked her gently, like a child, while she wept for what the fates had taken away. Then she slept, and when she woke Sam was gone, and the sheets were cold.

She got up, sliding her legs over the edge of the bed and padding across the room. There was a robe on the back of the door, and she slipped it on and belted it tightly, then went looking for him.

Sam was gutted.

If he'd only known—if he'd had the slightest idea of how much she still loved Mick, he wouldn't have touched her. He couldn't have. That precious gift she'd given him last night had been Mick's, and Mick's alone, and he felt like a grave robber.

Oh, she'd participated willingly enough, but she was a young, healthy woman. Of course she'd been willing. It was biology, nothing more, and if he'd allowed himself to read anything more into it, well, this morning had certainly shown him the truth. He couldn't do it again. He'd been married to Crystal when she'd been in love with another man, and this was ten times worse. He couldn't compete with a ghost, and he had no intention of trying.

He felt a huge, raw pain inside, a pain like nothing he'd ever felt before, and he slipped quietly out of bed, amidst the burned-out candles and the bruised rose petals, and went downstairs, still naked.

He went into the shower off the utility room, closed the door and went into the cubicle, turning the water on full and standing motionless, head bowed, under the spray.

A sob fought its way free, and then another. Turning his face into the wall, he gave himself up to the pain.

Common sense resurrected itself before he drowned. He wasn't married to Molly, she didn't want that from him. She'd suggested an affair, and he'd taken her up on it. He was being stupid. Nothing had really changed, except his feelings.

OK, that was a pretty big nothing, but even so, he wasn't sure that a more permanent relationship between them would be a good idea. There were still all the complications of Jack.

'You're justifying it unnecessarily, Gregory,' he told himself angrily, slamming the lever down and cutting off the tepid water. 'It's an affair. You're both adults. So she's got baggage—so what? So have you. Just enjoy it while it lasts, and to hell with commitment.'

He towelled himself roughly dry, found some clothes in the tumble-dryer that would do, and started clearing up.

Molly found him in the kitchen, up to his elbows in suds, and she went up behind him and slipped her arms around his waist.

'You should have called me, I would have helped you,' she said.

He grunted, but he didn't speak. He didn't stop, either, just carried on washing the pans until he'd finished, then dried his hands and turned into her arms.

'You needed to sleep,' he said, but so much later she'd almost forgotten what she'd been talking about. 'Coffee or tea?'

'Oh, tea. I can't start the day with coffee.'

She perched on the edge of the table, her legs crossed, and watched him while he made it, wondering if she was imagining it or if he was in a strange mood. When he turned, mugs in hand, he gave her an odd, unreadable look and set the mugs down.

'Oh, Molly.'

He walked over to her, put his arms round her and cradled her against his chest.

She tipped her head back and looked up at him. 'Sam? What is it?'

'Nothing. It must be all those aphrodisiacs we had last night.'

His smile was faint and didn't reach his eyes, and she lifted a hand and cradled his cheek. It was rough with stubble, but he smelt of soap and his hair was damp.

'I need a shower,' she said. 'Come and help me.'

'I've showered.'

'But I haven't,' she said. Slipping off the edge of the table, she held out her hand. 'Show me where it is.'

'There's one here—it's got better water pressure than the one upstairs.'

'But is it near the bed?'

Sam's eyes darkened. 'No—but I'm sure we'll manage.'

He took her hand, and led her through into a bright little room, fully tiled and still steamy from his shower. He flipped the lever, stripped off his clothes and eased the dressing-gown from her shoulders. Then, closing the cubicle door behind them, he turned her away from him and soaped her thoroughly under the stinging spray.

Her thighs clenched on his hand, and she turned in his arms, her eyes searching his. There was nothing there but desire, hot and raw and hungry, and as the water pelted down on them, he lifted her and lowered her down onto him.

She gasped aloud, and his mouth found hers and he drove into her, again and again and again, until she felt the ripples start. She clung to him, her nails biting into the hot, slick flesh of his shoulders, striving...

'Sam?'

'Come for me, Molly,' he said roughly. 'Come for me...'

She felt herself fall apart, felt his response, instant and so powerful she was almost afraid, and then his voice, muffled by the water, saying her name in a rough, strained whisper that she could hardly hear.

Then something else that could have been 'I love you...'

CHAPTER TEN

MOLLY was puzzled.

She didn't know what had happened, but something had, and the more she thought about it that night, the more convinced she was that it was something to do with Mick. It had been fine until Sam had asked about him, and then it had all gone pear-shaped. Well, not pear-shaped, exactly, but different.

But why? Because she'd cried? Even with her lack of experience she realised it was pretty lousy etiquette to cry about another man all over the man you'd just made love with, but he'd asked her about Mick, and she'd just told him.

Too much detail? Too much everything, probably, and then crying about it had just been the finishing touch. Sam was probably sulking because he'd made so much effort and then she'd cried about someone else. To be fair, she might have sulked, too.

Oh, well, it was no use crying over spilt milk. She'd talk to him in the morning at work. In the meantime she needed to get some sleep before she went quite insane. She turned over, thumped the pillow again and closed her eyes.

Pointless.

She went downstairs and made herself a cup of tea, then took it into the sitting room and sat down on the sofa, right opposite the pictures of Mick. She studied them thoughtfully.

'I wonder what you'd make of him,' she asked him, but

there was no answer. There never was. She was truly on her own now, and after eight years she was pretty used to it. She looked at the photos again, photos of another Molly at another time, and thought that if it wasn't for Libby, she'd put them away. She didn't need them to remind her of Mick. She carried him in a special place in her heart and always would, but she'd moved on years ago.

Four years, to be exact—the time she'd met Sam.

Oh, Sam, she thought, and her throat clogged with tears. What have I said to hurt you? Something, but what? Is it just your ego?

There was no point in asking him, either. He wouldn't talk to her, any more than Mick used to. What was it about men that they couldn't talk about their feelings? Women did it all the time—and men committed most of the violent crimes in the world. Because of pent-up emotion?

Probably.

Molly put her empty mug back in the kitchen and went back to bed, finally falling asleep some time after two. She woke at seven, hustled Libby off to school and went to work. She was on a sensible shift today, office hours, and although it meant that Libby had to walk to her grandparents' after school, at least they didn't have such a revoltingly early start.

There was no sign of Sam, but she'd deal with him later. First of all, she needed to find out how Rosalind had got on over the weekend, and if she was going to keep her beautiful little daughter, and if her parents were able to support her through it.

She was sure they would, once they'd got over the shock of knowing that their granddaughter had been born in a cubicle in a public toilet.

She went down to the nursing station and was told that Rosalind and her baby were fine, and they'd gone home with her parents the day before, all rifts if not healed, at least on the way to it. Molly was sorry not to have seen her again, but at least the outcome was a happy one and the newshounds weren't still haunting the department.

She was called down to A and E during the course of the morning to attend to a woman who'd gone into labour following a fall. She was being stitched, and they wanted Molly's assessment of her labour to know whether they should keep her there a little longer or transfer her straight to Maternity.

The first person she saw as she went in was Nick Baker, and he greeted her with a warm if weary smile.

'Hello, Dad,' she said, and he chuckled.

'Hi. Come to see our pregnant lady?'

'I have. How are things at home?'

'Wonderful. Sally's shattered, but the baby's lovely. He's as good as gold. Thank you for putting up with us, by the way, and being so good to Sally.'

She laughed. 'My pleasure. I'll look forward to delivering the next one.'

'Oh, give us a little while to get over the shock,' he said with a rueful chuckle. 'Your lady's in here.'

He drew back the cubicle curtain. 'Ann, this is Molly. She's a midwife. She's come to have a look at you and see if you need to be transferred to Maternity or if we can finish you off first.'

The nurse who was stitching her arm snipped the suture and stepped back out of the way, and Molly gave her a fleeting smile and took her place beside their patient.

'Oh, dear, you have had a bit of a tumble, haven't you?' Molly said, looking at the cut. 'I'm just going to take a quick look at you, and see how your labour's coming on. Is this your first?'

'No—my third. I feel really odd, though. I didn't feel

like this with either of the others. I don't know if it was the fall, but I feel so breathless and dizzy, and I've got this abdominal pain now that just won't go away—it doesn't feel like a contraction.'

Molly didn't like the sound of that, and clearly neither did Nick.

'That's a change from a few minutes ago. I think we could ask Sam to come down and take a look, and I'll rustle up a consent form,' he said.

While he was doing that, Molly kept a close eye on Ann's blood pressure and respiration rate, as well as the foetal heart rate.

It wasn't a good picture. Her blood pressure was falling, her resps were going up, and the baby's heart was slowing. On top of that her abdomen was rigid. It was looking more and more like a placental abruption, and Molly wanted Sam there fast. 'I think we need to get some fluids into you,' she said, and put a large-bore cannula in her hand in readiness.

She was about to find out what had happened to Sam when he appeared round the curtain, and her heart thumped. 'This is Ann,' she said, and quickly filled him in.

He didn't hesitate. 'Get some plasma expander into her, stat, Molly, please,' he murmured, and then, laying one hand on Ann's rigid abdomen, he took her uninjured hand in the other and explained the situation.

'Ann, I'm sorry, we're going to have to take you up to Theatre and deliver your baby by Caesarian section. Your placenta may be coming away, and we have to move fairly quickly.'

Fairly quickly? Molly all but ran to keep up with him as he strode along the corridor to the lift, the bag of plasma expander held aloft and the consent form lying unsigned as yet on Ann's chest. She went up to Theatre with them, leaving them at the door and going back down to the ward with a heavy heart.

Sam hadn't even glanced at her, except to find out information about their patient. OK, it had been fraught, but it had been fraught before and he'd always found time for a smile. So, was she just imagining it, or had she really upset him?

Unless it was nothing to do with Mick and she'd just put two and two together and made five. Maybe he was just bored with her—he'd got what he wanted, and now he'd lost interest.

No. She didn't want to think that, it was too painful, even though she acknowledged that it was quite likely to be true. After all, a man with the skill and expertise to set up a seduction scene like that wasn't likely to be satisfied for long with a fumbling novice, was he?

Especially if he was still in love with his wife. Maybe her talk of Mick had brought back memories of Crystal, and although her behaviour had been less than perfect, perhaps he still loved her anyway.

Love was a funny thing, there was no accounting for it.

She resolved to talk to Sam the first chance she could find, and then lost herself in her work.

Sam opened Ann up, removed the baby and handed him to Josh Lancaster who was standing by to resuscitate him, then removed the placenta manually. The uterus contracted, the bleeding slowed and then stopped, and he heaved a sigh of relief.

That had been close—too close for comfort, he thought, finally hearing the baby cry.

'How is he?' he asked, and Josh shrugged.

'Not great. He's coming up, though. He's a few weeks early—have we got a gestation?'

'Not that I know of. They might have something in her notes.'

'Hmm.' Josh continued working on the baby while Sam tidied up the mother and closed, and then she went through to Recovery and Sam watched Josh as he worked.

'Were we too slow?'

Again, Josh shrugged. 'Hard to tell. I hope not. He'll need to be in SCBU for a few days, though, I think, at the very least. How's Mum?'

'OK. She'll need transfusing, but she'll be fine. I think it was just the fall. There was a lot of bruising on the abdominal wall over the placental site, but I had a look round and couldn't see any other damage. There didn't seem to be any other bleeding, anyway. Is there any evidence of trauma on the baby?'

'No—just the anoxia. He's responding, I'm pretty confident now that he'll be all right.'

Sam nodded. 'I'll go and tell his mother, and get her admitted to the ward. I'll see you. Thanks, Josh.'

He went down to the ward, but Molly was busy, and he wasn't sure he wanted to see her anyway. It was too difficult at work, and he was beginning to think the whole thing had been a lousy idea. Maybe he'd give them both time to cool off.

It was two days before Molly saw Sam, and she got the feeling he was avoiding her again. This time, though, when she managed to corner him in the canteen, she didn't beat about the bush.

'Sam, what's going on?' she asked quietly but firmly. 'Last weekend you couldn't seem to get enough of me. Now you won't talk to me. I want to know why.'

He shook his head. 'I'm sorry, I owe you an apology. I've been really busy at home. I've been decorating in the evenings, and I've had a lot to do here.'

'That much?' she said sceptically. 'So much that you didn't have time even for a quiet hello?'

He sighed and rammed his hand through his hair. 'It's not that I won't talk to you, Molly. I just haven't had time, and I don't think we should seek each other out at work. It isn't good for our professional relationship.'

She laughed a little bitterly. 'That didn't seem to trouble you on Saturday when you were kissing me in the ward kitchen,' she said in an undertone.

'Saturday was different.'

'You're telling me. And now you've got me out of your system.'

He shook his head. 'Molly, that's not it. I haven't had time for anyone, it isn't personal—'

'Well, it damned well was at the weekend!' she said shortly. 'It's all right, Sam. I'm a big girl, I can take it. I threw myself at you. Only a fool would have turned me down, and you were never that.'

'Molly, stop it,' he said impatiently. 'I really have been busy.'

'So when are you free?'

He hesitated for a moment, then sighed. 'Tonight? Can you get a babysitter?'

'Libby's at her grandparents' until seven. I'll cook you supper, if you can get away.'

'I'll do my best.'

She stood up. 'You do that. And in the meantime, I'd like to make arrangements to see Jack again at the week-ends.'

'Of course. Tell me when, and I'll see what I can do.'

Sam got to his feet, and for the briefest moment their

eyes met. She could have sworn she saw pain in their cobalt depths, but then that blank look was back, and he walked away, leaving her standing, shaking, in the middle of the canteen.

'Molly? Are you OK?'

She looked round blindly, and saw Nick Baker coming towards her, concern etched onto his handsome features.

'I'm fine,' she lied. 'How are you all?'

'Oh—great. How's Ann?'

'Ann?'

'The lady with the antepartum haemorrhage.'

'Oh. She's fine. The baby's OK. Sam got her in the nick of time.' Her voice trembled on his name, and she rammed her hands in her pockets and stepped back. 'Well, if you'll excuse me, I have to go. Patients to see.'

She turned and walked away, resisting the urge to run. She wanted time to herself, to think through her conversation with Sam and work out what she was going to say to him tonight, but she didn't get a chance. The rest of the day was chaotic, and she rushed home, threw together a risotto and bathed in no time flat.

And then the phone rang. It was Sam.

'Molly, I'm sorry, I won't be able to make it. Something's come up at work and I won't get away until much later.'

'So come later.'

'I can't. I'm sorry. I'll see you tomorrow.'

She cradled the phone, stared at it for a moment and then rang Angie.

She didn't beat about the bush. 'Is there a difference,' she asked bluntly, 'between making love and sex?'

There was a moment of startled silence, then Angie said cautiously, 'I don't know. Yes, I think so. Molly, what happened?'

She gave a hollow laugh. 'I don't know. On Saturday night we made love—quite definitely. On Sunday morning—it felt different. Colder. More desperate. I don' know.'

'Desperate? That's an odd word to use.'

Molly sighed. 'I think I hurt him. He asked about Mick, and...'

'And?' Angie prompted.

'I cried. I told him things I've never told a soul, and then I cried.'

'Oh, Molly. Have you talked to him?'

She shook her head, then remembered she was on the phone and Angie couldn't see her. 'No. I can't. He won't talk to me.'

'Oh, men. Couldn't you shoot them? Look, Molly, you have to talk to him—if you want to sort it out, that is. I take it you do.'

'Oh, lord, yes. Angie, I love him. I thought I loved him before the weekend, but now...'

Her control shattered, and the strain of the last few days caught up with her. 'I'm sorry. I have to go,' she said, and hung up, tears pouring down her cheeks. She needed him, and because she'd pushed it, moved their relationship onto a different level, she'd lost him.

Well, she thought she'd lost him. From where she was standing, it certainly felt like it, and the pain was unbearable.

When she'd recovered enough to speak, she phoned her in-laws and asked them if they could keep Libby for the night. 'Something's come up,' she said. 'I have to work late.'

'Sure. We'll take her to school. Is everything OK?'

'Yes,' she lied. 'I'll see you tomorrow. Thank you for your help.'

'Any time. Looking after her's a pleasure. She's all we have of Mick, don't forget that.'

As if she could. Molly hung up, took the risotto out of the oven and went upstairs, holding a cold flannel over her face to soothe her red-rimmed eyes.

Pointless. It would take more than a cold flannel when she kept aggravating them again with another bout of tears.

'You're a fool,' she told her blotchy reflection. 'Go and eat that risotto, see if there's anything on television, and then get an early night.'

She didn't bother to get dressed. What was the point? Sam wasn't coming. She'd stay in her comfy, ratty old dressing-gown and slum it.

Sam felt like a heel.

He'd hurt Molly, he knew that, but he couldn't talk about it. What could he say? 'You're in love with a dead man, and I can't deal with it'? Hardly.

Debbie, of course, didn't beat about the bush. He thought he'd scoured all trace of Molly from the house, but she found the condom packet on the floor in his bedroom and put it back conspicuously on his bedside table.

'Things looking up, then?' she asked, and he grunted. 'I just wondered—what with the condoms appearing over the weekend.'

'Mind your own damn business,' he growled, and she blinked and stared at him.

'Oops. Didn't it go well?'

He laughed without humour. 'Not exactly. Put it like this—I'm not in the market for competing with her dead husband. I've already played second fiddle once. I'm not doing it again, and certainly not to a ghost.'

'Second fiddle? Are you kidding? The way she looks at you?'

'It's just sex, Debbie, believe me,' he said bluntly. Was he hoping to shock her into leaving it alone? If so, he'd reckoned without her Cockney grit.

'You're nuts. Did you blow it or what?'

'No, I didn't blow it,' he said emphatically. 'Debbie, leave it. She's coming over some time to see Jack, and I won't be here. Could I leave him with you to deal with it?'

She eyed him steadily. 'Have you told her how you feel?'

'There's nothing to tell her, Debbie. It's irrelevant. It isn't that sort of relationship.'

He left the room, Debbie's snort of derision ringing in his ears, and plunged himself into a needless reorganisation of his computer files. Anything rather than think about Molly sitting on the kitchen table in his dressing-gown, with her legs showing where the fabric had parted, and the shadow of her breasts visible in the deep, gaping V of the neck...

Or then there was the sitting room, where they'd danced together, or the dining room, scene of the greatest seduction of all time—and he couldn't even go in his bedroom. He avoided it until late at night, and went in there in the dark with the benefit of a few glasses of wine to knock him out.

It didn't work, though. Nothing worked, and he wondered if playing second fiddle would actually, in the long run, be worse than playing nothing at all.

He looked at his watch. Eight-thirty. Libby would be in bed. He could go and talk to Molly, apologise for being such a bastard. After all, it was hardly her fault that she was still in love with Mick!

He grabbed his jacket, tapped on the communicating door and told Debbie that he was nipping out.

'Finally,' she said, and he closed the door with a defiant click and let himself out. He changed his mind about a hundred times on the short drive over there, and when he arrived, he hesitated on the road outside until someone wanted to come out of their drive and he had to move.

'Oh, hell,' he muttered. Turning into her drive, he cut the engine and strode to the door without any further prevarication. He leant on the frame, his finger poised on the bellpush, but before he could press it the door swung open and Molly stood there in a disreputable old dressing-gown with a wary look on her face that made him feel a complete rat.

'You said come later. Am I too late?'

Her smile was faint, and just made him feel worse.

'Of course not. Libby's not here, she's staying with her grandparents. Come in.'

Sam stepped over the threshold, closed the door behind himself and drew her into his arms with a ragged sigh. 'I'm sorry, Molly,' he said gruffly. 'I haven't been very good to you this week.'

'No, I'm sorry. I shouldn't have gone on about Mick.'

'Forget it. I don't want to talk about it.'

He threaded his fingers through her hair, lowered his mouth to hers and kissed her tenderly. 'Forgive me,' he murmured against her lips, and with a little sigh she moved closer into his arms.

'There's nothing to forgive,' she said, and eased away, looking up at him. 'Have you eaten? There's some risotto left.'

He shook his head. He hadn't eaten, but he didn't feel hungry. Not for food, anyway. He kissed her again, and she melted against him for a moment, then drawing away she held out her hand.

'Come on,' she said softly. He placed his hand in hers

and she led him upstairs to her bedroom, closed the door and turned to him. The bedside light was on, casting a soft glow over the room, and she slipped off the dressing-gown and reached up for him, pushing his jacket off his shoulders, stripping off his sweater, unfastening the stud on his jeans and sliding down the zip, her fingers so near to him he could feel the fire.

They closed round him and he groaned and took her mouth, cupping her bottom in his hands and rocking her against him.

So it was just sex for her. So what? Suddenly it didn't feel so bad...

Molly saw Jack at the weekends, but Sam wasn't there.

'He had to go out,' Debbie said the third time it happened, but something about the way she said it made Molly wonder. He was still being a little distant at work, and the only time she got anywhere near him was when they made love.

Or had sex, or whatever he wanted to call it. At that time, he let down his guard, and for a few brief moments she had the real Sam, the Sam she loved from the bottom of her heart.

Still, she put the thought aside and concentrated on Jack, and it was a bitter-sweet experience. He was mangling some play-dough in the corner of the kitchen at his little table, and she was sitting at the big table, watching him. He was a lovely child, just like a miniature of his father to look at, and every bit as stubborn. She wondered—

'Tea?'

She shook her head. 'No, thanks, Debbie. I'm—not drinking tea at the moment,' she said, avoiding the woman's eye, but she may as well not have bothered.

'If you're not drinking tea for the same reason I'm not

drinking tea, then you've got to tell Sam,' she said in a low voice.

Her eyes flew to Debbie's, startled, then she looked away, colour running over her skin. 'How?'

'I don't know. When you've worked it out, you can tell me. I daren't tell Mark, he's under so much pressure at the moment. He's trying to set up this business, and the last thing he needs is me losing this job because of that.'

'Would you? Surely not. You can look after Jack and a baby. Women do that all the time—it's what we do best.'

'My baby, or yours?' Debbie said drily, and got up to put the kettle on. 'Herbal tea?'

Molly laughed wryly. 'Please. And then go and tell Mark.'

'He'll just worry.'

'I'll talk to Sam for you.'

Debbie shook her head. 'No. I'll do it. You talk to him about you, because you look like hell, you know, and so does he.' She sat down again, eyeing Molly thoughtfully. 'Can I ask you something really personal? Are you still in love with your husband?'

'Mick? No, of course not. I mean, I treasure his memory, but—Debbie, I've been in love with Sam for years, ever since we first met and talked about me having a baby for them.'

Debbie nodded. 'I thought he was talking bull. He told me to butt out.'

Molly laughed, then thought about Debbie's words for a moment and froze. 'Hang on. Does he think I'm still in love with Mick?'

Debbie nodded again. 'Yeah. Talked a lot of rubbish about second fiddle.'

'What?' Molly was stunned, but, thinking about it, it all made perfect sense. It had been after she'd told him about

Mick that it had all gone wrong, and she'd sensed it was something to do with him, but that? Never. 'He's crazy.'

'So tell him yourself. Maybe he'll believe you. He'll be back in an hour. What about Libby? Do you need to get back for her?'

Molly shook her head. 'No, she's gone to a sleepover party.'

'Right. We'll take Jack, and you can have the house to yourselves. We'll give you till nine tonight. If you need longer, ring my mobile. The number's in the phone, it's memory two.'

Molly nodded, then swallowed hard. Make or break, she thought, this was it. By the end of the evening she intended to have this sorted out, or she was leaving.

Baby or no baby.

Sam turned into his drive and stopped dead. Molly's car was there, and the lights were on, but there was no sign of Debbie and Mark and he wondered what was wrong.

Jack, he thought, fear clawing at his throat. He'd left his mobile behind by accident—had they been trying to contact him?

He let himself in and strode through to the kitchen, to find Molly sitting there at the table, her hands folded in her lap, her face pale.

'What is it? What's wrong with Jack?'

'Nothing's wrong with Jack.'

'Mark, then.'

'Nothing. There's nothing wrong with anyone—only us. Debbie and Mark have taken Jack out so we can talk.'

Her words registered slowly, and he hooked out a chair and sat down opposite her, relief wiping the strength from his legs. Then the relief faded, replaced by a sickening dread.

She was going to tell him to go to hell. He deserved it, the way he'd treated her for the past three weeks, but he couldn't seem to help himself.

'Can you just do one thing for me?' she asked him, the apparent calm of her voice betrayed by a slight tremor. 'If I ask you a question, will you answer it honestly? And I'll do the same.'

Sam hesitated for so long she thought she'd lost him, then he inclined his head a fraction.

'If I can,' he said.

Well, that was a start, she supposed.

'Do you want to go first?'

Again he hesitated, then he shook his head. 'No. You go first.'

Molly took a deep breath, then plunged in, her heart hammering.

'What do you want most in the world, Sam?'

His head came up, his eyes locking with hers, and this time she knew she hadn't imagined the pain in them.

'You,' he said unevenly, 'but I don't know if I'm strong enough to live in Mick's shadow. He was obviously a hell of a man, and I had no right to ask you about him that night. It made me feel...' He broke off, shaking his head and searching for words. 'As if I'd intruded in something I had no right to. That night belonged to you two, Molly. It should have been yours. I had no right to touch you.'

'Sam, that's nonsense. I wanted you, and you gave me a wonderful night—a night to remember. It was everything I'd wanted, for four long years.'

'Four?'

She nodded. 'Four. Since I met you. There is no shadow from Mick, Sam. He's gone, and I accepted that ages ago. I've loved you for years, ever since our first meeting.

That's why I agreed to have a child for you, because I wanted to carry your child inside me—because I loved you.'

His eyes closed fleetingly, and when he opened them his lashes were clumped with tears. 'Oh, God, Molly. I wanted to share it—to touch you, to hold you, to feel my baby kick against my side at night—but I couldn't. You weren't mine to touch, and I needed you. When he was born, I wanted to take you home with me. I wanted to watch you suckle him, but it just couldn't happen. That's one of my greatest regrets, amongst many, that you never suckled him.'

'I did,' she confessed. 'I know Crystal didn't want me to, but that night he cried, and I went to him in the nursery, and I fed him. It was the last thing I could give him.'

She closed her eyes, hot tears spilling down her cheeks, and then she was in his arms, gathered up against his chest as he carried her through to the study and sat down with her cradled on his lap.

'I love you,' he said unsteadily. 'Oh, God, Molly, I love you.'

His mouth found hers, his kisses tender, cherishing, almost reverent. He kissed away her tears, then rocked her gently against his chest.

'Can I ask you something?'

She nodded. 'If you promise to talk about my answer.'

His smile was crooked and a little strained. 'I'm sorry.'

'Don't be. What was it?'

'What do you want most in the world?'

'Apart from you? For us to be a family.'

His arms tightened convulsively. 'Oh, thank God. And maybe, when we've been married for a while—you will marry me, won't you?' he asked, breaking off to look down at her, sudden uncertainty in his eyes.

She smiled, her hand coming up to cup his rough jaw, reassuring him. 'Of course I'll marry you.'

'And then, after a while, how would you feel about having another child?'

'Wonderful. I'm glad you brought that up.' She laughed softly. 'Because a little under eight months should do it.'

'Eight...?' He lifted his head and stared down at her, puzzlement giving way to pure, unadulterated joy. 'Oh, Molly...' His hand slipped between them, coming to rest over their child. 'Are you sure?'

'I've done it before, I recognise the symptoms. And anyway, there was this little blue line on the test—'

'But you're on the Pill.'

'I had that bug—I didn't even think about it. I'm a bit of a novice like that.'

'Thank goodness.' Sam's hand splayed over the baby, and his eyes settled on the flat plane of her abdomen. 'We're going to have a baby,' he said incredulously. 'A real baby—our baby, yours and mine. Oh, Molly, I can't believe it.'

His arms tightened round her, and his lips found hers and brushed them tenderly. 'It's crazy but I always felt that Jack was your son, that you were his mother, and having you back in our lives somehow seems so right, but to go through the pregnancy and the birth with you, knowing we'll be together afterwards—you can have no idea how I've longed for that.'

'Me, too,' she said, resting her face against his shoulder, drawing comfort from his warmth. 'To have a baby, knowing I won't have to give it away at the end, will just be bliss, and to be back in Jack's life... I've worried so much about Jack—he will be all right with this, won't he?'

Sam nodded. 'Oh, yes. He's said the odd thing about some of the pregnant mums at nursery—like, could we have a mummy and a new baby, too, for instance. Throw a big sister into the equation as well, and he'll be delirious.' He chuckled, then looked down into her eyes again, that gentle concern back. 'How about Libby? Will she be all right about it?'

'She'll be ecstatic. She's always wanted a little brother or sister, and now she'll have two. And a father. She's missed having a father.'

Sam's face clouded. 'I'm not Mick, Molly.'

'I know. I don't want you to be. I want you to be yourself—stubborn, awkward, close-mouthed—'

'That's changing, I promise. I'll talk to you whenever things feel wrong. I've lost one marriage because I had no idea of my wife's feelings. I don't intend to do it again.'

She kissed him. 'Good. We won't have to fight about it.' She kissed him again, and again, and then glanced at her watch. 'We've got two hours before Debbie and Mark get back. Got any ideas?'

His smile was slow and lazy and worth waiting for. 'The kitchen table,' he murmured. And standing up, he carried her down the hall...

EPILOGUE

IT WAS a glorious September day, the first anniversary of their first night together, and they were all gathered in the garden at the cottage for the baby's christening.

Debbie was running round waiting on people in a—for her—demure cerise T-shirt dress that almost matched her hair, and Mark was propped against the apple tree, their six-month-old son Jordan squirming in his arms and threatening to dislodge the ring in his eyebrow.

Their business was flourishing, and between them and Molly, they were caring for all the children on alternate days. A bit of a nightmare in the holidays, but Molly was only going to be working two days a week, and Debbie was around to help on the other three as well, and so far it seemed to be going fine.

Sam ran his eye over the rest of their friends: Angie and Doug, the baby's godparents, with little Laura, Molly's first surrogate baby; Lyn, Molly's friend from her surrogacy support group, with her new partner; Nick and Sally Baker, with one-year-old Joshua; Sue, one of Molly's colleagues, with her husband and child; and, of course, all the grandparents—including the Hammonds and, unbelievably, Crystal's parents, who'd asked humbly if they could share in the celebrations.

The children were having fun—Libby and Jack and the others—giggling and chasing each other round the apple tree, their faces glowing with health and happiness and mischief. Sam smiled indulgently, and looked down at the baby in Molly's arms, a lump in his throat.

They'd called her Bonnie, and she was well named. She was perfect—a miniature Jack, but with something of Libby about her, too, and Molly was the picture of contentment. She was feeding Bonnie now, the baby's pink rosebud mouth fastened on her nipple and suckling hungrily, her fingers tiny and creased against the blue-veined smoothness of Molly's breast.

Her little eyes drooped shut, and her mouth stopped working as she slid into sleep.

'I'll take her,' Sam murmured, and lifted her from Molly's arms to cradle her against his shoulder. Their eyes met, and he smiled, a great tenderness welling inside him. 'All right?'

'Never better. The perfect end to a perfect year.'

He bent and kissed her, just the lightest touch of his lips to hers, a promise—and a thank you for a future he'd never thought he'd have.

A mother for his son, a child of their own, a beautiful stepdaughter—and the woman dearest to his heart to walk by his side every day for the rest of his life.

As she'd said, the perfect end to a perfect year...

The Pregnant Tycoon

CAROLINE ANDERSON

CHAPTER ONE

HAPPY Birthday, Izzy. The big three-O. Terrific.

Izzy felt her smile slipping and yanked it back with effort. Any minute now her face would start to crack. For what felt like hours she'd laughed at the witty in-jokes, picked at the delicate and hideously expensive canapés and now she'd had enough. If she didn't get out of here in the next five minutes, she was going to scream.

Loudly.

It was her thirtieth birthday, and she was at a party. Not her party, though, although it was in a way her celebration. No, this was a party to celebrate the phenomenally successful flotation on the stock market of yet another company she'd rescued from certain death.

Been there, done that, she thought tiredly, but everyone was on a high, and only a real party-pooper wouldn't want to celebrate with their friends.

Friends? She gave a quiet, slightly despairing little laugh. Apart from Kate, she hadn't known any of them for more than a year at the most. Were they really friends? Or were they only there because of who and what she was?

And who was she? She knew *what* she was, and if she ever lost sight of it, the press would lose no time in reminding her with one of the selection of nicknames they thought so amusing.

5

The Stripper, The Assassin—Godzilla was the latest in a long line. And all because she went in where angels feared to tread, and restructured ailing companies, turning them around and pointing them in the right direction. And, of course, because she was a woman, and because she was so young, she'd attracted a lot of attention in doing it.

More, really, than was warranted. Plenty of people did what she did, but not many, she was forced to admit, with such startling results. She'd been lucky—very lucky. Her instincts had only let her down once, and the press had loved it.

But not this time. This time it had been another runaway success, and she knew she'd never need to work again.

She would, of course, simply because if she didn't work, then what would she do with her life? Without work, it was empty.

Barren.

Nonsense, she told herself. You've got a great apartment overlooking the river near Canary Wharf, a fantastic assistant in Kate, you can have anything you want—except privacy.

That was the penalty. She had more appearances in the society rags than the average royal, every date she went on was turned into a full-blown affair—which was a joke, because most men were so terrified of her they'd run screaming before they got to her bedroom door—and she was standing there surrounded by people who didn't even know her.

Heavens, *I* don't know me. Where are my real friends? Do I have any?

'Excuse me,' she murmured with a vague smile, and headed for the ladies' loo. A few minutes alone—

'You OK?'

She glanced at Kate, her right-hand-woman—and the closest thing she had to a real friend—and dredged up a smile. 'Yes, I'm fine.'

'Great party. They're a super bunch—I'll miss them. Still, there's always the next lot.'

She fell into step beside Izzy, going with her into the cloakroom, chatting to her over the top of the cubicles so even that moment of respite was denied her.

She was wondering where on earth she *could* go to be alone when Kate erupted out of the cubicle and joined her at the washbasins. 'So, how's the birthday going? I remember being thirty. Shattering. I went on the internet—that website for contacting old school-friends and so on. Found out what they were all doing. Weird.'

She chattered on, telling some involved story about a couple who'd rediscovered each other through the internet, but Izzy wasn't listening any more. Her attention had been caught by the words 'old schoolfriends', and she was miles away. Light years.

Twelve, to be exact, up in Suffolk in the long, glorious summer between leaving school and going off to uni, camping by the river in a field owned by Will's parents, all of them laughing and telling jokes and chasing each other around in the long, sweet grass, full of the joys and without a care in the world.

Where were they all now?

Rob and Emma and Julia and Sam and Lucy—and Will. Her heart lurched. Where was Will?

He'd kissed her there, down by the river in the shelter of the willows. That had been their first kiss—the first of many that blissful summer, and a prelude to more than kisses. Much, much more than kisses, she remembered with a pang of longing.

And then she'd gone to university, driven by the need to get on with her life, and he'd gone away with Julia and Rob and Emma, travelling around the world, and come back at the end of the year with news that had shattered her dreams. Her friend Julia, with whom she'd shared everything—including, apparently, Will— was pregnant with his child, and he loved her and wanted to marry her.

Her world had fallen apart that day. She'd spent the next few years reconstructing it brick by brick, until the wall she was hiding behind was so high nothing and no one could get over it. She hadn't seen him since.

Where was he now? What was he doing? Was he still with Julia? And the child—a girl or a boy? Had there been others? Little dark-haired boys and girls with his quick wit and sparkling eyes, and a smile that left her breathless...

A familiar ache of longing settled in her chest, and she dragged in a deep breath and forced her eyes to focus.

Her reflection stared back at her solemnly and did nothing to improve her humour. Mouse-brown hair, curly on a good day and like wire wool in the rain, relieved by a few delicate highlights to give it a bit of lift and stop it looking like an old pan scourer, topped a face set with dull grey-green eyes splodged with brown. A kind person would call them hazel. Her mother called them muddy. Small, even features did nothing to draw attention to her, but at least she supposed she wasn't actively ugly, and her smile, when she could be bothered to produce it, was OK.

She practised it fleetingly, and scowled. OK? Just barely.

'All done?'

Her eyes swung across to meet Kate's in the mirror and she summoned that elusive and barely OK smile. 'Yes, I'm all done. Let's go back to the party.'

Steve was waiting for her—suave, sophisticated, and relentless—and for some reason totally unable to light her fire.

Not that he was alone. Nothing and no one seemed to light her fire these days, either personally or professionally. She'd lost interest in everything, and she was filled with a strange restlessness that made her snappy and short-tempered.

'I thought you'd deserted me, Isabella,' he said with a smile that made her skin crawl.

She gave a brief, humourless laugh. 'No such luck,' she said, and he gave her a rather peculiar look, as if he couldn't quite work out if it was an insult or not. Her head was starting to ache, and she knew it would be at least another two hours before she could get out of there.

'Are you OK, Bella?' he asked her, apparently genuine concern showing now on his smooth, rather characterless face. He was probably just looking for an excuse to take her home, she reasoned, but repelling his advances yet again was absolutely the last thing she needed. Knowing her luck there'd be a photographer lurking, anyway, and she didn't believe in the old maxim that there was no such thing as bad publicity.

There was, and she'd had enough of it to last her a lifetime. A single glimpse of her on the arm of the very recently divorced CEO would be enough to put another notch on the imaginary bedpost that the gutter press had dreamed up out of thin air, and there was no way she was adding any more fuel to that particular fire.

'Just a bit of a headache,' she said, digging out *that smile* again. 'I'll be fine—and don't call me Bella. You know it's not my name.'

He laughed, quite unmoved by her reprimand. He seemed unmoved by most things, she thought, and not for the first time she wondered what made him tick. Money, probably—lots of it, and preferably somebody else's. Still, he wouldn't need to worry about that now, not since her makeover of his company. She'd made him rich beyond his wildest dreams, and women would be all over him like flies on a muck heap.

He trailed a finger up her bare arm, pausing thoughtfully at her shoulder before slipping his fingertip under her strap and toying with it absently. 'We ought to get together, you know, Isabel,' he murmured, getting her name right for once. 'How about Friday evening? We could do dinner—somewhere quiet.'

'Quiet sounds good,' Izzy muttered under her breath, not really referring to his suggestion, but he pounced on it like a terrier with a rat, and she couldn't be bothered to argue. Before she could draw breath he'd arranged the venue, the time and told her what to wear. If she hadn't had such a headache coming on, she would have told him what he could do with his quiet night. As it was she just stifled a sigh and nodded.

She persevered until midnight, then, excusing herself, she took a taxi home and let herself into her cool, tranquil apartment with a sigh of relief. *This* was quiet. This was what she needed.

She heeled off her shoes, padded over to the kitchen and filled a glass with iced water from the cooler in the fridge door, then dropped gratefully into the corner of the comfortable sofa, her feet tucked up underneath her on the butter-soft leather as she stared blindly out over the city skyline.

Lights twinkled, millions of them. All those people out there busily getting on with their lives, she thought, the clubs and bars in this thriving corner of the capital throbbing with life. It was still early by their standards, merely the beginning of the night. Even the thought exhausted her.

She rubbed her temples, pulling out the pins that held her unwilling hair in place. It sprang free, a wild tangle of curls tumbling down over her shoulders, and instantly her headache eased. She sighed and dropped her head back against the soft cushion of the sofa and closed her eyes.

She wanted to open the window, to slide back the big glass pane and step out onto the roof garden, but all she would hear would be the honking traffic and the sirens, the sounds of the city by night.

It would be quiet in the country, she thought, the only sounds the rustlings and cries of the animals. Perhaps quiet wasn't the word. She thought again of their campsite by the river all those years ago, the astonishing sounds of the countryside at night, and she had a fierce longing to return, to hear the sounds again.

Kate's words came back to her, piquing her curiosity, and she got up and went over to her computer.

With a few keystrokes she connected to the internet, and within minutes she'd registered with the website Kate had talked about and was scanning a list of once-familiar names.

Rob's name sprang out, and she clicked on the envelope beside it to read his message. It was so much like him that she could almost hear his voice. He was a solicitor now, married to Emma, they had three children, and they still lived in the village.

How incredible, after all this time, that they were still there in the same place. She felt a little stab of something that could have been envy, but crushed it ruthlessly. What was she thinking about? She had a fantastic life—success, wealth beyond her wildest expectations, a full and hectic schedule.

What more could she possibly want?

Will.

She ignored the curiously painful thought, dismissing it before it took hold. She'd e-mail Rob, and ask him how everyone was. Without stopping to think too much, she wrote a quick e-mail and then as an afterthought included her telephone number.

Maybe he'd ring and they could have a chat.

'Michael, I'm not telling you again, do your homework or that GameBoy's going in the bin. Rebecca? Beccy, where are you? Your stuff's scattered about all over the place.'

She wandered in, her mouth formed in a sulky pout around her thumb, and with ill grace she shovelled her books back into her school bag and flounced off again.

Will sighed and rammed a hand through his hair. He had the accounts to do, another endless round of forms to fill in for yet another set of regulations—and when he'd finished that, he'd have the ewes to check—again. Still, at least it was warm now. Lambing in April, even if it was by accident, knocked spots off lambing in February.

The phone rang, freeing him from the paperwork he hated, and he scooped up the receiver almost gratefully.

'Hello, Valley Farm.'

'Will—it's Rob. Just making sure that you haven't forgotten the party.'

His heart sank, the gratitude evaporating. 'No, I haven't forgotten,' he lied. 'When is it?'

'Friday—seven-thirty onwards, at the house. You are coming, aren't you? Emma will give me such hell if you don't.'

And him too, no doubt. 'I'll try,' he promised evasively. 'I might be able to get away for an hour or so, but I'm still lambing, so don't rely on me.' He didn't need anyone else relying on him. He felt as if the weight of the world was on his shoulders as it was, and the party was just one more thing he had to do out of duty.

'Stuff the lambs.'

'With garlic and rosemary?'

'Smartass. Just be there,' Rob said firmly, and the dial tone sounded in his ear.

He dropped the receiver back into the cradle and

scowled at it. If it was anybody else, any way on God's earth he could get out of it, he'd do exactly that. He couldn't, though. It was Rob and Emma, their tenth wedding anniversary and thirtieth birthday joint celebration, and he had no choice.

That didn't mean, however, that he had to enjoy it or stay longer than was strictly necessary!

Two hours, tops, he promised himself. And duty done, honour satisfied, he'd be able to come home and—

And what? Sit here in the empty house on his own and stare morosely at the four walls? Go alone to his big, empty bed and lie staring at the ceiling, equally morosely, until sleep claimed him?

He snorted. He could always tackle some of the endless paperwork that dogged his life and drove him to distraction. God knows, there was enough of it.

Shooting back his chair, he went through to the kitchen, noting almost absently that Michael was now doing his homework, albeit in front of the television, and Rebecca was curled in the big chair with the dog squeezed up beside her and a cat on her lap, her eyes wilting.

'I'm just going outside to check the sheep,' he told them, hooking his elderly jacket off the back of the door and stuffing his feet into his muddy Wellington boots. 'Beccy, bed in twenty minutes. Michael, you've got one hour.'

He went out into the cold, quiet night and made his way across to the barns. There were warm sleepy noises coming from the animals, soft bleats and shufflings in the straw, and he could hear the horses moving on the other side of the partition that divided the barn.

He did a quick check of the lambs, made sure none of the ewes was in trouble, then, satisfied that all was quiet, he cast an eye over the other stock: the chickens and ducks all shut up for the night, the house cow and the few beef calves out in the pasture behind the house. Then he checked the horses that were not his but were there on a DIY livery. He always included them in his late-night check, just to be sure they had water and none of them had rolled and got themselves cast, stuck firmly up against the side wall and unable to stand up again.

All was well, though, and with his arms folded on the top of the gate he paused for a moment, drinking in the quiet night.

A fox called, and in the distance he could hear a dog barking. Owls hooted to each other, and the pale, ghostly shape of a barn owl drifted past on the night air, on the lookout for an unwary mouse.

Vaulting over the gate, he left the stockyard and walked round to the old farmyard on the other side of the house, looking round at all the changes that had been made in the last few years.

The old timber cowshed and feed store had been turned into a thriving farm shop and café, selling a range of wonderful mainly organic foods, many of them cooked by his mother. She ran that side of the enterprise, while his father supervised the timber side of the business, the garden furniture and wooden toys and willow fencing which were now manufactured on-site in the old milking parlour.

Diversify, they'd been told, and so they had. Instead of boggy, indifferent grazing down by the river, only usable in the height of the summer, they now grew coppiced willow, cutting it down to the ground every winter and harvesting the supple young shoots while they were dormant. They were used to make environmentally friendly and renewable screens and hurdle-style fencing panels, now hugely popular, and all sorts of other things, many to special order.

He still grew crops on the majority of the farm, of course, but it was going organic, a long process full of bureaucracy and hoops of red tape that he had to jump through in order to satisfy the stringent requirements of the food industry, and then there were the sheep. In a few weeks, when the lambs were a bit tougher, he'd move them down to the saltmarsh pasture on the old Jenks' farm, because organic saltmarsh lamb fetched a huge premium in the specialist restaurant market.

Buying up the farm from Mrs Jenks had been a major investment at a time when they couldn't really afford it, but it had been a one-off opportunity and there had been no choice. It had spread their resources even further, however, and made more work, and it would be years before they got a return.

Small wonder, he thought, that he was tired all the time. Still, the farm was thriving again, their futures were secure, and that was all he asked.

With one last glance round to make sure that nothing had been overlooked, he went back inside. There was a little scurry and he saw the tail-end of his daughter disappearing through the doorway. He suppressed a smile and laid a friendly hand on Michael's shoulder.

'How're you doing, sport?'

'OK, I suppose. Just got my French to do now.'

Will chuckled ruefully. 'Not my strong point, I'm afraid. You'll have to ask your grandmother if you get stuck.'

He put the kettle on, and went upstairs to check on Rebecca. She was already in bed, with very little sign of having washed her face or cleaned her teeth, and he chivvied her through the bathroom and then tucked her up in bed.

'Read me a story,' she pleaded, and although he was exhausted, he picked up the book from beside her bed, settled down next to her with his back propped against the headboard and his arm around her shoulders, and started to read.

'Dad?'

Will sucked in a deep breath and forced his eyes open. 'Michael? What time is it?'

'Nearly ten. You've been here for ages.'

Will glanced down at Rebecca, snuggled against his chest fast asleep, and gently eased his arm out from behind her and settled her down onto the pillow. 'Sorry,' he murmured, getting to his feet. 'I just sat down to read her a story—I must have dropped off.'

'You look knackered,' his son said, eyeing him worriedly. 'You work too hard these days.'

Will ruffled his hair affectionately and gave him a brief hug. 'I'll live,' he said, and wondered if it was only to his own ears that it sounded like a vow.

'Good grief. Emma?' Rob pushed his chair back from the computer and turned towards the study door as his wife came in.

She propped herself against the doorframe, arms folded across her chest, and tipped her head on one side. 'What is it?' she asked him. 'You look as if you've seen a ghost.'

He gave a shaky chuckle. 'Well—in a way. It's Isabel Brooke. She's sent me an e-mail. She wants to get in touch. I've got her phone number—shall we ring her?'

Emma shrugged away from the doorframe and came and stood beside him, her hand on his shoulder, peering at the screen. 'Well. Wow—the famous Isabel Brooke! You could always ask her to the party.'

Rob gave a startled cough of laughter. 'You have to be joking! Why on earth would she want to come up here to our boring, pedestrian, provincial party?'

Emma slapped him lightly on the shoulder. 'Hey! This is *our* party. It's going to be the best party this county has seen in a long while. Boring and provincial, my foot. Anyway, she might like it.'

Rob chuckled again. 'I stand by to be amazed. So, shall I ask her?'

Emma shrugged slightly. 'Why not? She'll either say yes or no.'

'Sometimes, my darling, you are so profound.' Rob stood and wrapped his arms around his wife. 'It's too late tonight. I'll ring her tomorrow. Just now, I have better things to do…'

'Isabel? There's a call for you—somebody called Rob. I told him you were in a meeting, but he said it couldn't wait.'

Kate was hovering, her head stuck round the meeting room door, waiting for her answer. Izzy frowned and rubbed the little crease between her brows with a small, blunt fingertip. 'Kate, I really don't have time for—' She hesitated, a thought occurring to her. 'Did he give a surname?'

Kate shook her head. 'He just said you go way back.'

Izzy smiled apologetically at the people gathered around the table. 'Would you excuse me?' she murmured. 'I won't be a moment. Kate, could you be a love and see if anyone needs more coffee?'

She went out into her office and picked up the phone. 'Isabel Brooke,' she said, curiosity vying with wariness.

'I was beginning to think you weren't serious about getting back in touch with us—or were you just making me cool my heels so I know my place?' the familiar voice said laughingly, and Izzy felt her mouth kick up in a smile.

'And hello yourself,' she said, settling down in her chair with her feet propped on the edge of her desk, crossed at the ankles. A smile played at the corners of her mouth. She picked a little bit of fluff off her trousers and smoothed the fabric absently. 'I'm sorry, I really was in a meeting, and I'd said no calls. I didn't realise I'd given you my office number.'

'You didn't, but I didn't want to leave it too late, so I got my secretary to do a bit of sleuthing. How are you?'

'I'm fine. Great. How are you? And Emma? Three kids now! I'm impressed.'

He laughed. 'Don't be. They were the easy bit. We're all fine—really good, but nothing like as spectacular as you! Talk about a meteoric rise in the world.'

Izzy shrugged, then realised he couldn't see her. 'It's only money,' she said dismissively, realising that it was true. What was her success when measured against Rob and Emma's happiness and the birth of their three children? She swallowed a lump of what had to be self-pity, and put her feet back on the floor.

'Look, Rob, I really am rather tied up this morning, but I'd love to see you all. Is there any way we can meet up?'

'Actually, that's why I'm phoning you. Emma and I are having a party to celebrate our tenth wedding anniversary and our thirtieth birthdays, and we want you to come. The trouble is, it's tomorrow night. Not very much notice, I'm afraid, and I expect you're so busy you won't be able to make it, but loads of us will be there and it would be really great to see you.'

Something big and awkward was swelling in her chest, making it hard for her to breathe, and there was a silly smile plastered to her face that she couldn't seem to shift.

'That would be fantastic. Of course I'll come—I wouldn't miss it for the world. I'll hand you back to my secretary and you can give her all the details, and I'll see you on Friday. Thanks, Rob.'

She spoke briefly to Kate and asked her to get all the relevant information from Rob and book her a hotel room nearby, and then, ruthlessly suppressing a twinge

of guilt, she also asked her to contact Steve and cancel
the dinner engagement he'd talked her into at her party.
Then, forcing herself to concentrate, she went back into
the meeting and smiled brightly at the assembled company.

'Sorry about that, everybody. Now, where were we?'

Izzy was a mass of nerves. It was quite ridiculous. She
did very much more scary things than this every day
of her life, and yet, for some reason, this whole event
had taken on the most enormous significance.

Because of Will? What if he was there? And Julia?
Oh, Lord.

She checked the address and eyed the house warily,
reluctant to go in there yet. Twelve years was a long
time, and a lot had happened. Too much? They always
said you should never go back, but maybe it was time.
Maybe this was just what she needed to get closure.

She checked her appearance one last time in the little
rearview mirror of her car, and then with a mental
shrug she abandoned any further prevarication, got out
of the car and strode purposefully towards the open
front door, the flowers she'd brought clutched just a
little tightly in her hand.

As she drew nearer she could hear the sounds of a
party in full swing—loud voices, shouts of laughter,
the insistent rhythm of music that invaded her blood.
It would be pointless to ring the doorbell, she realised,
and so, her heart pounding in time to the beat, she
walked down the hall and through the open door at the
end, a smile plastered to her face.

For a moment no one noticed her, then a sudden

silence fell, and everyone seemed to turn towards her. Her smile was slipping, brittle, and she stared at the room full of strangers and wondered what on earth she was doing there.

Then a man detached himself from the crowd, shorter than she remembered, his body more solid, his hair thinner, but the sparkling green eyes and the smile that encompassed the world were just the same, and he strode towards her, arms outstretched.

'Izzy!'

'Rob,' she said with relief, and went into his arms with a sense of homecoming that took her by surprise.

He released her, holding her at arm's length and studying her, then dragging her back into his arms for another bear hug. 'Emma!' he called. 'Look who it is!'

Emma hadn't changed at all. She was still the friendly, lovely girl she'd always been, and she hugged Izzy, took the flowers with an exclamation of delight and dragged her off to meet all the others.

Well, most of them. There was no sign of Will, and Izzy suppressed the strange sense of disappointment that prickled at her. She'd had no reason to suppose he would be there, so it was ludicrous to feel so bereft at his absence.

Anyway, if he'd been there, Julia would have been, as well, and she wasn't sure that she was ready to meet her again, even all those years later.

And then there was another sudden silence, and her eyes were drawn to the doorway.

A man filled it, his dark hair untidy and rumpled as if he'd just combed it with his fingers, although they were now rammed firmly in his pockets. He looked awkward and uncomfortable, ready for flight, but before he had the chance to make his escape the spell broke and the crowd surged round him, wrapping him in a welcome as warm as it was inescapable.

And then he looked up across the crowded room and met her eyes, and her heart jammed in her throat.

Dear God, after all these years. He hasn't changed, she thought, then shook her head slowly. No, he has changed, but he's still—Will. My Will.

No.

Yes!

Stop it. Never mind that. Look at him. Look at the changes. He's bigger—taller, heavier, older. His eyes look tired. Beautiful, still staggeringly beautiful, but tired.

Why so tired?

She wanted to cry, to laugh, to hug him—and because she could do none of them, she retreated, through a door she found conveniently placed behind her, and fled into the sanctuary of another hallway.

She needed time—time to think. Time to get her ducks in a row and her heart back under control before she said or did something stupid.

Oh, Lord. Will…

CHAPTER TWO

WILL was stunned. He wouldn't have imagined in a million years that Izzy would be here. Of all the places, all the ways he'd imagined meeting her again, this hadn't even been on the list. Somebody was pressing a drink into his hand, somebody else was slapping him on the back, saying how good it was to see him again, but all he could think about was Izzy.

His Izzy.

No. Not now. Not any more. Not for years—not since he'd betrayed her trust—

Hell, why hadn't Rob warned him? Would he still have come?

Fool. Of course he would have come. Wild horses wouldn't have kept him away. He needed to speak to her, but first he had to greet all these people who were so pleased to see him—good people who'd supported them through the nightmare of the last few years. So he smiled and laughed and made what he hoped were sensible remarks, and when he looked up again, she was gone.

Inexplicably, panic filled him. 'Excuse me,' he muttered, and, squeezing his way through the crowd, he went through the doorway at the back of the room that led out to the side hall. It had been the door nearest to her, and the most likely one for her to have used to make her escape, but he couldn't let her go until he'd spoken to her. He was suddenly afraid that she would have slipped out and gone away, that he wouldn't have a chance to speak to her, and he had to speak to her.

There was so much to say—

She hadn't gone anywhere. She was standing in the side hall looking lost, absently shredding a leaf on the plant beside her, her fabled composure scattered to the four winds. The powerful, dynamic woman of the glossy society magazines was nowhere to be seen, and in her face was an extraordinary and humbling vulnerability. His panic evaporated.

'Hello, Izzy,' he said softly. 'Long time no see.'

Her smile wavered and then firmed with a visible effort. 'Hello, Will,' she replied, and her voice was just as warm and mellow and gentle as he'd remembered. 'How are you?'

'Oh, you know,' he said with a wry smile. 'Still farming.' He ran his eyes over her elegant and sophisticated evening trousers and pretty little spangled top, and his gut tightened. 'You're looking as beautiful as ever—not the least bit like an assassin.'

'Still the old sweet talker, then,' she murmured, her lips kicking up in a smile that nearly took his legs out from under him. 'Anyway, I'm surprised you remember. It's been a long time—twelve years.'

'Eleven since I saw you last—but I've got the newspapers and the glossies to remind me, lest I should forget,' he told her, trying to keep his voice light and his hands to himself.

She rolled her eyes expressively, and a chuckle managed to find its way out of the constricted remains of his throat.

'So—how's Julia?' she asked, and he felt his smile fade. Oh, hell. There was no easy way to do this.

'She's dead, Izzy,' he said gently. 'She's been dead a little over two years. She had cancer.'

Even though his words were softly spoken, he felt their impact on her like a physical blow. Her eyes widened, her mouth opening in a little cry as her hand flew up to cover it. 'Will, no—I'm so sorry. I had no idea. Oh, Will—'

If he'd had any sense he would have kept his distance, but he couldn't. She looked so forlorn, so grief-stricken. He took one step towards her, and she covered the ground between them so fast he barely had time to open his arms. She hit his chest with a thud, her arms wrapping tightly round him in a gesture of comfort that was so typically Izzy it took his breath away.

Dear God, he thought wildly. She felt the same—she even smelt the same. It was almost as if the last twelve years had never happened—his marriage to Julia, the two children, her slow, lingering death, the long fight back to normality—all that swept away with just one touch.

Her body trembled in his arms, and he tightened them reflexively around her. 'Shh—it's all right,' he murmured softly, and gradually her trembling body steadied and she eased away from him. Reluctantly, yet knowing it was common sense, he let her go and stepped back.

Her hand came up and caught a tendril of hair, tucking it back behind her ear, and her smile was sad. 'I'm sorry. I really had no idea, Will. It must have been dreadful for you all. Why didn't Rob tell me? I can't believe it—I'm so sorry I brought it up like that, spoiling the party.'

He laughed, a rough, scratchy sound even to his ears, and met her anguished eyes with a smile. 'You haven't spoilt the party. I hate parties anyway, and besides, mentioning Julia doesn't change anything. We talk about her all the time. Her death is just a fact of life.'

He wanted to talk to her, to share the huge number of things that had happened for both of them in that time, but people were coming through the hall, heading for the cloakroom or the kitchen, and they all paused for a chat.

He felt the evening ebbing away, and panic rose again in his chest. He couldn't let her go again without talking to her, properly, without constant interruptions. There was so much to say—too much, and most of it best left unsaid, but still—

'Look, it would be really nice to catch up with you—I don't suppose you've got any time tomorrow, have you?' he suggested, wondering as he said the words whether he himself could find any time in the middle of what was bound to be a ridiculously hectic schedule.

'I'm staying at the White Hart for the night,' she said. 'I was going to head back some time tomorrow, but I don't have any definite plans. What did you have in mind?'

He crossed his fingers behind his back and hoped his father could help out with the children. 'Come for lunch,' he suggested. 'You'll know how to find the farmhouse—it hasn't moved.'

His smile was wry, and she answered with a soft laugh. 'That would be lovely. I'll look forward to it.'

They fell silent, the sounds of the party scarcely able to intrude on the tension between them, but then the door opened behind him yet again and Rob came out, punching him lightly on the arm.

'Here you both are! Come and circulate—you can't hog each other, it's not on. Everyone wants to talk to you both.'

And without ceremony he dragged them back into the party and forced them to mingle. They were separated from each other within moments, and when Will's phone rang to call him back to a difficult lambing, she was nowhere to be found. Still, he'd see her in the morning.

He shrugged his coat on, said goodbye to Rob and Emma and went back to the farm. It was only later, as he crawled into bed at three o'clock with the lambs safely delivered, that he realised they hadn't discussed a time.

Izzy pulled up outside the farmhouse and stared around her in astonishment.

Well, it was certainly different! The house looked pretty much the same, and the barns behind it, but beyond the mellow old brick wall dividing the house from the other side of the farmyard there had been some huge changes.

The weatherboarding on the old farm buildings was all new and freshly stained black, sharp against the soft red of the tiled roofs, and on the front of one was a sign saying, 'The Old Crock's Café'. There was a low fence around an area of tables and chairs, and though it was still only April, there were people sitting outside enjoying the glorious sunshine.

There were other changes, too, beyond the café. The farm shop beside it seemed to be doing a brisk trade, and on the other side of what was now a car park the big building that she was sure had once been the milking parlour now housed an enterprise called Valley Timber Products. She could see chunky wooden playground toys and what looked like garden furniture in a small lawned area beside it.

There was a basket shop, as well, selling all sorts of things like willow wreaths and planters and wigwams for runner beans, as well as the more traditional baskets, and she could see that, at a quarter to eleven on a Saturday morning, the whole place was buzzing.

A thriving cottage industry, she thought, and wondered who ran all the various bits and pieces of this little complex and how much of it was down to Will. He probably let all the units to enterprising individuals, she reasoned. There wouldn't be enough hours in the day to do anything else.

She turned back to the house, conscious of the fact that it was still not eleven o'clock and she was probably rather early for lunch, but she'd been asked to vacate her room by ten, and after driving somewhat aimlessly around for half an hour, she'd decided to get it over with and come straight here.

Get it over with, she thought. *Like going to the dentist.* How strange, to be so nervous with Will, of all people, but her heart was pounding and her palms were damp and she hadn't been so edgy since she'd held her first board meeting.

At least then she'd had an agenda. Now she was meeting the widowed husband of her old schoolfriend, father of the child whose conception had been the kiss of death for their relationship.

Bizarre.

'If you're looking for Will, he's in with the lambs,' a woman called, pointing round the back of the house, and with a smile of thanks, she headed round towards the barns.

'Will?' she called. 'Are you there?'

A dog came running up, a black and white collie, grinning from ear to ear and wagging at her hopefully, then it ran back again, hopping over a gate and heading into a barn.

She eyed the mud thoughtfully, glanced down at her Gucci boots with regret and picked her way over to the gate.

'Will?'

'In here,' a disembodied voice yelled, and she wrestled with the gate—why did farm gates never swing true on their hinges?—and went through into the barn. It took her eyes a moment to adjust, and when they had, she spotted him crouched down on the far side of the little barn with a sheep. It was bleating pitifully, and as she picked her way across the straw bedding, Will grunted and glanced up, then rolled his eyes and gave a wry smile.

'Hi,' he said softly. 'Sorry, didn't realise it was you. Welcome to the mad house. You're early.'

'I know. I'm sorry—do you want me to go away?'

He shook his head. 'No. Can you give me a minute? I'm a little tied up.'

She suddenly realised what he was doing, and for a moment considered escaping back to the café to give him time to finish, but then the ewe tried to struggle to her feet, and with his other hand—the one that wasn't buried up to the elbow in her back end—he grabbed her and wrestled her back down to the straw.

'Anything I can do to help?' she found herself asking, and he gave her a slightly incredulous look and ran his eyes over her assessingly.

'If you really mean that, you could kneel on her neck,' he said, and she could tell he expected her to turn tail.

She did, too, but then, to her own amazement as much as his, she gave a little shrug, dropped her Louis Vuitton bag into the soiled straw and knelt down in her Versace jeans and Gucci boots and put her knee gently on the ewe's neck.

'By the way, good morning,' she said, and smiled.

Will was stunned.

If the paparazzi who hounded her for the glossy society mags could see her now, he thought with an inward chuckle, they'd never believe it.

'Morning,' he said, and then grunted with pain as the ewe contracted down on his hand and crushed a sharp little hoof into his fingers. Well, at least he knew where one leg was, he thought philosophically, and the moment the contraction eased, he grabbed the offending hoof, traced it up to the shoulder, found the other leg, tugged them both straight and then persuaded the little nose to follow suit.

Moments later, with another heave from Mum and a

firm, solid tug from Will, twin number one was born, followed moments later by the second.

And the third.

'Triplets?' she said, her voice soft and awed, and he shot her a grin and sat back on his heels, using a handful of straw to scrub at the soggy little morsels with their tight yellow perms and wriggling tails.

'Apparently so.' They struggled to their feet, knees wobbling, and made their way to their mother, on her feet by now, and Will got up and looked ruefully at his hands.

'I'd help you up, but—'

She grinned up at him, her soft green eyes alight with joy, and his heart lurched, taking him by surprise. She stood easily, brushing down her knees with a careless hand. 'That was wonderful,' she said, the joy showing in her voice as well as her eyes, and he wanted to hug her.

Instead he took a step back, gathered up his bucket of hot water and soap and towel, and quickly made a pen around the little family.

'We'll leave them to it. They've got all they need for now.'

'Why isn't that one feeding?' Izzy asked, staring worriedly at the lambs as one of them stood by bleating forlornly and butting its mother without success.

'They've only got two teats, but she's had triplets before. They'll take turns and she'll sort them out. She's a good mother. Come, Banjo.'

He ushered her towards the back door, the dog at his heels, and, kicking the door shut behind them, he stripped off his padded shirt and scrubbed his arms in the sink.

'Don't mind me,' she said dryly, and he looked up, suddenly self-conscious, to find her laughing softly at him across the kitchen.

He felt his mouth quirk into a grin, and he shook his head. 'Sorry. Didn't think. Actually, I could do with a shower. Can you give me five minutes?'

'Of course.'

'Make yourself at home,' he told her, and then, as he ran up the stairs, he remembered the photos of Julia and the children all over the piano in the corner.

He shrugged. What could he do? She'd been his wife, the mother of his children. She deserved to be remembered, and he couldn't protect Izzy from that reality any more than he could have prevented Julia's death.

She looked around the kitchen, so much as it had been all those years ago, and felt as if she was caught in a time warp.

Any minute now Rob and Emma and Julia, and maybe Sam or Lucy, would come through that door from the farmyard, laughing and chattering like magpies, and Mrs Thompson would put the kettle on the hob and pull a tray of buns out of the oven.

She'd always been baking, the kitchen heady with the scent of golden Madeira cake and fragrant apple pies and soft, floury rolls still hot in the middle. She'd fed everybody who came over her threshold, Izzy remembered, and nobody was ever made to feel unwelcome.

And at Christmas they'd always come here carol-singing last, and gather round the piano to sing carols and eat mince pies hot from the oven.

With a tender, reminiscent smile still on her lips, Izzy turned towards the piano—and stopped dead, her heart crashing against her ribs. Slowly, as if she had no right to be there but couldn't help herself, she crossed the room on reluctant feet and stood there, rooted to the spot, studying the pictures.

Julia and Will, laughing together on the swing under the apple tree. Julia with a baby in her arms and a toddler leaning against her knee. Will on the swing again, with the toddler on his lap, laughing, and another one with the baby, nose to nose, his expression so tender it brought tears to her eyes.

What am I doing here? I don't belong! This is her house—her husband.

She turned, stumbling blindly towards the door, and Will caught her and folded her into his arms, cradling her against his chest as the sobs fought free and racked her body.

'Shh. I'm sorry. I should have realised it would upset you. I'd forgotten how much you loved her.'

Loved you, Izzy corrected silently, but she couldn't speak, and anyway, it didn't seem like the smartest thing to say under the circumstances.

Her sobs faded as quickly as they'd come, the shock of her reaction receding in the security of his arms, and gently he released her and stood back, looking down at her with worried eyes.

'OK now?'

She nodded, scrubbing her nose with the back of her

hands, and he passed her a handful of kitchen roll and waited while she blew her nose and mopped her eyes and dragged out that smile.

'Sorry,' she mumbled. 'Too many memories.'

He nodded and turned away, his face tight, and she could have kicked herself. If she had too many memories, what on earth did he have?

'Tea?'

'Please.'

He put the kettle on, then turned and propped himself against the front rail of the Aga and studied her thoughtfully. Uncomfortable with his scrutiny, she studied him back and fired off the first salvo.

'You've changed,' she said, her voice almost accusing.

He snorted softly. 'I should hope so. I was a puny kid of nineteen the last time you saw me. I've grown two, maybe three inches and put on a couple of stone. I work hard—physical stuff. That builds muscle.'

It did, and she'd seen the evidence for herself just a few moments ago when he'd stripped off at the sink. Putting the disturbing memory away, she shook her head, studying the lines on his face, the lingering trace of sadness in his eyes. 'I didn't mean that,' she said, and then gave a short, hollow laugh. 'I'm sorry, I'm being a real idiot here. Of course you've changed, after all you've been through. Who wouldn't?'

His smile was wry. 'Who indeed? Still—it's all over now, and we're moving on.' He cocked his head on one side and his smile softened. 'You don't look any different,' he said, his voice a trifle gruff, and she rolled her eyes.

'All that money, all that sophistication, and I don't look any different?' She'd meant to sound a light note, but instead she sounded like a petulant little toddler. How silly, to feel hurt. After all, she probably hadn't changed that much. Nothing had touched her as it had touched him.

Not since he'd gone away.

But Will was looking embarrassed, and she wanted to kick herself again. He scrubbed a hand through his hair and gave an impatient sigh. 'I meant—oh, hell, I don't know what I meant, except it wasn't an insult— or not intended to be. I'm sorry if it came over like that.'

His eyes were full of remorse, and she shook her head and reached out, laying a gentle hand on his arm. 'Of course it didn't. I just feel different, and I suppose I thought it might be reflected in my face, but a sensible woman would be flattered. Anyway, I wouldn't want my money to have changed me, and I certainly don't want to look like Godzilla, so perhaps I should just be grateful!'

His mouth lifted in a wry smile, and his eyes swept her face, their expression tender. 'I suppose you have changed, a little, but you're still you, every bit as beautiful as you ever were, and it's really good to see you again. That's what I was trying to say in my clumsy, inept way.'

She laughed, her turn now to be embarrassed, and shook her head. 'I'm not beautiful—'

'I'm not going to argue with you,' he said, but his thumb came up and brushed away the last remnant of her tears, and the tender gesture nearly brought her to her knees. Then he dropped his hand and stepped away, ramming it into his pocket, turning away.

When he spoke, his voice was gruff. 'It's a bit of a shock, really, seeing you again—takes me back all those years. But that's never a good idea, and you can't really go back, can you? Too much water under too many bridges.'

And just then some of that water came pouring into the kitchen in the form of a tidal wave of giggling and chasing and high-pitched shrieks that skidded to a halt the moment they saw her.

The little girl she was ready for—dark-haired, blue-eyed, the image of her father. The boy, though—he stopped her in her tracks. His colouring was almost the same, but it was the shape of his face, the expression, the vulnerable tilt to his mouth.

Julia.

Will straightened up, looking down at them with pride in his eyes.

'Izzy, meet my children—Michael and Rebecca. Kids, this is Isabel. She was at school with me and your mother. Say hi.'

'Hi,' they chorused, and then their four eyes swivelled back to him and mischief sparkled in them again. 'Grannie says can we ask you for some more eggs, because everybody wants egg sandwiches today and she's run out,' Rebecca said in a rush.

'And Grandad's sold a climbing frame and a tree house this morning, and you know old Mrs Jenks?' Michael said, his eyes alight. 'She's having a willow coffin. She's going to have a woodland burial, and her son's up in arms. I heard Grannie telling Grandad.

They were arguing about it in the café, and she said it was her body, she could do what she wanted with it. And Grannie said to tell you there's roast pepper flan today,' Michael added inconsequentially, and Izzy felt her lips twitch.

Will was smiling at them, ruffling Michael's hair and slinging a casual, affectionate arm around his daughter's shoulders, and Izzy felt suddenly empty.

I've got nothing. Thirty years, and I've got nothing. Nothing to hand on except money, and no one even to give that to. No wonder I haven't changed.

The kettle boiled, its shrill whistle fracturing the moment and freeing her.

'I'll make the tea—you get the eggs,' she said, and opened the cupboard the mugs had always lived in.

'Try the dishwasher,' he said over his shoulder as they went out, and she pulled down its door and found mugs—lots of mugs, unwashed, even though the machine was full. She put powder in the dispenser, shut the door and set it going, then washed the two mugs she'd rescued and made the tea, lifting out the teabags just as he came back in.

'Find everything?'

'Just about. I put the dishwasher on.'

'Oh, damn,' he said. 'I meant to do that.' His grin was wry. 'I meant to do all sorts of things, but you were early and the ewe was late, and—' He broke off, the grin widening as he shrugged, and then he sighed and wrapped his arms around her again, and hugged her briefly against that wonderfully solid chest that she had no rights to.

'It really is good to see you again,' he murmured,

releasing her to look down searchingly into her eyes. 'Are you OK? Really OK?'

She found that smile somehow, and the lie to go with it. 'I'm fine. How about you? You've had so much more to contend with.'

His eyes tracked away, then back, and his smile was fleeting. 'Yes. I'm OK now. It's been a rough few years.'

'Tell me,' she said softly, and he picked up his mug and pulled out a chair for her, then sat in the carver at the head of the table, his father's chair if she remembered right, and stared down into his tea.

'It was nearly three years ago. She'd been having difficulty swallowing, and she felt as if there was something stuck in her throat, so she went to the doctor. He referred her to the hospital, and they diagnosed cancer of the oesophagus. She had treatment, but it was only to make it less uncomfortable for her. We knew that right from the beginning. She reckoned it was because of the chemicals in our food, and she'd had concerns about that for some time, so by then we were already eating only organic stuff and the farm was in the process of going organic.'

'And there was nothing they could do for her?'

He shook his head. 'Only short-term and then it was all down to the Macmillan nurses and ultimately the hospice. It was agony to watch.'

Izzy could hardly imagine it. 'Did the children know?' she asked, thinking of the bright, bubbly young things who'd burst in on them just a few minutes earlier and chattered about coffins, of all things, and he nodded.

'Yes. Eventually. We told them she was sick, and then when it was inevitable and the end wasn't far away, we told them she was dying. She made them scrapbooks—snippets of herself for them to keep, memories they'd shared, things they'd want to know about themselves that only she could tell them. Some of it will only make sense to them when they're older, of course—things about their births, philosophical stuff about being a mother and what it meant to her—but lots of it was very ordinary and just things she'd treasured about them.'

Something splashed on Izzy's hand, and she blinked and swallowed. Tears. Tears for Julia, who'd always wanted to save the world, and for the children—and for Will, his voice quiet and thoughtful, telling her about Julia's last days. He had loved her, she realised with shock. Really, genuinely loved her. She hadn't wanted to believe it, but now she did.

She blinked again, squeezing the tears from her eyes and letting them fall, and then he made a soft, clucking noise with his tongue and handed her another fistful of kitchen roll.

She sniffed, scrubbing her nose with the tissue. 'I'm sorry. It's just all so sudden. I mean—I didn't even know until last night, and now, talking to you like this—it's all so real.'

'It seems light years ago,' he said gruffly. 'We move on. Time heals, Izzy. The kids don't stop growing just because their mother's died, and they've dragged me with them. I've had to cope because of them, and we've got through it together. It's been very positive in a lot of ways.'

'And all I've done is make rich people even richer and rescue reputations that probably didn't deserve rescuing, and acquire some of their wealth along the way. My God.'

Her voice sounded hollow, and it seemed appropriate. That was how she felt inside—hollow and empty and worthless.

'I shouldn't be here,' she said, the tears welling again, and then his arms were round her again—again!—and he was cradling her against his body, standing in front of her so her cheek was pressed against his board-flat abdomen, just above his belt, the buckle cold against her chin.

'Don't be silly,' he murmured gruffly. 'Of course you should be here. It's lovely to see you, Izzy. It's been too long.'

It had, she thought sadly. Much too long. So much too long that it was years too late.

Too late for what?

She didn't want to think about it—not with his belt buckle pressing into her chin and his arms around her and the solid beat of his heart sounding through that wall of muscle. And then his stomach rumbled, deafening her, and she laughed a little unevenly and eased away.

'You sound hungry.'

He laughed with her, propping himself on the edge of the table just in front of her and staring down into her eyes. 'I am. I missed breakfast—and, come to think of it, I don't know if I ate last night. I missed the food at the party. Come on, we'll go over to the café. Mum'll feed us.'

'In the café?'

'Mmm—the Old Crock. That's what she calls herself, and it seemed like a bit of fun to call the café the same thing. She runs it—and the farm shop. Dad's in charge of Valley Timber and the willow business.'

'The climbing frame and the tree house and the coffin,' she said, remembering Michael's words, and she wondered uneasily where Julia was buried. The churchyard, probably, since her father had been the vicar. She'd have to ask him some time—but not now. Now she'd heard and seen enough, and she needed time out to absorb it all and put it into place in her head. And her heart.

'He makes more than coffins. He broke his leg and was in hospital, and he did basket weaving for occupational therapy. He loved it, but it was a bit time-consuming and not really cost-effective, and then he discovered willow hurdles. It's all come from there, really. But it's not just him; there are lots of people working for him, many of them disabled. It's a thriving business and it puts something back into the community, and we're all really proud of it. Come on. I'll show you round after we've eaten.'

He held out a hand, large and strong and callused, so different from the soft city hands she was used to, and pulled her to her feet.

'It's changed so much,' she said as they went out into the yard and she looked again at all the new enterprises.

'Not really. Not in the ways that matter. It's still home.'

Home. Could he have found a word more calculated

to tear a hole in her heart? She thought of her apartment, high up in the polluted air above London's Docklands, with the deli and coffee shop and restaurant just inside the entrance, the health complex in the basement, the home shopping service, the weekly delivery of organic vegetables in a box to her kitchen, the concierge to run errands and fix stuff that went wrong—was that home?

A cow mooed, and under the bushes just in front of them chickens were scratching in the leaves.

No, she thought. *Not home. This is home.*

But not yours. Never yours.

'You're lucky,' she said to him, suddenly choked again. 'To live here, surrounded by all this.'

'I know,' he said softly, and she could see the pride and the affection in his face. Then he turned to her and grinned. 'Come on, come and see Mum. She'll be delighted to see you again. She loved you.'

You loved me. Or I thought you loved me. I loved you—

'I'll be delighted to see her again, as well. She's a darling,' Izzy said firmly, and, straightening up, she threw back her shoulders and headed across the yard beside Will.

CHAPTER THREE

AS THEY crossed the farmyard, Izzy was struck by the hail of friendly greetings from everyone they passed. It was obvious that Will was well liked and respected by the community—and equally obvious that word of her presence here had spread like wildfire.

For the most part their friendly curiosity was harmless, and some of them remembered her family from all those years ago. They were kind and welcoming, if a little wary, which she could understand.

That dratted reputation again, she thought philosophically, and smiled back until her face felt like cracking.

Others, though, were not quite so tactful or kind—like the two old crones who stopped them just a few feet from the café entrance.

'What a lovely day, Will.'

'Isn't it?' he said, and made to walk on, but one of them stopped him with a hand on his arm.

'Aren't you going to introduce us to your friend?'

He sighed and gave a rather polite smile that made Izzy want to laugh.

'Sorry, ladies. Mrs Jones, Mrs Willis, this is Isabel Brooke.'

Mrs Willis nodded sagely, smiling at Izzy in a way that made her instincts prickle. 'Of course. You've been busy since you left here—the papers don't think much of you, do they, dear?'

44

Izzy smiled sweetly in reply. 'Don't they? I wouldn't know—I have better things to do than read the gutter press.'

The woman sucked in her breath, but any reply she might have made was drowned out by Will, coughing suddenly and turning away, and Izzy had to fight the urge to laugh.

'Sorry—choked—need a drink,' he gasped, and, grabbing her elbow, he steered her towards the café.

As they made their escape, Mrs Willis got her breath back. 'Well, really!' she muttered.

'Of course, they used to run around together—if you ask me, he had a narrow escape,' Mrs Jones chipped in. 'Julia was a lovely girl.'

Here we go, she thought. They're going to start on my mythical conquests in a minute.

A minute? They didn't wait that long.

'That one's a nasty piece of work,' Mrs Willis went on. 'Supposed to have a revolving door on her bedroom.'

'Oh, I believe it, and it isn't hard to work out what she's after now,' Mrs Jones said spitefully, her voice carrying clearly across the farmyard, and Will gave an exasperated sigh and shot Izzy an apologetic look.

'Hell, Izzy, I'm sorry,' he muttered. 'I didn't imagine even those two would be quite so harsh.'

She shrugged. 'Don't worry. I'm used to it. I've heard the revolving door joke so many times I'm immune,' she lied. And yet, even though she heard it every day, even though she was constantly sniped at by thwarted business rivals and the press took endless potshots at her reputation, still, to hear it up here in

what had always seemed like the ultimate sanctuary—
that hurt.

It wouldn't be so bad, she thought, if there was any
truth in it. If she had even one per cent of the fun she
was supposed to have, she wouldn't feel so hard done
by—and maybe that was the trouble.

'Come on, we'll get you a nice cup of coffee and a
menu to look at, and you can say hello to Mum. She'll
be pleased to see you.'

'Is she expecting me?'

'I told her I was bringing a friend in. I didn't tell
her who, but the rest of them seem to have found out.'

'Won't the children have said something anyway?'

'Maybe, but they probably got distracted and forgot.
We'll surprise her.'

Izzy was suddenly reluctant to enter the café. What if
Mrs Thompson felt the same way as those women—?

'Stop it. She loves you.'

'Does she? She must be the only one.' Izzy didn't
mean to sound so bitter, but after the latest barrage of
press coverage, weeks of working much too late every
night and trying to cram far too much into every day,
to have her morals raked over and be compared to a
dead woman and found so badly wanting was more
than she needed right now.

She was beginning to regret coming up here for the
party and was wondering how quickly she could make
her escape, but as Will ushered her through the door
of the café, Mrs Thompson looked across, put down
the coffee pot she was pouring from and came round

the counter, wrapping Izzy in a huge and very welcome hug.

'My darling girl, how lovely to see you!' she said warmly, and, holding her at arm's length, she studied her face, tutted and folded her back against her soft and motherly bosom. 'You've been overworking,' she chided, then released her, studying her again. 'But still as beautiful as ever.'

'You're very kind, but I know I look dreadful,' she corrected, unable to wipe the smile off her face. Her eyes were filling—again!—and that warm and motherly embrace was just about the last straw. She stepped back and looked around. 'Um—you look really busy. Do you want us to come back later?'

Mrs Thompson was having none of it, though. 'Good heavens, no, I'm never too busy for old friends. I'm taking a break,' she told her assistants. 'Coffee, Izzy?'

'Please, that would be lovely.'

'Three coffees, Jo, and we'll have it outside.'

Izzy didn't fancy that. It was warm enough, on this lovely April day, but she didn't really want to sit out there with those nasty old gossips in range and become the object of their continued attention.

Mrs T, however, had her own plan, and she ushered them out, settled them down in a sunny spot and fussed over Izzy so that it was clear to everyone that she was not only welcome, but *very* welcome.

And that, of course, was exactly what she was intending. 'Have those old bitches gone away yet?' she asked Will conversationally, and he gave a wry smile.

'I think so.'

'Good. I saw them homing in on you and knew they

were up to something. I think I might ban them. They're bad for trade.' She switched her clear blue gaze to Izzy and scanned her face thoughtfully. 'I'm sorry about them. I hope they didn't say anything too hurtful.'

Izzy shook her head. 'They've got a way to go before they can compete with the gutter press,' she said with a slight smile. 'I've heard it all before.'

'But not here, in your old home.'

For a moment she thought Mrs T meant the house, but then she realised she was talking about the village, and she felt a moment of confusion. Because if anyone asked her to define home, it would be the farmhouse she thought of…

'I don't really think of it as home any longer,' she confessed. 'My parents moved away during my first year at university, and—there was never anything to come back for.'

There was a sudden, awkward silence, then Mrs Thompson looked up at Will. 'Darling, go and chivvy up the coffee, could you? And ask how much of that pepper flan there is. I wanted them to save some for you; I know Izzy loves it.'

After a second's hesitation, he shrugged slightly and went, and Mrs T turned back to Izzy and took her hand. 'I'm really sorry about what happened that year. Julia was a wonderful mother, and she did everything she could to be a good wife to Will, but you were missed, Izzy—by all of us. Don't ever think you weren't.'

Oh, Lord. Her eyes were filling again, and she gave a shaky laugh and brushed away the tears with an impatient swipe. 'I swear I haven't cried so much since I was a baby,' she said with a vain attempt at lightness, but it blatantly failed and Mrs T clicked her tongue just like Will and patted her hand comfortingly.

'Poor girl. It's been tough for you, hasn't it? All the adverse publicity? Do they really think you're so hard and mercenary?'

Izzy shrugged and tried for another smile. 'I don't know. Does it matter? It's all good sport, I suppose.'

Again the tongue-clicking, and then she sat back with a smile as Will set the tray of coffee on the table, sat down again and sent Izzy a searching look.

'All right?'

'Of course I'm all right.'

'Of course she is—what did you think I was going to do to her?' Mrs T asked briskly, and handed Izzy a mug of steaming, fragrant coffee. 'Black or white, sweetheart?'

'Black, please. I think I could do with a shot of caffeine to give me back some spine!'

Will frowned fleetingly, but his mother was moving on with the conversation, leaning back in her chair and looking round. 'So, Izzy, what do you think of all the changes?'

She latched onto the impersonal shift gratefully. 'Amazing,' she confessed. 'I expected it to all be the same, but of course it isn't. Nothing's the same.' Rats. Back to that again.

She was conscious of two pairs of identical blue eyes homing sharply in on her, but she only spoke the truth.

What was it Will had said? Too much water under too many bridges?

And so much of that water in the form of tears—

She found her smile again. 'So—tell me all about the business. You run the farm shop as well as the café, Will tells me. When do you find time to sleep?'

Mrs T laughed. 'Oh, there are a few hours between midnight and dawn that come in handy.'

'She does too much,' Will growled affectionately.

'I always have done. I'm fine. I'm fit, I'm well and I'm active. That's all I ask. When I'm ready for my rocking chair, I promise you you'll be the first to know.'

Will chuckled and sat back, his coffee propped on his belt buckle, and Izzy dragged her eyes away from that firm, flat abdomen and the intoxicating fit of his jeans. She looked up and met his eyes, and something in their expression held her transfixed.

She'd seen it before, years ago, and it had been as mind-blowing then as it was now. Heat washed over her and she looked hastily away, pretending interest in the Valley Timber operation.

'So—how's your husband?' she asked Mrs T, and totally failed to hear the answer. All she could think about was Will, and the heat in his eyes, and the way he'd looked at her that long-ago summer...

He wanted her.

He'd always wanted her, right from the first moment he'd seen her when they were sixteen, but she'd been focused on her studies and had hardly noticed him.

Until that last summer. She'd noticed him then, and he'd engineered a camping party down by the river, and in a quiet moment, when the others were laughing

and fooling around, they'd gone for a stroll alone together under the willows, and he'd kissed her.

Only once, then, and it had nearly blown his socks
off. He'd retreated, shocked by the force of his feelings,
and she'd blushed prettily and laughed and backed
away, equally shocked. They'd got over the shock,
though. Got over it and come back for more—and
more, and more. Until one night, when they were alone
in the house, he'd taken her to his bedroom and made
love to her.

It had been a disaster that first time—he'd been fumbling, inept, and too eager to last more than a second
or two, and she'd cried, not with pain but with frustration. So he'd tried again, and despite her shyness he'd
learnt what pleased her, and it had blown his mind.
Making love with Izzy had uncovered a tenderness and
passion in him he'd never known existed, and he'd
fallen head over heels in love with her.

From then on they'd been inseparable. They'd spent
time with the others, but there had been no question
that they were an item, and even though he'd planned
six months of travelling round the Far East and
Australia during his forthcoming gap year, he had seriously considered staying behind.

She'd considered going with him, but they'd talked
it through, and in the end she'd stayed at home and
he'd gone with Julia and Rob and Emma—and the rest
was history.

He wondered how different his life would have been
if he'd stayed behind that year, or if she'd gone too, if
they would have been together, and he realised with

something akin to shock that they wouldn't. Of course they wouldn't.

Look at them now—poles apart.

She lived in London, she was a mover and shaker in the business world, and he was a struggling farmer with two kids and a pile of paperwork so high he could scarcely see over it.

They had nothing in common, no meeting ground, nothing—except the lingering embers of a fire so hot it had burned in his heart for years.

And talking of hot—

He leapt to his feet, cursing softly under his breath and brushing at the searingly hot coffee he'd just slopped onto his jeans, a little below the belt and in a critical and highly delicate place.

Effective, though. It put the fire out even more efficiently than a cold shower, and after a moment of mopping and blotting he sat down again cautiously and shot them a wry smile. 'Sorry—I must have dozed off,' he lied, and avoided his mother's hard, knowing stare.

'Are you all right?' Izzy asked, concern in her eyes, and he just wanted to grab her and kiss her.

Damn. He all but ran his finger round under his collar. 'I'm fine,' he muttered, even though he wasn't. The coffee on his jeans was now cooling fast in the fresh April breeze, but even the combination of hot and cold wasn't enough to settle him down.

'I need to check on the kids,' he said, even though he knew they were perfectly safe, but he had to get away from Izzy for a moment and get his head in order.

'They're fine,' his mother said firmly. 'You sit down. I'll go and organise your lunch.'

And she walked off and left him alone with Izzy, not knowing where to look or what to say, conscious only of the heat rising up in him again and threatening to consume him.

Hell. It had been years since he'd even thought about sex—three long, tragic, lonely years—and now suddenly, like opening a door on a blast furnace, there it was, hot and raw and aching, and all because of this pretty and surprisingly vulnerable woman sitting beside him staring down unhappily into her coffee cup.

'I shouldn't be here,' she said, her voice soft, puzzled, and she looked up then, meeting his eyes, and a lump formed in his throat. Lord, she was lovely—and he was suddenly afraid for her. She seemed so vulnerable, so fragile, and now he could see the change in her.

That lovely, spontaneous warmth was tempered by caution, and he could see that the adverse publicity had wounded her deeply, making her uncertain and withdrawn. It was a tragedy, a crying shame, and he had to stop himself from reaching across and hugging her.

Or kissing her.

Instead he smiled, a crooked, slightly off-kilter smile that was all he could get past the emotion choking him.

'Of course you should be here. I'm sorry, I'm not being a very good host. Out of practice.' He put his coffee cup down before he did anything else stupid with it, and sat forwards, folding his arms on the edge of the table and leaning on them, to hide his misbehaving body. 'Tell me about what you do.'

'What I do? You know what I do. I'm an asset stripper.'

He snorted. 'Rubbish,' he said bluntly, and her eyes widened. 'I know you better than that,' he went on. 'You can't lie to me. Tell me about it. Why do you do it? And don't say for the money, because I know that's not true, either.'

She smiled reluctantly. 'For the challenge?' she offered. 'Because there's something incredibly satisfying about turning a company around and making it work when it's destined for the scrap heap?'

'So how do you know what to take on and what to leave?' he asked.

She shrugged. 'Instinct. A good product and lousy management and marketing are usually the keys. If the product's useless, there's no point, but if it ought to work and something's stopping it, then I'll take it on.'

'For a price?'

'Sure. And I'm ruthless. I try not to be unkind, but if someone's in the wrong job the chances are they aren't happy, anyway, so I don't have a problem with helping them relocate to something they're better suited to, either in the company or out of it. I have a recruitment agency as well, and I use that to help people find the right slot to fit them if I can.'

He chuckled. 'Be careful, you'll have me believe you're Joan of Arc in a minute.'

'Hardly. I can be pretty tough.' Her laughter was soft, and he felt a hard, tight knot in his chest ease a fraction at the sound.

'But not quite Godzilla.'

'Not quite.'

Their eyes met and locked, and he felt the heat again, searing through him, making him want things he had no business wanting, things he'd put out of his mind for years. Just when he thought he would have to kiss her or die, his mother appeared at his side, a tray in her hands and a beaming smile on her face.

'Here we are, darlings. Roasted pepper flan, green salad and fresh, crusty bread just out of the oven. More coffee?'

And that was it. They spent the next few minutes eating, and all he had to do was watch her tucking into her food as if she hadn't eaten for days. And for all he knew she might not have done. She was slim enough, goodness knows. If she ate like that all the time she'd be huge, surely?

And she certainly wasn't, although she went in and out in all the right places—

No! Not that again!

He pushed his empty plate away, wrapped his hand round his coffee cup and took a gulp of the fresh, scalding brew that brought the tears to his eyes and helped his mind to focus on something other than Izzy's body.

'Wow. That was even more gorgeous than I remember!' she said with a little laugh, and sat back, her plate scraped clean and her eyes alight.

She looked gorgeous, her mouth soft and full and moist with the sheen of oil from the salad dressing. How would it taste—?

'Fancy a guided tour?' he asked, smacking his cup down on the wooden table with a thud. The coffee slopped over the side onto his hand, and he winced. Perhaps he should give up on coffee for a day or two—

Her slender, eloquent brows pleated together over

puzzled, wary eyes. 'Am I holding you up? You must have things to do, and I'm taking hours of your time—'

'Don't be silly,' he said, feeling instantly guilty and hating himself for it. He tried for a smile. 'I'm sorry. I'm just used to eating and running—as I said, my social skills are getting rusty. There's no rush. Finish your coffee.'

'Your social skills are fine and I've had all I want,' she said, her mouth curving in a tentative answering smile that made the urge to kiss her even worse. 'If you're sure you've got time, I'd love a guided tour, but don't let me hold you up.'

'There's no rush,' he said again. 'Come on. My father will be looking forward to saying hello. He would have come over, but I expect he's busy keeping the kids out of mischief.'

'They seem full of it,' she said softly, and she sounded wistful.

Did she regret not having children? He didn't imagine so. Where on earth would she have fitted them into her lifestyle?

Where on earth would she have fitted *him* in, come to that, or vice versa?

Nowhere. They simply wouldn't ever have had time, either of them, and they didn't now. Not today, not any other day. This was strictly a one-off, and cherishing any illusions about seeing her again, about tasting that soft, ripe mouth or holding her firm, taut body in his arms was just a waste of breath.

He stood abruptly, scraping his chair on the paving and only just catching it before it toppled.

'Come on,' he said, more tersely than he'd meant to. 'Let's go and find my father.'

What on earth had she said? Something, that was for sure. His brows were dragged together in a frown, and he towered over her, big and intimidating and impatient.

She got slowly to her feet.

'I think I should go.'

'What?' His frown deepened, then cleared, and he sighed softly and gave a wry smile. 'I'm sorry. I'm assuming you've got time to burn and you're probably in a hurry to get back.'

'No. I just don't want to outstay my welcome.'

His eyes searched her face, and he sighed again and rammed his hands through his hair, tumbling the soft dark strands and leaving it spiked and unruly. 'You aren't. It's me. It's just seeing you again—bringing everything back.'

Julia, she thought. She was reminding him of Julia, of happy times when they were young, and she swallowed a sudden lump in her throat and straightened up.

'Come on,' he said gently, taking her elbow. 'You can't go without seeing my father, and I really would love to take you round the farm and show you everything we've done.'

He seemed to mean it, so with a little shrug she put away her doubts and smiled at him. 'I'd love that.'

'Then let's go.'

They crossed the yard to the old milking parlour, and his father came out with the children in tow. 'Isabel.

How nice to see you,' he said, and kissed her cheek lightly. 'You're looking well.'

'And you look just the same,' she said, scanning him quickly with affectionate eyes. A little greyer, perhaps a little more solid round the middle, but still the same man she remembered. He was a little shorter than Will—he'd been taller before, she thought, but Will had overtaken him, grown and filled out. They were still the spitting image of each other, though.

'I gather you've built an empire,' she teased gently, and he laughed.

'Someone's been talking it up,' he said wryly, and he led her through and showed her where they made the furniture and the garden toys.

'The toys are all modular—you can extend the climbing frames and ladders and make forts and tree houses and all sorts. And the timber's treated to last thirty years, so it's a pretty good investment.'

She looked at the play equipment, then at Mr T, obviously proud of his achievements, and nodded. 'It looks good. How do you market it?'

Two pairs of brows creased in a puzzled frown.

'Market it?' Mr T said. 'Well—people know we're here, they come and buy it.'

'So you don't advertise?'

'Locally, occasionally. We don't really need to do more.'

'And then there's the willow business,' Will said. 'So we've got more than enough to keep us occupied.'

She was sure they had. 'It's impressive,' she said honestly. 'Really good stuff. You should be proud of it.'

'We are,' Will said. 'Come and see the farm. Dad, are you OK to keep the children a little longer?'

His father nodded, and Will led her back to the house and round to the yard. 'We'll go in the Discovery,' he said, opening the door for her, and she climbed up into the big off-roader and strapped herself in, grateful for the space between them.

Or she would have been if it had been enough. Once he went round to his side of the car and slid into his seat, though, she realised that nothing short of a couple of miles would be enough.

Good grief! She hadn't realised the pull between them was so strong—at least, as far as she was concerned. She couldn't speak for him, and of course he was still grieving for Julia, so it was probably all one-sided.

She stifled the pang of sorrow and tried to concentrate on the maze of tracks he drove her down, pointing out all the things they'd changed, the crops they were growing, the difference because of going organic.

She tried to listen. She really, really tried to listen. But all she could hear was the sound of his voice, soft and low with a slight rasp of gravel now and then, and then they were heading downhill towards the river, winding their way around the fields until he stopped in the shade of the big old willows along the riverbank and got out.

She slid down from the car and followed him as he strolled slowly towards the water, pausing to pluck a blade of grass and twirl it absently in his fingers.

'We camped down here,' he said, his voice gruff. 'Do you remember? That summer?'

She nodded, unable to talk because his eyes were hot and tracking slowly over her, and everywhere they touched her, her body caught fire.

'I thought you'd be growing the willow here,' she said, struggling for normality but sounding breathy and desperate, like a sad old maid.

He shook his head. 'No. Not on this bit. I saved this bit.' He didn't smile. Instead he reached out, lifting a hand and brushing a callused thumb over her lips. 'I kissed you here, under this tree,' he said, his voice taut, and her breath jammed in her throat.

'I remember.'

They stood spellbound, trapped by something much stronger than themselves, and then he dragged himself free of the spell and strode back to the car.

'Will Thompson.'

His mobile. His mobile had been ringing, and he'd heard it.

She'd heard it too, but only dimly over the pounding of her heart. She realised she was holding her breath, and sucked in a great lungful of air, then another.

'We have to go,' he said tersely. 'I'm needed back at the farm—a ewe's in trouble.'

Not only the ewe, she thought with irony.

'Don't worry, I ought to be getting on anyway.'

He nodded, and before she was properly in her seat he was heading up the track, taking a shorter route back to the farm.

He slammed to a halt outside the house and turned to her, his hand on the doorhandle. 'I need to go and change and check this ewe,' he said. 'I'm sorry, I'd like to see you off properly, but I really—'

'Just go. Don't worry about me.'

He hesitated for a fraction of a second, then he leant over and pressed his mouth to hers in a hard, swift kiss that sent her pulse off the Richter scale.

'You take care,' he ordered gruffly.

'You, too. Thanks for today.'

'Any time.'

His door opened and slammed shut, and she was left sitting there watching him run towards the house. She followed slowly, retrieving her bag from the kitchen and scribbling him a note on the back of a business card.

Thank you for everything. If you're ever in London, here's my number. Be good to see you. Izzy.

And without further ado, without waiting for him to come down, she went back over to the café, thanked his mother for lunch and said goodbye, and headed back to London, her heart in turmoil. So much to absorb, so many things to take in and deal with.

Julia. The children.

And Will. Will, if anything even more attractive to her now than he had ever been, and even further out of reach. He didn't even have time for lunch and a little drive around the farm on a Saturday afternoon. What hope was there for any kind of relationship?

She lived in London, worked all over the country, sometimes out of it. On Monday she was flying out to Dublin to talk to a man about his ailing firm. She could be working there for weeks—months.

If Will didn't have time for a relationship, the same

was certainly true of her, because she was ridiculously busy.

And anyway, there was Julia, canonised in the village, her spectre hanging over the possibility of any relationship that they might have. How could she deal with that? Not even she needed a challenge that great.

No. She'd go back to London, and put Will out of her mind, and get on with the rest of her life.

CHAPTER FOUR

'SO—GOOD party?'

Will eyed Rob warily. 'You tell me—it was your party.'

Rob chuckled, his eyes altogether too searching for Will's peace of mind. 'Oh, I know what it was like from my point of view. I was actually talking about Izzy.'

Will knew perfectly well what Rob was talking about, and he had no intention of being led into such incredibly dangerous waters. Instead, he turned the tables on his old friend.

'Did you know she was coming?' he asked.

Rob shook his head. 'No—not when I last spoke to you. She got in touch a day or so later, just by chance.' Will's face must have showed his scepticism, because Rob threw up his hands in the air in a gesture of total innocence. 'Really, I swear. It wasn't planned—just a happy coincidence.'

Happy? Will wasn't sure about that. For the last couple of days he'd felt unhappy and unsettled, filled with a strange restlessness, and his nights had been rife with dreams. He didn't even want to think about those. Much too dangerous.

He made a noncommittal noise that didn't fool Rob at all, and made a production of looking at his watch. 'I have to get on,' he said, carefully avoiding Rob's eyes, but the soft snort indicated that his friend didn't believe a word of it.

'So, when are you seeing her again?'

Will stifled a sigh. 'I'm not.'

Rob stared at him. 'Why ever not?'

'What do you mean, why ever not? Why ever should I?'

'Because there's still something there between you?'

Will rammed a hand through his already rumpled hair, and glared at Rob. 'How on earth would you know that?'

Rob shrugged slightly and smiled. 'Because I'm not blind?' His smile faded, concern showing in his eyes, and he scanned Will's face searchingly. 'I know you loved Julia,' he said softly, 'but she's gone, Will, and you and Izzy always had something special. I often wondered—'

'Don't go there,' Will growled at him. 'It's none of your damn business. Just keep out of it, Rob, I'm warning you.'

Rob threw up his hands in defeat and stood up, slinging the chair back underneath the edge of the table and heading for the door. 'OK, OK, I know when I'm not wanted, but just do me a favour. At least think about it.'

He was out of the door before Will could reply, which was just as well. He wouldn't have wanted to hear what his old friend had to say about him. Then Will sighed and pressed his lips together into a hard line. Think about it? His laugh was short and bitter. He'd thought about nothing else for days. He knew the phone number by heart, he'd studied it for so long.

Several times his hand had reached out to pick up the phone, only to withdraw at the last minute.

Once, he'd even dialled the number and hung up before it could ring.

He was obsessed by her, tormented by the futility of his attraction for a woman so totally out of his reach. He wasn't fool enough to imagine it could be anything other than a passing physical attraction, at least on her side. If she felt anything at all, it was probably just curiosity, an urge to revisit once-familiar territory.

She was a powerful, sophisticated woman, and she would have better things to do with her time than spend it with a frustrated, overworked farmer—at least once that curiosity had been satisfied.

There was no way he was leaving himself open to that kind of heartache. Besides, he didn't even have time, so what on earth was he thinking about?

Izzy. That was what he was thinking about, all day and all night—she was driving him mad, and he almost wished he hadn't seen her again.

Almost.

With an impatient sigh, he pulled on his boots and coat, slapped his leg for the dog and headed out of the door. Forget Izzy, he told himself sternly. Forget the intoxicating scent that surrounded her. Forget the sound of her laugh, the soft curve of her lips, the gentle swell of her breasts.

But, try as he might, he couldn't forget the haunted look in her eyes when those two old bitches had been gossiping about her. She wasn't nearly as tough as she tried to make out, he realised, and for all her success he'd sensed a strange restlessness in her, a lack of fulfilment.

She seemed somehow sad inside, and he didn't think it was simply because she'd just heard about Julia. Instinctively, he knew it was more than that, and, fool that he was, he wanted to reach out to her, to help her. What on earth he thought he could do to help her he had no idea, and anyway it was a crazy notion. She'd probably find it highly amusing.

He climbed up into the tractor, the dog scrambling up beside him, and fired up the engine. It started with a roar that drowned out his thoughts, and just to be on the safe side he turned on the radio good and loud and listened to a political debate that was about as interesting as watching paint dry.

It was, however, a darned sight safer than thinking about Izzy.

'Mr O'Keeffe, if I'm going to be able to help you, you're going to have to provide me with a lot more information.'

'Ah, Miss Brooke, but what information would that be?' he asked in his soft Irish brogue.

Izzy stifled her exasperation and tried very hard not to grind her teeth. 'Well, Mr O'Keeffe, until I have it I won't know, will I?' She smiled sweetly at him and thought if he answered with yet another question, she'd probably have to stab him with the letter opener that was lying on his desk.

Fortunately for both of them, he simply smiled enigmatically and pressed the button on his intercom. 'Deirdre, would you come in, please?'

His secretary came in with no evident haste, and eyed Izzy without curiosity. 'Yes, Mr O'Keeffe?'

'Miss Brooke would like some information,' he said. 'Do you suppose we could help her?'

'Now, then, which information would that be, Mr O'Keeffe?' Deirdre asked him innocently.

Izzy decided that if she didn't take the matter into her own hands, she was going to be there for the next five years just trying to get a glimpse into the filing cabinet.

'I'll need the last three years' accounts, financial reports, audit reports and sales figures—oh, and the personnel files.'

Deirdre's eyes widened. She looked worriedly at Mr O'Keeffe, but he merely raised his hands palm-up and shrugged.

'You heard the lady, Deirdre,' he said. 'She'd better have what she needs.'

And yet the information was not forthcoming. Deirdre couldn't find this, that was missing, the other was still with the accountant—the excuses were legion and relentless.

'Mr O'Keeffe, if I'm going to be able to help you, I'm going to need information,' she told him firmly. 'Now, either you are going to be able to provide me with that information, or I'm going to go home. I'm simply not going to be messed around by you any longer. Either you want my help or you don't.'

Deirdre was beginning to look faintly panic stricken, but Mr O'Keeffe seemed to take it all in his stride.

'Well, now, it seems we may have a little problem

there, Miss Brooke. Perhaps if you came back to-morrow—'

'I have a meeting in London tomorrow,' she pointed out. 'I have come here, as arranged, for a brief preliminary meeting to decide whether or not it's worth considering my involvement in the resuscitation of your company. Without information I can't do that, so it's up to you. If I leave you now, then I won't be back.'

He paused thoughtfully for a moment, then nodded to Deirdre. The woman left the room, and a few minutes later came back, her arms piled high with files.

Izzy eyed them sceptically. 'A CD or floppy disk would have done,' she said, trying hard to keep the sarcasm out of her voice.

'Ah, but there's nothing like a piece of paper for making things clearer,' Mr O'Keeffe said. 'Now, Miss Brooke, how about a nice cup of coffee?'

'I understand you want to talk to me, Mrs Jenks?'

'Well, actually it was me,' her son said, and Will could see from the way he squared up his shoulders that he was spoiling for a fight.

Not again, he thought with an inward sigh. Ever since they'd bought Mrs Jenks' farm and allowed her to live rent-free in her old home for the rest of her life, her son had been on Will's case. If it wasn't one thing, it was another. What was it this time? The windows? The heating system? The elderly Rayburn in the kitchen?

'About the Rayburn,' Simon Jenks began, and Will suppressed the urge to roll his eyes. 'Now the summer is coming, she really could do with it taking out and replacing with a decent cooker—'

'But I like the Rayburn,' Mrs Jenks protested. 'I don't want another cooker; I'm used to it.'

'But it's awful, Mother,' Simon said vehemently. 'It always goes out, you have to keep putting fuel in it all the time, and it's too much to expect of you in your state of health.'

She glared at her son. 'My state of health? What would you know about my state of health? You only turn up when you want to make a nuisance of yourself. I tell you, Simon, I like the cooker the way it is, and I don't want Will being put to a lot of trouble messing about and changing things just for the sake of it. I'm too old. I can't be bothered with it.'

Simon bristled a little, but was undeterred. 'Well— how about the windows?'

'How about the windows? The windows are fine. Simon, leave it,' Mrs Jenks said firmly. 'Now, if you've finished your coffee, why don't you go and get on? I'm sure you're very busy.'

He opened his mouth, shut it again and stood up abruptly. 'I'll pay for the coffee,' he said, but Will waved him away.

'Forget the coffee. It's on the house,' he said, and watched the man go with a quiet sigh of relief.

The sigh Mrs Jenks gave, on the other hand, was heartfelt and a great deal louder. 'Oh, that boy will be the death of me!' she said with a chuckle. She laid a gnarled old hand over Will's and patted it gently. 'You do know, don't you, that I'm quite happy with every- thing as it is? I'm an old woman, Will. I just want to be left in peace. I'm not interested in a new cooker or having the builders in. Don't let him browbeat you, will you?'

Will smiled at her understandingly. 'No, I won't let him browbeat me. I know he only wants the best for you, but sometimes when we're close to people, we can lose sight of what that is.'

The gnarled hands tightened on his. 'But you know, don't you?'

He turned his hand over and gripped hers gently. 'Don't worry, Mrs Jenks, I'll look after you.'

Her rheumy old eyes filled without warning, and she blinked and looked away. 'Oh, look, here are the children. I swear, they grow every time I see them. They were delightful earlier. I was talking to them when I arrived. Charming little things.'

Will looked at them, their eyes sparkling with mischief, and thought 'charming' wasn't perhaps quite the word he would have used. They were filthy, and the aroma drifting off them was something else.

He stood up and smiled down at the elderly woman. 'I think my charming little things need dealing with,' he told her dryly, 'if you'll excuse me?'

She chuckled, smiled benignly at the children and waved him away. 'Don't be too hard on them. They're just children.'

Just children? He nearly laughed out loud. Certainly they were children, but just? Just? Hardly.

He chivvied them across to the house, made them strip in the utility room and sent them to wash and change into clean clothes. They came down a few minutes later, smelling slightly better, and Rebecca said brightly, 'I like Mrs Jenks. She gave us some sweets. She said Simon is a pain in the neck. What's a pain in the neck?'

'She means he's a nuisance,' Michael said scornfully. 'I expect he wanted her windows mended.'

'No, actually, he wanted her Rayburn replaced,' Will told them, struggling to keep a straight face.

'I knew it was something like that,' Michael said. 'She was ever so cross with him.'

'He means well,' Will said, and closed the subject. 'So, are you two going to tell me how you got quite so filthy?' he asked mildly, and their faces were twin pictures of guilt.

'I dropped something in the pond,' Michael said, avoiding looking at his father. His tone was innocent enough, but Will wasn't fooled.

'Something?'

Michael shuffled unhappily. 'Beccy's shoe,' he confessed.

'And what were you doing with Beccy's shoe by the pond?'

'He stole it and ran off with it, and threw it at me, and it fell in the pond.'

'But I found it,' Michael said, as if that would make it all right again. 'It was a trainer, so you can wash it.'

'No,' Will said firmly. 'You can wash it.'

'Ah, Dad!' Michael wailed in protest, but Will was adamant. They had to learn the consequences of their actions, and if that meant scrubbing a stinking, filthy shoe retrieved from the bottom of the pond, then so be it.

He sent him off to do it, and Beccy, sitting at the

table scribbling with a pencil on the back of an old envelope, said innocently, 'Is Izzy your girlfriend?'

Will nearly choked. He opened his mouth to reply, then shut it again until he'd thought of something to say.

'Why on earth would you think that?' he asked after a moment, trying to keep a slightly wild note of panic out of his voice.

'Mrs Jenks said you were sweet on her. I didn't understand, so Michael explained.'

'Mrs Jenks said it was years ago, before you married Mummy,' Michael chipped in from the other room. 'She was talking to Grannie.'

How ridiculous to feel guilty for something that had happened so long ago, and yet, confronted by the innocence of his children, guilt was exactly what he did feel. Perhaps his recent thoughts and dreams were also partly responsible.

'She's an old schoolfriend,' he said firmly. 'I told you that.'

'But was she your girlfriend?' Beccy asked, reluctant to give up, but Will refused to be drawn any further.

'She's a friend—nothing more. Michael, have you finished that shoe yet? If so, you need to go over to the café and have some lunch quickly. You're going out this afternoon, don't forget.' And not a moment too soon, he thought, with questions like that cropping up right, left and centre.

'I wouldn't mind—I thought she was nice,' Beccy said, scooting out of the door before he could get another word in.

He gave a slightly strangled laugh. Nice? 'Nice'

wasn't the word he would have used. Gorgeous, maybe. Beautiful? Intoxicating?

Damn. Back to that again. He stomped into his study and flicked through his diary, checking the date of the next farmers' market, and a note caught his eye. There was a meeting in London, later in the week, about obtaining funding for certain organic projects, and he had pencilled it in without any real intention of going. He wasn't sure if it even applied to him, but it might be interesting.

And if he was going to be in London, then what would be the harm in meeting Izzy for a drink afterwards?

No. Too dangerous.

But as he went about his work for the rest of the day, the idea niggled at him, and by the time he'd put the children to bed at the end of the day, he could hardly think about anything else.

Just a quick drink—nothing formal or too elaborate. Keep it light.

If she was even there, of course, on Thursday evening. There was no guarantee that she would be. And anyway, he probably wouldn't even go.

It was just one of those days, Izzy decided. She'd waded through some of the paperwork she'd brought back from Ireland with her, and she still had far more questions than answers.

Not surprising, really, considering how evasive Mr O'Keeffe had been, but that still didn't help her to decide whether or not she was going to take up the challenge.

She was just debating phoning him and telling him where to stick his firm when Kate stuck her head round the door, her face alive with curiosity.

'There's a man here to see you. He hasn't got an appointment, but he's got the most gorgeous eyes. You ought to see him just for that!'

Izzy chuckled and leant back in her chair, swinging it round to face Kate and propping her feet on the corner of the desk. 'Gorgeous eyes, eh? Perhaps you'd like to give him coffee and keep him waiting so you can chat to him yourself?'

Kate laughed wryly. 'Love to, but it's you he wants. His name's Will Thompson.'

Her feet hit the ground so hard her ankles jarred. 'Will?' she squeaked, and hauled in a steadying breath. 'Will's here?'

Kate tipped her head on one side and eyed her even more curiously.

'Uh-huh. Still want me to entertain him?'

She stared at Kate. 'Um—no. Can you knock up some coffee?'

'You've got an appointment in twenty minutes.'

'With?' she asked, her mind completely blank.

'David Lennox. It's about the Dublin deal.'

The accountant. She paused for a second, then shrugged. 'I'll see Will—find out how long he's around. I may have to reschedule David.'

'He won't like it,' Kate warned, but Izzy shrugged again. David needed her business more than she needed him, and they both knew it.

'He'll live. Anyway, I'm not sure I'm ready to talk

to him—that paperwork's utterly impenetrable, and I think it's deliberate.'

She stood up, tugged her soft sweater straight and ran the tip of her tongue over her suddenly dry lips. 'Right. Let's see what Will wants.' She went past Kate, her heart hammering, and walked into the reception area on legs that had suddenly turned to jelly.

He was standing by the window, looking out over the city with a brooding expression on his face, and as she crossed the room, her footfalls muffled by the thick carpet, he saw her reflection and turned to her, one corner of his mouth kicking up in a wary smile.

'Izzy.'

'Will.' Her chest rose and fell rapidly. Crazy, but those eyes— 'What a lovely surprise.'

'I'm sorry, I should have called, but I was at a meeting today just a few minutes away from here, so I thought I'd drop in and say hi.'

She could feel herself smiling inanely. 'I'm glad you did. Come on into my office. Kate'll make us coffee.'

'Have you got time?'

'Sure,' she lied blithely. 'It's nearly the end of the day, and I haven't got anything important on.'

David Lennox wouldn't have thanked her for that, but it was just tough. And besides, the way Will's eyes were tracking over her put a whole new slant on her words. She was suddenly acutely conscious of what she *had on*—the soft cashmere sweater in the same muddy green as her eyes, the beautifully cut black trousers that did amazing things to her figure. And most particularly the fine silk and lace matching underwear she had put on this morning without any thought—

She swallowed and turned away from those searching eyes, leading the way into her office and closing
the door behind them, then instantly regretting it, because now she was alone with him and—

'Izzy?'

She whirled round and stopped, trapped by those
eyes, by the gentle puzzlement in them.

'I've just dropped in to say hi. That's all. I thought,
if you weren't busy, maybe we could have a drink. But
if you've got something on, don't be afraid to say so.'

Something on. Like the matching underwear? She
closed her eyes briefly and feigned concentration.

'Nothing that I can think of. A drink would be
lovely. Do you want coffee here first? How are you for
time?'

He pulled a face. 'Time's fine. I can go on any train.
I'll fit in with you, Izzy. I don't mind what we do.'

'We'll skip it, then—'

'Coffee,' her PA said, breezing in brightly at that
moment and flashing Will a smile that made Izzy want
to smack her. Good grief! The girl was besotted, and
Will was smiling back, and she was—

Jealous. That was what she was. Jealous. How stupid.

'I've spoken to David—he was going to be late anyway, so you're seeing him tomorrow morning at seven-
thirty. Will that be all right?'

Kate's question was seemingly innocuous, but Izzy
read all the right meanings into it. Would she be available at seven-thirty tomorrow? Or still tied up with
Will—?

'That'll be fine. Thank you, Kate. I think, though,

actually, we'll skip the coffee. I'm sure you can find some willing takers. I'm going to take the rest of the afternoon off. Can you field my calls and hold the fort?'

Kate grinned. 'I expect I'll manage. Have a nice time.'

Her dancing eyes showed exactly how she thought Izzy and Will were going to spend the afternoon, and Izzy was torn between whacking her over the head with the telephone directory and wailing with frustration.

She did neither. Instead, with considerable poise and sang froid, she unhooked her jacket from the back of her chair, slipped it on and smiled up at Will. 'Ready when you are. Where are you taking me?'

He laughed and rolled his eyes. 'It's your city. You tell me.'

She shrugged. 'OK. There's a little wine bar just round the corner that serves light snacks, unless you fancy anything a bit more substantial?'

'Sounds fine,' he said, and as they passed Kate, Izzy could see the curiosity bubbling behind those clear, intelligent grey eyes.

There'd be hell to pay for this, she thought, but suddenly she didn't care. She felt as if she were bunking off school, something she'd never done and had always fancied doing, and she had an overwhelming urge to throw back her head and laugh.

And then they were in the lift, going down to the foyer, and in the small confined space she was suddenly so utterly aware of him she could hardly breathe.

'Smart office,' he said into the silence, rescuing her just when she thought she'd start to hyperventilate.

'You like it?'

'Very impressive.'

She laughed. 'You have to look the part. Evidence of success is important, otherwise people think you aren't any good, but you have to get it right. Too much marble and gleaming steel and two-inch-thick carpet and they feel they're being ripped off—and God forbid they should realise the truth!'

He chuckled, the sound strangely soft and intimate in the enclosed space, and just when she thought she'd make a fool of herself the lift doors opened and they stepped out into the bustling foyer.

Will smiled at the receptionist. 'Found her,' he said, and Ally smiled back and coloured slightly. Another conquest, Izzy thought crossly, and resisted the urge to grab him by the arm and hustle him out.

Ally, though, didn't give her the option. 'So I see. Izzy, I've got something for you,' the girl said, and stood up and leant over, an envelope in her hand. 'This just came for you—Kate said you were on your way down.'

She took it, ripped open the envelope and scanned it, then stuffed it into her bag. It was another note from Steve. Really, she'd have to talk to him. Just not today.

'Thanks,' she said, flashing a smile at the girl. 'I'm not coming back tonight, Ally, if anyone calls, by the way,' she added, and Ally flicked an appraising glance at Will and smiled back.

'Sure. Have a great time.'

She didn't quite grind her teeth. Instead she made herself smile politely and whisked him out of the door.

CHAPTER FIVE

THE wine bar was heaving.

Izzy stared at it blankly, and Will thought she seemed flustered. Come to think of it, she'd seemed flustered since he'd arrived unannounced in her office, and now her composure was threatened again.

'It can't be this full. It's usually busy, but not like this. There must be an impromptu party or something.'

'It doesn't matter. We can go somewhere else, surely?' he said, trying not to sound too enthusiastic. Not that there was anything wrong with the wine bar, but a pub might be preferable. He might feel less out of place. As it was, amongst all the city types thronging the bar he was beginning to feel distinctly under-dressed. His usual jacket and trousers had seemed fine this morning, and he'd put on his favourite tie. He'd even dug out a new shirt from the bottom of his drawer in honour of the occasion.

But, looking around him now, he felt like a country cousin, positively middle-aged compared to the frighteningly young executives swarming around them in pinstripe suits like upwardly mobile ants. There couldn't be anyone there a day over twenty-five, he thought in horror, and they were flashing credit cards around in their soft city hands, their designer watches and diamond-studded rings glinting in the sunshine.

79

Izzy stared at the crowd for another few seconds, then seemed to come to a decision.

'We can go to my place,' she suggested. 'There's a coffee shop and a restaurant in the complex, and I've got beer and wine in my apartment if you'd rather be there. I can probably find you something to nibble on if you're hungry.'

He didn't want to think about that one too hard.

'Your place sounds fine,' he said. 'I'd like to see it—so I can picture where you live.' That sounded dubious, so he qualified it hastily. 'I always think it's easier if you can visualise someone in their own environment. Sort of fixes them in their own place in the great scheme of things.'

And it would add another layer to his dreams.

Oh, hell.

'My place it is, then.' She shrugged, smiled and set off along the pavement at a fast clip, as if she wanted to hustle him out of sight of all the bright young things in the bar. She probably knew most of them, he realised—or maybe she was hustling him away from one in particular?

'Is there a fire?' he asked mildly, keeping up with her easily but just curious about her sudden haste.

She laughed and slowed down. 'Sorry. I always power-walk to work. It's good for me.'

He ran his eyes down her legs, clad in beautifully cut and incredibly sexy trousers, to her feet, and did a mild double-take. 'In those shoes?'

She looked down at the impossibly high heels and smiled. 'These? I always wear shoes like these to work. I need to look tall or people won't take me seriously.'

He snorted softly. 'I can't imagine that. They've only got to glance at your list of achievements to feel suitably intimidated. I'm sure your height's got nothing to do with it.'

'I just feel happier,' she said firmly.

'Whatever. I couldn't stand in shoes like that, let alone power-walk.'

Her grin was infectious. 'I'd love to see you try,' she teased, and he chuckled.

'I am not cross-dressing for your entertainment,' he retorted, and when she responded with a delicious gurgle of laughter, he suddenly began to relax. She was still Izzy, still capable of teasing him and having fun, and he stopped thinking about her meteoric success and concentrated instead on her and what she was saying.

'I nearly bought a place in here,' she told him, waving at a tall glass and brick structure that looked like an old industrial building.

He said so, and she nodded. 'It is. It's all very loft-style and open plan, but I didn't fancy rough blockwork walls and steel girders all over the place, and anyway, it didn't have a river view.'

And, of course, a woman of her substance would have a river view, he thought dryly.

You've got a river view, his alter ego prodded.

But in the country. That's different. And it's not quite the Thames.

They arrived at a discreet glass and steel entrance door in the side of a tall building. 'Here we are,' she said, and they went into the foyer.

His jaw must have sagged visibly, but he clamped his teeth shut and took it all in, in minute detail.

A broad, elegant sweep of marble served as a reception desk, concealing a uniformed security guard and a concierge, and off to one side a coffee shop, a restaurant and a little deli bustled with activity.

'We could eat here if you'd rather,' he suggested, hoping she'd disagree, and to his relief she shook her head.

'We're here, we might as well go up. Afternoon, George.'

The concierge smiled. 'Good afternoon, Miss Brooke. Your vegetable box arrived. I had it put in your kitchen.'

'Thank you. Any messages?'

'No. Just your post.'

He handed her a thick stack of envelopes, and she threw him a smile that would have ensured any man's undying devotion and led Will towards the bank of lifts on the opposite side of the foyer.

A man in gym gear with a towel round his neck appeared beside them and grinned at Izzy.

'Hiya, Iz. Haven't seen you in the gym this week. Everything all right?'

'Fine. I'm just busy. I will come, Freddie, I promise.'

'Mind you do. I don't want that shoulder playing up again.'

He winked at her and went off. Izzy stepped into the lift and swiped a card, and the doors hissed shut. Seconds later they opened, and Will followed her across a hall and through a door, opened with another swipe of the card.

Pale gold. That was what he saw. Gold from the sun on the walls, streaming through the floor-to-ceiling windows and flooding the room with light. And there below them was the river, stretched out in both directions and dotted with little boats.

'Come and see my garden and have a look at the view,' she said, and at the touch of a button the big doors slid open and she stepped out onto a roof terrace lush with plants.

He followed her and fingered a leaf thoughtfully, trying not to think how much such an apartment must cost to rent. He couldn't even begin to contemplate the freehold value. He glanced down at the slim, straplike leaf in his hand and recognised a cordyline. There was a yucca beside it, and beyond that a fatsia with huge, brilliant green leaves, startling against the concrete backdrop that was London. 'Nice plants. Watering them must be a nightmare,' he said, but she shook her head.

'There's an irrigation system. I'm away a lot. They'd die.'

Of course. What else? He crossed to the edge of the roof garden and leant over, peering down several floors to the riverside below. People moved like ants, and even the noise of the sirens and honking horns was muted this far up.

It was still there, though, and the air, although clearer, was still tainted with exhaust fumes.

He hated it.

He turned, brushing against a viburnum that responded with a wave of heady scent from the pink-blushed flowers, and he breathed deeply and the world righted itself. What a miracle, in this desert of brick and glass and seething bodies.

He touched it gently, almost thankfully, and went back inside, into the climate-controlled stillness of the apartment, and looked around.

Quiet understatement. Elegance, good taste and a great deal of money had created a beautiful environment. Only the teetering shoes cast aside on the rug and the bag dropped nearby on a butter-soft suede sofa made it look lived in, and he thought of his chaotic and untidy house and groaned inwardly.

What had she thought of it?

Of him?

Not that it mattered. If he hadn't realised before just how far apart their lives had taken them, he would have realised now.

'What can I get you to drink?'

He stiffened. Her voice was right behind him, so close he could hear her breathing. Or maybe he just imagined it. He stepped away, just to be sure, and turned.

'What are you having?'

She shrugged. 'Water, probably, for a start. I've got a water cooler.'

Of course. He looked across at the kitchen area of the big, open-plan living space and saw a gleaming steel American-style fridge with a water dispenser in the door, built into a wall of units in dark cherrywood.

'Sounds good.'

She laughed. 'You don't have to have water. You can have tea, or coffee, or beer, or wine—whatever.'

'Water's fine,' he said, and wondered how long they could continue talking about nothing when there was so much to say.

Or maybe there wasn't. Maybe it was all best left buried in the past, because the past was, after all, all they could ever have...

Will was looking distinctly uncomfortable. He'd downed the water as if he'd just been rescued from the desert, and she'd refilled his glass and gone over to the sofas, settling cross-legged into the corner of one and patting the cushion for him to join her.

'Mind if I sit here? I can see the river.' He shed his jacket and tie and took the other sofa, sitting with one leg hitched up, his ankle propped across the other knee, and, although apparently relaxed, she could feel the tension coming off him in waves. Because of her? Surely not. If so, why would he have come to see her?

He looked around, his face strangely expressionless. 'Nice place.'

Nice plants, nice place. She made a rude noise. 'You hate it.'

He blinked in surprise, but then laughed softly. 'No. I'd hate to live in it, which is just as well, since I wouldn't have a prayer of affording it, but I don't hate it. It's interesting—and if you're busy, and you've got to live round here, I guess this is the way to do it. I'm just glad I don't have to—not enough trees and animals for me.'

She could understand that. There weren't enough trees and animals for her, either, but that was one of the trade-offs. And if she needed trees and animals, she could go and find them easily enough. 'There's always the zoo,' she told him, but he winced.

'Not quite the same as having the cat on your lap while you're watching the telly in the evening.'

'No—but you don't have to feed them, either. I couldn't have a cat if I wanted one. I'm away far too much on business.'

He shook his head slowly from side to side, as if he was trying to understand. 'That must be hell. I'd hate to be away from the farm, but some of that is dreading the chaos I'll go back to.'

She laughed softly in sympathy. 'I can understand that. Luckily I have a brilliant PA—Kate. You met her. She keeps everything ticking over for me.'

He grunted. 'I need a Kate—think she'd come and work for me? I could pay her in eggs.'

Izzy chuckled at the thought. 'I think Kate might want rather more than eggs.' She tipped her head on one side. 'So what happened to all your plans? How come you ended up farming? You were so dead set against it. Surely you can't blame that on Julia and the baby?'

He gave a rueful smile. 'No. My father broke his leg just a few days before our wedding and ended up in a wheelchair for four months. I had to take over the farm, and by the time he was up and about again I'd realised it was what I wanted to do with my life.'

He settled back against the corner, some of the tension leaving his body, and she doodled in the condensation on the glass and watched him.

'So did you go to college?'

He nodded. 'Yes—the local agricultural college. It's attached to UEA in Norwich, and I did a degree in agriculture and land management.'

'Not quite the same as civil engineering.'

'No—but I'm happy, Izzy. I never thought I'd be happy staying in one place and doing one thing all my life, but now I can't imagine doing anything else.' He cocked his head on one side. 'What about you? Are you happy? All this—' He waved a hand around '—success. Has it made you happy?'

She looked down, suddenly struck by the realisation that, no, it didn't make her happy. It made her busy, and it made her rich, but happy?

Not in the ways that mattered.

'Mostly,' she replied, unwilling to give him total honesty. 'There are still things I want from life.'

You, for instance. To wake up to the sound of birdsong and find myself in your arms. To be pregnant with your child—

Good grief! That was too much honesty, even for her! She catapulted to her feet. 'I'm going to open a bottle of wine—what do you fancy? Red or white, or maybe something sparkling? We could break open a bottle of champagne, if you like. Sort of a late birthday celebration.'

He eyed her oddly. 'Red, please, if you've got any open. Nothing too heavy, though. I've got to drive when I get home.'

'I've got a nice light Merlot.'

He nodded. 'Do fine. Thanks. Want me to open it?'

He followed her to the kitchen without waiting for an answer, and she had the bittersweet joy of watching those strong, capable hands deftly stripping the seal and twisting out the cork.

He put the bottle down on the worktop just as she

turned with the glasses, and her elbow caught it. Only his lightning reflexes stopped it from crashing to the floor, and he righted it and smiled at her and her heart crashed against her ribs.

'Whoops.'

Whoops, indeed. He was standing just inches away from her, and as she watched, his smile faded. Very slowly, very deliberately, he released the bottle and moved his hand towards her face, turning it so that his rough, workworn knuckles grazed feather-light over her cheekbone.

'I've missed you, Izzy,' he said, his voice low.

She couldn't answer. Her heart was wedged up in her throat, and as he turned his hand again and trailed the tips of his fingers over her jaw and down to her suddenly dry mouth she thought she'd never be able to breathe again. Her tongue flicked out to moisten her lips, and she felt his thumb drag over the soft, damp skin.

A tiny moan escaped from her throat, and her eyes fluttered shut.

For what felt like for ever he did nothing, then his fingers slid round and threaded through her hair, anchoring her tenderly as his lips whispered over her jaw like the brush of an angel's wing.

'I've missed you,' he said again, his breath puffing softly against her cheek, and then his other hand wrapped warm against her shoulders and drew her to him.

She went willingly into his arms, her own stealing round him to cradle him against her heart as her lips parted for him and she felt again the gentle touch of his mouth settling on hers for the first time in so many years.

So sweet. So dear. So very, very welcome. She felt the coaxing invasion of his tongue, but there was no need to coax. She forgot all the reasons why this was a bad idea, all the reasons why she should run a mile.

She forgot Julia. She forgot the pain of losing him, the pain of knowing he loved another woman. She forgot the long, lonely, agonisingly bleak years without him.

And she forgot the sheer impossibility of a relationship with a busy man tied down by duty and responsibility and the demands of a farm and a family, not to mention her own duties and responsibilities and silly-hectic schedule.

Instead, she gave herself up to the warmth of his mouth, hard and yet yielding, demanding and yet giving so much more than he took. His body cradled hers, rocking her against him, and her body responded to his as a desert flower responds to rain.

And then he was releasing her, his hands cupping her face, his kisses light again, tender, soft little sips as he retreated, and she opened her eyes to find him looking down at her with regret and confusion in his eyes.

'I'm sorry. I don't know what I was doing.'

She tried for a smile. 'I thought you were kissing me,' she said, trying to make light of it, but all the reasons why it was such a lousy idea were crashing back into her scrambled brain like logs tumbling from a woodpile, and she pulled back, dropping her arms to her sides and resisting the urge to hug them around herself defensively.

He stared down at her sorrowfully. 'Izzy, I'm sorry. I shouldn't have done that.'

She turned away. The only way she could deal with the pain surging through her. 'Don't beat yourself up about it. It was only a kiss. It's hardly the first time.'

That wasn't the thing to say. She shouldn't have harked back to their earlier relationship. It was over, forgotten—or should have been. And yet wasn't that what this was all about? Laying the ghost?

Was that why Will had come here today? To lay the ghost? If so, his tactics were way off beam. Her ghosts, all of them, were running round her head screaming blue murder, and she gave her head a little shake to clear it.

'Wine?' she said brightly, and reached for the glasses.

'Thanks.'

He'd retreated, standing staring sombrely out over the river, his eyes hooded and his expression forbidding.

Idiot. Why had she thrown herself into it with so much enthusiasm? She could have kept it light, kissed him back and moved away.

No, she couldn't. Even she couldn't lie to herself like that. She'd been waiting for that kiss for twelve long years, and the moment he walked out of the door she was going to relive every precious second of it.

'Here.'

She handed him his wine and he took it, careful not to touch her, and retreated back to his corner of the other sofa as she curled into her usual place again and watched him warily over the rim of her glass.

'So—you never did tell me what brought you to London. You said something about a meeting?'

'Oh—yeah. It was a conference about ways of accessing funding for various farming initiatives.'

'Useful?'

He shrugged. 'Not overly. Quite interesting, but most of it was irrelevant to us.'

He fell silent again, giving the simple Merlot very much more attention that it actually warranted, and Izzy wondered what he was thinking.

Regretting the kiss, most probably, because until then they could have just picked up their friendship and carried on.

'I shouldn't have come,' he said suddenly. 'I thought I could do this—see you from time to time, chat with you, be a friend. But it's difficult. Much harder than I thought. We've got too much history to ignore it, and there's no way we could have a relationship now. We're just light years apart.'

He looked up from the wine and met her eyes, and she read regret and sadness in his gentle gaze.

'I don't want to have an affair with you, Izzy,' he said softly. 'It wouldn't be fair on any of us. So I think I'd better just go, and I don't think I should see you again for a while.'

'Another twelve years should do it,' she said, and even she could hear the ache in her voice.

His sigh was ragged and heartfelt. 'Izzy, I'm sorry.'

He got to his feet, set his wine down on the granite slab that served as a coffee table and came over to her.

'Don't get up. I'll let myself out.'

He picked up his jacket, tucked his tie more firmly into the pocket and then stooped and pressed a gentle, chaste kiss to her lips.

'You take care. And if you ever need anything, give me a call.'

'I thought we weren't going to see each other again,' she said, fighting to hold back the tears, but his hand touched her cheek and one spilled over and he brushed it away tenderly.

'I'd never turn you away if you needed me,' he said, his voice rough, and then he went, the door closing behind him with a soft click. She heard the faint whirr of the lift, and he was gone.

She brushed the tears away angrily.

'You're such a fool,' she told herself, scooping up the glasses and going into the kitchen to tip the wine down the sink. Freddie was right; she hadn't been in the gym for a while. She'd go and have a good work-out, and then a swim, and then she'd grab something simple to eat from the deli and have an early night.

'So how was the conference?'

'Oh—quite interesting,' he told his father, but couldn't for the life of him remember anything except seeing Izzy. 'I've brought some handouts back to look at.'

'See anyone you know?'

He nodded. 'One or two. I had a drink with an old friend afterwards.'

'Anyone we know?'

He felt his mother's eyes boring right through him, and he shrugged evasively.

'Don't think so,' he lied, and wondered if this was going to become a habit. 'Any phone messages? Anything happened I should know about?'

'Not really. The stock are all bedded down for the night. Why don't you stay for a drink?'

He shook his head. 'It's been a long day, and anyway, I need to get the kids home to bed.'

'Leave them here,' his mother suggested. 'They're in the middle of a video, and they're no trouble. It's the school holidays; it won't matter if they stay up late, and they love being here.'

'They love you spoiling them,' he corrected fondly, and gave in. He found them in the little television room, curled up under quilts, and kissed them both goodnight, then went back to the farmhouse and let himself in, Banjo at his heels.

'You're supposed to be an outside dog,' he told the animal, and was rewarded by a lashing tail and a swipe of a wet, pink tongue across his hand. He patted the dog's head absently and went upstairs and hung up his formal clothes, tugging on an old rugby shirt and a pair of worn jeans with a sigh of relief.

He could still smell London in his airways, hear the noise and bustle, feel the vibration of the underground trains coming up through his feet.

He didn't know how Izzy could stand it, although he had to admit she certainly made the best of it. Her apartment was hardly subsistence living, and she had the money to take advantage of all the shows and exhibitions and other wonderful cultural things that London had to offer.

If you could stand the press of people and the constant noise.

He pulled on his boots and went out with Banjo, doing the usual late check and then standing, arms folded on the top of the gate, just listening to the cacophony of sound that was night time in the countryside.

The owl swooped overhead again, as it often did, and his mouth twisted into a parody of a smile. He'd asked Izzy if she was happy, and she'd said mostly, or something like that. He'd told her he was, and yet he wasn't sure if it was happiness or contentment.

Recently, though, even contentment had eluded him, replaced by a strange restlessness.

Hormones? He'd been alone a long time, and before then Julia had been very ill for several months. No wonder he'd responded as he had to Izzy.

He shouldn't have kissed her, though. Big mistake. It had brought back all sorts of memories that were best left forgotten, and opened wounds that surely were healed by now.

And yet she'd cried. As he'd been leaving her, she'd cried, a solitary tear trailing down her cheek and nearly crippling him. He'd almost stayed, then. Nearly thrown away all his resolve and taken her back into his arms and made love to her.

He propped his hands on the top of the gate and hung his head, staring down at his feet and wondering if he would ever truly get her out of his system.

He had a terrible feeling that he wouldn't, and he wasn't even really sure he wanted to. At least this way he still had his dreams.

CHAPTER SIX

SHE went to Dublin on Monday, as promised, to see Daniel O'Keeffe.

Not that she held out any great hope of being able to work with him. The man was a nightmare, and she had a feeling she was simply acting as an expensive courier to return his impenetrable documents.

David Lennox had been suitably pithy about the lack of transparency in the information she'd been given.

'They're trying to pull the wool over someone's eyes. Maybe yours, maybe someone else's, but if I were you I'd steer clear. I don't like the look of them.'

The accountant never liked the look of any of the firms she took on, but she'd be a fool to ignore him on this one. Her instincts were screaming, and if she didn't get some straight answers today, she was walking.

Definitely.

'Forty-nine per cent?'

She sat back in her chair, folded her arms and met his eyes fair and square. 'Forty-nine per cent. I'll give you my time for nothing, and at the end of the day, if my strategy's failed and the firm's in the state it's in now, I'll be out of pocket. If it works, and I believe it could, we'll all be a lot richer.'

'Fifteen.'

She laughed. 'Not a chance. I wouldn't do it for

fifteen per cent if it was a dead cert, and the only certain thing about your operation, Mr O'Keeffe, is that nobody will give me a straight answer to my questions. I don't like that—it makes me uneasy.'

Her words made him uneasy, too, for all the charm and the ready smile. She was getting too close to something, and all of a sudden the hairs on the back of her neck started to prickle.

'Tell me about Cork,' she said, and if she hadn't been watching him so carefully she would have missed the tiny flicker of alarm in his eyes.

'Cork? Ah, now. Beautiful place. Beautiful county— wonderful scenery. You'd love it—'

'I wasn't asking for a tourist information sales pitch,' she told him dryly. 'I was curious about your transactions with a firm there—DOK Logistics. You see, I can't find any record of them. I just wondered if you'd care to shed any light?' Yep, he was definitely looking shiftier by the minute.

'You can't find the records? How strange. They're there, to be sure. You must have looked in the wrong place. Haulage firm. We use them from time to time.'

'Expensive haulage.'

'You have to pay for the best,' he assured her, but he couldn't quite meet her eye, and she hadn't got past the fact that DOK just happened to be his initials.

'I don't need this,' she told him, finally coming to her senses. She didn't need the money, it was too big a risk, and she didn't trust him. He had all the charm the Irish were renowned for, but he was lying like a rug and she'd had enough.

She stood up, clipped her briefcase shut with a defiant click and held out her hand. 'Goodbye, Mr O'Keeffe. I hope you find someone to help you sort yourself out—I'm afraid it won't be me.'

He looked at her hand for a long moment, then gave a wry smile and stood up, shaking it gravely. 'I'm sorry we won't be doing business. I was looking forward to it. Thank you for your time.'

Looking forward to the money, more like. And as for her time—! 'My pleasure. I'll be sending you my bill.'

Not that she had any hope of it being paid, but it was the principle—something O'Keeffe seemed a little short on, for all his charm.

She took a taxi to the airport, took the first available flight and landed at Stansted airport at four that afternoon. The sun was shining, but the ground was soaking wet, and as they were transferred to the main terminal building from the arrivals satellite they were informed that there would be hold-ups in getting away from the airport because torrential rain had caused havoc and the county's roads were gridlocked due to a spate of major accidents.

Great, she thought. Just when she was looking forward to getting home and having a nice cup of tea and a long, hot soak in the bath.

She had no luggage to collect, so she headed straight for the exit to find out just how bad the situation was. One look, however, at the mass of people thronging the information desk and stacked up outside all the food outlets, and she had her answer.

There was an information board giving further details, and as she walked she stared up at it, silently

cursing herself for ever getting involved with O'Keeffe.
If she'd followed her instincts—

She didn't see the ice cream the child had dropped.
She found it, though. One minute she was striding towards the information board, the next she was on the
floor, her arm doubled under her and pain like she'd
never felt in her life surging through it, robbing her of
everything except the need to die.

Will walked into the kitchen, glanced at the answer-
machine and saw the blinking light. He sighed.
Probably something else he'd forgotten to do, he
thought with resignation, and hit the 'play' button.

'Will? This is Izzy. I was just ringing to hear a
friendly voice. I'm stuck at Stansted—I've fallen down
and broken my arm, and I can't get an ambulance for
hours because the roads are in chaos and all the hospitals are implementing their major incident plans because of the rain, and I hurt, and I just wanted to talk
to you. Sorry, I'm rambling. I'll go.'

Her voice had a quiver in it he didn't like, and it
rose towards the end, as if she had been struggling for
control. He frowned at the answer-machine, pressed the
button to listen again, then dialled 1471 and called her
back on her mobile.

She answered after a few rings, sounding woozy, and
his concern accelerated. 'Izzy? What's going on?'

'Oh. Hi, Will. Sorry about the pathetic message. I
was just feeling a bit lost. I couldn't get Kate, my PA,
and I just wanted to hear a friendly voice, really.'

Her voice wobbled, and he felt the adrenaline begin
to pump round his body. 'Tell me about your arm,' he

said, wanting her to focus and needing to know how bad she really was. She sounded horrendous. 'Izzy? Talk to me.'

There was a pause. 'Well, it's—broken.'

'You're sure?'

Her laugh was slightly manic and worried him. 'Oh, yes,' she said. 'It's sort of bent, just above my wrist, and it hurts.' Her voice wobbled again, and she went silent.

'How's the traffic situation? Any news on your ambulance?'

The laugh was definitely desperate this time. 'Oh, it gets worse. About seven hours, they think. I don't think I can sit here for seven hours—well, that's silly. Of course I can. I don't have a choice. I wonder if there are any heroin addicts about that want to share?'

His imagination ran riot until he realised she was joking. 'Haven't they given you anything for the pain?' he asked, wincing as he imagined what she was going through.

'Oh, yeah. There's a paramedic here, and he's been brilliant. He's had a look at me and said it needs hospital, but I just can't get there, so I'll have to wait. All the roads are at a standstill; it's hopeless. I've had some pain relief, but nothing short of oblivion will be good enough for a while, but it's better than it was and at least it's in a splint. I'll live.'

'Where are you?' he asked, an idea forming in his head.

He could almost see her shrug. 'Oh, I don't know. In some office somewhere in the main terminal. At least it's quiet. It's bedlam out there. Will, don't worry.

I'll be OK. Look, I have to go; my battery's getting low and I might need it. I'll speak to you later.'

She cut him off, and he stared at the phone for a second, then punched in another number. Two minutes later he'd made the arrangements, changed into clean clothes and headed out of the door.

'Izzy?'

She opened heavy lidded eyes and stared blankly at him. Was he real, or had she conjured him up out of the drug-induced haze that was enveloping her? Whatever, he was the most welcome thing she'd seen in a long while, and she reached out her good hand, the one that wasn't dying with pain, and touched his hand. It gripped hers back. Real. Amazing.

'Will?'

'That's me.'

She tried to think, but it was too hard. There was something, though. Something important. Yes, that was it. The roads. 'How did you get here?'

His grin widened and he crouched down in front of her and pressed her fingers to his firm, warm lips. 'Friends in high places,' he said enigmatically. 'Come on, I'm taking you home.'

She thought she'd never heard anything so wonderful in all her life, but she still had no idea how he could do it.

'How?' she asked, puzzled and unable to think clearly because of the painkillers.

'Same way I got here—helicopter. Told them it was a mercy mission—got air ambulance clearance to land.'

'You've got an air ambulance?' she said incredulously, but he just laughed and shook his head.

'Not quite. It's Rob's brother's toy. Remember Andrew? I twisted his arm.'

She winced at the thought, and he pulled a face. 'Sorry. Inappropriate metaphor. Luggage?'

She shook her head. 'No luggage. Only that bag.'

'Come on then. Your chariot awaits, ma'am.'

She stood up and swayed, and he took her good arm firmly and clamped her against his solid and very welcome side.

'Whoops,' she said, and tried to smile, but the room was spinning. She sat down again abruptly, and after a moment tried again.

'OK now?'

She nodded. 'Better.'

'Come on, then, Dizzy Izzy,' he said with a tenderness that brought tears to her eyes. 'Let's get you out of here.'

There was a car waiting for them, and they were whisked across to the north side, to the old terminal building the private flights operated from, and within moments she was strapped into a seat in a little helicopter and Rob's brother Andrew was grinning at her.

'I've always wanted to rescue a damsel in distress,' he said with a laugh, and she smiled back weakly and sagged against the seat.

'Happy to oblige,' she said, but her voice sounded slurred with pain and drugs, and saying anything else was just too much effort.

Will strapped himself in beside her, and held her good hand while Andrew went through the pre-flight checks, then got clearance for takeoff. There was that horrible sickly moment when the aircraft tipped forward and surged away from the ground, and then everything righted itself again and she could see straight.

Well, straightish. The painkillers must be something else, she thought, and closed her eyes. The vibration of the helicopter was giving her arm grief, but in what seemed like seconds, but was probably minutes, they were setting down in what looked like a playing field.

'Where are we?' she asked, puzzled.

'Ipswich Hospital—well, a school right behind it. Look, there's someone there with a stretcher.'

She sighed quietly with relief. She didn't want to make a fuss, but her legs didn't really seem to belong to her, and the idea of lying down was starting to appeal more and more.

Will helped her down the steps out of the helicopter, the person with the trolley manoeuvred it under her, and as she sat down on the edge of it everything faded away and went black.

'Will?'

Her eyelids fluttered open, and he leant forwards and took her good hand, glad to see her back in the land of the living. 'Hi, there, Sleeping Beauty. How are you feeling?'

'OK. You must be tired, all this hanging around. What about the children?'

'With my parents. Don't worry about them. How are you, really?'

'Sore. Hand hurts.'

'That's because they've sedated you and straightened your arm. You've got a temporary cast on, but you've got to go down to Theatre tomorrow and have an operation to pin it.'

She blinked and stared at him, trying to focus. 'Can't. I've got a meeting—'

He laughed and shook his head. 'Not any more, you haven't. Sorry, old thing, you're out of commission for a few days at least. They'll let you out tomorrow evening, if you're all right and have someone to look after you.'

'But—where will I go?'

'Home with me,' he said firmly. She opened her mouth to argue, shut it again and smiled weakly.

'Thanks.'

He nodded. 'My pleasure. Now, you need some sleep, and so do I, but I'll see you in the morning.'

He pressed a chaste and friendly kiss to her forehead, and went quietly out, leaving her alone.

Silly. She missed his presence even while she could still hear his footsteps retreating down the hallway...

She didn't want to go through those next few hours and days ever again, Izzy thought when she woke on Wednesday morning. She could hardly recall the previous thirty-six hours, but there was a lingering memory of pain and hideous nausea, and through it all Will, beside her whenever she woke, holding her hand, holding her hair when she was sick, holding a glass and making her drink cool water—holding her together.

She opened her eyes, and for the first time in what felt like days she was alone. How silly, to feel that sudden emptiness because he wasn't there.

He had work to do, a farm to run, children to take to school—or was it the holidays? She didn't know for sure. Not being a parent, she was out of touch with these things. They'd need feeding and dressing, though. Did you dress children of ten and eight or whatever they were? She had no idea.

She looked around the room, taking in the simple furnishings and restful colour scheme. Pale blues and creams, with old honey pine furniture that looked hand-waxed. By Will? Maybe. She was in a double bed, the mattress gently supportive, the quilt softly snuggled round her. Was that why she'd slept so well, or was it the painkillers? Probably.

There was a pretty chair in the corner, and a robe was laid over the end of the bed. Not hers, because all of her things were in London, but someone's.

Julia's?

A chill ran over her. Had this been their room? Or had Julia decorated it, not knowing that Izzy would end up here, staying in it?

She threw back the quilt and sat up slowly, swinging her legs over the side of the bed and pausing while the world righted itself. She really didn't need to fall over again.

'Izzy?' There was a tap on the door, and Mrs T poked her head round and smiled. 'You are awake. I thought I heard you move. I was in the kitchen down below you. How are you feeling?'

She gave a wry smile. 'I don't know. I'll tell you when I try to walk. I need the loo.'

'And a cup of tea, I expect, in that order. Here, slip this on. It's my spare dressing gown—the respectable

one I keep in case I have to go into hospital. It'll probably drown you, but it's not full length so you
shouldn't trip up in it.'

Izzy slid her good arm into it, relieved that it wasn't
Julia's, as she'd feared, and Mrs T settled it around her
shoulders over the baggy old T-shirt that was probably
Will's, and helped her to the bathroom just next door.

'I'll be in your room, straightening your bed. Give
me a call if you need me,' she said to Izzy. 'Oh, and
there's a toothbrush and toothpaste on the windowsill
for you if you want them.'

'Thanks,' she said, touched by their thoughtfulness.

She managed without help—just. It was the silly
things, though. How did you tear off the loo paper with
one hand? Fortunately the fracture was in her left arm,
because she was most profoundly not ambidextrous,
but even so it was a nightmare.

Pulling up the hospital-issue paper knickers.
Squeezing the toothpaste. Drying one hand without the
other to help.

Weird. Very unnatural. It dawned on her that her
plan of going back to London either today or tomorrow
might be a little ambitious.

Which posed a problem, of course, and one she'd
have to discuss with Will when he reappeared.

She went back to her room, to find that Mrs T had
fluffed up her pillows and propped them up, and turned
back the quilt so she could get back into bed easily.

She eyed the bed with longing, but she was hungry
and thirsty and she ought to get dressed and think about
breakfast.

'Come on, back into bed and I'll bring you up something nice. What do you fancy?'

She felt her brows pleat a little with worry. 'You haven't got time to run around after me.'

'Nonsense. I've got lots of staff over at the café. Let them earn their keep. Now, what'll it be? Tea, coffee, or something milder? We've got green tea, or fruit tea of various denominations, or I can find you some fruit juice?'

'Tea, please, if you really have got time. Just ordinary tea, not too strong, not too milky, no sugar. That would be lovely.'

'And what about something to eat?'

She opened her mouth to say she wasn't hungry and her tummy rumbled.

'I think that's a yes,' Mrs T said with a chuckle. 'Come on, back into bed and I'll see what I can find. Will's cupboards tend to be a bit bare, so I might have to nip over to the café. I won't be long.'

Will's cupboards? She went out, leaving Izzy to think about that one. She'd assumed that all of them lived together, but maybe they didn't. How odd, to think of Mr and Mrs T anywhere else. And that meant she was here alone with Will and the children.

A little shiver of something ran over her, and she bit her lip. Not that he was about to take advantage of the situation with her arm in plaster, but it made her feel uneasy. What would those old busybodies in the village be thinking of her? Of them?

She rested her head back against the pillows and stared blindly out of the window. All she could see was rolling fields stretching away into the distance, punctuated by woodland and hedges that criss-crossed the landscape like seams on a patchwork.

Beautiful. The window was open, and she could hear the lambs bleating outside. She sat up and peered down, but the angle was wrong. Was Will out there with them? Maybe.

She leant back again, conscious of the pain in her arm and a slight prickling where the wires holding the bones together came out of the skin. At least, she thought that was what it was, but her memory of the post-op chat with the doctor was patchy and she didn't really want to think too much about it. She concentrated instead on keeping her hand very still.

Mrs T reappeared in the doorway, a tray in her hands, and settled it on the bedside table. 'Tea, and fingers of French toast with honey. You always used to like that.'

How amazing that she remembered. Izzy smiled her thanks and wriggled further up the bed, taking the tea she was offered and sipping it gratefully.

Odd how nothing in her life had ever tasted so welcome. Before she knew it the mug was empty, and she rested it down on her lap and smiled at Mrs T. 'Gorgeous. I was ready for that.'

Mrs T's smile was approving. 'Good. Now, tuck into this and see if we can't get a bit of colour back into your cheeks.'

She handed Izzy the pile of French toast, cut into convenient fingers so she could manage it with one hand, and while Izzy ate she told her that Will was out on the farm with the children, checking the fencing over at the Jenks side of the farm, because he was going to move the sheep over there now they'd finished lambing and were all outside again.

'The name's familiar. Do I remember Mrs Jenks?' she asked, and Mrs T shrugged.

'Probably. She's always been around. All my life, certainly, and probably my mother's, too. She's a wonderful character, and what she did to deserve her son I can't imagine. He's such an old woman. She sold the farm to Will on condition she can live there for the rest of her life, and her son nags him constantly to replace the Rayburn in the kitchen and change the windows and refit the bathroom, and she doesn't want to know.'

'So what does Will do?'

She laughed. 'Nothing. And then the son thinks he's being a negligent landlord—even though he chases round after her and is there more often than her own son. And not only does he not charge her rent, he provides her with wood cut to the right size for her stove and stacks it just by the door. He clears her snow in winter, cleans her windows, takes her shopping—he's wonderful to her, and her son just drops in from time to time and complains.'

'Why doesn't Will tell him to take a hike?' Izzy asked in astonishment.

Mrs T just looked at her. 'Because he's not like that. He says the son's just concerned, but he's not. He's trying to milk the deal for all he can, even though he's got his hands on the money for the farm already, from what I've heard. I try not to listen to the gossip, but there's a lot of it, of course, in the café.'

Which reminded Izzy of the two old women who had been so bitchy the last time she was here.

'Mrs T, is my being here going to be a problem for Will? I mean, with the village? People will talk, and I don't want to cause trouble.'

'Good grief, child, you've broken your arm! Of course you're here; you need help. You can't possibly manage on your own.'

Nobody had called her a child for years, and Izzy had to struggle not to smile. There was something comforting about it, though—about being taken care of generally. Nevertheless, she was still worried about Will's reputation, and she needed to know about his domestic arrangements.

'You said something about Will's cupboards. Do you not still live here?'

Mrs T shook her head. 'No. When he and Julia got married they took over one of the estate cottages, and when they had Rebecca, and the people in the other half left at around the same time, it seemed sensible to knock the two halves together and make one decent-sized house. When Julia got very ill, they moved in here, and she had a room downstairs until she had to go into the hospice.

'Then last year, when the children seemed to be coping without her, and because Will needed to be here running the farm and we didn't, it seemed to make sense for us to take over the cottage and leave the house to him. Peter said us being here might cramp his style, and they needed to be independent, but we aren't far away and we muddle along somehow.'

She patted Izzy's hand. 'Don't worry about the gossips. You leave them to me. Our house is too far from the café for me to pop across like this and keep an eye on you if you were there, and Will's busy so he can't do it. Anyway, it won't be for long, and it's lovely to have you here, so don't you give those silly old gossips another thought. You just concentrate on getting better. More tea?'

And that was the end of that.

She ate her breakfast, drank two more cups of tea and then Mrs T left her to sleep.

She did, as well, to her amazement, but not for long. Her young, fit body was recovering fast from the shock and the anaesthetic, and, rather than sit there and think about how much her arm hurt, she got up and went over to the window and sat on the wide sill and looked down at the sheep.

She was still sitting there when Will came back with the children, and he looked up at her window and waved at her, and she felt as if the sun had come out.

How foolish. Less than a week ago he'd been at pains to point out to her that there could be no future for them, even in the short term, and now here she was, a guest in his house, utterly helpless and unable even to dress herself without assistance!

So how was that going to work?

She had no idea. All she knew was that she wanted to be here—no, needed to be here. Her body needed to rest and recover, and so did her heart. It had been years since she'd done nothing for a while. Two years since she'd taken so much as a few days off.

It wouldn't hurt her now.

But Will might. He'd hurt her before, and she wasn't foolish enough to believe he couldn't do it again.

Would she survive this time?

She got up and walked back to the bed, her legs a little unsteady, and moments later she heard him run up the stairs two at a time. There was a knock on the door, and it opened a crack.

'Izzy? You decent?'

She chuckled. 'Not according to Mesdames Jones and Willis, but I'm covered from neck to ankle. You can come in.'

The door swung wider and he appeared, his smile apparently warm and genuine. 'How are you?'

'Fine,' she lied. She could have said she'd missed him when she'd woken, but there was no way she'd confess to being so pathetic and needy, and anyway, if he didn't want a relationship, she had no intention of pushing it.

'Did Mum look after you?'

'Of course. Don't you trust her?'

His smile grew wry. 'Sorry. Of course she did. I expect she forcefed you.'

'Almost,' Izzy admitted with a grin. 'Tea and French toast. She remembered I love it.'

'She's like that.'

He perched carefully on the end of the bed and pursed his lips, studying her. 'You OK, really?'

She shrugged. 'Hurts a bit. I'll manage.'

'That was never in doubt. You ought to let go, you know—let someone else take over for a while.'

Her smile was slow. 'I'm a control freak. It's hard for me.'

'I know, but sometimes things happen that are bigger than us, and we have to go with the flow.'

'Like breaking my arm and ending up here? I really

only rang you because I just felt so stranded and lonely. I didn't mean to trouble you, especially after what you said about not seeing me again for a while. I'm sure you didn't mean four days.'

He made a sound that was half-laugh, half-sigh, and rammed a hand through his hair. He looked away, then looked back, his hand locked around the back of his neck, and the teasing light had gone from his eyes. 'I said if you ever needed me, give me a call. I meant that, Izzy. I really meant that, and I'm glad you felt you could do it.'

'You also meant what you said about not seeing me again, though—didn't you?'

He shrugged dismissively. 'Forget that. You needed getting out of there fast. It was a hellish situation, and I only did what any friend would have done.'

'And if I'd thought about it I could have arranged a charter flight myself into City Airport, got a taxi to a hospital in London, then gone home the next day.'

'And then what? How would you have looked after yourself? You aren't dressed yet. Can you do it?'

She thought of her clothes—the jacket they'd had to cut off her in Casualty, the trousers with the side zip that she'd never reach with her other hand, the blouse with the fiddly buttons. Not a chance. She didn't even know where they were.

'I'd have my tracksuit bottoms and a baggy T-shirt at home,' she reasoned, and he got off the bed and went out, coming back a few minutes later.

'Michael's jog bottoms and a rugby shirt of mine that's shrunk in the wash. Fresh socks. I think Mum washed out your underwear. If you can manage to get that lot on without help, you'll be doing well. And how would you cook, and shop?'

She shrugged again. She seemed to be doing that a lot lately. 'I wouldn't. I'd eat downstairs, or get stuff sent in.'

That was the easy bit. It was the other things she was beginning to wonder about, like doing up her bra and opening jars and cans and all the things one just took for granted. Washing. Showering. Hair-washing. That was going to be interesting, with her hair turning into a scouring pad at the first sign of water.

'Not easy, eh?'

Was he reading her mind? Probably. He used to.

'I'd manage,' she said again, more firmly. 'And, talking of rescuing me, that kind gesture—for which, by the way, I'm profoundly grateful, because I don't know how much longer I could have stood it—must have cost someone a small fortune in fuel and airport fees. You must let me know how much, and who I owe, so I can sort it out.'

'Andrew,' he said. 'But don't worry. He owes me shedloads of goodwill. He keeps his helicopter here on the farm. We'll call it rent.'

'Then you should have it—'

'Izzy,' he growled warningly. 'Let it go. It's not often I get to play the hero. Just let me do it, eh? Just this once?'

She felt the smile start at her toes and work its way up.

'My pleasure,' she said. 'Now, if you'll find me my underwear, I'd like to get dressed.'

And, of course, she'd forgotten it was the little

scraps of Janet Reger. He came back in with the tiny garments dangling from a fingertip and a smile lurking in his eyes.

'Underwear?' he said questioningly, and she pressed her lips together to keep in the sassy retort and snatched them out of his hand.

'Thank you. You can go now. I can manage.'

His lips twitched, but without a word he turned and went out.

'I'll be here when you need help,' he said, and it was all the challenge she needed.

The bra didn't make it on—much too hard—but the little lace thong and the rest of the clothes she managed, with some difficulty, and when she emerged on the landing, sore and exhausted but victorious, his smile was one of reluctant admiration.

'Stubborn woman,' he said gently, and brushed her cheek with his knuckles.

Mistake. Her knees were already weak, and that was almost enough to send her tumbling head-first downstairs. She swayed, and he grabbed her and tucked her firmly into his side, then walked her downstairs, his hard, lean hip bumping into her softer one with every step, until by the time they reached the bottom she was ready to scream with—

What? Frustration? Longing?

Disappointment?

He let her go, and she followed him into the kitchen and sank gratefully into a chair. The children were nowhere to be seen, and he explained he'd sent them over to the café for lunch.

'Do you want to join them, or can you make do with bread and cheese and my company?'

Cheese gave her indigestion, but she wouldn't pass up on the offer of his company for the world.

'Oh, I guess I can make do,' she said softly, and he met her eyes and smiled, and her heart sank.

She'd known all along that she was in hot water. It was only then that she realised just how deep it was.

CHAPTER SEVEN

SHE needn't have worried.

After that morning, and once he was satisfied that his mother was looking after Izzy properly, Will avoided her whenever possible.

Whether he was avoiding her or simply getting on with his work she wasn't sure, but he was never around, and Izzy took to spending several hours at a time curled up on the sofa in the kitchen, with a cat on her lap and a book taken from the selection in the study.

She needed to rest, not only to get over the anaesthetic but because her sleep pattern was shot to blazes by the awkwardness of the cast and the pain in her arm, but the enforced holiday was anathema to her.

When the inactivity got too much, she went over to the café and sat in the corner, people-watching and chatting to Mrs T when she could spare the time. She couldn't help much, of course, because there was little that could be done one-handed, but if she could do anything she did, and if it got busy she took herself off for a little walk to get out of the way.

And she spoke to Kate, of course, on a daily basis, and went to the hospital in a taxi for her check-up at the fracture clinic, and went to physio, and by the end of the weekend she was tearing her hair out.

'Is your arm sore?' Rebecca asked on Sunday evening.

She looked at the little girl, so like her father that it hurt, and summoned up a smile.

'A bit. Why?'

'Because you're crabby. Mummy was always crabby when she was sore.'

A huge wave of guilt washed over Izzy, and she sat down at the table next to her and gave a wry grin. 'I'm sorry. I'm just feeling a bit trapped and bored.'

'Like wet play,' the child said sagely. 'I hate wet play. We have to stay inside and read or something, and the boys get horrible, and then the teachers get mad with us.'

'You ought to go out with Dad round the farm,' Michael said, wandering in on the tail-end of the conversation and dropping into the chair opposite. 'He likes company. He gets bored on his own, too. Dad, Izzy's bored. You need to take her round the farm with you.'

Izzy's head whipped round. She hadn't realised Will was there, too. How much had he heard, and how ungrateful would he think she was?

She dredged up an apologetic smile. 'I'm sorry. I'm just not used to doing nothing. I don't make a very good patient. I should go back to London, really.'

He looked puzzled. 'And do what?'

She shrugged. 'I could go into the office.'

'Is there anything going on at the moment that only you can do?'

She thought about it for a moment, and was a little shocked to realise that, no, there was nothing that would grind to a halt without her. The only thing she could be doing—would be doing—was drumming up more business, and they frankly didn't need it.

'No,' she replied. 'They can manage without me, I'm sure. Probably glad to be shot of me.'

His mouth twitched into a smile. 'So relax. How are you sleeping?'

She rolled her eyes. 'Not wonderfully well. I wake up early, when the painkillers wear off, and can't get back to sleep again. I'm usually awake when you get up.'

'So come down and have tea with me, and if you feel really energetic you can come out when I feed the stock and let the hens out and milk the cow. Nothing exciting, but it might beat lying in bed bored and hurting.'

It certainly would, for a whole raft of reasons she didn't really want to go into, either with Will or in front of his children, and none of them was anything to do with boredom or pain!

'I'm moving the sheep tomorrow,' he told her. 'The kids will be back at school, so I'll have to get them up and out in time for the bus, but after that I'll be putting the ewes and lambs into the trailer in batches and shipping them over there. You're welcome to join me.'

And so she found herself up at five-thirty the next day, sipping tea while the painkillers kicked in, walking round the yard with Will and watching as he checked the animals, scrubbed out water troughs, mixed feed, forked silage and all the other innumerable things that seemed to be necessary so horribly early in the morning.

Then she sat on a straw bale and watched as he hand-milked Bluebell, the house cow, and the gentle rhythmic slosh of the milk into the bucket nearly sent her to sleep.

It was hardly even light, and yet he'd done half a day's work, and she knew he didn't come upstairs to bed until at least eleven, if not later, shut away in his study battling with the paperwork that she knew he hated.

She was always in her room before he came up, because the pain in her arm was tiring and she was ready to escape from it by nine-thirty or so. She always saved her strongest painkillers for the night, and although she was worried they might be addictive, she thought the most addictive thing about them was the blissful oblivion they brought.

There was no way Will would need anything to bring him oblivion, she thought. No wonder he'd struck her as tired when she'd first seen him at the party the other week. He must be exhausted, and she wondered how on earth he kept going. Will-power and grim determination, most probably, and her lying around all day with a book and a sour expression was probably the last thing he needed.

The milking finished, they went back in and had breakfast with the children. She sat nursing a cup of tea while Will chivvied and coaxed them out of the door with their packed lunches and bags and PE kit, and then, while he made a few phone calls and in an effort to give something back for all his kindness, she loaded the dishwasher one-handed and put it on, then tried to sweep the kitchen floor.

Difficult, with Banjo barking and bouncing round biting the end of the broom and turning the whole procedure into an enormous and very noisy game.

'Banjo, stop it!' she said, laughing helplessly at the dog as his tail lashed and his eyes sparkled with mischief, and when he let go to bark she made a quick swipe for the crumbs under the table. Not quick enough. He seized it again and she shook her head and gave up.

Her hair was sliding out of its band, and she lifted her cast to brush it out of her way and caught sight of Will, standing in the doorway with a curious expression on her face, watching her intently.

Slowly she straightened, the dog and his game forgotten, conscious only of her wildly misbehaving hair and the hectic colour she could feel in her cheeks.

'What is it?' she said, her voice sounding strange to her ears, and he shrugged away from the doorframe and came over to her, taking the brush from her hand.

'Banjo, in your bed,' he said quietly, and the dog turned and walked reluctantly out to the utility room and flopped down with a grunt. Will propped the brush up against the wall, eased the band out of her hair and ordered her to sit. She felt his fingers against her nape and a shiver of something indefinable ran over her skin.

'What are you doing?'

'I was going to brush it.'

'You'll never get a brush through it. It needs a wash, but I can't manage. I can only just about cope with the shower. Your mother helped me with it last week, but it needs doing again desperately and I don't like to ask her. She's so busy.'

'I'll do it for you later,' he promised, and with gentle fingers he drew it back and secured it once more in the band. Then he stepped back, and she had an odd feeling that he was distancing himself from her. It felt curiously lonely.

'I'm going to do the sheep. Still want to come?'

She nodded, and felt her hair trying to escape again. Oh, well, there was nothing she could do about it. Maybe she should have it cut—or get Kate to send her hair straighteners on. In fact, there were so many things she was going to need if she was staying here that it would be impractical to ask Kate to deal with it.

'I'm going to have to go back to London,' she told him, and a quick frown flitted across his face and was gone.

'I thought we sorted that one out yesterday?'

She nodded. 'Yes—but there are things I need if I'm going to stay. I'll have to go back and get them. I can get a minicab to take me.'

The frown was back in force. 'Don't be silly. If you need to go, I'll take you.'

'But you can't! You're busy.'

'No. The weekends are impossible, but I can get cover during the week,' he told her. 'Once the lambs are out at pasture I can get Tim to do most of the work, and my father's always willing to pitch in with enough notice. It won't be a problem. Just give me a couple of days' notice.'

'Wednesday, then?' she said with a wry smile, and he gave a grunt of laughter.

'Take me literally! But Wednesday will be fine. I'll sort it out.'

'I'll ring Kate later—get her primed. I'll need to go in and do one or two things in the office.'

'Fine.' He looked up at the clock. 'Right—we need to move the sheep. You up for it?'

'Just call me Bo Peep,' she said with a grin, and he laughed and squeezed her shoulder briefly before heading for the door.

He kitted her out with boots—his mother's, he said, to her relief—and a thick jumper she'd seen him wear, because although the sun was shining it was only April still, and he'd warned her it could be cold down on the salt marshes at the far side of the farm.

She was glad of it. It took hours, and she saw Banjo's ability to round up the kitchen broom put to good use.

'So he's not just a pretty face,' she said to Will, and he chuckled.

'He's all right. He's young, and a bit too enthusiastic, but he's a good boy, really. He'll be a good sheepdog when he's settled down a bit.'

She thought he seemed pretty darned good now, but what did she know? She just trailed along, keeping Will company and trying not to get too sidetracked by the sight of his muscles rippling as he caught an escaping ewe and manhandled her into the trailer, or picked up a big metal hurdle and swung it round to create a funnel to drive the sheep towards the trailer.

Eye candy. That was what the Americans called it.

She sighed quietly. She might as well enjoy the view. She'd never get close enough to touch.

'How on earth do you get a comb through it?'

'Slowly and carefully and bit by bit,' Izzy replied,

and he stared down at the tangled mess in his hands and sighed.

'Well, I'll try,' he said, not willing to promise anything, and she sat at his feet on the rug in the kitchen, with him on the sofa behind her, his knees bracketing her shoulders and the heat from her body searing him through the fabric of his jeans, and slowly, inch by inch, he worked his way over her hair and turned it from wire wool to smooth, shining wet tresses that lay heavily in his hands.

'Now what?'

She shrugged. 'Don't know. I always put something on it to help style it, either to straighten it or to let the curl out. I don't have anything with me. Try finger-scrunching it.'

He tipped her head back with a blunt finger and brought his head down beside hers so she didn't have to dislocate her neck to see him. 'Finger-scrunching?' he said, a trifle desperately.

'You know, sort of cobble it up in your hands and put the bounce back.'

He gave a strangled laugh. 'I've just spent nearly an hour getting the bounce out of it!' he protested, but nevertheless he tried, and, sure enough, it started to dry with curl rather than frizz. Probably because he'd put half a bottle of conditioner on it to try and settle it down, but now it was drying, and it had shine and bounce and curl, and he sifted his fingers slowly through it over and over again, feeling the weight and texture of it, enjoying the quiet moment with her.

Dragging it out, in fact, because it was the only fee-

ble excuse he had to touch her, and he'd been aching
to touch her for days now.

Weeks.

Hell, years. Twelve long, agonising years.

'Ouch!'

'Sorry.'

He disentangled his finger from the rebellious strand
that had caught it. 'I think that's all I can do,' he said,
and, standing up, he stepped round her and went out
into the study, leaving her sitting on the floor staring
after him and wondering, probably, what on earth she'd
done wrong.

Nothing. Nothing, that was, short of looking too
damn beautiful for her own good, and smelling of soap
and shampoo and warm, desirable woman.

'I'm going to tackle some paperwork,' he growled,
and shut the study door behind himself with a defiant
little bang.

Izzy stared at the door for several long seconds. Well.
So much for thinking they were having a relaxing, intimate little interlude.

He'd dried her hair, and now it was dry he'd gone.
Job done.

She pulled a face, her mouth tucking in at one side
ruefully. One step forward, half a mile back. He hadn't
been slamming doors this morning.

Oh, well. He was taking her back to London on
Wednesday, and if he was as grumpy as this on the
way there, she might not bother to come back.

He wasn't grumpy. He was friendly enough, but a
little distant, and she thought it would have been easier

with a minicab driver. At least she wouldn't have felt obliged to entertain him or worry about his mental health!

They went straight to her apartment, taking the lift up from the underground car park. She'd thought she'd have to bribe the man on the barrier to let them in, but one look at her arm and he agreed they could use one of the empty slots.

'Hussein's away. You can have his space. As it's you, Miss Brooke,' he said, and eyed Will with undisguised curiosity.

She could have done without that, but it was too late now. A cab with a plate on, of course, would have occasioned no comment whatsoever, but Will's elderly Land Rover Discovery, with mud up to the window line, was a bit of a giveaway.

Her apartment looked as if she'd never been away. More correctly, she thought, looking at it in dismay, it looked as if she'd never lived there—as if no one lived there. Where were the personal touches? The piles of books, the clutter of photo frames, the school bag slung in the corner with its contents spilling out?

She even missed the smell of wet dog.

'I need to change out of these things, and I'd better do something with my hair—spray something in it to tame it again. Can you give me a hand to do that in a minute?'

'Sure,' Will said. 'Holler when you need me.' He let himself out onto the roof garden and went over to the railing, leaning on it and staring out across the river with a strange look on his face.

Izzy didn't have the mental energy to work out what

was wrong with him. He was such a complex man, with so many layers, she was discovering, that she had no idea where to start. Had he always been so private, so withdrawn?

No. That had happened some time in the past twelve years, since he'd left her. Probably since Julia's illness. Many people withdrew when they lost a loved one. He might even have depression as a result.

What a curious thought.

She went into her bedroom and opened her wardrobe, and was faced with row upon row of business suits, blouses, skirts, smart trousers, endless high-heeled shoes and boots and strappy sandals. She wouldn't need them on the farm!

She turned instead to her gym kit, and found what she was looking for. Jog bottoms—ones that fitted her, rather than Michael, although she'd been very grateful for them—and wide-sleeved tops that would go over her cast.

She dug out a pair of jeans and some trainers with Velcro, because she'd been wearing a pair of Michael's trainers for the past week, and they were a touch on the small side as well as having laces which she had to have help with.

Then, just out of vanity and to counteract the hugely unsexy outer layers, she opened her underwear drawer and hooked out a heap of froth. Pretty lace, slippery silk, warm to the touch and soft to the skin, gleaming satin and fine, transparent mesh. Nothing weighed more than a few grams, and it would make her feel better.

And her hair straighteners. She threw them on the

pile, although she couldn't use them one-handed, but maybe she could talk Rebecca into helping her.

She gave the door a dubious look, but there was no way Will would come in unless she called him. She stripped off her clothes with difficulty, although she was getting better at it, and went into her bathroom. She couldn't use the power shower, but the hand-held spray over the bath might be quite useful.

She washed herself as thoroughly as she could without soaking the cast, then dried and put on her own deodorant, her own moisturiser, her own perfume—it was wonderful. She started to feel human again, and she was just humming gently as she put the finishing touches to her make-up when there was a tap on the door.

'Just a minute,' she called, and picked up the towel. 'OK.'

He came in and hesitated, his eyes raking over her, and then he closed them and let out a ragged sigh. 'Izzy, for God's sake,' he groaned. 'Give a man a break and cover yourself up.'

And then she realised with dismay that she was standing in front of the mirrored wall behind the basin, and although she was holding the towel up in front, there was nothing behind her but the lingering mist from her shower to keep her from his eyes.

'I'm sorry,' she muttered, flustered now, and went out into the bedroom and reached for the pile of underwear. She picked up the first pair of knickers she found, if you could call them that. A thong, the briefest briefs in all the world, designed to wear under a lace dress and be invisible.

Oh, well. She pulled them on one-handed, muttering at the elastic which managed to twist as she pulled them up, and then she was dragging on her jeans and the loose cotton top that she'd found which would hopefully go over the cast.

But, of course, she couldn't do up the jeans one-handed, especially not since Mrs T's cooking, and with a sigh of exasperation she turned to Will.

'OK, you can open your eyes now. Can you help me with the zip, please?'

He looked down at the yawning vee in the front of her jeans, the skin behind so slightly covered by the fine mesh and lace of her invisible underwear, and his mouth tightened.

He's angry, she thought, but his hands were gentle. He drew the edges of her waistband together, fastened the stud and slid up the zip without comment, then stepped back out of range.

'Is this what you're taking?' he asked, looking at the bed.

She was sitting on the edge of the bed, shoving her feet into the trainers, and she glanced over her shoulder at the heap of clothes. 'Yes. There's a soft bag in the bottom of the wardrobe at that end. They should all fit in there.'

He produced it, his fingers automatically caressing the butter-soft brown leather, and she remembered how tactile he'd always been, how sensitive to texture. Was that still true, with his hands so calloused from working on the farm? Or was the pleasure of touch now lost to him?

How sad that would be, she thought.

He held the bag open with one hand and stuffed the clothes in with the other, handling her underwear as if it contained live snakes. She suppressed the urge to laugh, but then he looked up and his face was tautly controlled, and she felt the laughter drain away. He probably thought she was hopelessly frivolous and impractical.

'That everything?' he asked, and she nodded.

'My wash things are ready, on the side in the bathroom. I'll get them.'

She went round him, careful to give him a wide berth, and retrieved her toiletries from the shelf. They slotted neatly into another little bag made for the purpose, and then she truly was ready.

'Nothing else?'

She shook her head. 'I don't think so. Do you think I've forgotten anything?'

'Nightclothes?'

She shrugged. 'I thought I'd carry on sleeping in a T-shirt. It's easy.'

He growled something under his breath and hoisted the bags into one hand. 'Right. Let's go.'

He left her to follow him, and she caught up with him in the big open living room.

'Do you want a drink before we go, or shall we get something downstairs?'

'What about going to the office?'

She shrugged again. 'I thought we could do that after lunch, if you're not in a hurry, but since you obviously are we can go now. We'll grab something to eat on the way home.'

She pressed the button to close the roof garden door,

then found her lift pass and opened the door with a smile. 'Shall we go?'

Definitely should have come in a minicab, she thought as they threaded their way through the traffic. He got lost once, because she was distracted, and had to go a longer way round. It didn't matter, really, but it obviously irritated him, and she was getting ready to tell him to go back alone when they arrived at the office.

There was no problem with parking there, of course. They went straight into her space, since her car was at her apartment, where she kept it, and up in the lift to her office to be greeted with delight and concern by Kate.

'How long are you going to be?' Will asked when the kerfuffle had died down a little and everyone had exclaimed over the cast and tutted at the bags under her eyes.

'Not long. Why? Did you want to do something?'

It was his turn to shrug. 'Thought I might take a stroll—too much sitting about.'

'Give me an hour,' she said, and he nodded and went back out to the lifts, leaving her at Kate's mercy.

Kate took her by the arm and all but towed her into her office. 'How *are* you? It's really good to see you again—I've been so worried. How does it feel?'

Izzy scowled at her hand and flexed her sore, swollen fingers in disgust. 'Not wonderful. It keeps me awake at night.'

'Sure it's not him?' Kate teased, and Izzy felt her colour rise.

'Don't be ridiculous. Didn't you see how impatient

he was? He's a reluctant hero if ever I met one. I think he's feeling a bit trapped by his better nature at the moment, so we'd better not take too long. What's been happening?'

Kate rolled her eyes. 'Where do you want me to start? I've had Daniel O'Keeffe on the phone at least twice a day, begging you to go back. I've explained you've broken your arm, and anyway you aren't interested, but the man seems to have gone deaf. And Steve is driving me crazy. He wants you, Izzy, and you're going to have to tell him to take a hike. I can't, and he's pestering me for your landline number. I told him I don't know it and your mobile's broken.'

'Oh, damn, I forgot the charger,' she said. 'We're going to have to go back to my place.' She thought of Will's reluctance to spend any more time in there, but it was too bad. She needed her phone, she needed her independence, and she needed—

She needed to be back here, with her arm working and her freedom back, she thought, but it was curiously unappealing. Out of the blue she had a much better idea, and it didn't necessarily involve Will at all.

'How do you fancy closing the office and having a few weeks off, Kate? We can leave Ally to tell everyone that we're on annual shutdown, or something, and we can keep in touch with the employment agency staff and make sure there aren't any problems. It's years since we played hooky. I reckon it's time.'

Kate's jaw dropped. 'Close the office?' she squeaked, and opened and shut her mouth a few more times without saying anything at all apart from 'But—!' and 'I mean...' and things like that.

Izzy grinned at her. 'I take it that's a yes?'

'Oh, yes! Oh, boy, is it a yes! And you know what? I'm going to go to Australia to see my mother. I haven't seen her for two years, and she keeps nagging. Izzy, I love you!'

She hugged her, suddenly remembering her arm when the cast caught them both in the ribs, and then she stood back and looked long and hard at Izzy.

'Will you be all right? Truly? He looked a bit cross.'

'Will?' She shrugged. 'He's just in a bit of a grump for some reason. I may not include him in my plans. I mean, he's been very kind to me, but he obviously doesn't want me around. I'll go away somewhere—lie in the sun somewhere exotic and read trashy novels and drink blue cocktails and fend off the press. I might even find a man to rub in my sunscreen,' she joked.

Then she noticed a fleeting panic on Kate's face and turned to see Will standing in the doorway, his eyes curiously expressionless.

'I did knock,' he said. 'You didn't hear me. I'm ready when you are.'

And he turned on his heel and walked out.

'Oops,' she said softly, wondering just how much he'd heard. 'Better go. I'll leave you to tell everyone about the office—keep them all on full pay, and tell them we'll be back on the first of June. Dream up something appropriate for the answer-machine so Ally doesn't have to deal with all the calls for this office as well as the other one. You'd better tell her to contact me on my mobile, initially, until I know where I'll be. And have fun, and thank you for everything.'

She kissed Kate's cheek and hugged her briefly, then went out into the reception area.

Will was standing there staring out of the window again, and she smiled at him brightly. 'All set,' she said, and he nodded curtly and headed towards the lift.

Oh, rats. Whatever he'd heard hadn't improved his mood at all, she realised, and could have kicked herself for making that stupid crack about finding a man. Nothing could have been further from her thoughts, and the idea that he would now think that of her was curiously painful.

Still, trying to explain would only make the hole deeper. The only thing to do was to stop digging, and so she followed him in silence, suddenly aware of the unfamiliar sensation of butterflies dancing madly in her insides.

CHAPTER EIGHT

HE WAS silent in the lift, all the way down to the car park level, then helped her into his car and edged out into the traffic without a word.

'I need to go back to my apartment,' she told him. 'I've forgotten my phone charger.'

Did he sigh? If he did, it was under his breath, but it was irrelevant. She was well aware of the fact that he was less than happy. What she didn't know was why, but it didn't matter. She'd be out of his hair soon. She had a check-up at the hospital on Friday, and after that she'd go away and leave him in peace. She couldn't see him complaining.

'Have you had anything to eat or drink yet?' she asked, hoping he'd say no so she could suggest popping into the café in her apartment block, but he nodded.

'I grabbed a coffee and a roll round the corner,' he said, and fell back into silence.

So much for that idea, then.

They turned into the underground parking lane and were waved through with a broad smile. The lift whisked them silently up to her apartment, and she left him hovering in the living room while she went into the bedroom to pick up her phone charger.

It was plugged in, of course, down behind the bedside cabinet, where she could only reach it with her left arm. Her right just couldn't get round the corner, and there was no way she had the strength in her left hand even to flick the switch, far less pull the plug out of the wall.

And that meant asking Will.

She went back out and found him on the roof terrace again, staring blindly out over the horizon, his face forbidding.

'Will?'

He turned, and for a second there was a raw pain in his eyes that took her breath away. Then it was gone, replaced by a half-smile that barely touched his mouth. 'What is it?'

The pain had shocked her, and for a second she couldn't think straight. 'Um—I can't unplug the phone charger. It's behind the bedside table and I can't reach with my right hand.'

Was that alarm that flickered in his eyes? Surely not. Had he really been so embarrassed by the incident earlier that he was worried about being in her bedroom? How silly. He hadn't shown any sign of worrying in her bedroom in his house, so why here? It wasn't as if he'd seen anything he hadn't seen before, after all.

And what had that pain been about? He must have been thinking about Julia, missing her, desperate to get Izzy out of his life so he could go back to grieving alone. Oh, damn. And she was making it so much harder for him.

He followed her back to her room and hunkered down by the bedside cabinet, pulling out the plug and coiling up the flex without a word.

'Thank you.'

He didn't even look at her. 'Right, is there anything else, or can we get the hell out of here now?' he asked bluntly, and the shock of it brought her to her senses.

She'd had enough. She'd loved him, for heaven's sake. He'd loved her. She was the injured party in all this, and there was no justification for giving her the cold shoulder. If he didn't want her staying with him, all he had to do was say so, not just freeze her out.

'You didn't have to be here,' she reminded him just as bluntly. 'I suggested a minicab. This was your idea.'

'Well, it was a lousy one,' he growled.

That was it. She tipped her head on one side, put her hands on her hips and glared at him. 'Have I done something specific to make you hate me, or is it just habit?' she asked without preamble.

His hands stilled, and then he rose slowly to his full height, the charger dangling forgotten from his fingers.

'What makes you think I hate you?' he asked, his voice incredulous.

She laughed shortly. 'The fact that you've hardly spoken a word to me all day? The fact that you can't seem to stand to look at me? You *asked* me to stay, Will. It wasn't my idea—but you don't have to worry. I'm leaving, just as soon as I've had my check-up on Friday—maybe even before then.'

'And going on holiday somewhere exotic to drink cocktails with some man you've picked up on the beach—what's the matter, Izzy?' he said bitterly. 'That door not revolving fast enough for you these days?' He gave her bedroom door a pointed look, and she stared at him in astonishment.

'You bastard,' she said slowly. 'You know that's just empty rumour.'

'Do I?' He gave a hollow, strangled laugh and rammed one hand through his hair. 'I'm not sure I know anything any more, except that this is tearing me apart. You really think I can't stand to be around you? I must be a better actor than I thought.'

The anger drained out of her, and the butterflies started up again in earnest. 'I don't understand,' she said unsteadily.

He put the phone charger down and moved towards her, slowly but surely. 'Don't you? Look at me, Izzy. Really look at me. What do you see?'

She looked, and her breath jammed in her throat.

Hunger. Dear God. Raw, elemental hunger—a hunger so great it should have terrified her. It didn't. It was her own hunger that did that—hunger for a man who'd already told her there was no future for them. Hunger for a man she hadn't forgotten in twelve years, and never would.

She lifted her hand towards him, then it fell to her side.

'Can you see it, Izzy?' he asked softly, his voice changed almost beyond recognition. 'How much I need you? You see, the simple truth is I can hardly keep my hands off you. Helping you, having you around for the last few days and having to do things for you—that's been bad enough. Drying your hair the other night was torture—and coming in here earlier and seeing you wearing little more than your cast and a squirt of perfume—I nearly lost it, Izzy. And I'm going to lose it now if we don't get out of here soon.'

The butterflies disappeared, banished at a stroke by his words. He wasn't angry with her. He didn't hate her. He wanted her—wanted her, for heaven's sake! She nearly laughed aloud with relief.

Instead she lifted her hand again, and this time she slid it gently but firmly round the back of his neck and drew him down to meet her mouth.

'So lose it, Will,' she said softly. 'Lose it with me.'

He sucked in his breath sharply, but then let it out on a ragged sigh and lifted his head. 'I can't—we can't. Not unless you're on the Pill or whatever.'

She dropped her head forwards against his chest and let out a groan of frustration. 'I'm not. Why would I be? I don't do this, Will. Ever—despite what the gossips say.'

He stepped back. 'Then let's get out of here—now, while we still can.'

But she didn't want to. She shook her head and smiled. 'No. Wait. I've got an idea. There's a machine in the gym.'

She backed away from him, then turned and ran out of her apartment, grabbing her bag and her key on the way. She went down in the lift to the gym, and as luck would have it bumped straight into Freddie.

'Iz—hey, what have you done?'

'Broken my arm. Sorry. Won't be in for a while. I've just come to see if I left something in the changing rooms,' she ad-libbed. 'Sorry, Freddie, got to fly. I'm going up to Suffolk in a minute. I'll see you when I'm back.'

And she shot into the changing room with a sigh of relief, then rummaged in her purse for money.

Amazingly she had the right change, and there was no one about. She shoved the money in the slot, pulled open the drawer with shaking fingers and reached in just as a voice called her name.

Damn. Of all the times—!

'Izzy! How are you? Haven't seen you for ages!'

'Oh, hi, Maggie,' she said, slamming the drawer shut and dropping the condoms into her bag. 'I'm fine.'

Maggie's eyes went from the dispenser to Izzy and her brows arched as her smile widened. 'Yes, I can see that. Well, well.'

Inspiration struck. Izzy looked at the dispenser, smacked her forehead with her palm and laughed. 'What an idiot! I've used the wrong machine—I wanted tampons! Oh, rats.'

She rummaged again for change, but then didn't have enough, and Maggie kindly lent her some.

'Thanks. You're a star. Sorry, got to go—personal emergency!' she said breathlessly, and all but ran out. She made it back to the apartment without bumping into anyone else, and went back into the bedroom on a bubble of laughter.

'You won't believe it—'

Will wasn't there. He wasn't in the living room, either, and panic started to rise in her chest—and then she heard the shower running. Her heart slowed and she closed her eyes. Thank God. For a horrible moment—

She went back into the bedroom and perched on the end of the bed, kicked off her trainers and waited. Moments later he emerged, a towel tied round his waist, his hair roughly dried and dripping rivulets down over his broad, solid chest.

'Any joy?'

She waggled the packet at him, and his shoulders dropped about three inches. His sigh of relief was heartfelt, and with a laugh she went into his arms.

This was Will—the Will she'd fallen in love with when she'd been just a girl on the brink of womanhood.

He'd been little more than a boy then, but not now. Now he was most emphatically a man, and for all the burning hunger that blazed in his eyes he didn't seem in any hurry. He lowered his head slowly and brushed her lips with his once, twice, before he settled his mouth over hers and kissed her thoroughly.

He didn't touch her elsewhere, except to steady her shoulders with his strong, hard hands, and the urgency went out of her.

He was right. They'd waited twelve years for this. There was no hurry now. She gave herself up to sensation...

She was beautiful.

He propped himself up on one elbow and waited patiently for her to wake. There was no rush. He was enjoying the view—not the glorious panorama of the river through the window, but the lush, tender curves and softly shadowed hollows of her body. He felt his own stirring again, and smiled sadly.

To think he'd imagined he was strong enough to walk away from this again.

He'd done it once, and it had been the hardest thing

he'd ever done in his life. He couldn't do it again, and yet he knew it would come to that.

Whatever. He'd take what he could get, and deal with the other later.

He trailed a finger up the underside of her arm, flung above her head like a sleeping child. Yet she was no child, this woman who'd taken him into her body with such tenderness and rapture. He felt his heart contract. There was so much she didn't know, so much he should have told her.

But there was time. He'd tell her when she woke.

Leaning forwards, he pressed his lips to the soft, cool skin of her midriff. She stirred, murmuring his name sleepily, and he moved up, trailing his tongue over her nipple and blowing over the damp skin. It puckered, and her eyes fluttered open, soft and unfocused.

'Well, hello there,' he murmured, his mouth kicking up in an involuntary smile.

Her mouth curved in answer, and she lifted herself on her right elbow and kissed his lips. He toyed with her mouth, savouring the moment, then lifted his head, staring down at her in wonder.

'We need to talk,' he said softly.

She lay back against the pillows. 'No.'

'Yes. There are things you need to know—about me and Julia—'

'No.' She put her finger on his lips, silencing him. 'No, Will. Please. It's over—in the past. I don't want to know. It doesn't matter any more. All that matters is this—what we are to each other now. Please—just give me this.'

He couldn't argue—not when her eyes were still

glazed from their loving. With a quiet sigh he drew her gently into his arms and covered her mouth with his.

The journey home—odd how she thought of it as home—was nothing like their journey into London that morning.

They didn't talk much this time, either, at least at first, but their silence was one of contentment. They didn't need to talk. Their bodies had said all there was to say, and for a large part of the journey their hands lay linked together between them, his fingers idly caressing hers as he drove one-handed up the A12.

The traffic was reasonably light at that time of the evening, and there was no hurry. He'd phoned his parents earlier, and asked if they could watch over the children and make sure the stock were all OK, and they'd been all right about it, he said.

Izzy looked across at him now, the strong planes of his face visible intermittently in the headlights of oncoming cars.

'OK?' she asked, and he threw her a smile.

'Never better. You?'

Her smile grew wider. 'Me too. How long till we're there?'

He shrugged. 'Half an hour? Three-quarters, maybe?'

'What about the children? Are they at your parents' house or yours?'

'Ours,' he said, and for a moment she thought he was referring to them as a couple. Then she realised he was talking about him and the children—his immediate family, to which, of course she didn't belong. It was a sobering thought.

'I would have thought your mother would want to be in her own home,' she said, and he gave her a slightly crooked smile.

'Well, it is, in a way. Was for years. And it's easier during term-time to get the kids settled in their own beds and make sure their homework's done. They'll use any excuse to fail to do it.'

Izzy tried to imagine babysitting her grandchildren at some point in the future and couldn't. It was too far removed from everything that was familiar to her, and she wasn't sure she'd know where to begin. 'Won't she be bored?'

He laughed. 'Not a chance. She's doing a bit of baking, but she's had to bring everything with her. She wanted to try out some recipes and she needs all her strange ingredients. I don't tend to have a lot in the house.'

Izzy chuckled. 'She mentioned that,' she said, and then she wondered what Mrs T was thinking about their delayed return. 'When you asked her to babysit—what did you tell her?' she asked him thoughtfully.

He shrugged. 'Oh—just that you'd had more to do in the office than you'd anticipated, and that we were hungry and we'd decided to stop to eat and give the traffic time to die down.'

'The truth, then,' she teased with a smile, and he laughed.

'You want me to tell her the truth?'

She thought of their wild and passionate lovemaking and felt her colour rise. 'Good grief, no!' she said firmly. 'Anything but! On a need-to-know basis, your mother doesn't.'

'Well, at least we agree about that. In fact, since we're on the subject, we could do with some ground rules here, Izzy.'

Ground rules? A line drawn in the sand that she wouldn't overstep? She was hurt that he should consider it necessary to mention it, and so her tone was sharper than it might have been. 'Let me guess—no sex in the house, no cuddling in front of the children, no talking dirty in the utility room when we think the kids are out of earshot—what kind of an idiot do you think I am, Will?'

He had the grace to look embarrassed. 'I'm sorry, but—they're my kids, Izzy. They've been through a lot. This is their mother we're talking about.'

Actually, she'd thought they were talking about themselves, but apparently not. She sighed deeply and rubbed her good hand over her face. 'I'm sorry, too. I didn't mean to snap. Of course we don't want to do anything to draw attention to our relationship, either in front of the children or anyone else, for that matter. I've had enough attention from the media about affairs I *haven't* had without drawing their attention to one I am having.'

He looked slightly startled. 'Media?' he said, as if the thought hadn't even occurred to him. But why should it? He didn't live in the glare of publicity like she did.

'That's why I don't like eating out anywhere except the apartment block, or very occasionally that wine bar if it's quiet,' she explained. 'I should be safe up here, because the local press aren't looking for me. I'm not nearly as interesting as an oil spill in the North Sea or a thatched cottage on fire. I'm sure they won't bother with me if I keep my head down, but if I start making waves—well, they'll have a field-day, and you'll be the ones to suffer.'

His mouth tightened. 'So let's not do anything to provoke it. I don't want the kids involved in anything sordid like that.'

'And I do?' she said, piqued again. 'Don't worry, Will. Like I said, *I* won't be doing anything to attract attention.'

They fell silent again, but this time it wasn't a comfortable silence. Their conversation had simply served to underline the huge gulf between them. For a short while Izzy had allowed herself to believe that everything would be all right, but now she could see that she'd been wildly optimistic.

It was an affair—that was all. Nothing more, nothing less, and there was no point in trying to talk it up to herself. She was his house-guest, an old flame, and a willing one at that. They had been thrown together, and only a fool or a saint would turn down an opportunity like that.

And Will Thompson had never been either.

Will was finding it increasingly difficult to stick to those stupid ground rules. He was up at five-thirty, and sometimes Izzy came down to the kitchen with him, warm and tousled from sleep, and the urge to drag her straight back up the stairs and into his bed was practically overwhelming.

So he'd growl at her, and then he'd feel her withdrawing from him, and he'd want to kick himself for being so insensitive. Or over-sensitive, more like—over-sensitive to her presence, her wide-open smile and the promise in her eyes.

He ached for her with a physical pain, and working himself to death was the only way round it. So he worked. He shifted the muck heap, a messy job he'd been meaning to do for ages, and relocated the chickens onto fresh ground, and tore the roof off the old cow barn and replaced it—all on top of his normal hectic workload—just so he didn't have the time or the energy to think about her.

It was a week before she pulled him up on it.

He was in the study, struggling with the endless paperwork and hardly able to keep his eyes open, and she came in, dressed in a pair of loose pyjama trousers and a baggy T-shirt, and perched on the edge of his desk, right in his way.

'We need to talk,' she said firmly, and he slammed down the pen and glared up at her.

'No. We need to make love,' he said, and the expressions chasing across her face would have made him laugh if he hadn't been so desperate.

And then she smiled. 'I agree. But when? And where? You haven't sat down in the last week—you've hardly paused long enough to swallow your food. Your children don't recognise you any more—do you know how much time I've spent with them in the evenings?'

Guilt washed over him, and he scrubbed his face with his hands and pressed his fingertips into his tired, tired eyes.

'Izzy, I'm sorry,' he said gruffly. 'I didn't mean to do that to you—I just wasn't thinking. I was trying not to, in fact. You're driving me crazy.'

She bent over and pressed her lips to his. 'Shh. Don't worry. What are you doing tomorrow?'

'Tomorrow?' He felt his body stir with reaction. 'I don't know. You tell me—you've obviously got something up your sleeve.'

'I'd like to visit the lambs with you, and take a picnic, and go down to the river and have lunch. We could spread a blanket out under the trees—'

'And make love in broad daylight? Are you crazy?' He laughed, his bottom lip caught between his teeth, the idea hideously appealing. That was where he'd kissed her the first time, where it had all started, and he only had to think about it and he needed her. 'Hell, Izzy, don't do this to me.'

'We could just spend time together—eat, rest a little. We don't have to—well, you know.'

'Yes, we do,' he said softly. 'I need to hold you so badly.'

'You can hold me. You can hold me now.'

He shook his head. 'The kids,' he said, conscious as ever of their presence just overhead. He couldn't do that to them—not with Izzy, who could never settle here with them and be part of a permanent family. If they walked in they'd start asking questions, and they'd be entitled to answers.

And he had none to give them that were even remotely suitable for their ears.

'A picnic?' he said, going back to Izzy's earlier suggestion, and she nodded.

'I thought I could get some things from the café during the morning and we could set off late morning. Do the lambs first—'

'No. We'll have lunch first, then check the lambs. If I'm going to get that close to you, I want a shower first.'

Probably a cold one.

He looked down at the desk and sighed. 'If you could just get that delectable bottom off my paperwork, I'll be able to finish off here and get some sleep, or I'll be dozing off in mid-picnic.'

She chuckled and stood up, turning to look down at the endless piles of stuff.

'Good grief,' she said weakly. 'What is this lot?'

He shrugged. 'Mostly dealt with but unfiled. There's all sorts of stuff that could be thrown out, I expect, but I don't know where to begin. Paperwork's not my thing.'

'But it is mine. Could I help you? Sort through it, try and make some sense of it? Have you got a filing cabinet?'

'Yeah—behind the door. It's virtually empty.'

She looked from the cabinet to the desk to him, and shook her head in mock despair. Or maybe not mock. He felt his mouth tighten.

'I'm sorry. It's not my strong point.'

'It isn't, is it? But don't worry, you have all sorts of other sterling qualities which more than make up for it. I'll have a look through it all tomorrow and see if I can tackle it. I might need your help for some of it.'

He snorted. 'I don't doubt it. My mother used to do it all, but she's too busy now, and anyway, it's all farm stuff and she's got enough to do with her own accounts and records.'

'I'll do it. Don't worry. Why don't you come up to bed now? You look shattered and it's after midnight already.'

'Come up to bed?' he said weakly. 'Hell, Izzy, you know how to push my buttons, don't you?'

She coloured softly. 'You know perfectly well what I mean,' she said, her brisk voice quite at odds with the warm blush on her cheeks and the sensual aware- ness lingering in those beautiful soft green eyes. 'I'm going up. I'll see you tomorrow.'

He pushed the chair back and drew her into his arms. 'I'm sorry—sorry it's so difficult, sorry I'm so tired, sorry I'm so crabby. How's your arm these days? I haven't even asked.'

Her smile was gentle and forgiving, and just made him feel worse. 'It's OK. Hurts a bit sometimes if I overdo it, but otherwise it's all right.'

He nodded, then, unable to help himself, he bent his head and kissed her. His hands slid down over her bot- tom, cupping the firm swell and easing her against him. Heat rocketed through him, and with a ragged groan he dragged his mouth away from hers and stepped back.

'Go on—go up. We'll continue this tomorrow.'

'I'll hold you to that,' she said softly, and her smile nearly had him reaching for her again. It would have done, if she hadn't slipped through the door and pulled it firmly closed behind her.

He sat down carefully at the desk, conscious only of

the tightness of his jeans and the promise of tomorrow. To hell with the paperwork. He couldn't concentrate.

Yanking the door open, he strode through to the kitchen, tugged on his coat, shoved his feet into his boots and did one final and quite unnecessary stock check.

Anything rather than stay in the house and listen to Izzy's bed creaking gently as she climbed back into it and snuggled down under the quilt alone.

'Tomorrow,' he told himself, and Banjo wagged his tail and grinned. He ruffled the dog's ears. 'You don't know the half of it, mate,' he said affectionately. 'Come on. Time for bed.'

And, please God, he'd have the self-control to walk upstairs past her door and keep on going.

CHAPTER NINE

Izzy couldn't believe it. He'd actually gone along with her plans for the picnic and not found some feeble excuse!

She hadn't really expected him to agree. He'd done everything in his power to keep out of her way since they'd come back from London, and she'd been starting to wonder if he was regretting making love to her. Talking to him last night, she'd decided that the only thing he was regretting was that they couldn't find the opportunity to do it again.

She'd spent the week wandering aimlessly about, chatting to Mrs T, reading and trying to keep out of his way. Emma had rescued her on Monday and taken her out for lunch, and they'd had a long chat which had done nothing more than underline for Izzy just how far removed her lifestyle was from that of all her old friends.

Emma had asked about Izzy's job, and looked stunned and dumbfounded when she'd explained what she actually did with her days.

'Good grief! I couldn't do that.'

'And I couldn't bring up three children.'

'How about two?' Emma asked, and Izzy just laughed at her friend's unsubtle fishing.

'I don't think so.'

'So—how are things with Will?' Emma asked, apparently changing the subject and yet not doing so at all, and Izzy just shook her head in apparent amusement and took the remark at face value.

'Will's fine, as far as I know,' she told her. 'To be honest, I hardly ever see him. He's so busy on the farm it's ridiculous, and he works in the office until after midnight.'

Emma tutted. 'He always looks exhausted. I used to think he was trying to get over Julia, but maybe it's just that there's too much to do and not enough people to do it.'

And, with that in mind, on the morning of the picnic Izzy went over to the café early to organise the food so she could go and make a start on the office as soon as it was all arranged.

'A picnic?' Mrs T exclaimed, and beamed hugely. 'What a wonderful idea! Oh, Izzy—now, what have we got? Pepper flan's on again, or there's a chicken and bacon tart, and I can always make you up some sandwiches. I know what Will likes—how about you? What should I put in for you?'

She shook her head, totally bemused by the choice. 'Everything looks wonderful,' she said, staring into the chiller. I can never decide. Just give us whatever you've got too much of.'

Mrs T clicked her tongue disapprovingly. 'Nonsense. You go. I'll find you something not too messy to eat that you can manage with one hand, and I'll put in a bottle of water and a flask of coffee. All right?'

'On one condition.'

'What's that?'

'This is my treat for him. I want you to let me pay for it.'

Mrs T looked at her sternly and drew herself up. 'You'll do no such thing. You're a guest here, and a very welcome one, and Will's my son. I wouldn't dream of charging either of you for any of it, and I'm insulted that you should find it necessary.'

Izzy closed her eyes and sighed. 'I'm sorry. I didn't mean to offend you, but I've been here day and night, abusing your hospitality—'

'Fiddlesticks. I'm not offended. I'm just not letting you pay. Go on, go and make yourself beautiful—not that that will take you long.'

Izzy laughed wryly. 'I don't know so much. My hair—'

'I'll come over and give you a hand with it again tonight,' she promised.

'Thanks. Right, I'd better go, I promised Will I'd have a look at the study for him and try and sort out that mountain of paper.'

'Good grief! Well, if you're going to tackle that lot I'd better put in a few extra calories and a dash of brain-food! I don't envy you, dear. I don't suppose you have the slightest idea what you've taken on.'

Oh, she did. Or she thought she did, until she went in there and started sifting through the piles. It seemed to fall into three groups—obvious rubbish, domestic paperwork and things related to the farm.

Rubbish first, she thought, and, retrieving a bin bag from the kitchen drawer, hung it over the front of one of the filing cabinet drawers and heaved all the junk mail, newspapers, three-year old telephone directories and the like into it.

That made a huge difference. Then she separated farm from home, and then subdivided home again, into things about school, utility bills and so on.

The farm would be harder, and she'd need to take advice on that, but by the time Will came in at twelve and stuck his head round the door a goodly portion of the massive oak desk was visible.

'Good grief!' He did a mild double-take and stared at her. 'Where did it all go?'

She pointed at the bin bag, and a look of panic so great it was almost comical crossed his face. 'It's all right. Anything I wasn't utterly sure of is still here on the desk.'

His shoulders dropped and he grinned faintly. 'OK. Sorry. Right, going to shower—if the picnic's still on?'

She smiled. 'Oh, yes.'

'Right.' His eyes closed, and his Adam's apple worked furiously for a second. 'OK. Give me two minutes.'

He was at the top of the stairs in three strides, and as she walked through to the kitchen a moment later he crossed the landing wearing nothing more than the water from the shower. Smiling to herself, she retrieved the picnic basket Mrs T had packed from the stone shelf in the larder, where it was keeping cool, and by the time she'd closed the larder door he was back in the kitchen, his jeans yanked up more or less over his hips, his shirt being roughly tucked in as he hopped across the floor putting on his shoes.

'I would have waited,' she said with a smile, and he gave a wry chuckle.

'I just don't want to waste any time,' he said, and, taking the basket from her, ushered her out to the Discovery.

And there, on the passenger seat, was a bunch of willow catkins and hawthorn tied round with a long blade of grass to make a posy.

She picked it up reverently and turned to him, going up on tiptoe and kissing his cheek wordlessly. Then she climbed up into the car, and he slammed the door and went round to his side, sliding in beside her and firing up the engine in one. He dumped the basket on her lap, almost crushing the posy in his haste, and then headed off down the field behind the farm and over the rise towards the river.

'We used to take the tractor—can you remember?' he said with a grin, and she nodded.

'With a flat trailer on the back, and we'd all sit on it and bounce about. We were younger then.'

'Yes.'

Such a world of meaning in one small word. Younger, and free of responsibility and thought and care. They'd had no idea then how fate would take their carefully made plans and turn them on their heads.

In the past, she reminded herself. Live for now.

He was pulling up in the glorious sunshine just beside the willows and alders in their special place. He cut the engine, and they sat for a moment just listening to the beautiful sounds of the day.

Miles away on the other side of the river someone

called their dog, and the spell was broken. Will looked across at her and gave a grim smile.

'You do realise that if we spread that blanket out on the grass, I'm going to make love to you.'

'I'm counting on it,' she said softly.

'It's broad daylight.'

'There's no one here. That person was miles away.'

He swallowed hard, his throat working. 'If I had any sense at all, I wouldn't even take off my seat belt.'

'That would be very uncomfortable,' Izzy said with an impish grin, and he gave a resigned laugh and unclipped it.

'You're a wicked woman.'

'And you love me,' she said, quite without thinking, but he was already getting out of the car and either didn't hear or chose to ignore it, to her great relief.

He took a blanket from the back, told the dog to stay and relieved Izzy of the basket. He spread out the blanket on the soft, sweet spring grass, and set the picnic basket down right in the middle of it, then sat cross-legged on one side.

Hiding a smile, Izzy sat on the other side facing him, and uncovered the basket. 'Goodness knows what's in here; it was your mother's choice.'

'If it's food, it'll be wonderful,' he said, and took a slice of the chicken and bacon tart. 'Dig in. You're going to have to eat loads so she's not offended.'

'Don't. I've already offended her once over this by trying to pay—'

'What? Izzy, you should know her better.'

'I would have gone to the supermarket but I can't drive.'

He shook his head. 'Just eat—but not too much. You can have more later.'

He broke off a piece of the tart and fed it to her, making her lean across and take it with her mouth, and she realised he was looking down her top.

'What is that?' he asked, his voice gruff.

'What?'

'That thing that under other circumstances I might have called a bra.'

She laughed self-consciously. 'It is a bra.'

He shook his head. 'No. It's closely related, by the look of it, to that crazy scrap of nonsense that nearly drove me mad last time, when you made me zip up your jeans. You remember?'

She remembered. 'Close. Same make.'

He groaned and put the slice of tart down. 'To hell with food. Come here. If I don't kiss you I think I'm going to die.'

'I doubt it,' she said, but she went anyway, shifting the basket out of reach and lying down on her back beside him.

'Better,' he said, and then his mouth came down and claimed hers in a fiercely passionate kiss that started as it meant to go on. There was nothing subtle or coaxing about it, just hot and hungry and demanding, and it drove her wild with desire.

'Will?'

'It's OK. I'm sorry. I've just wanted to do that so much.' His fingers were busy sliding up her top, unfastening the front clip of her bra, brushing aside the insubstantial wisp of cleverly cut lace that somehow managed to support her and yet could reduce him to this. How amazing.

His mouth was busy with one breast, his right hand with the other. Then he switched breasts, and his hand was free to roam. He pushed down her jog bottoms and groaned.

'Hell's teeth, they're *worse*,' he muttered gruffly, and dropped a hot, heady kiss on the tiny panel of lace. Then he lifted his head. 'I want you, Izzy,' he said, and his voice was taut, his face expressionless except for the blue fire burning in his eyes. 'I want you like I've never wanted anyone, but we can't do this here.'

Disappointment washed over her, but then common sense followed and she drew him down into her arms, careful not to scrape him with the cast, and cradled his head against hers.

'It's all right,' she said. 'Just hold me.'

He wrapped her against his chest and rolled onto his back, taking her with him. 'If things were different,' he said after a long silence, 'if I didn't have the kids, and you didn't have the press after you everywhere you went, and our lives ever touched—'

He didn't say any more, but he didn't need to. He was telling her yet again that this was all they could have, and she already knew that.

'Shh,' she said, pressing a kiss to the hard, rough angle of his jaw. He'd showered, but he hadn't shaved since the morning, and the slight scrape of stubble on her lips was curiously intoxicating. She kissed him again, trailing her lips over his skin, enjoying the sensation, and he turned his head and captured her lips with his.

This kiss was soft and tender, a gentle unwinding, although she could tell his body was still as taut as a bowstring and raging with need.

'We ought to eat something,' he said after a while, 'and then we should get on. We've got the lambs to check, and I've got a million and one other things to do before I milk Bluebell.'

'You ought to teach me to do it one-handed,' she said with a grin, and he laughed softly.

'You've got quite enough to do in the study—if you can bring yourself to tackle it.'

'I'll tackle it. It won't take long,' she promised, and levered herself up. 'You stay there. I'll feed you.'

He was going to scream with frustration. Her picnic had been a lovely idea, but it had just cranked up the heat another notch and left him even hungrier for the things he couldn't have.

'We're going to have to go back to London,' he said. 'Invent an excuse—you might need the office,' he suggested.

She laughed. 'They all know it's shut. They'd see straight through it.'

'Shopping?'

She gave him a blunt look. 'You, shopping? If I was going shopping, I wouldn't take you. I'd be allowed chainstore white underwear.'

'Don't. It can be very sexy.'

'You think all underwear's sexy,' she said, and he chuckled and turned down the track towards the sheep, glancing as he always did towards Mrs Jenks's cottage.

Funny. He slowed the car and looked again, and sure enough, there was no smoke.

'What is it?'

'Mrs Jenks. She always has the fire lit. Always.'

Izzy shrugged. 'Perhaps she felt it was warm enough.'

He shook his head. 'No. She feels the cold. I think we should check on her.' He turned down her track, and when he reached the end her little dog came running out whining.

'The door's open,' he said. 'I don't like it.'

He headed for the open door at a run, leaving Izzy to follow, and as he went into the kitchen he found the reason for the dog's concern. The old woman was lying back in her chair by the side of the Rayburn, her eyes closed, and for a moment he thought she was dead. Then her eyes fluttered open and she stared at him unfocused.

He crouched down beside her and took her hand. 'Mrs Jenks? It's all right, we're here now.'

'Will?'

He was relieved to hear her voice, but it was thin and reedy, and he knew she was dying. 'Don't talk,' he murmured, squeezing her hand gently.

'Why not? So much to say.' Her fingers tightened on his. 'Thank you for looking after me.'

His throat closed. 'Don't. It's been a pleasure. Let me get Simon or the doctor—'

'No! Not Simon, and the doctor can't help me. I'm dying, Will. Just stay with me. It hurts.'

'What hurts, my love?'

'My heart. It's the end. I know that. I want to die

here, not in some horrible ambulance, bumping along the track with a mask on my face—oohh.'

'Shh. Don't talk now. Just rest. Can I get you anything? A drink?'

'Water.'

Izzy put a glass in his hand. She must have been waiting with it. He held it to her lips, but she only wet them, nothing more.

After a moment she opened her eyes and looked over his shoulder and smiled. 'Izzy,' she said unsteadily. 'You look after him. He's a good man, and you deserve each other after all this time.'

Her eyes closed, and she gripped his fingers for a moment, then looked at him again. 'Is it sunny?'

'Beautiful.'

'I think I'd like to die with the sun on my face,' she said, and gently, as carefully as he could, he lifted her and carried her out into the garden. There was a seat by the back door, and he sat down on it with her cradled on his lap, and she rested her tired white head against his shoulder and sighed.

'That's lovely,' she whispered. 'Thank you.'

Moments later Izzy touched him gently on the arm.

'Will? She's gone.'

'I know,' he said. He felt the tears slide down his cheeks, but he didn't have a free hand to brush them away, and anyway, he reckoned Mrs Jenks had earned them. He stood up and put her carefully down onto the seat, propping her up with cushions that Izzy brought out for him. 'I'll just let her sit here in the sun until they get here.'

He walked away, bracing his arms against the roof

of the car and staring at the ground. Izzy put her arms around him from behind and hugged him gently.

'Are you OK?'

He nodded. 'Yes. Simon will give me hell for not calling him, but he wouldn't have got here. Nor would we—if we'd made love, we wouldn't have been here now, and she would have died alone.'

Izzy released him, and for a moment he thought he'd upset her. Then she opened her side of the car, reached in and brought out the posy he'd made her. Without a word she handed it to him, and he took it and tucked it into Mrs Jenks's hand.

'Thanks,' he said gruffly. Then, and only then, he called the police.

If she thought he'd been busy before, the next two weeks were hell. Simon Jenks wanted to clear out the house immediately, and there were heated discussions about what items of furniture were his and what were not. The executors were involved, and Will was kept running backwards and forwards to the little farmhouse to sort out one dispute after another.

Izzy was feeling much better now, and the pain of her arm was giving way to frustration and discomfort. Still, at least she'd been able to get the office work cleared for him, and his study was now a lovely room with everything in its place.

He was stunned. 'I won't know where to find a thing,' he told her, and she opened the filing cabinet and gave him a quick guided tour of her carefully labelled pockets.

'Good grief,' he said faintly. 'Thank you, Izzy.'

He kissed her—just a quick brush of his lips, but then he hesitated and drew her into his arms, kicking the study door shut behind him and plundering her mouth, threading his strong fingers through her hair and holding her still while he drank from her as if he couldn't help himself.

By the time he lifted his head his chest was heaving and his eyes were dark and smouldering.

'We need to find an excuse to get to London,' she said with a wry, breathless little laugh, and he just rolled his eyes and chuckled grimly.

'I wish. I can't get away from things here long enough to eat at the moment. The chances of a day off are just so remote they aren't worth considering.'

'It'll get better,' she reminded him.

'I'll hold that thought. I have to fly. I've got another meeting with Simon Jenks and the executor—that man will take the wallpaper if I let him. What she did to deserve a son like that I cannot imagine, but God had better have a very good reason.'

'I thought she didn't believe in God?'

'She didn't. She believed in love and human kindness. It's her funeral tomorrow. Will you come with me, Izzy? I don't think I can do it on my own.'

And so, the next day, she found herself standing beside Will during the simple ceremony. Mrs Jenks had elected to have a green burial, and she was laid to rest on the edge of a wood, her simple willow coffin interwoven with flowers from her garden. She knew Will had done that, his last gift to the woman. He held himself firmly in check until the coffin was lowered into the grave.

Then he turned away, and she knew he was thinking of Julia. What could she say to him? How could she comfort him?

She couldn't, but she could take him home. 'Come on,' she said gently, and. slipping her arm through his, she led him to the car. 'I can't drive you, Will. Are you OK to do that?'

He nodded. His eyes were dry, but his face was drawn and haggard and for the first time she understood just how deeply he was grieving for his wife.

She was just a passing diversion, an itch he hadn't finished scratching in his teens. Julia had been his real life, and she was truly deluded if she imagined that she could in any way take the woman's place.

He disappeared the moment they got back to the farm, not even waiting to change but whistling up the dog and striding off across the fields without a word. She let him go. She had no choice, she couldn't have caught up with him if she'd tried, but she didn't want to try.

The funeral breakfast was being held at the Old Crock, courtesy of Mr and Mrs T, and nothing to do with Simon, for all the fuss he'd made—and now it seemed he was contesting the sale of the property, saying she'd been there so long that it still belonged to her and Will had no right to the house. So the café was seething with people who'd genuinely loved the old woman, and she was being given a send-off she would have been proud of.

It was too much for Izzy. The accumulated emotion of the past few days and weeks was getting to her, and the thought of eating anything much was distinctly unappealing. Instead she phoned Emma and arranged to walk over there for lunch. A little exercise and fresh air was exactly what she needed, and she set off over the fields in the opposite direction to Will. There was a track that led down to the village, and she took it, walking out and pushing herself to get her heart pumping and her legs working again after her long period of inactivity.

By the time she reached the village she was regretting it. She felt distinctly light-headed and queasy, because of the lack of food and the heat of the day. It was only early May, but the temperature had soared in the past day or two and it was hotter in the sun than she'd realised.

She knocked on Emma's door and went gratefully into the cool kitchen on the north side of the house.

'You look rough,' Emma said candidly, scanning her face with searching eyes.

Izzy scanned her back and took in the pallor, the circles round her eyes, the hollow cheeks. 'You don't look so great yourself. What's happened, Emma?'

Emma gave a rueful laugh. 'The usual. I'm pregnant again.'

'What? You said you weren't having any more— that three was more than enough—'

'Yes, well, tell it to the fairies. They must have had other ideas. And don't ask me how it happened. I have no idea. We must have made love in our sleep. That's what you get for so many years of harmony. You don't even have to be conscious.'

They laughed, and Emma opened the fridge. 'You need feeding. Fancy helping yourself? If I look at anything more highly flavoured than an ice cube I'll heave.'

But curiously Izzy didn't feel like much either. 'Have you got any fruit?'

'Yeah, sure—in the fruit bowl, or I think there's some melon in the fridge somewhere. And there should be slices of apple in lemon juice and water. When I'm feeling strong I eat them.'

Izzy had a slice of melon and felt better, but sipping iced water and sitting in Emma's lovely cool kitchen were probably also partly responsible. She found herself telling Emma about the funeral, and Will's reaction.

'Poor Will. I wonder if he'll always feel guilty.'

'Guilty?'

'He and Julia weren't always happy. I think he blamed himself. Personally I don't think either of them were to blame. He did his best to be a good husband, and Julia was a dutiful wife and a wonderful mother to those children, but they didn't have any sparkle.'

'But he loved her.' Izzy was sure of that.

'Oh, yes, he loved her,' Emma agreed. 'Just not enough. But that's what you get for "having to get married". Being pregnant is a lousy reason to get married. Do you remember Cathy Bright? Her younger sister got married three years ago because she was pregnant, and they've split up already. She's had another baby, too—trying to patch up their marriage. I often wondered if that's why Will and Julia had Rebecca, but I didn't like to ask, and Julia didn't talk about it very much. She was a very private person.'

How strange. Izzy found it hard to imagine Will and

Julia unhappy. Nothing he'd said had given her any indication of that, and at the graveside today, and again in her roof garden in London, she'd seen real pain in his eyes, the sort of pain that took your breath away.

And besides, he'd told her himself that he loved Julia, eleven years ago, when it had all happened. He'd come to see her, to tell her that he and Julia were getting married, and he'd told her he was in love with her best friend.

Will had never lied to her. She hadn't wanted to believe it, but she'd had no choice. And she had no choice now. Maybe Julia had been unhappy, but it hadn't been for lack of love, of that she was sure.

Emma was in the fridge, raiding the ice cube tray and complaining bitterly about Rob.

'I can't imagine what I saw in him,' she was grumbling. 'I thought he was the sexiest man alive—and look where it's got me! Pregnant for the fourth time, for heaven's sake. It's a good job I love him so much or I'd kill him.'

She sat back down at the table with a handful of ice cubes and offered one to Izzy.

She chuckled and took one, sucking on it while Emma carried on, an ice cube stuck in her cheek while she talked. 'It's knowing it's going to go on for the next few weeks that I can't stand. I mean, I know the routine inside out now. Dizziness, nausea, tiredness—all the time the tiredness, but that might be something to do with all the other kids!—and then the nipples kick in. Sore, tense, prickly—they itch and tingle in the night, and my bra always feels too tight even when it isn't, and then in five minutes or so it will be, and I'll have to go back into my huge bras again for the next few months—oh, I could scream if I had the energy. I loathe it. I loathe Rob. It's all his fault.'

Izzy laughed. There was nothing else to do at such a litany of disaster. 'I'm sorry,' she said, covering her old friend's hand and giving it a squeeze. 'But just think, you'll get a baby out of this. Isn't it worth it?'

Emma snorted. 'Ask me in seven months. No, better still, ask me in ten months. By then it'll be going through the night, if it knows what's good for it, and I might have caught up on some sleep.' She sighed. 'So—tell me about you. How's your arm?'

Izzy looked at it disparagingly. 'Hopeless. It hurts a little still, but mostly it itches and prickles where the wires are. I should have the cast off tomorrow, and it'll hopefully feel better then. I should have gone today, but with the funeral and everything I've had to change the appointment. I'm just hoping Will can take me.'

'Don't bet on it. I heard Rob talking to him on the phone the other night. Simon Jenks is getting right up his nose and I think he's seeing Rob to get all his facts straight about where he stands on the property. Rob doesn't think there's a problem, but he's certainly going to be busy. Want a lift to the hospital?'

Izzy was tempted, but she took one look at her friend's drawn face and shook her head. 'Don't worry, I'll get a taxi. I might go shopping afterwards.'

She didn't go shopping. Instead, once the cast was off and the wires removed—amazingly painless and simple—she took herself off into town, found a beauty salon and begged a manicure. The skin on her arm was horrible, and she needed her nails attended to drastically. The arm was terrifyingly weak, but the girl who did it was very gentle and thorough, and after she was finished Izzy felt more human.

She went back to the farm in a taxi, and she realised when she arrived that she was feeling peckish. She walked into the café, intending to order something light, and the smell of frying bacon hit her in the back of the throat.

She swallowed hard and backed away, turning and running across the yard to the house and only just making it into the bathroom in time. Minutes later, her stomach thoroughly empty and her legs like jelly, she sat down on the edge of the bath, hung her head over the sink and splashed her face with cold water.

It was having the wires removed, she thought. It must have affected her more than she'd realised. She lifted her head and rubbed absently at her breasts with her arm. They were tender. She must have a period due. Thank goodness she'd had the cast off. She'd been wondering how she'd deal with that particular problem one-handed—

She felt the blood drain from her face.

Her cast had been on five weeks. She'd had a period the week before she'd gone to Dublin, just after the party. That had been six weeks ago.

And her cycle was as regular as clockwork. She'd never been a day late in her life.

It must be the shock of seeing Will again, and the fracture, and the change of routine, she told herself. But what routine? She had no routine. Her life was in a constant state of flux.

Which left only one answer.

CHAPTER TEN

SHE couldn't tell Will. Not after what Emma had said yesterday.

Being pregnant is a lousy reason to get married... He loved her—just not enough... I often wondered if that's why Will and Julia had Rebecca... I wonder if he'll always feel guilty—

No. She couldn't tell him. She'd always thought they'd been happy together, and nothing he'd said had given her reason to doubt it. If Julia had been a private person, then so, too, was Will, and she didn't think he'd talk about his marriage.

Although he'd tried to tell her something about Julia before, of course, and she'd stopped him. She'd told him it was in the past, and so it was, but that didn't mean it wasn't still affecting him. Had he been going to tell her that they hadn't been happy?

She worried her lip with her teeth, not knowing what to do and yet knowing that she had to get away. Now her cast was off, although her arm was desperately weak she could use it a little to do things, if she had to, and it would be fine soon, surely?

In direct contrast to her nausea. She'd hardly made it to the bathroom earlier, and if she stayed here any longer Will would cotton on. He'd had two children with Julia, and his mother would start to notice that she wasn't drinking coffee even if Will didn't. It wouldn't take them long to put two and two together, and until she'd got all her ducks in a row she didn't want him knowing about the baby.

Baby.

Her hand went down instinctively to cradle it, her palm lying flat over her taut abdomen. It wouldn't be many more weeks before it started to show, though.

She packed her few things, went round the house gathering together all the little bits and pieces that always seemed to disperse themselves, and then she went out of the back door and round the side, to go across to the café and tell Mrs T she was going, and found herself faced with a barrage of cameras.

Fortunately they were pointing towards the café, but at least it gave her a good excuse for leaving. She hurried back inside, shut herself in the study, pulled down the blind and rang the café. The phone, of course, was engaged, and seconds later there was banging on the front door.

Damn. Was it locked? The back door was never locked, and she couldn't remember locking it just now. She wasn't even sure it had a key. Would they just come in?

She phoned Mr T in the Valley Timber workshop.

'Mr T? It's Izzy. What's going on?'

'Oh, Izzy—you've seen them. I was going to call you. Someone caught sight of you at the funeral yesterday,' he told her, 'and Mrs Willis confirmed your identity, apparently.'

She sighed raggedly. She'd hoped it was nothing to do with her, but that had been too much to expect, and anyway, she needed the smoke screen. 'I need to get away. They won't give up, and I promised Will this wouldn't happen, for the sake of the children.'

'Want a lift?' Thank God he didn't argue.

'I'd love one.'

'Go round the back and wait in the kitchen. Give me a few minutes—and keep out of sight.'

'OK.'

She dragged her things downstairs with her good hand, and lurked in the utility room, bent down behind the freezer, out of line of the window.

The door slammed open and Will came striding in. He caught sight of her and pulled her gently to her feet. His eyes were troubled. 'My father says you're going.'

She nodded. 'I have to, Will. For the kids.'

Emotions chased across his face, but not least was relief, and he didn't try and talk her out it. Quite the opposite. 'I'll take you to the station,' he said firmly.

She shook her head. 'No. It'll just add fuel to the fire, and anyway, I hate public goodbyes. Let your father do it.'

He hesitated, then nodded agreement. 'You're right. Take care, Izzy. I'll miss you.'

He was swallowing hard, and so was she. 'I'll be in touch. Thank you for everything you've done. You've been wonderful.'

God, her heart was breaking, but she wasn't going to cry. She wasn't. She went up on tiptoe and kissed his cheek, and then he handed her bags out to his father and went round to the front to create a diversion while they made their escape over the fields in the Discovery.

Mr T took her to the station and hugged her as he

said goodbye, and there were tears in her eyes then, tears she couldn't hold back.

'Thank Mrs T for me for all her kindness. She's been so good to me. I'll miss her.'

'She'll miss you, too. Don't you be a stranger, now, Izzy. We'll expect you back just the moment this has all settled. You're good for Will. He needs you, and so do the children. They've really taken to you.'

She couldn't speak. Her throat was closed up so tight she thought she'd choke, and she hugged him back hard, then all but pushed him off the train. 'Go on, or you'll be coming to London with me.'

'That'd give them something to talk about,' he said with a wink, and stepped off the train just as the guard blew his whistle and the doors started to slam.

He lifted his hand to wave, but she'd turned away, struggling with tears and the rising nausea that the smell of the train had brought on.

She didn't enjoy the journey.

'So that's that. Simon Jenks hasn't got a leg to stand on with this nonsense. Will? Will, are you paying me any attention?'

Will stared at Rob and scrubbed a hand over his face.

'Sorry. Yes, I'm listening.' In between feeling empty because Izzy was gone and relieved that the press had also gone away.

Still, he'd always known she was going. It had only been a matter of time, and now her cast was off she didn't need them any more. She could wash her hair and dress herself, and shower and all the other things that had been tricky, and for the last few days she'd been looking a bit peaky.

Missing her old life, not unnaturally. She'd be glad to be back, and once he'd talked some sense into himself he'd be glad she was gone.

And he'd do it. Give or take another twelve years.

Izzy was lost. There was nothing to do in London, nowhere to go that she could cope with. Everything either made her feel sick or sad, and above all she was lonely.

She'd never really been lonely before, or if she had, she hadn't really put a name to it. Now, though, she was bereft. Will had only been in her life again for a few short weeks, but the impact had been huge.

Without the baby to think about life would have been unbearable, but now, with this little person slowly developing inside her, the child she'd always longed for in a way she'd never understood, gradually the blackness started to recede and she could see the light again.

And with the dawning of that light she realised that she would have to make some drastic changes in her life.

She was spending all her time in the roof garden, in the shade under the grapevine, sipping iced water and listening to the endless hubbub of the city, longing for the tranquillity of the countryside.

And that was what she'd have to do. She'd move to the country. She would close her business. There was nothing to sell. It was Isabel Inc. Without her it was nothing. She'd terminate her lease, sell on the employment agency and retire to the country with her baby.

The idea held huge appeal, and when Kate rang her and gently broke it to her that she'd met a man in Australia and wouldn't be coming back, she was able to wish her well and genuinely mean it.

'How's that gorgeous man of yours?' Kate asked, and Izzy, who didn't feel up to dealing with Kate's curiosity even long-distance, said he was fine. For all she knew, he was.

He hadn't phoned her, though, and she hadn't rung him. Let sleeping dogs lie. There'd be time. More than enough time. So long as she told him about the baby before it was born, to give him time to get used to the idea, that would be enough.

She was realistic enough to know he'd want to be involved with it, but she wasn't going to give him a chance to bully her into marrying him just to salve his conscience, and so she had to wait until she was strong enough to stand up to him before she told him.

With any luck it would be before the baby went off to university!

She laid a hand on the gentle curve that was their child. 'Where are we going to live, baby? Near your daddy, I suppose. Then you can be friends with Rob and Emma's baby, and Emma will be there for me, and at least I won't be lonely. And your grandparents will spoil you to bits, and you can play with your brother and sister, and it should be a good life. We'll be fine.'

And if she told herself that enough times, maybe it would be true.

She'd have to tell her own parents at some point, as well, but as they didn't approve of her lifestyle, and had chosen to believe a lot of the rubbish that appeared in the press, she felt no need to live near them. They could see their grandchild on carefully edited occasions, and that would be enough. She didn't need their disapproval on a daily basis.

But, of course, she'd need somewhere to live—and to find somewhere she'd need an agent she could trust.

Tom Savage. He'd been at school with them, he'd been at the party at Rob and Emma's, and she knew he dealt in the sort of country property she was looking for.

So she rang him, and told him she was looking for a house close to the village. 'Within, say, five miles?' she suggested, and he promised to call her back. Twenty minutes later the phone rang.

'Izzy. It's Tom. Look, I've got an idea. There's a farmhouse come on the market—it's close to the village, just about three miles south. You might know it. Wildmay Farm. It used to belong to Mrs Jenks.'

Her heart stopped. 'That's Will's,' she said, and he confirmed it.

'He's selling it. The thing is, it needs a great deal of work, but I know money isn't something you're worried about, and it's in the most wonderful spot.'

'I know. I know the house.' She'd been there when Mrs Jenks died. She'd never forget the image of Will sitting there with the dead woman in his arms and tears streaming down his face. 'I'll have to think about it.'

'Well, don't think too long. There's a lot of interest. You might need to move fast. It's got all the barns as well, of course. I don't know why he's selling it; I didn't speak to him for long. He was a bit—short, really. I think he's had a lot of hassle from the son and he just wants to be shot of it.'

Izzy had other ideas, but she wasn't sharing them with Tom Savage. 'Can I buy it anonymously?' she asked. 'Or under a business name?'

'Sure. Can I ask why?'

'Just privacy. I don't want everyone knowing my business.'

'No problem.'

'Good. Tom, we'd better meet. Do you want me to come up?'

'Sure. I can show you round the property if you like.'

'Don't bother. I'll see it later. I don't need to see it before I buy it.'

'In which case, why don't I come to you? I've got to go to the London office on Monday. Why don't we meet for lunch?'

And, of course, as luck would have it, the place he chose was heaving with celebrities and they were spotted by the ever-present paparazzi.

'Oh, damn,' she muttered. 'Why don't you come back to mine for coffee and to do the paperwork? We aren't going to get any peace here.'

'Miss Brooke! Isabel! Is it true that your affair with Will Thompson is over?'

'Is this the new man in your life?'

'Sorry, I'm happily married,' Tom said, and threw a handful of notes at the waiter.

'Excuse me,' she said, as one of the men shoved a microphone under her nose and started asking her more questions about Tom, and he neatly and none too gently deflected him out of her way as he ushered her out of the door. Behind her she could hear camera flashes popping, but they headed out into the sunlight and Tom hailed a taxi, helped her into it and slammed the door behind them.

'Canary Wharf,' he said, and then let out his breath in a rush. 'Are they always like that?'

Izzy laughed. 'Sometimes. Usually they're rude.'

He gave a strangled laugh and ran his finger round his collar. 'How do you cope with it?'

'I don't. That's why I want to buy this place anonymously. I really don't want publicity, Tom.'

He nodded his understanding of the situation, and then pulled out the details again. 'They're only sketchy details as yet, we haven't got the others back from the printer, but they give you information about the barns. I don't know if it's even suitable for you, but it could be a lovely house. Not big, of course, but it used to be two cottages. With a bit of work it could have a sensible layout and there's nothing you'd want to change about the surroundings.'

'Location, location, location,' they said together, and laughed.

'Tom, I'll have it. It's ideally situated for what I want, and I might turn the barns into holiday retreats for stressed executives. You never know, I might end up running it as a bed and breakfast!'

He gave her an odd look. 'I thought you wanted somewhere as a weekend retreat?'

She shook her head. 'No. A lifestyle change. I'm sick of London, sick of my job, sick of being hounded by the press. Hence the secrecy. I want some peace.'

Peace to bring up my child, she added silently.

He nodded. 'I can understand that—but surely, if you're going to be living there, Will's going to know, so what's the point of the anonymity thing on the purchase? It doesn't have to be public knowledge.'

She'd been waiting for that, and she was ready for him. 'I don't want him feeling he's got to let me have it at a good price. I know Will, and he would do something silly like that. If he thinks I'm just another Londoner, with more money than sense, he'll get the going rate, and that's only fair.'

Again, Tom nodded. 'Right. OK, I'll keep it quiet.'

They arrived at her apartment block, but of course the press were there by then and they were photographed going in.

'It would drive me crazy,' Tom said, looking at them over his shoulder as they hurried in.

'It does. Hello, George. Sorry about the fuss outside.'

'No problem, Miss Brooke. I'll get rid of them for you and let you know when the coast is clear.'

'Thank you.'

She took Tom up to her apartment, made him tea and apologised for not having coffee. 'I've run out,' she said, although in fact it was simply that she couldn't yet tolerate the smell. They looked at the paperwork, she contacted her solicitor over the phone and he met them there, and when Tom left two hours later he had an offer thirty per cent over the asking price.

'That's a good margin,' her solicitor said curiously.

'Because I don't want to lose it in a contract race. I want that property, Bill. I intend to have it.'

He nodded. 'Leave it to me. What about the lease on the office? And what about severance packages? Want me to get David Lennox in on this?'

It took days of sorting out, during which the gutter press had a field-day with her 'relationship' with Tom, but finally the business was closed, and the house was secured. All she had to do was sign the papers and transfer the money. She went up in a private car to Tom's office and bumped into Rob, of all people.

'Izzy! How are you?'

'Oh, I'm fine. Just up here to see a friend.'

And then Tom walked out behind her and came over and greeted her, and she could hear the maths going on in Rob's head. Between the fact that Will was selling the little farmhouse, the papers were linking her to Tom and she was standing here in his office, there was plenty to work on.

Rob wasn't stupid—and two and two, in this case, were definitely going to make a lot more than five. However, he didn't stay to air the result of his equation, just smiled briefly and went away, a puzzled frown on his face. She had the feeling she hadn't heard the last of it.

'Damn,' Tom said, and Izzy echoed it a thousand-fold. Of all the people to run into, only Will could have been worse.

'Fancy a look at the house, since you're here?' Tom said after they'd finished their business and put the paperwork away.

She suppressed a little quiver of excitement. She'd been itching to see it, but until now she hadn't liked to. But now it was hers, the money transferred, and Will was unlikely to be there. He would have finished clearing it out ages ago.

And it would have been fine, of course, if he'd hadn't just finished checking the sheep and been heading back to Valley Farm. The cars stopped nose to nose on the track, and Will got out, his face carved from stone, and walked up to her open window. He raked her with expressionless eyes, then looked across at Tom.

'This is private land. I don't want either of you on it.'

She had no idea how Tom was reacting. The shock of Will's words had her reeling, though, and it was a second before she got her composure back. By the time she had, Tom was out of the car and speaking to Will a few feet away.

'The house is sold,' she heard him say. 'The money was transferred to you today.'

'So what the hell are you doing here?'

Tom caught Izzy's eye. 'I'm acting for the new owner.'

'And did you have to bring *her* with you?' He jerked his head at Izzy, and she felt herself recoil from his anger. 'I mean, it's not up to me that you're cheating on your wife, but you don't have to rub my nose in it with the woman I love. Now, get the hell out of here, Tom, before I do something I'll regret, and don't come back.'

The woman I love.

Had he meant to say that? Was it true?

Izzy got out of the car, her legs trembling.

'Tom, you go. I'll talk to Will.'

'I have nothing to say to you.'

'But I have something to say to you, and I'd appreciate an opportunity to say it.'

Tom looked from one to the other, and folded his arms. 'I'm not leaving her with you. You're too angry—'

'He won't hurt me. Not like that, anyway. You go, Tom. Please.'

'Ring me. You've got my mobile number,' he said, and got back into his car reluctantly and backed slowly away, leaving Izzy standing just feet away from the man who, only moments before, had said *the woman I love*.

'Is it true?' she said softly. 'Do you love me, Will?'

He turned to her then, and the pain she'd seen in his eyes before was back in spades. 'I've never stopped loving you,' he said, his voice taut with emotion. 'In all the years I was with Julia, all the time we spent together, always in the centre of my heart was my love for you. And I really, really don't need to see you running around my land with another of my old schoolfriends—'

'I bought the house,' she said, and for a moment he was motionless. Then he lifted his head and stared at her, his face puzzled.

'You?' he said incredulously. 'It was you?'

'Yes. That's why I saw Tom in London, why I'm here today.'

'But—why? A weekend cottage, so you can come up here and jerk my emotions around when it suits you?'

'I've never jerked your emotions around, Will,' she told him flatly. 'It was you that did that to me. You that went travelling the world with my best friend and came back in love with her.'

'No.'

'Oh, yes.'

'No. I told you that because I thought if you hated me it would be easier for you. It's the only lie I've ever told you, Izzy. I didn't love her. I never loved her, not like that. Not in the way she deserved. And I'll regret it for the rest of my life, because she was worth more, but she didn't love me, either, in the end. It took her a while to realise, but then of course it was too late. She was already pregnant.'

'But you'd still had an affair.'

He shook his head. 'No. We slept together once. We were young, we were drunk, and she came on to me. She did it deliberately—said she wanted to know what it was like, just once. But it was enough, and because she was the vicar's daughter, and I'd promised I'd look after her, I had no choice but to marry her—and I've paid for that night over and over again.'

'You've got beautiful children,' she reminded him.

His hard, craggy face softened. 'Yes. I've got beautiful children, and I grew to love Julia and understand her, and she gave me a great deal. I don't regret it, but I regret what I lost, and it's cost me dear. And to see you with Tom—'

'I've told you about Tom and why I was with him.'

His brow creased. 'So why buy the house? If it's not a weekend cottage, then why?'

'Because I wanted to be near you. I've given up my

business. I'm selling my apartment. When the house is done up I'm moving up here.'

'Then why not live with me?'

She laughed unsteadily. 'Because you've never asked me?'

'Because I know I have nothing to offer you— you've got everything, Izzy. I've got nothing.'

'Except my heart.'

She blinked, because she could no longer see him, and then somehow she was in his arms.

'Oh, dear God, Izzy,' he said, and his chest heaved. His trembling hands cradled her face and he stared down at her, wonder dawning in those beautiful, sparkling blue eyes. 'I love you,' he breathed, and then his mouth was on hers, desperate, hungry, then gentling as he folded her in his arms and rocked her against his heart.

'Marry me, Izzy,' he said. 'Be with me. Stay with me. Grow old with me. Have babies, if you want, but for God's sake don't leave me again.'

'Before I say yes, there's something else,' she said, her heart in her mouth. This was so hard. What if he thought she'd done it on purpose?

'Something else?'

'Another reason why I was coming up here to be near you.' She took a steadying breath. 'Will, we're having a baby.'

He stared down at her in confusion. 'But—we can't be. There was only that day in your apartment, and we used something both times.'

She lifted her shoulders in a little shrug. 'I don't know. Maybe there was a fault. The doctor said it sometimes happens. It's rare, but not unheard of—and it's happened to us.'

'So you decided to come back.' His voice was flat.

'No. I decided to leave. And then I decided to come back, because I didn't feel it was fair to you or the child not to be together. I've seen you with your children, Will. You're wonderful with them. I couldn't deny our child that same love, just because we didn't share it, but I couldn't trap you, either. You've been caught like that once. I didn't think it was fair to trap you again. I want you to have the choice, and you still have it. I've bought this house and I can live here, and you can have your child. You don't have to marry me.'

'Oh, yes, I do,' he said. 'I do because I love you, and I've always loved you, and I'm not losing you again. The first time was bad. The second was intolerable. The third time would kill me—so you will marry me, Izzy, if you love me, and you'll let me show you how much I love you.'

'And the baby?'

'Of course I'll love the baby,' he said softly, his hand sliding down between them to rest against her womb. 'How could you doubt it?'

'So what will we do with the house?' she said thoughtfully.

He laughed. 'I don't know. Turn it into a retreat, so we can sneak down here away from the screaming kids and get a bit of one-to-one from time to time?'

She smiled up at him. 'Sounds good,' she said contentedly, but her mind, still tuned to business, refused to switch off. If they were together, she could become properly involved in the running of all the Valley Farm enterprises. While she'd been doing his paperwork, all sorts of strategies had occured to her, but they all needed money—and that she had in abundance. Mrs Jenks's little house and barns were only the start of it, but she didn't bother to tell him her ideas now. There would be plenty of time to discuss it later. Years. For now, she was just enjoying being close to him.

They strolled up the track, arms locked round each other, and when they came to the house he took her hand and led her to the bench outside the door, where he'd held Mrs Jenks in his arms to die.

He sat down and patted his lap, and she curled up against his chest and thought how lucky Mrs Jenks had been, to die like that with the sound of his heart under her ear. Did Will have any idea how much he had to offer?

'You're a good man,' she said softly. 'I love you.'

'I love you, too. I was so sure I'd lost you—even more sure there was no way round it. I never dreamt for a moment you'd give up everything to come up here and be with me.'

'Give up everything? I've given up nothing. You're my everything, Will. You, and our baby, and your children, and your parents, and Rob and Emma and Tom. It's people that matter.'

'There are people in London.'

'Not that I care about. Kate's in Australia, and she's met a man and not coming back. She was my only real friend. This is my home—up here, with all of you. Especially with you.'

He lowered his mouth and kissed her tenderly. 'Then welcome home, my darling,' he said softly. 'Welcome home.'

The Baby from Nowhere

CAROLINE ANDERSON

CHAPTER ONE

'I SEE your new neighbours are moving in.'

'About time. It's been empty for nearly a year.' Maisie lowered the wallpaper sample and peered out of the bedroom window, eyeing the hive of activity below with interest. 'Good grief! Is that a big enough removal van?'

Kirsten, with no attempt at subtlety, was leaning out of the other little window and openly studying events as they unfolded. 'There's some nice stuff coming out of it.'

The cavernous interior of the huge lorry was being systematically emptied by a fleet of bulky, sweating men. It was these contents that were attracting Kirsten's interest, but Maisie's had moved on in a different direction.

Supervising operations as the removal crew struggled with the contents was another man, standing to one side of the drive and scowling from time to time at the clipboard in his hand. No wonder he couldn't remember where everything was to go. The van was big enough to house the contents of a stately home!

'If that lorry was full, they must have been at it all morning,' Kirsten mused.

It was quite possible, if the number of pages flapping around on the clipboard was anything to go by. Maisie had only come back with Kirsten in her lunch-break to let the dogs out and get her friend's opinion

5

on the wallpaper, and it seemed she'd missed much
of the action.

Pity. Her eyes flicked back to the man again, scanning his tall, lean frame, checking out the way the
sun gleamed on the ruffled strands of his dark blond
hair, and her heart did a little shimmy in her chest.

Lord, girl, you need to get out more, she told herself in disgust.

'Oh, that's pretty.'

She gave Kirsten an odd look. Pretty? She wouldn't
have called him pretty. Architectural, maybe, but
pretty? Definitely not—unless Kirsten was talking
about the dog.

'The little desk. It's gorgeous.'

Maisie looked again. Gorgeous? Not by her standards. Sure, the desk was OK, but the dog that had
appeared at Mr Clipboard's feet—a delightful golden
retriever with floppy ears and a daft grin and a wet,
lolling tongue that she'd just bet could lick you for
England—now, she was gorgeous, but even she
couldn't hold a candle to her master in the eye-candy
stakes.

He'd exchanged the clipboard for a huge pot plant,
some kind of palm or tree fern, and as he strode towards the conservatory with it, the dog bounced
around under his feet and nearly sent the man and the
plant flying. He said something to the dog, but whatever it was it didn't have much effect, and after another couple of strides he gave up and put the plant
down, ruffling the dog's ears affectionately and laughing.

And it was so infectious. Kirsten could feel the

smile starting deep inside her, and she couldn't take her eyes off him. He was *beautiful*...

'Mmm,' she said appreciatively, and earned her own odd look from Kirsten.

'I thought you didn't like dusty old antiques?'

'What?' Maisie stared at her blankly, then realised her friend was still talking about the furniture. Because, of course, Kirsten was stationed at the other little window and might not have noticed the man from her slightly different perspective.

Maisie, however, had most definitely noticed him, and had to drag herself away. In just a moment...

Which was, of course, too late. He looked up, and for a second she thought her heart was going to stop. He was staring straight at her, his ice-blue eyes hypnotic, mesmerising her so she couldn't break the contact.

Ice blue? He was miles away. Well, not miles, but far enough that she couldn't possibly see his eye colour. And yet she knew it, just as she knew the sun would rise in the east and come in that damned window and shine right in her eyes.

She sucked in some much-needed air and let it out on a quiet snort of disgust. So he was a hunk. So what? There were plenty of good-looking men around.

They just all seemed to be either married or so full of bull that she lost interest in the first few seconds.

'What on earth are you looking at?'

'Nothing,' Maisie denied, moving rapidly away from the window and heading for the stairs, her wallpaper samples forgotten. 'Cup of tea?'

'Mmm. You could take one round to him—he's

rather lovely. No wonder you were showing so much interest. Actually, on second thoughts, give me the tea, I'll take it. Is he single? No, don't answer that, it's irrelevant. I'll just kill his wife. What a scoop—the man *and* his fabulous furniture.'

Maisie chuckled. 'You're outrageous,' she told her friend, then almost stopped in her tracks as another emotion broadsided her. Jealousy? Was that strange urge to trip Kirsten up so she couldn't walk round there *jealousy*? Good grief!

'I'm sure they don't need tea,' she said firmly. 'Much too hot. And may I remind you it was you who started the curtain-twitching. And I believe he is single.'

The last was an afterthought, but Kirsten stopped dead behind her on the stairs and gave an accusing gasp of laughter.

'Well, you sly old thing, you *are* curious!' she said victoriously, and Maisie had to fight the urge to blush.

'Not at all. The builder said something about it, but I could be wrong.'

Actually, the builder had said he couldn't understand why a single man would want to live there, rattling around in a bloody great place like that all on his own, pardon my French, so Maisie had, hoping for further information, but her bleep had gone off and the opportunity for further revelations had been cut off in its prime. If only she hadn't been on call…

'Make lemonade,' Kirsten suggested, going tenaciously back to her passport onto the man's property. 'After all, it would only be neighbourly on such a hot day and I know you've got lemons, I saw them in your fridge. And, anyway, I'm sure you're dying to get a look at all the renovations.'

'It would be interesting. I doubt if poor old Miss Keeble would recognise it, though. It's been torn apart, but I'm sure it needed it. It must be years since the place had any real maintenance. So—lemonade, you think?'

'Absolutely.'

So she made some—a huge jug of it, with the fresh lemons that she'd bought on impulse to go with a rainbow trout and had then forgotten to use. She'd had to buy a net of them, because the single ones had sold out, and there they were sitting in her fridge, as Kirsten had said, needing a good home.

So she made lemonade, brimming with vitamin C and sharp tang and real flavour, and, trailed by Kirsten with a huge box of biscuits given to Maisie by a grateful client, she told Jodie and Scamp to stay and she and Kirsten trooped out of her gate and round and in through his, just as the removal men slammed their doors and drove away.

He was standing on the drive, hands on hips, looking around his garden with satisfaction, and as they approached he looked up and scowled.

Well, no, perhaps frowned was a better word.

She gave a mental shrug and put on her best neighbourly smile. 'Hi. Thought you could all use something cool to drink—it's a scorcher, isn't it? But we seem to be too late for your removal team. I'm Maisie, by the way—I live next door.'

'And I'm Kirsten,' Kirsten said, sidling round her and putting on her best *femme fatale* smile and holding out her hand. 'Welcome to Butley Ford.'

Maisie sighed inwardly and tried not to notice how Mr Drop-Dead Gorgeous ran his eyes—and, yes, they were quite definitely glacier blue—over Kirsten's bare, brown and endless legs and smiled. Still, at least the frown had gone. He shook her hand politely, but then his eyes flicked back to Maisie and the smile changed, becoming...

What? Less formal? Surprised?

Why surprised? There were no surprises about Maisie. Five-four, short unruly dark hair, toffee-brown eyes—she was pretty average, really, so why he was looking at her like that?

He extended his hand to her. 'Hi. I'm James. Nice to meet you. This is very kind of you, but you really didn't need to bother.'

Great. He was going to dismiss them, and now she'd feel a fool, not to mention the wasted lemons. Oh, well, they had started to wrinkle, so it wasn't really a waste, and it just went to show how wrong she'd been about him looking at her—

'Oof!'

The jug jerked and slopped, deluging her less-than-ample bosom with ice-cold lemonade, and she let out a little shriek.

'Sorry, blasted dog's got no manners. Tango, get *down*!'

He dragged the dog off, totally unabashed and still wagging its tail furiously, and then relieved Maisie of the jug and handed her a snow-white and immaculately laundered handkerchief. 'I'm sorry. She just gets a bit excited.'

A bit? Maisie blotted her chest ineffectually and

looked at the mutt with a jaundiced eye. So much for the elegant entrance!

'Is your wife inside?' Kirsten was asking politely, still concentrating on the core business while Maisie just went for damage limitation.

'No,' he said, in a tone that implied he knew exactly what Kirsten was up to and found it mildly amusing. He waited a heartbeat, during which she swore none of them breathed, then added casually, 'I don't have a wife.'

There was a rattle, and the lid was off the tin. 'Biscuit?' Kirsten said, almost as if she was rewarding him for being single, and Maisie nearly choked on her laughter.

His lips twitched briefly. 'Thanks. Look, why don't you both come inside? I don't know if I can find glasses...'

'We won't trouble you—'

'Oh, how nice—'

She and Kirsten spoke at once, and she gave her friend a sharp look that was ignored with a skill born of years of practice.

But James was looking at her, not Kirsten, one brow raised as if he was waiting for her answer, and with a faint smile she shrugged in defeat and trailed them both inside.

The dog, freed by now, was bouncing round their feet barking and grinning and lolloping like a baby— which, of course, Maisie could see she was. Nine months? Ten? She'd be a baby for a good few years yet. Retrievers only seemed to grow up when they got arthritis, and sometimes not even then.

She needed training—quiet, gentle, no-nonsense

training, not people shrieking and grabbing her and turning it into a game, so that she got rewarded every time she was bad.

Hobby-horse, she told herself, and concentrated on not making more of an idiot of herself than she already had.

She blotted once more at her soggy front and sighed. Of course, it would be her thin white T-shirt—the one that went totally transparent when it was wet. She said something very rude in her head and followed James through the door.

They'd gone in the back way—the tradesmen's entrance, her jaundiced little alter ego reminded her—through the old scullery now refurbished with what looked like solid oak units and a huge white china butler's sink big enough to bath an elephant, and into a kitchen that was to die for.

More of the lovely pale gold oak units bracketing a massive white four-oven Aga curled around one end of the room, and at the other end was a huge fireplace with a pair of sofas facing each other in front of it. Between the two areas, in the centre of the room, squatted a vast old refectory table piled high with boxes.

Miss Keeble would have approved, Maisie thought. She'd always regretted not being able to look after the place, and she would have loved the sofas. And so, of course, would her dogs!

Tango, however, possibly better trained than she appeared or maybe just too hot, flopped down on the stone-flagged floor, stretching out her legs frog-like so that her tummy was pressed on the cool stone and dropping her head between her paws with a great big sigh.

'Is that lovely?' Maisie said to her, and the dog wagged her tail lazily and grinned agreement.

'Stupid mutt. Only sensible thing she's done all day,' James said with a weary smile, and scrubbed a hand through his hair. 'The removal men had their own drinks and I've just stuck my head under a tap, so I'm afraid I have no idea where the glasses are.'

'In here?' Kirsten was pointing at a box, and he shrugged and peered at it.

'"Glasses",' he read, and pulled a wry grin. 'Bingo.'

He slit the packing tape with his keys, whipped open the lid and pulled out three tall tumblers. 'That's what you get for having packers—a bit of logic. I would have thrown them in any old box and spent weeks looking for them.'

'There's time for that yet,' Maisie said drily, remembering her own move. 'I've been in my tiny house for three years and I've still got boxes I haven't unpacked.'

'Here.' Kirsten had rinsed out the glasses and filled them with the lemonade, and Maisie took one.

'Please, ladies, have a seat,' James said, waving a hand at the sofas.

Maisie sat, and Kirsten, predictably, took the other sofa. So now where's he going to sit? Maisie wondered, but he didn't. Instead he propped his lean hips on the side of the refectory table and took a cautious sip. He gave a sensual groan that almost made Maisie whimper in reaction, then sighed and drained the glass.

'Oh, bliss. Real lemonade. My compliments, ladies.'

'Thank you,' Kirsten chipped in, before Maisie could even open her mouth, so she simply sighed and took a biscuit from the tin—her tin!—that he proffered, and resigned herself to yet another inch on the waist that seemed determined to grow almost daily. Still, at least she'd got her appetite back after her bug, even if it had taken weeks.

Kirsten, of course, refused a biscuit, but James took one and bit it cleanly in half with those dazzling, almost-too-perfect teeth, and Maisie had to stifle another whimper.

She drained her glass and stood up. 'Sorry, got to go back to work. I hope you don't have too much trouble settling in.'

'I'm sure it will be hell,' he said mildly, and put the lid on the biscuit tin. 'Here, take these back. I can't possibly eat them all.'

'Keep them,' Maisie pleaded, knowing perfectly well what would happen if she took home the opened tin. She was going to have to do something about her weight gain, and the biscuits wouldn't help at all. 'It'll save you having to cook for a day or two.'

'There are some good pubs and restaurants in the area,' Kirsten said, less than subtly. 'I could show you, if you like.'

His eyes flickered with amusement for a second, then went politely blank. 'I'm sure I'll find them when I need them,' he returned smoothly, and held the door so Kirsten had no option but to leave with her. 'Thank you again for your welcome.'

But this time his eyes were on Maisie, and the smile that crinkled them was genuine and warming.

Very warming. Oh, lord.

'My pleasure,' she managed. 'I'll wash your handkerchief and return it.'

'Don't worry about it. I'm sorry about your T-shirt.'

His eyes lingered for a second on the damp, translucent fabric, and the heat mounted. Then his eyes flicked up to hers once more and he smiled again, a polite social smile this time, and closed the door.

Her legs threatening to rebel, Maisie turned on her heel and headed round the side of the house and down the drive, Kirsten beside her chanting softly under her breath.

'Oh, boy. Oh, wow. I'm in love. He is—'

'Gorgeous,' Maisie finished for her. 'I noticed. I wonder what he does.'

'London,' Kirsten said firmly. 'Must be. Something big in the City. He's obviously got pots of dosh. Did you see that new kitchen? I'd die for a kitchen like that.'

'I'd die for the sink in the scullery, never mind the kitchen.'

'Pity we had to leave so soon—I was angling for a snoop round the house. All those priceless antiques—the man must be worth a complete mint. All that and those looks, too. There's no justice. God could have spread it around a bit!'

'I'll share,' Maisie promised, laughing. 'You can have the antiques.'

'In your dreams!' Kirsten retorted, and Maisie thought it was quite likely. It was the only way she'd come within spitting distance of that particular fantasy!

They turned up the lane beside the garden wall and walked up to Maisie's little house. 'You need a gate in the wall,' Kirsten teased. 'Think how handy that would be.'

'There is one,' she pointed out. 'It's covered in creeper, but it's there, from when the Lodge belonged to the house—it used to be the old doctor's surgery, and the doctor lived in the Mount and presumably just nipped through the gate to see his patients. Nice and handy.'

'Mmm,' Kirsten said, her eyes brimming with laughter. 'Perhaps you should dig out your secateurs.'

'Or not.' She checked her watch. 'Just got time to change my T-shirt and then I'll have to go back to the surgery. What are you doing?'

Kirsten laughed. 'Well, I know what I'd *like* to do, but I guess I'm going to come back to town with you unless I want to be stranded. There's an interesting thought…!'

'You're incorrigible. Don't you have any clients to see?'

Kirsten shook her head. 'No, just paperwork and orders and following up a useless builder.'

'Lucky you! I've got a full surgery—stitches out, inoculations, anal glands—I can hardly wait. I've got a follow-up of an intractable itchy coat—what do you bet me it's a wheat allergy and she won't stop feeding the poor dog the crusts off her toast? If you ask me, most pets would be better off without their owners.'

'All except Tango,' Kirsten chipped in with a grin. 'I wonder if he's going to take her to the vet any time soon? Or, better yet, I wonder if he needs any interior design advice? All those rooms—he can't possibly have got them all sorted yet and he'll need the right backdrop to set off his goodies.'

Her eyes sparkled with mischief, and Maisie chuckled. Her friend was relentless.

'Why do I get the feeling he'll get one of your flyers through his door in the next day or so?' she said drily, and Kirsten's eyes widened.

'What a wonderful idea! Maisie, you're a star!'

And Maisie, seeing the futility of setting herself up in competition with the beautiful and sparkling Kirsten when she was on a mission, gave an inward sigh and conceded defeat. Kirsten wanted James? She'd get him, regardless of his feelings in the matter. Of that Maisie had no doubt.

Hot, sweaty, his muscles screaming in protest, James wrestled the heavy mattress onto the old mahogany four-poster and sat down on the end of it to catch his breath. He must have been mad. Try as he might, he couldn't for the life of him remember why moving up here had seemed such a good idea. Why saddle himself, a single man, with a huge house and two acres of garden to rattle around in all alone, miles from all his old friends?

Just having a place to store the furniture he'd grown up with was no good reason, he thought, lifting his head—and there, laid out in front of him on the other side of the window, was the real reason, and they didn't come much better than that.

The salt marshes, dotted with sheep and a haven for birds at this time of the year, stretched away to

the left as far as he could see. To the right was the
pretty little riverside town of Butley Ford, loved and
remembered by him since his childhood, and straight
ahead of him a path led enticingly across the marshes
and joined up with the river wall where he'd walked
all those years ago with his grandfather.

Grandy was long gone, and so, now, were his parents. Only he and his sister were left, and she'd gone
off to the other side of the world to sail the Pacific
with the new love of her life, leaving Tango with
James—'just until I come back'.

If she ever did. She'd already put off her return
once, and James had a feeling that the next time he
heard from her, it would be to tell him she wasn't
coming back at all.

Ever.

He glanced down at the dog, sitting up at the window and staring hopefully out over the new and fascinating landscape. The tip of her tail was wriggling
with enthusiasm, and she turned her head and looked
up at him hopefully.

He sighed and hauled himself to his feet. He was
knackered, and absolutely the last thing he needed
was to take the dog for a walk, but she'd been good
all day—well, as good as she got—and it was a beautiful afternoon.

He looked out of the other window, the one on the
flank wall, and studied the little cottage that was his
nearest neighbour. Was that Maisie's? Curiosity
stirred in him, but the dog was jumping up and looking hopeful, and his attention was distracted.

He ruffled her soft, pretty head. 'Come on, then,

Tango. Let's go and find that walk I used to go on with Grandy.'

The dog bouncing round his feet, he found her lead and headed for the river.

'Let's go for a run, shall we?'

Jodie and Scamp were at Maisie's heels instantly, tails lashing. Scamp, the springer, squirmed with excitement while she changed her shoes and clipped on their leads, but the elderly lurcher just watched her as if butter wouldn't melt in her mouth, eyes bright in the amber fuzz that made up her coat, then they were trotting along quietly beside her even though they'd been waiting all afternoon for this.

They were good dogs, she thought, and even quite civilised now. Great friends and wonderful company in the evening, and they didn't chatter in the morning either. Maisie hated people that chattered in the morning—and that went double for the cockerel!

They walked down the lane to the end, crossed over to the path that ran between the fields and then followed it to the foot of the river wall, then up the few steps to the top. Once up there, she turned left and broke into a jog, heading inland, and they loped along beside her still on their leads.

It was the breeding season, and she wouldn't trust either of them not to disturb the nesting birds. She had enough trouble keeping them out of the chicken run! Well-behaved they might be. Saints they were not.

And neither was Tango. She came streaking towards them, barking wildly and lashing her tail, and skidded to a halt a few feet away as it if had suddenly dawned on her that she might not be welcome. Her tail was still waving, but she looked much less confident, and Maisie watched as her two dogs checked out the youngster, circling her and sniffing all those important places.

'Sorry—she got away from me.'

Maisie looked up, shielding her eyes from the sun, and found herself only a few feet from a gasping James. He'd obviously been running, and now he was bent over, hands on knees, trying to get his breath.

'You should keep her on a lead—the water birds are breeding, and she hasn't even got a collar on!' It came out sharper than she'd meant it to, and as soon as the words were out, she could have kicked herself.

He glanced up at her, arching a brow, then he pulled a lead from his pocket and dangled it in front of her, the collar still attached to it. 'I tried,' he said, his reproach mild, and she felt a pang of guilt. After all, they were going to be neighbours, and she didn't want to get off to a bad start.

It was going to be difficult enough when he encountered Hector!

She dredged up a suitably apologetic expression. 'Sorry—I didn't realise. It's just that so many people—'

'Don't worry about it.' He was still breathing a little hard, and Maisie crushed the urge to smile.

'Out for a run?' she asked innocently, and he snorted.

'Not exactly. That was all Tango's idea.'

Maisie's lips twitched. 'I bet she thought that was great fun.'

'I'm sure she did.' Hands on lean, jeans-clad hips,

he straightened his shoulders and gave a wry smile. 'Since I seem to be this close to her, I think I might put her back on the lead and quit while I'm winning.'

'Sounds like a plan,' Maisie said, letting the smile show now. 'Of course, if you tightened her collar the birds would be safe and you wouldn't risk a coronary.'

He stared at her for a second, then his mouth quirked and he gave a little huff of laughter. 'Do I look that unfit?' he asked, but she just shrugged.

'Are you?'

He slipped the collar over Tango's head and tightened it a notch, then straightened. 'Not really. We've just walked all along the river wall, back along Rectory Road and down to the Quay for a look at the boats, then out on the river wall again to the woods. That was when she slid off. I ran after her, and then she caught sight of you and legged it. Not surprisingly, I couldn't keep up.'

He fell into step beside her, and she turned down off the river wall and headed back towards Rectory Road along another path across the marshes.

'So—why Butley Ford?' Maisie asked, telling herself it was just to make polite conversation, and nothing at all to do with her ravening curiosity.

James shrugged. 'I've always liked it. I used to come here on holiday when I was a boy, and stay with my grandfather. I needed a lifestyle change, and this house came up, and I thought, Why not? A job fell in my lap—it was just...'

'Meant?'

He laughed a little awkwardly. 'Sounds so stupid, but that's what it felt like.'

'I don't think it's stupid. Sometimes it just happens.'

He shot Maisie a curious glance. 'And you? Why did you end up here? How long have you been here?' he asked.

'Three years. There was a job, and my house was just sitting there needing a tenant, and—well, it just happened, really, rather like yours.'

He nodded. 'Like so much of life.'

'Do you believe in destiny?'

He laughed. 'No. I believe in careless coincidence and random happenings. Fate, if you like. I think we make our own destiny in how we pick our way through the hand fate throws us. What about you?'

She shrugged. 'I haven't really thought about it. How's the unpacking going?'

'Oh, don't,' he groaned. 'I must have been mad to move. It's a nightmare.' They came to a halt by his back gate, and he looked down into Maisie's eyes and nearly took the legs out from under her with his wry smile. 'I seem to have most of a jug of lemonade in my fridge, and a whole heap of biscuits. Fancy sharing?'

She did—quite desperately—but she had the dogs and cats to feed and the chickens to do, and she'd promised Anna she'd pop over and check on the pony's breathing.

'Another time,' she said, and to her disappointment he seemed to withdraw.

'Of course. I could do with straightening a few things up before I call it a day anyway.'

He opened the gate and went through it with

Tango, lifting his hand in farewell before closing it and shutting her out behind the solid wall of wood.

Curious how lonely that made her feel but, short of banging on the gate and telling him she'd changed her mind, there was nothing she could do.

Maisie shrugged. Kirsten would never have wasted such a golden opportunity, she told herself, but, then, she wasn't Kirsten. With a little shrug, she trudged along the lane outside the high brick wall that enclosed his garden, round the corner into Doctor's Lane and down to the Lodge.

There would be other opportunities to see him. She could wait.

CHAPTER TWO

ANY hope Maisie might have been cherishing about bumping into James again over the next couple of days was soon crushed.

It was one of those nightmare weekends when she wished she'd been a landscape gardener or a window cleaner or a filing clerk. Anything rather than a vet, working alone and wondering every time she sat down or tried to catch a nap how long it would be before the phone rang again and there was yet another emergency.

Not long enough, was the usual answer.

The surgery on Saturday morning was straightforward enough, apart from the dog with a foreign body in his ear. He had to be admitted for emergency surgery to remove it as soon as her consults were finished. The rest were mostly routine, including two cats for inoculation because the owner was off on holiday that day and had forgotten until they were about to go that the vaccination certificates had to be up to date before the cattery would accept them.

Easy mistake to make, Maisie thought, but there was really no excuse because the surgery sent out reminders. She signed the cards, sent them off on their holiday with a gently worded slap on the wrist and went out into the back.

'All ready when you are,' Kathy, the head nurse, told her.

'I need a cup of tea,' Maisie wailed, and found a mug in her hand.

'How did I know you'd say that?' Kathy teased.

'Creature of habit. You're a darling. How's the dog?'

'Morgan? He's fine. He keeps shaking his head and scratching, but I've put a lampshade on him so he can't get to it. He's just whimpering and looking mournful.'

Maisie laughed. The little cross-breed was a charmer, and she couldn't leave him suffering any longer. She swallowed her tea hastily and put the mug down.

'Come on, then, let's sedate him and get this seed out. At least, I hope that's what it is. I'm pretty sure, but he wouldn't really let me get a look.'

'It's that time of year—bit early, but it's been a mild spring.'

'And it's working up to being a hot summer,' Maisie said with feeling. She hated the heat, and to-day it was getting to her. Ever since she'd had that bug, she'd been hot and cold all over the place. Today she'd just been hot, and she knew it was going to be one of those weekends.

She injected a small amount of sedative into the vein in Morgan's leg while Kathy held him firmly. 'Hope that's enough. I don't want to give him too much, I want to send him home with his owners in a couple of hours. We don't need anything else to baby-sit for the weekend.' As they watched, Morgan's eyes drooped and he keeled over, still semi-conscious but hopefully sufficiently unaware that she could pull out the foreign body without upsetting him.

She checked his heart again, made sure he was OK and then lifted up his ear flap and peered inside.

'Oh, yes, it's definitely a grass seed. Is he OK?'

Kathy nodded. 'Seems fine.'

'Right, hold him firmly, just in case he's not under enough,' she warned, and then with the long-nosed forceps she grasped the grass seed and pulled it out. He didn't even flinch, to her relief, and she examined the seed carefully to make sure it was intact.

'Right, that looks OK. It doesn't smell yet, so it can't have been in there long,' she said. The phone rang and as they were alone now in the surgery, Kathy answered it while Maisie carried on working. She listened for a moment, then cocked her head on one side and looked at Maisie.

'There's a horse with colic out at Earl Soham.'

There would be, she thought. It was miles.

'OK. Take all the details and tell them I'm on my way.' By the time Kathy had finished jotting down notes, Maisie was stripping off her gloves. 'Right, I've cleaned the ear out and given him a jab of anti-biotic and reversed the sedation, so if you could finish off here for me and keep an eye on him—what else have we got in over the weekend?'

'Nothing much,' Kathy told her. 'The little cat on fluids, the hedgehog that was brought in yesterday—that's all.'

'Right. If you could make sure they're all OK before you go, I'll leave Morgan here in your capable hands. Thanks, Kathy, you're a star.'

She checked the boot of her car for everything she might need for this next emergency, and then as an afterthought popped back in and used the loo. The tea seemed to have gone straight through her, and goodness knows when she'd get another chance.

She left for her colicky horse, wondering what she'd find. It could vary between a bit of mild tummyache from overeating to a massive impaction of the bowel contents or a twisted gut, both the last potentially fatal and requiring urgent referral to Newmarket for surgery—or, if the owner was unable or unwilling to pay for surgery, euthanasia.

In the end it was a fairly straightforward colic. The mare was sweating up and pacing restlessly, biting at her sides and unable to stand still, but she wasn't throwing herself on the ground or trying to roll, which was always a good sign.

Maisie passed a tube up the mare's nose and down her throat, and checked it was in her stomach and not her lungs by sucking on the pipe. If it didn't smell foul, it wasn't the stomach. Simple test, really, but it turned her own stomach every time and today was no exception.

Luckily—or unfortunately, depending on whose side you were on—she'd got it right first time, and all she had to do now was mix a litre or so of liquid paraffin and hot water, shake them up together to try and make an emulsion and then hold the ghastly mixture aloft until it had drained down the pipe, something it was always curiously reluctant to do.

'OK, little lady,' she said soothingly, as the horse stamped her foot and moved restlessly around the box. 'Just a little longer.'

Her owner snorted. 'They should tell you at vet school that oil and water don't mix,' he said sagely as she struggled to hold the funnel in the air and keep moving with the horse.

'I tell you what, I'll swap,' Maisie said. 'You hold this, I'll hold the horse. Your height might help. I can never do this bit.'

'You need wellies with stilts on,' he teased, but he took over, to her relief, and with his extra height the paraffin mixture seemed to give up its struggle and slid obligingly down the tube into the horse's stomach.

She'd given the little mare an antispasmolytic and a sedative already, and it seemed to be working. They watched her for half an hour, and finally Maisie was happy that she was improving slowly. The horse was less restless, and with instructions to the owner to watch her constantly and report back in a couple of hours or immediately if there was any change for the worse, she stripped off her overalls, packed up her equipment and went back to her car.

The first thing she did was check her mobile phone for messages, and of course there were some.

Three, in fact—all in different directions, and none of them anywhere near a loo, she thought as she bounced down the farm track to the road. Still, at least they were nearer home. She stopped at the gate and rang the callers, wondering if any of them could get to the surgery. At least it had plumbing, and she could kill three birds with one stone and reunite Morgan with his owners at the same time.

She was in luck. Two she could advise over the phone, and the third was able to come in to the surgery, so she headed straight there. It was the last thing she wanted to do. She ached from end to end, she'd got cramp in her arm from holding the funnel aloft and trying to hold the restless mare's head reasonably still, and if the nagging from her bladder was to be believed, she probably had a urinary infection.

Great. Still, at least she was headed for the surgery and not the middle of a field, she thought, and wondered if the rest of the weekend was going to be governed by her proximity to plumbing.

Oh, joy.

Sunday was no better, and by the end of Monday morning she was considering a career change. Either that or a week in bed. She came home for lunch, and while she was outside, doing the chickens and playing with the dogs, she could hear Tango barking. Funny. She'd been barking that morning when she'd left for work, but she'd assumed it had been because of the postman.

She went back for her afternoon surgery, leaving her dogs safely and happily enclosed in their outside run with their toys and plenty of water, but when she got back, Tango was still at it.

Not just once or twice, as if someone had rung the doorbell, but the sad, continuous barking of a dog left alone for hours.

James must have started his job, she thought, and she felt anger rising in her. He shouldn't have got a young dog if he didn't intend to give her time, and Tango was obviously unhappy.

She took her dogs for a walk, wishing she could take the young retriever too, and when she came back the barking had stopped.

Good. Finally, he must be home.

She would have gone up his drive and said something to him, but yet again her bladder was nagging,
and so she went straight home. Thank goodness she'd
phoned the surgery earlier and made an appointment
to see the doctor tomorrow, because this was getting
worse and worse, and there seemed to be pressure on
it rather than irritation.

From a mass of some sort?

No. She wouldn't let herself think about it, but at
the back of her mind was the subconscious fear. She'd
lost her mother to cancer when she'd been only
twelve, and then her father two years ago, just before
she'd moved here, but there was nothing to connect
her to either of them, because she'd been adopted.

Nevertheless, the fear was there. The Big C. She
saw enough of it at work, after all.

No! She wouldn't think about it. She'd discuss it
with Dr Shearer tomorrow. It was probably nothing
more or less than a simple urinary tract infection.

And what about the mass?

No. She was imagining it. There was no mass. It
was probably just because she was due for a period.

She cooked herself a meal, then debated going next
door to talk to James about leaving Tango, but she
was just too tired. She'd talk to him when she saw
him. She'd need plenty of energy for that particular
confrontation...

How did he know he was in trouble?

There was just something about the purposeful
stride of that diminutive little woman that made his
heart sink.

Only his heart, though. Everything else was rising.

His blood pressure, his interest, his— Damn. He didn't need to be that interested in his neighbour!

James stopped walking and let her come to him, and when she was just close enough that he could have reached out and touched that feisty little chin with his fingers, she came to a halt.

'About Tango,' she began.

'Good morning. Beautiful day.'

'She barks when you're out.'

'I know.'

'She's frightened.'

'And you'd know this.'

'Yes, I'd know this. I'm a vet.'

'Ah.' He tipped his head on one side and studied her. 'You don't look old enough—'

'Don't change the subject! You shouldn't be leaving her all day—you were gone yesterday before I left in the morning, and you didn't get back until after me last night—and I'd been home for lunch, so I know you weren't there then, and she was barking the whole time! You can't simply leave a dog for eleven and a half hours, it's criminal!'

He opened his mouth to correct her, then shut it again. He couldn't be bothered to argue. She'd already tried and sentenced him in one fell swoop without giving him a chance to put his case, and, anyway, he was tired. He'd been woken up at some ungodly hour for the last four mornings, and he'd had enough. To hell with neighbourly relations.

'I tell you what,' he said tightly, 'I'll shut my dog up if you'll shut your cockerel up.'

'It's not my cockerel,' she snapped.

'Well, it's not my dog,' he snapped back. 'And,

anyway, my personal domestic arrangements are none
of your damned business, so I'll thank you to butt
out—and while you're at it, you could return the
cockerel to the rightful owner so we can all get a bit
of sleep.'

'Not easy. She's dead.'

'Lucky her,' he muttered. He shut his mouth with
a snap and walked off.

At least, he would have done, but Tango and the
two scruffy mutts at Maisie's feet were inextricably
intertwined, and so his dignified exit on the moral
high ground was reduced to farce as he struggled to
separate the dogs without any help from the infernally
irritating woman standing in front of him.

'You could do something useful,' he snarled, and
one of her naturally pretty eyebrows lifted in an eloquent curve as she looked down on him.

She unclipped her dogs, removed their leads from
the tangled mess and turned on her heel, the dogs
falling into step behind her without a word from their
mistress as she stalked off in dignified silence.

Damn.

And she still had the sexiest bottom he'd ever
seen...

She was late, of course, because a rabbit had kindly
presented with an explosively full abscess that had
ruptured all over her as she'd palpated it and covered
her with about a gallon of foul-smelling goo. She'd
had to go home to wash, and yet again she'd heard
Tango barking.

So much for her lecture! Still, she didn't have time
to worry. She drove the short distance to save time,

and then, of course, she couldn't park the car. By the
time she had, it was six thirty-five and she would have
been quicker if she'd walked from home. She leant
on the counter, trying to get her breath because, of
course, she'd run from the side street where she'd
eventually abandoned the wretched vehicle. 'Maisie
McDowell,' she gasped. 'I've got an appointment
with Dr Shearer at six-thirty.'

The receptionist looked down at her computer
screen, then back up at Maisie with a frown. 'Six-
twenty, actually. I'm sorry, Miss McDowell, Dr
Shearer's left.'

'Left?'

'Well, you are fifteen minutes late.'

She dredged up a smile. 'I'm sorry. I had to go
home and change after work.'

The receptionist gave her a speaking look. 'I'm
sure Dr Shearer would rather have seen you on time
than not at all.'

'I doubt it,' Maisie muttered, and started to turn
away, but the thought of waiting any longer was too
much for her. She needed answers, and she needed
them tonight. She turned back. 'I don't suppose
there's another doctor still working? I really, really
need to see someone tonight,' she said, and she was
conscious of a tremor in her voice.

Perhaps the woman heard it too, because she un-
bent a little, albeit unwillingly. 'Well, Dr Sutherland's
still here, but he's been very busy and he has just
finished. I'll buzz him and see if he'll see you, but I
wouldn't hold out much hope.'

'Dr Sutherland?' Maisie said, puzzled. She'd never
heard of a Dr Sutherland, but the receptionist was

ignoring her, talking on the phone, and she looked up and gave Maisie a chilly smile.

'You're lucky. He says he'll see you if it's that urgent, just go straight in.'

'Thank you.'

Maisie turned and headed for the consulting rooms. Damn. She didn't mind seeing a male doctor really, but she had hoped to see Jane Shearer, just because being prodded about in that area was something she'd rather have done by a woman doctor, given a choice.

Still, better this Dr Sutherland than waiting any longer, she thought, and knocked on the door.

At the peremptory 'Come in!' she opened it, stepped inside and came to a grinding halt.

'Maisie?'

Of all people. He closed his eyes and counted to ten, then dragged in a good, deep breath and looked up into those startled toffee-coloured eyes. The last time he'd seen them they'd been spitting amber sparks, and absolutely the last thing he needed was another conversation with the neighbour from hell.

'I didn't know you were a doctor,' she said accusingly, and he gave an inward sigh.

'You didn't ask,' he pointed out fairly, but she wasn't in the mood to be fair, obviously.

'I thought you were working in London.'

'London?' He was astonished and perhaps a touch irritated, and he wondered if it came over in his voice. He decided he didn't much care. 'Why would I live here and commute to London?'

She shrugged. 'People do. Kirsten thought—'

'Ah. The lovely Kirsten. Kirsten seems to think I

want to have my house professionally co-ordinated—
by her, of course.' He swung his chair round and met
her eyes candidly. 'Presumably because I'm a fat cat
from the city.'

She had the grace to blush. 'I think it was the antiques,' she said, trying to explain and failing.

His mouth twitched. 'Ah, yes. The millstones.
Family heirlooms, actually. I'm sort of stuck with
them—a caretaker for future generations of little
Sutherlands, God help them. Anyway, now you're
here, and now you know I'm a doctor, which is presumably why you're here, why don't you sit down
and tell me the reason for your visit?'

It was obviously the last thing in the world she
wanted to do, but after an inward battle she sat,
looked him in the eyes and said candidly, 'There's
something pressing on my bladder. Some kind of
mass.' She hesitated. 'I think it could be cancer.'

He settled back in his chair, hands steepled under
his chin, and eyed her curiously.

'Cancer?'

She nodded, and he wondered what on earth made
her think it was cancer. Although, as she was a vet…

'Tell me your symptoms, from the beginning. What
was the first thing you noticed?'

She blinked and stared at him for a moment.
'Um…oh, well, I suppose feeling ill. I thought it was
a bug, but now I'm beginning to wonder. I felt dreadful for a few weeks, and I'm still not right. Some
things taste odd.'

'Odd?'

Maisie shrugged. 'I can't really explain. I just seem

fussier than I was. And then a week or so ago I started needing to pee very often—'

'Any pain or unusual odour?'

Dear God. He was talking about her bladder to the neighbour from hell, and judging by the look on her face she was not impressed!

'No,' she said. 'No pain, no odour.'

He moved on, wondering how this question would land. 'Bowels OK?'

She squirmed uncomfortably under his scrutiny, and despite her rising colour didn't allow her eyes to drop from his. 'Fine,' she said shortly.

'How about your periods? Regular? Lighter or heavier than usual, or any discomfort on intercourse?'

She sucked in her breath, and he found himself holding his. He really, really didn't want to know about her sex life.

'I don't have a regular cycle,' she told him. 'I must have a period due at any time, though.'

He noticed that she'd ignored the part about intercourse when she'd answered his question. Was that deliberate? 'So when was your last period?' he asked, dealing with that first.

She felt her brow crease in thought. 'I have no idea.'

'Before the onset of these symptoms?'

She nodded slowly. 'Probably. I had one during the snow—that would have been the first week in February.'

'You seem very certain of that.'

She looked acutely uncomfortable. 'I am. We had snow, I couldn't get out to go to the shops. I…um…'

She trailed off, and the penny dropped. He suppressed a smile. 'Right. And nothing since?'

She shook her head, puzzlement showing on her face. 'I don't think so.'

Good grief. It was now the beginning of June! Surely she was more aware of her cycle than that? Hardly anybody was *that* irregular. Unless...

'Just hop up on the couch and let me have a look at you,' he said, and she undid her jeans and he slid his hands under the edge of the denim and probed and prodded her abdomen. She avoided his eyes, staring fixedly at the wall, and just to be certain he was very thorough. He could feel her heart pounding, though, and the fear he could sense in her was climbing higher with every passing second.

'Any pain?'

She shook her head and squirmed as he pressed down just under the rim of her pubic bone. 'Just pressure.'

Lord, it was so obvious. How had she not noticed? 'What about clothes—everything still fit you?'

She frowned at him. 'Clothes? Of course they still fit—well, except for the fact that I've gained weight. I haven't started losing it yet, if that's what you're getting at.'

He turned away to hide his smile. 'Not at all. Quite the opposite. You can get down from there now, I'm pretty sure I know what's wrong.'

'And?' she said, sliding off the couch and fastening her jeans with trembling fingers. She had one foot half in, half out of her trainers when he sat down again and studied her thoughtfully.

'Well, you're right, of course, there is a mass in

your abdomen, but it's nothing to worry about. At least, it's not going to kill you, and it's a self-limiting condition.'

'So you think it's an abscess?' she said, and he could see the relief in her eyes. 'Thank God for that. I'd managed to convince myself...' She sat down, wriggling her foot into her shoe and tugging up the laces with one hand while she smiled at him in relief.

'No, I don't think it's an abscess,' he said, returning her smile wryly. 'But I estimate that it will have resolved itself in about four to six months—well, all bar the next eighteen years, or so. That could be a little more tricky.'

'Eighteen...? What on earth are you talking about?'

He arched a brow. 'Call yourself a vet, Maisie?' he said softly. 'I should have thought it was obvious. You're pregnant.'

The blood drained from her face, and for a second he thought she was going to pass out. Then her colour returned, and she sat up slowly and stared at him, her shoe forgotten.

'Don't be ridiculous! I can't possibly be pregnant.'

'They all say that, but unfortunately no method of contraception is infallible.'

'Mine is,' she said tightly.

'Apparently not. Just because you don't want to admit it, that won't change the facts. I'm sorry, Maisie, you may not like it but you're going to have a baby. I'd stake my career on it.'

She got to her feet, and gathered herself up to her full five feet four. 'Good,' she said clearly. 'It may come to that, because there's no way on God's earth

I can be pregnant, *Dr* Sutherland, because I haven't been in a relationship for over two years, and not even elephants are pregnant that long!'

'Nevertheless—'

She cut him off, the bit between her teeth and determined to have her say. 'I *know* I can't be pregnant,' she said emphatically, 'and if that's the only thing you're prepared to consider, then you deserve to be struck off for incompetence, and I shall do my best to make sure it happens! I knew GPs were hard to come by these days, but I didn't realise they were scraping quite *that* far down into the bottom of the barrel!'

And wrenching the door open, she stalked out.

James sat back in his chair and winced. Ouch. The bottom of the barrel, eh? Nice one, Sutherland. Very well handled.

Oh, well, she'd get over it. She'd remember her one-night stand eventually, and come crawling back for antenatal care.

Or a termination.

He didn't want to think about that one, but it was Maisie's problem, not his, and he had no intention of provoking any further discussion with her on the subject. She could see someone else next time, he'd had it with going head to head with a woman whose tongue could lash the skin off you at fifty paces.

Let her deal with it herself.

He packed up his desk, shut down his computer and picked up his bag.

No. He wouldn't feel guilty. It was hardly his fault she couldn't remember having had sex. She'd only remembered her last period because she'd obviously had a supplies crisis when she'd been cut off by the snow. Not much of a boy scout, our Maisie, he thought wryly. Anyway, she should be grateful to him for putting her mind at rest. Pregnancy, even unplanned and evidently unexpected, was a damned sight better than cancer.

He headed for home, his conscience clear.

Sort of.

Maisie slammed the consulting-room door behind her—or she would have done, but the door-closer resisted her efforts and all she got for her sins was a tearing pain in her wrist and a broken nail.

Damn. Damn, damn and double damn.

Tears blurring her vision, she ran out into the street, one foot still half in, half out of her shoe, found her car more by luck than judgement and drove blindly home, her wrist still stabbing with pain.

He was crazy. There was no way she was pregnant, she thought, sitting in the car on her drive and still seething with anger, and only one way to prove it to him. She'd go and buy a pregnancy test.

She backed out into the lane, scrubbing the tears from her cheeks, and drove one-handed to the supermarket in a nearby town.

Twenty minutes later she arrived home, went into the bathroom armed with the test and the instructions and set out to prove him wrong.

CHAPTER THREE

SHE wasn't at home.

James stood at her front door, eyeing her car thoughtfully and listening for the dogs, but they were silent. He pressed the doorbell again and heard it echo, as doorbells always seemed to in an empty house.

She wasn't there. And somehow he just knew where she'd be.

Ignoring Tango and his guilt, because he had enough guilt about Maisie to sink a battleship and Tango, bless her heart, would survive a little further neglect, he headed down the path across the marshes and up onto the river wall, and there in the distance was a small hump.

As he walked towards it, his guilt prodding at him, the hump resolved itself into a person seated on the edge of the path. Another minute and he could see it was her, and the dogs were with her. They turned their heads towards him, watching him intently, but she didn't so much as glance his way.

He didn't fancy his reception, but he couldn't leave her here and ignore her—not after the way he'd broken the news to her. He'd been hugely unprofessional, because he was nothing like detached enough, and once he'd got over his self-righteous fit and had had time to think about it, he'd been disgusted with himself.

41

Disgusted, and worried about her.

And anyway, what if he *was* wrong? If, as she'd said, she hadn't had a relationship with a man for two years, then there was no way she could be pregnant.

Unless the unthinkable had happened.

No. Don't be melodramatic, he told himself. She's just shocked because some one-night stand she's almost forgotten about has had repercussions.

The thought of her having a one-night stand brought bile to his throat, but he swallowed it and carried on walking slowly towards her, stopping only when he was a mere stride away.

She didn't look up, but the dogs wagged their tails, to his relief. He didn't fancy being eaten by them, and he didn't put it past Maisie to have trained them to attack.

He lowered himself to the path beside her and sat staring out over the river. She still didn't acknowledge his presence but, then again, she didn't get up and walk away either, and he hadn't really expected her to greet him with open arms.

'I owe you an apology,' he said softly. 'I handled that consultation with all the skill and tact of a bulldozer.'

'You were right.'

'Pardon?'

'You were right. I am pregnant. I bought a test.'

He turned his head and studied her, and saw the lines of strain etched on her face. Tears had dried on her cheeks, the moisture stripped out of them by the sun and the wind, and the salt trails ran down to her chin. His heart went out to her.

'Maisie, I'm really sorry. I don't know what to say.'

'You could tell me how,' she said, her voice stunned with disbelief. He stared at her, the flippant reply hovering on the tip of his tongue, but the utter bewilderment on her face stopped it in its tracks. She looked shocked to the core, and James realised that he was dealing with something very much more complex here than simple denial, something that was going to take all his skill and understanding to help her through.

Maisie really didn't seem to have any idea how she could have become pregnant.

And that left only one—highly unpalatable—answer.

She felt his hand under her elbow, and realised he'd stood up. 'Come on. I'm going to take you home and make you something to eat and drink.'

'I don't want anything—'

'Tough. Come on.'

His voice was gentle but implacable, and she let him lift her to her feet and lead her home.

His home, not hers, she noticed vaguely as they turned up his drive.

'I need to feed the cats.'

'Later. They'll manage a bit longer.'

He led her in through the scullery with its wonderful sink, and Tango greeted them rapturously.

'Hello, silly dog,' she said gently, rubbing the dog's head quite automatically when she found it almost in her face. 'Get down.'

She got down, but probably because James had

hauled her off and sent her out into the enclosed rear garden with the other two to let off steam together. Of course, Jodie and Scamp knew exactly where they were, and rushed off to smell all the new and exciting smells.

How wonderful to have such simple things to worry about, when she—

'How?' she said to herself for the hundredth time, but James must have heard, because he took her elbow again and led her through into the kitchen and pushed her gently into one of the sofas.

'I don't know. We'll talk it through. Let me make some tea.'

'I don't want tea. I just want answers.'

'You need both.'

He filled the kettle, and she watched him absently and wondered why he was bothering to be nice to her when she'd been so rude to him that morning.

Even if he had deserved it.

And she'd been rude to him this evening as well. Oh, lord.

'Look, I'm really sorry about today. I shouldn't have said what I did about scraping the bottom of the barrel.'

His mouth quirked. 'I've heard worse things, and I have to say this time I had it coming,' he said gently. Then he was pushing a mug of tea into her hands and sitting down beside her, one arm resting on the back and his body turned so he was facing her. He hitched a knee up onto the cushion, his foot tucked behind the other leg, and settled back, studying her with those extraordinary ice-blue eyes.

'Do you believe in virgin births?' she asked suddenly before he could speak, and he smiled, a rueful, regretful smile, and shook his head.

'No, I don't.'

'So—how, James? How on earth have I got pregnant? I mean, it's not like I get drunk and sleep around—I couldn't live a more blameless existence.'

'Nobody's trying to blame you, Maisie. Let's get that clear right from the start.' He paused for a moment, his lips pursed, then met her eyes. 'Your last period.'

'Back to that again?'

'You're sure it was in January or February?'

She nodded. 'Yes, quite sure. I can even tell you the day. It was a Sunday—the first Sunday in February.'

'OK. Well, from examining you I would say you're about somewhere between fifteen and twenty weeks pregnant. If we take that first Sunday in February as day one, that makes you about seventeen weeks pregnant, according to my ready reckoner, which is spot on for how you felt. I'd say your baby's due in early November.'

She stared at him numbly. It all seemed so unreal. How could she be having a baby? She couldn't look after a baby and go to work. And anyway, there was still the insurmountable problem of how it had been conceived. There was no way—

'Now, I want you to think back. You say your cycle's irregular, so working forwards from that last period, can you think of any time in the following few weeks when you woke up in the morning and didn't remember going to bed? Maybe if you'd been out, or away...'

'I don't go out, not like that, and I haven't been away—'

She broke off, a sudden, shocking thought occurring to her. It must have shown in her face, because James removed the mug gently from her trembling fingers and set it down, then took her hands in his. His grip was warm and reassuring, an anchor in a suddenly wild sea.

'What, Maisie? What have you remembered? Tell me.'

She shook her head. 'I can't tell you. I don't know,' she said, and her voice sounded strange and far-away. 'I don't remember anything—well, nothing significant, really.'

'Try,' he urged.

So she tried, scraping about in her patchy memory for as much information as she could muster.

'I was at a conference—an equine anaesthetics symposium in Newmarket. One of my old lecturers was there, too—a clinical pharmacology professor. I hadn't seen him for years. He was alone, and we were drinking in the bar. He was telling me all about his wife leaving him.'

She shook her head to clear it. 'I felt sorry for him. He'd had a car accident, and he said things had gone wrong from then onwards. We had quite a few drinks, I suppose, and I woke up in the morning feeling really rough and wondering why I'd let him get me so drunk. It never occurred to me, not even when I saw it in the paper, but— Oh, God.'

She felt his hands tighten on hers reassuringly. 'What did you see in the paper?'

'He hanged himself,' she said slowly. 'In police

custody. He'd been arrested for putting something in a girl's drink—the barman had seen him and called the police, and they'd arrested him. It was a couple of weeks after the conference, and I was really shocked. I remember telling Kirsten, laughing about it a bit hysterically, saying I'd had a lucky escape—but I hadn't, had I? I hadn't escaped at all, I just hadn't remembered.'

She turned blindly to him, locking onto his eyes for confirmation of what she already knew.

'Oh, my God. He must have put something in my drink, and then...'

James nodded, his eyes full of compassion and something else that she didn't quite understand. She felt her eyes fill with tears, and as the first one slid down her cheek, she felt his arms come round her and wrap her safely against the hard, solid warmth of his chest.

James wanted to kill someone.

The bastard who had done this to her would be a good start, but he was already dead. Probably a good thing. Murder didn't sit well with the Hippocratic oath.

Her hands tightened convulsively on his shirt and he heard her gulp on the sobs that were fighting their way out of her body.

'Do I have to tell the police?' she asked, her voice filled with dread, and he forced himself to breathe nice and deep and steady, and rubbed a hand gently over her back.

'Not if you don't want to,' he said, not sure if it was true but sure that, for now at least, it was what

Maisie needed to hear. 'What would it achieve? He's dead, Maisie. You can't press charges against a dead person. The only person this affects is you. If you want to go to the police, then I'll support you, but I don't think there's any point. I think you should concentrate your energies on dealing with the here and now.'

She stayed rigid for a minute more, then he felt the sobs rising in her again and she collapsed against his chest. He shifted, easing her closer, and somehow she ended up on his lap, burrowing into his shoulder, her body heaving.

He held her for what seemed like an age, until the sobs died away and she was still, then she pushed up and turned her head away.

'I'm sorry... I don't know why I— Oh, hell, I never cry.'

'I think you have a pretty good excuse.'

She sniffed, and he pulled a spare, clean handkerchief out of his pocket and put it in her hand.

'Thanks,' she mumbled. She blew her nose and scrubbed at her eyes, then looked at the handkerchief and laughed unsteadily. 'You're going to run out at this rate.'

'At least you'll know what to buy me for Christmas,' he teased, and she smiled, but then the smile faded and she shifted away from him, into the corner of the sofa.

James let her go, sensing that it was all part of the process of coming to terms with what had happened to her. For a moment she chewed her lip, then she looked up at him, then away again, as if she was struggling with her words.

Finally she spoke, her voice quiet and strained. 'I feel—is violated too strong a word?'

He crushed his anger. 'No. No, I don't think it is. I think I would feel the same.'

She shot him a surprised look. 'Really? I thought men didn't worry about that sort of thing. Sex at any price and so on. I would have thought the average man would simply be annoyed that he couldn't remember it.'

He gave a short, startled laugh. 'Well, I don't know about the average man, but that certainly doesn't apply to me. The idea of anyone drugging me so they could use my body for something so essentially private and personal would make me very deeply angry—but, then, I may be a bit of an oddball. I can't imagine wanting to get that close to a woman with whom I wasn't involved body and soul. I just don't do it. So, no, I don't think violated is too strong a word.'

A shudder ran through her, and she wriggled further away from him, hitching herself right up into the far corner of the sofa as if their conversation had brought it home to her that she was alone with him, and how vulnerable that made her. He wanted to reassure her, to tell her that she was safe with him, but he knew she wouldn't believe him yet, and possibly never after this, simply because he was a man.

Except that this man wanted nothing more than to hold her and protect her and cherish her...

Hell's teeth. Where had that come from?

He stood up abruptly, moving away from her to give both of them more space. 'Another cup of tea?'

She shook her head. 'I should go home.'

'Not until you've eaten.'

And there were things they needed to discuss, tests that needed to be run to make sure that she and the baby were safe, but now was not the time to introduce any other fears or to consider whether or not she was going to continue with the pregnancy. For now, she needed to know that there was one person in the world she could trust absolutely, and he intended to make damned sure she could.

And that meant that, for now at least, he'd have to put his own personal interest very firmly on hold.

Maisie knew what he was doing.

Slowly, reassuringly, he moved about the kitchen, throwing together something that smelt absolutely wonderful and keeping up a steady stream of meaningless conversation while she sipped her third cup of tea and the dogs lay in heaps around her feet. She'd behave the same way with a wary, injured animal, and the thought made her smile a little inside.

'I'm not going to fall apart,' she told him softly, and he paused for a moment, then shot her a crooked smile.

'I didn't think you were.'

'You're cosseting me.'

'Don't you think you deserve it?'

She laughed a little raggedly. 'Probably not. I was stupid, wasn't I? Putting myself in that position.'

'What—having a few drinks with someone you'd learned to respect? I wouldn't say you'd done anything wrong at all.'

'Except leave an unguarded drink.'

'Were you in a nightclub or drinking with strangers?'

The ragged laugh sounded again in her ears as she remembered the very sedate and civilised surroundings of the hotel bar. 'Hardly. We were in the hotel lounge.'

'I rest my case. Do you like ginger and garlic?'

'Love them.'

'Good, because it's just occurred to me I've put rather a lot in if you don't like it.'

'What about your patients?' she asked, and he just shrugged and grinned.

'I tell them all to eat lots of garlic because it protects the heart and is a wonderful natural antibiotic. The flip side is they hopefully don't notice if I smell of it.'

She chuckled, then her smile faded as the reality of her situation came crashing back. Oh, lord...

'Come on. It's ready.'

She looked up, to see two plates on the table heaped with a colourful extravaganza. Her stomach rumbled, and she got up and went over, deliberately shutting her mind to unwelcome thoughts. 'Looks good. Miss Keeble would be scandalised at you, though, eating in the kitchen,' she said with a weak attempt at a smile, and he chuckled.

'Miss Keeble would no doubt be scandalised at all sorts of things that I've done, but fortunately for me she isn't here to worry about it.'

'I think she would have liked you. You're a good cook—that would help. This is delicious.'

He smiled, his eyes softening, and she felt hugely guilty for the way she'd criticised him.

'I'm so sorry about the way I spoke to you,' she said, putting her fork down. She couldn't eat until she'd got this off her chest, but he just waved his own fork at her and shook his head.

'Don't worry. Eat.'

But there was something else troubling her, and she ploughed on. 'About Tango barking...'

'Tango hates being left alone. I'll come back before I go on my calls, if I can, and take her for a run, then after my calls I'll come home for lunch and take her out again, or play with her in the garden. Then she'll be alone again while I do my evening surgery and any other calls, but that's only a couple of hours, four at the most if I'm the duty doctor. Besides, it's only temporary and it's probably better than being in kennels. She's not mine, she's my sister's. When she comes back, Tango goes.'

And now she felt really bad.

'Stop it. Eat your food.'

He must have read her mind. Maisie had another forkful and tipped her head on one side, meeting his enquiring eyes. 'How about if she spent the day with Jodie and Scamp in the run in my garden? They get on well, and mine are so laid-back they'll help her settle. Then I wouldn't have to worry about her. I come home for lunch, too, after we finish operating, and I take them for a walk then. There's usually a lull until afternoon surgery, unless I've got a large animal call, so there's plenty of time.'

'Whatever. Eat, for goodness' sake, it'll be cold. We'll worry about Tango later, if you insist.'

'I do.'

He threw up his hands. 'Fine. Have her. Do whatever makes you happy. Now, eat, woman, for goodness' sake.'

She nodded, relieved that the dog, at least, was sorted for now. Her own problems—well, she just wouldn't think about them for a little while. There'd be plenty of time later.

'Tell me about Miss Keeble,' he said suddenly.

She looked up and found him watching her again, a thoughtful expression on his face.

'Miss Keeble? She was a treasure. Lonely—bit of a funny old stick. Not everyone liked her, but she was very good to me. We got on really well, and I did what I could for her.'

'Did she have money? There was very little evidence of it being spent on the house in recent years, but some people get a little eccentric in their later years.'

Maisie laughed. 'No, she didn't have any money at all. I don't think she'd ever owned her own home, she'd gone from her parents' home straight into service.'

His eyebrows shot up. 'So how did she end up with this house? Was she a drug baron or something exciting?'

Maisie chuckled. 'Hardly. She was the doctor's housekeeper. He used to live here in the Mount, and the Lodge was his surgery. There's a gate in the wall—'

'Yes, I've seen it. Perhaps we should get it working again if I'm going to keep Tango in your garden with your dogs. Save having to take her out on the road.'

'Good idea. Anyway, he retired, but Miss Keeble carried on looking after him until he died, and he left her both houses, in gratitude for services rendered. Rumour has it he was a cantankerous old man, but they looked after each other till the end, and she spoke very fondly of him.'

'And she had no money to maintain it all.'

'That's right. He only left her the houses, and she didn't have any money to keep them up. That's why she took in paying guests in the summer, and rented out the Lodge. When I moved here three years ago, she let it to me, and when she died, I found she'd left it to me in her will.'

'Good lord. None of my landlords have ever given me so much as a lightbulb, never mind a house!'

Maisie laughed. 'I know. The distant cousin who got this house queried it, but not as hard as I did. Believe me, nobody was more surprised than I was. I'm still waiting for someone to come along and tell me the will was dodgy and it's not mine. I have to pinch myself sometimes, but maybe she felt she'd been given it herself and she could do what she liked with it—and don't forget, I got the animals, too, so it wasn't quite the open-handed gesture it sounds like!'

'Animals?'

'Yes. Jodie and Scamp were hers, but there were also the cats—three of them, a ginger kitten and two elderly tabbies. Not that the kitten's a kitten any more. You're bound to have seen them. They haunt your garden.'

'Tango chases them.'

She chuckled. 'I'm sure. And then there were the chickens.'

'Ah.' James tipped his head on one side and gave her a wry smile. 'The cockerel with the dead owner.'

'Mmm. Hector.'

He snorted. 'Hector? How appropriate. I think it means bully, doesn't it?'

'He's glorious.'

'Not at four o'clock in the morning,' James said sternly, and if she hadn't seen the glimmer of humour in her eye, she would have thought the old cock's days were numbered.

'I could try shutting him in, but with these light mornings they get up early to enjoy the day...'

He made a rude noise and topped up her water glass, only the trickling sound breaking the sudden slightly tense silence.

She had a wonderful idea. 'Do you like eggs?'

He eyed her suspiciously, and she felt the smile tugging at her mouth as he set down the water jug. 'Going to bribe me? Or trying to kill me with cholesterol?'

She shook her head. 'Old wives' tale. They've changed their minds. Dietary cholesterol is almost insignificant compared to the amount made by our own bodies, and anyway it's saturated fat you need to cut down on. Eggs have good cholesterol and are very healthy.'

He chuckled. 'You're very convincing. I understood the jury was still out.'

She shrugged and smiled. 'Some sceptics like to hang onto the old myths...'

'Thank you. Eggs would be lovely. I eat about two a week.'

'But have you ever had a real egg? From a real, happy, free-range chicken?'

'Would they be the free-range chickens I found in

the borders the other day and had to chase out of the garden before they ate all the flowers?'

She felt her colour rise. Oh, dear, was there no end to the havoc she was causing in his life? 'I'm sorry. They still think they live here. I have to rescue them all the time.'

'Can't you clip their wings?'

'But the wall's so low at the side they can hop over it,' she explained. 'They'd need cannon-balls tied to their feet to stop them.'

'I'm sure it can be arranged,' he said drily, and she wasn't sure if he was joking. 'Although if we get the gate working, no doubt they'll just drag themselves through it, cannon-balls and all.'

'I'll do something about their run,' she promised. In fact, she'd been meaning to, because she was losing eggs and one of the chickens had disappeared, probably courtesy of Mr Fox.

'So, how about a cup of coffee and some of those delicious biscuits of yours to finish off?' he suggested, and she realised to her amazement that she'd eaten every scrap on her plate. How she'd found time to do that and talk so much she didn't know, but he'd successfully distracted her from the chaos her life had so recently descended into.

Not any more, though. Her hunger taken care of, reality had come crashing back with all the subtlety of an express train, and she pushed her plate away and shook her head.

'No. Really. That was lovely, but I couldn't eat another thing. I have to go back and feed the chickens and shut them up in their useless run, and I still haven't done the cats, and the dogs will be hungry—'

'I doubt it. They've had some of Tango's food—'

'Did you feed them?'

He smiled wryly. 'They seemed to think it was a good idea.'

'I'm sure.' She was debating pointing out that he shouldn't have fed them without consulting her, and then abandoned the idea. He'd been kindness itself, and without him she'd probably still be sitting on the river wall, contemplating throwing herself in or selling her story to a Sunday paper. She could see the headline now—VIRGIN VET IN PREGNANCY PUZZLE.

Well, hardly a virgin, but she might as well have been for all the difference it would have made.

'I still can't believe that such a respectable, decent person as Phillip Stevenson would have done that.'

'Phillip Stevenson?'

'My pharmacology professor—and, if the evidence is to be believed, the father of my baby.'

Baby. Dear God. She got up abruptly and walked out into the garden, suddenly feeling shut in. What had happened that night? Had she fought him? Passed out?

Enjoyed it?

She shuddered. Most unlikely. She'd respected him—well, until she'd seen the paper—and he'd always seemed a nice enough guy. Certainly clever, and reasonably good-looking when he'd been younger, she was sure. But she'd absolutely never seen him in anything other than his professional capacity as a lecturer when she'd been a student, and she certainly wouldn't have entertained a relationship with him—

'Penny for them.'

She sucked in a huge deep breath and let it out

with a whoosh. 'I was thinking about Phillip. He'd always seemed so decent. He said his marriage had fallen apart after the accident. I wonder if he had a head injury—if it changed him.'

'Possibly. It can certainly cause personality changes. Did he seem different?'

She nodded slowly, thinking back. 'Yes. More…I don't know. Intense, perhaps? I felt a little uncomfortable. I remember that.' She wrapped her arms around her body, hugging herself. 'I think I want to go home.'

'Sure. I'll walk you back.'

He locked the door with Tango on what she obviously considered to be the wrong side of it, and, gathering up the dogs, he shepherded them all home, pausing at her front door while she rummaged in her pocket for the keys. Finally she found them and opened the door, then hesitated.

'Thank you for everything,' she said quietly. 'I don't know what I would have done if you hadn't come and found me.'

'Don't thank me. I should have listened to you more closely, but I was still feeling mad about you telling me how to look after Tango.'

'I'm so sorry about that.'

He laid his finger on her lips, cutting off the words. 'No. Forget it. It's all past.' His eyes were troubled, searching her face, and she felt curiously naked. 'Will you be OK on your own?'

She nodded. 'I feel safe in my house. I've got the dogs.'

'I thought they lived outside?'

Her laugh sounded strained, even to her ears. 'Only

when I'm at work. At night they sleep outside my bedroom—unless I forget to close the door properly, and then they sneak onto the bed in the night and I find them there in the morning. I think tonight I might forget to close the door.'

His chuckle was warm and gentle, his breath puffing against her cheek. He was standing close to her, but she didn't feel threatened. Odd, that. She would have thought she might have done, under the circumstances, but she seemed to know instinctively that she was safe with James.

She turned to push the door open, and gasped as pain stabbed through her wrist.

'What is it?'

'Nothing. My wrist twinged—I hurt it earlier.'

Not for the life of her could she tell him that she'd strained it trying to slam the door of his consulting room, but then he took her hand in his, turning it over, carefully flexing it, his fingers probing. It might have hurt. She had no idea. All she was aware of was the warmth of his hands around hers, the firm yet gentle touch that made her want to cry.

'Put some ice on it now and before you go to bed, and put a support bandage on it before you do anything. If it's still sore in the morning let me know. I can let you have some anti-inflammatory gel to put on it if you need it. I don't want you to take anything like ibuprofen—not with the baby.'

Baby. Oh lord.

'I've got arnica and witch-hazel gel—I'll use that,' she said, and gave him what felt like a very brittle smile. 'Thanks again. I'll see you in the morning with Tango, shall I?'

'Sure. About half-seven?'

'OK.'

He lifted a hand in farewell and turned, walking the few steps to the lane and then turning the corner out of sight.

She closed the door slowly and sagged against it.

Baby. My God, she thought, and her hand slid down and cradled it. I'm going to have a baby.

CHAPTER FOUR

IT WAS a strange night.

Maisie couldn't sleep, probably not surprisingly, and she gave up in the end and curled up on the window-seat in her bedroom, the dogs at her side, staring out over the eerie silver landscape.

She could see the moon's reflection on the river as it snaked through the marshes, and beyond it in the distance, at the north end of Orford Ness, on the spit of land that separated Orford and Butley Ford from the sea, was the lighthouse, winking its warning every few seconds as the beam swept across the horizon.

It was peaceful, and she sat there with the window open and listened to the quiet rustlings and occasional cries that broke the silence.

And as she sat, contemplating the moonlit marshes, peace seemed to steal over her, calming her anger and soothing her fears, so that all she could think about was the baby growing within her, the innocent life that Phillip's actions had inadvertently created.

No. She wouldn't dwell on that. She wasn't ready to think about him yet, so she shut out any thought of the man who'd done this to her, and concentrated instead on the knowledge that in a few more months she'd be a mother.

How amazing. And she'd be a good one, not like her own mother, who'd abandoned her, given her up for adoption when she'd been just hours old and walked away without a backward glance. When she'd turned eighteen and had tried to contact her birth mother, the woman hadn't been interested, and Maisie could still remember vividly the pain of that rejection as her dreams of a loving reconciliation had crumbled into dust.

Deprived of the possibility of a relationship with the woman who'd given her life, she'd clung to memories of her *real* mother, the woman who'd opened her heart and her home to another woman's child, and who'd been the most loving and caring and understanding person she'd ever met. Losing her to cancer had been devastating to Maisie, but she'd never forgotten the warmth and generosity of her love, and she vowed that her own baby, too, would know that same unconditional love.

And thanks to Miss Keeble, bless her heart, at least she had a home to offer her child, a home that she owned free and clear. If she was careful, she could possibly cope on a part-time salary. It would be tight, but she'd manage.

'We'll be all right, baby,' she said softly, her hand creeping down to cover the tiny bulge that was her child. 'We'll be all right.'

The quiet night was giving way to dawn, and down in the garden she heard Hector's early morning call. She sighed. So late already? If she was going to get any work done today, she ought to try and catch a couple of hours' sleep, at least.

As she stood up stiffly, stretching to ease out the kinks induced by sitting there for hours, she glanced across at James's house. Which was his bedroom? She'd thought it was the one on the front corner, the one she could see from her room, but in the few days since he'd moved in the lights had been on in so many of the rooms when she'd gone to bed each night that she'd never managed to work it out.

Now, though, she could see that the windows of that corner bedroom, with the lovely views over both the river and the town, were open, and as she stood there, she saw a shape move inside the room, backlit by the moonlight from the other window.

The sash slid shut with a little thump, and she suppressed a guilty smile.

Oops. Hector had got him up again. She stood motionless, watching the window for any further sign of movement, then after an age a dark shape detached itself from the glass and moved away, silhouetted again by the moonlight flooding through the room.

Seeing him there was curiously comforting—reassuring, somehow. She felt less isolated, less alone in the world, knowing he was there. Ridiculous, really. He was only a neighbour, another GP in the practice she was registered with. Nothing more. She'd only seen him in his professional capacity by accident, and yet they'd argued about Tango and Hector, and he'd taken her into his home, fed her, cared for her, talked to her patiently and sympathetically through the most difficult moment of her adult life.

Why? No doubt he was asking himself that at that very moment, wondering what on earth he'd done to deserve her. Probably still feeling guilty about his less-than-sympathetic consultation, but to be fair there was no way he could have told her that would have made any difference.

Poor James. She'd keep out of his way for a while, try and cut him a bit of slack.

Starting by shutting Hector up at night.

'Bloody chicken!'

James stood at the window, glowering down into Maisie's garden and contemplating murder.

He'd had little enough sleep as it was, with Maisie's problems milling round and round in his head, and now that dratted bird had started with the crowing. If he had any sense at all he'd move into another bedroom. There was a wonderful one at the other end of the house, the mirror image of this one, with the same stunning views out over the marshes to the front but over the woodland at the side instead of towards the town.

And Maisie.

He glanced at her house, and for a moment he thought he saw her there at the window, her face ghostly pale in the moonlight.

No. He'd imagined it, poor, sad old fool that he was. He went back to bed, chastising himself soundly for fantasising about her in her bedroom, and spent the next two hours wide awake thinking about nothing else, while Hector went almost unnoticed.

'Good morning.'

She smiled up at him, that sassy mouth tilted at the corners, and only the dark smudges under her eyes gave away the momentous revelations of the past twelve or so hours.

'Hi,' she said softly.

'How are you?'

The smile wavered a little. 'I'm fine, thanks.'

'Really?'

She nodded. 'Really.'

'Did you sleep?'

She shrugged, her smile slipping a little more. 'Not really.'

'Neither did I.'

Maisie sighed and threaded her hand through the wild ebony strands of her hair, tousled by the early-morning breeze that tugged at them as they walked along the river wall. 'Look, I'm really sorry about Hector—'

'No. No, it wasn't Hector. Not really. He was just the icing on the cake. I was...' What? Fantasising about her? Wishing that he had a right to be involved with her, that they'd made this baby together?

'You were...?' she probed, and he shrugged and laughed a little awkwardly.

'Just a bit restless. It was hot.'

In fact, the sea breeze across the Ness had kept it beautifully cool, but what was a little white lie between friends?

'You should open the windows,' she said guilelessly. 'Then the breeze would cool you.'

'And then I'd hear Hector,' he said. She coloured softly and he almost groaned aloud. Lord, she was gorgeous, and he was going to have to keep a nice, safe, professional distance—starting now.

'Maisie, come and see me tonight, at the surgery. What time do you finish?'

She shrugged. 'I don't know. Why do I need to see you?'

James hesitated a moment. This was difficult.

'There are things we need to consider—things that might threaten your health.'

Her colour disappeared, leaving her pale and visibly shaken. 'I hadn't even thought—you mean HIV?'

'Amongst other things, all of which are far more likely. We should do a urine test to make sure it is just the pressure of your uterus and you don't have an infection, and you need blood tests for all the routine things like haemoglobin, blood sugar and so on, never mind any sexually transmitted infections. You'll need swabs and smears, too, so I'll arrange for a nurse to be there to do those for you.'

She'd stopped walking, but now she started again, just slowly, as if she was in a daze.

'Good grief. I hadn't thought it would be so complicated.'

'And there's also the question of whether you want to keep the baby.'

Again she stopped, but abruptly this time, her eyes widening. 'Keep it? Of course I'm going to keep it!' she said indignantly. 'What kind of a person do you think I am?'

'The sort of person who's been drugged and—well, raped, for want of a better word,' he said gently. 'The other day you were using the word "violated". A lot of people under those circumstances would be desperate to have the baby taken away.'

'No way,' she said firmly, shaking her head to emphasise the point. 'Nobody's taking my baby away from me. And anyway, it's not like I don't have a clue who the father is. I've been thinking—he was a good man, James, highly respected in his field, a brilliant academic, an excellent clinician.'

'Good genetic material,' he said thoughtfully, and wondered why that mattered to her. Almost immediately, he had his answer.

'Exactly. She'll be able to be proud of him, not wonder—'

She broke off, and he pondered her strange choice of words and the use of 'she', not 'it'. It sounded curiously autobiographical.

'And I'm sure it wasn't really like him to do that,' she went on. 'I'm certain that it was just because of the head injury. So it's not as if there's even a reason to consider—'

She broke off, as if she couldn't bring herself to say the word, and he smiled, suddenly realising how glad he was to hear her decision and the conviction behind it.

'Good for you,' he said softly. 'Will your family be able to help you?'

She shook her head, and her eyes clouded over. 'I don't have a family any more. My parents have both died, my mother when I was twelve, my father two years ago. They had cancer.'

'Is that why you thought you had it? Because of family history?' he asked, but she shook her head again.

'Well, possibly, but not because of a genetic link. I'm adopted.'

And her remarks about the baby's father suddenly fell into place.

'So you're all alone.' It wasn't a question, but she lifted her chin as if defending her decision, and determination flashed in her eyes.

'I know it won't be easy,' she said, 'but I'll manage. I'm going to do this, James. I'm going to be a good mother.'

'I'm sure you will,' he said, believing it. This tough, determined young woman had guts to burn, and he felt suddenly irrationally proud of her.

'So—what time tonight?' she asked, as they arrived back at her house and put the dogs in the run.

'Six-thirty? Or whenever. I'll wait for you. Ring the surgery if you're going to be later than that, because I don't want to keep the nurse hanging around.'

She stroked Tango's head absently, reassuring her, and the simple act gave James a warm, fuzzy feeling inside.

Hell. He was getting too involved—and certainly far too involved to continue to act as her doctor. 'Can I talk to Jane Shearer about you?' he asked abruptly, and she looked up, her eyes wide and worried.

'Do you have to?'

He shrugged. 'I just feel— We're neighbours, Maisie. More than that—friends, almost. It's not appropriate.'

'Appropriate? Why on earth not?'

He shifted awkwardly. 'Maisie, you're pregnant. You'll need antenatal care—regular examinations—and I don't think I...'

He saw the moment light dawned, and colour ran hot and swift over her cheeks. She turned away.

'Of course. How silly, I didn't even think about that. Um. Does she need to know everything? It's just...the circumstances are a bit...'

She trailed off, and he concluded, 'Unusual?'

She laughed, a brittle sound, and he realised that for all her courage, she was hanging on by a thread.

'I tell you what. I'll do the first tests, and get a nurse to take any necessary swabs. I'll simply say you're overdue for a smear—that should cover it. And then I'll hand you over to Jane and I'll keep an eye on your notes if you like and discuss anything you're worried about. Will that do?'

She looked up at him, her cheeks a little warm still and her eyes over-bright. 'Thank you,' she said, so quietly that if he hadn't seen her lips move he wouldn't have known she'd spoken.

'My pleasure. Right. If you think the dogs will be OK, I'd better get off to work. What about you? Are you all right to work today? I can give you a sick note if you want.'

She shook her head. 'No. I'm pregnant, not sick. I'll be fine. I'll save my sick leave for when I need it. And anyway, I could do with being busy. Give everything time to settle in my head before I have too much time alone to think about it too much. Thinking won't change it, James, so I'd rather not waste the energy.'

He nodded slowly, then with a reassuring squeeze to her shoulder he turned on his heel and walked swiftly away, before he gave in to the urge to pull her into his arms and kiss her better.

'Kirsten? Are you busy?'

'Maisie? Hi. Are you OK? I tried to ring you last night but you were out.'

'I was with James.'

She almost heard Kirsten's ears prick. 'James? Oh, my God! Mr Body-To-Die-For James next door?'

'Yes. We had supper. Look, can you come round?

I'd come to you but I'm really tired, and I want to talk to you. I've got something important to tell you.'

'I'll be right there.'

There was a click, and the line went dead. Maisie smiled wryly. Kirsten was so predictable. Give her the slightest little hint of mystery and she was in there without hesitation.

It only took her ten minutes to arrive, by which time Maisie had put some popping corn in the micro-wave and made a jug of coffee. It was decaf, but even full strength wouldn't keep her awake tonight, she was so tired.

The door banged open and shut again, and Kirsten was there, eyes sparkling with curiosity. 'Well?'

'And hello to you, too,' she said with a chuckle. 'Coffee?'

'Mmm. And is that toffee popcorn I can smell? This must be serious.' But the sparkling in her eyes didn't diminish. If anything, it grew brighter, and Maisie suddenly found herself wondering how to say the words.

'It is,' she began, and then Kirsten looked at her— really looked at her for the first time—and the sparkle went.

'Oh, God, Maisie, what is it? What's happened?'

And just like that, the floodgates opened, and she found herself wrapped in Kirsten's slender but com-forting embrace.

'Tut-tut, silly girl,' Kirsten said, rocking her, and after the initial flood of tears, Maisie eased out of her arms and reached for a tissue.

No James this time to proffer an immaculately laundered hanky, she thought with a touch of hysteria, and blew her nose vigorously. Kirsten was watching her worriedly, her hand moving up and down Maisie's arm in a comforting gesture.

'Are you OK, Maise?'

'I'm fine. Just—a bit shocked, really. Come on, let's take the coffee and the popcorn and go and sit down.'

Once they were settled on Maisie's old sofa, the popcorn wedged between them and steaming mugs of coffee cradled in their hands, Kirsten fixed her with a searching look.

'OK. Give.'

Maisie shrugged. Where to start?

'Try the beginning,' Kirsten said, reading her mind, and she gave a shaky laugh and tipped her head back against the sofa.

'The beginning. OK. Do you remember, a few months ago, I showed you that thing in the paper about my old college professor?'

'The guy who topped himself in a police cell because he'd been caught drugging some girl?'

'That's the one. We had a laugh about it.'

'Yeah, because you'd been drinking with him a few days before and you said what a lucky escape—'

Kirsten broke off, her eyes widening. 'Oh, God. It happened to you, didn't it? And you've caught something off him—not HIV. Tell me it's not HIV.'

'No. Well, I don't know yet. That's being tested. No, it's worse than that.'

'How can it be worse? Oh, no, you're pregnant!'

Kirsten sat bolt upright, sending coffee and popcorn flying in all directions, and stared at her in horror. 'You are, aren't you? You're pregnant!'

She shrugged. 'So the test said. I went to the doctor, but I was late, and Jane Shearer had gone, but I saw James—'

'James? *Our* James? He's a *doctor*?'

'Yes—not a fat cat from the city at all, so I'm sorry to ruin your illusions,' she said wryly, remembering James's slightly bitter words. 'The antiques are inherited. Anyway, he told me I was pregnant, and I didn't believe him,' she said, leaving out the hideous scene and her temper tantrum. 'So I did a test, to prove him wrong.'

'And it didn't.'

'No, it didn't. That's what I was doing there last night—talking it through, because I just had no idea how it could have happened.'

'You don't remember?'

She shook her head. 'Only drinking with him and feeling sorry for him because his life had gone pear-shaped since the accident.'

Kirsten slumped back against the sofa, crushing popcorn into the upholstery and staring at Maisie, wide-eyed. 'So what are you going to do?'

'What do you mean, what am I going to do? I'm going to have a baby—the first week in November, apparently.'

'Oh, my God. Can I be godmother?'

'Only if you learn to moderate your language,' Maisie teased gently, and Kirsten, the queen of cool, actually blushed.

'God, I'm sorry—there I go again! You'll have to have a swear box.' She fished some of the popcorn out from behind her back and ate it absently. 'So what will you do about work? November—grief, it's already June! That's not so long, really, is it? I'm amazed you don't show.'

'I do.' She stood up, pulled up her top and turned sideways to Kirsten, peering down as she did so and looking in wonder at the gentle swell of her abdomen. Her friend's eyes widened.

'Wow. That wasn't there last week.'

She laughed. 'Oh, yes it was, it was stuck in my pelvis pressing on my bladder and making me pee every five minutes.' Her smile faded. 'It's almost as if, now I know, it's allowed to show—does that sound silly?'

Kirsten shook her head, as much in bewilderment as anything, and stared at Maisie's no-longer-flat tummy as if she couldn't quite take it all in. 'So what have they said at work?'

Maisie pulled a face and plopped back onto the sofa, spilling the rest of the popcorn. 'I haven't told them. What do I say? It was a one-night stand but I don't know who it was? I was drugged? It was an old boyfriend but we aren't seeing each other again? They know I'm not in a relationship.'

'So tell them nothing. Leave them guessing—it's nobody's business but your own.'

'Funny you should say that. It's exactly what James said this evening.'

'So believe us. We can't both be wrong.' She tutted and reached out her hand, rubbing Maisie's arm again in support. 'Are you OK? Really? I mean—that's like rape, isn't it? Don't you need counselling?'

She shook her head. 'No. I'm fine—and, anyway, talking to James is like seeing a counsellor. He's been brilliant but, really, I'm all right. I can't remember it,

I don't know anything about it. It's like it's happened to someone else. At first I felt as if my body had been, I don't know, burgled or something, but now—I know it's silly, but I feel like this is my baby, nobody else's. Just mine.' She gave a little laugh. 'I know it's crazy, but I'm really quite excited, now it's sunk in. Kirsten, I was adopted. I've never had a relative before—not a blood relation. And now I will. It's fantastic.'

Kirsten stared at her in amazement, then a smile broke out on her face.

'You really mean it, don't you? Oh, Maisie, I'm so glad you're OK.'

Kirsten leant over and hugged her, then sat up abruptly and sniffed, blotting her eyes with the backs of her hands and streaking her make-up everywhere. 'Look what you've made me do!' she wailed, laughing, and Maisie smiled and scooped up another handful of popcorn and ate it while Kirsten pulled herself together and scrubbed mascara off her hands.

'So—what now?'

'Now I have to go to antenatal classes and learn how to give birth and how to be a mother, and I have to sort out some kind of maternity leave and part-time stuff for later with my boss, and it's going to be chaos.' Her smile faded. 'I'll need help, Kirsten. I hate asking, but if I need anything…'

'Then ask. Never mind hating it. You just ask. And I don't want to hear that you can cope.'

Maisie laughed, and stood up. 'More coffee?'

Kirsten shook her head. 'No. You need to take your baby to bed. You look bushed.'

'I am bushed. I didn't sleep very well last night.' That was an understatement. She'd had about an hour of sound sleep before the alarm had rudely woken her at six. After Kirsten had left she put the dogs out, checked that the chickens were all in the run and shut them in. Not that it worked.

She was still one down, a pretty little Light Sussex hen called Helga. She was always going broody, and she suspected that she'd taken herself off somewhere and the fox had got her.

'Poor Helga,' she murmured, and felt the prickle of tears.

For a chicken? Good grief. These hormones were going to be the giddy limit. How was she going to feel when she had to put down someone's beloved dog or horse? It didn't bear thinking about.

Whistling for the dogs, she went back inside, stroked Max, the ginger cat, in passing, and went up to bed, the dogs trailing hopefully behind her.

'Sorry, darlings, not tonight,' she said, and closed the door firmly on their noses. She didn't put the light on, but instead crossed to the window and looked over at James's house. It was ten-thirty, but there was no light on in his bedroom. She could see light spilling out over the lawn at the back of the house, though, and as she stood there, she heard him call Tango.

A minute later the light came on in his room, and he crossed to the window, closed it firmly and shut the curtains. She felt stupidly shut out, and to her disgust her eyes filled with tears.

How ridiculous! She was turning into a watering-can! She got into bed, turned out the light and was asleep in moments.

He had a flea bite.

He couldn't believe it. He'd been scratching his leg in his sleep and, in fact, at one time it had been so bad it had woken him. James glared down at the flayed skin and swore colourfully.

Tango. It had to be—and she'd probably got the fleas from Jodie and Scamp. They'd been shut up together now for two days.

Great. Infested by a vet's dogs! What kind of an advert was that?

Still, he had the morning off today, so he'd take himself off to the vets' and get some spray. But which practice? Maisie had gone off to work ages ago, so he couldn't ask her. That would teach him to have a lie-in!

He looked in the *Yellow Pages*, but it was singularly unhelpful. None of them listed Maisie's name, so he picked one at random and phoned.

'Do you have a Miss McDowell working for you?' he asked, and, of course, he was fielded by a protective receptionist.

'Who's calling?'

'The name's Sutherland. I'm her new neighbour.'

Immediately her tone changed, becoming concerned. 'Is there a problem?'

So she was there. He gave a wry smile. 'No. No problem. I need to see a vet with my dog, so I thought I'd come to her.'

'She's got an appointment free in fifteen minutes. Can you make that?'

'I'll do my best.'

'I'll tell her to expect you, Mr Sutherland.'

The phone went dead before he could ask directions, but he thought he knew where it was. He called

Tango, got the car out of the garage and set off, the dog breathing heavily down his neck all the way there. He really, really needed to get a carrying cage or harness, he thought as her tongue swiped wetly across his ear. Or at the least a blanket for the back seat.

'Don't crawl to me, you've got fleas,' he told her sternly, and she grinned at him in the rear-view mirror and looked utterly unrepentant. 'You wait,' he said. 'I'll get Maisie to vaccinate you. That'll teach you.'

He found the practice without difficulty and took his place in the waiting room. A few moments later Maisie came out and crouched down in front of the dog, throwing James a puzzled smile.

'Tango! Hello. What are you doing here?'

'Fleas,' he said expressionlessly, and Maisie looked up again, her eyes brimming with laughter.

'Fleas?'

'So it would seem.'

'Well, we'd better go and have a look.'

She led him through into the consulting room, helped him lift Tango onto the table and got a telling-off from him for picking her up.

'Don't be ridiculous, I have to do my job,' she said dismissively. 'Right, why do you think she's got fleas?'

He hitched up his trouser leg and she winced. 'Ah. Right. OK, I'll check her, but I don't know where she's got them from. Mine haven't got fleas.'

He grunted under his breath, but she must have heard because she shot him a look.

'Mine *haven't* got fleas,' she repeated, and ran her fingers through Tango's coat, brushing it backwards.

'There we are,' she said, and plucked a flea from the dog's back. 'And it's a chicken flea—and before you say it, mine are treated. I wonder where she's got that from?'

'Heaven knows. What's the difference?'

'In the type of flea? Slight but noticeable.'

'Not to my leg,' he grumbled gently, and she laughed and turned to her computer.

'She's not the natural host, so they will migrate onto anything else living to see if it's better. Hence your bites. I'll get you some flea treatment that should sort her out. It'll kill any fleas on her and prevent reinfestation.'

'Not organophosphates?' he asked, checking, and she shook her head.

'No. Not any more.'

'Good.'

She turned back to him, a smile on her face, and was about to speak when the door flew open.

'Maisie, it's David. He's operating, and he says he's feeling really ill. He's dizzy, and he looks awful. Can you come? He wants you to finish up for him, he just can't do it.'

She glanced up at James. 'Would you mind if I abandon you?' she said. 'Kathy will look after you and get you the flea stuff.'

'Of course,' he said, conscious of a ludicrous and quite unwarranted disappointment. 'You go and take over.'

Then he heard a man groan and retch, and his professional instinct kicked in. That wasn't ordinary nausea—not unless the man was a total drama queen.

'Do you want me to take a look at him? He sounds really quite ill.'

Maisie, her face concerned, threw him a grateful look. 'Would you mind?'

He thought of his morning off, already eaten into by the fleas, and the mountain of unpacking and sorting out he'd intended to do, but then the man gasped and groaned again, and he gave a wry smile. 'Of course I don't mind,' he lied, and, Tango in tow, he followed her through the door into the back of the practice.

CHAPTER FIVE

THEY went through a dispensary and what looked like a surgical preparation area into an operating theatre. There, propped up against the operating table, hands braced against the side of it and his eyes firmly shut, stood a man in green scrubs.

His skin matched the colour pretty well, and James didn't like the look of him at all.

'David?' Maisie said, and the man opened his eyes, turned his head a fraction and retched helplessly.

'Lay him down,' James said quickly, and took hold of David's shoulders, easing the man down onto the floor. Someone took Tango away, to his relief, and he knelt down on the floor beside the man and took his wrist.

'Pulse is nice and regular, but a bit fast. David, can you hear me?'

'I can hear you, but I'm not opening my eyes.'

'OK. That's fine. My name's James Sutherland, and I'm a doctor. Can you tell me how you feel?'

'Dreadful. Sick. So, so sick.'

'Is it worse when you move?'

'Yes.'

'Any chest pain?'

'No.'

'Headache?'

'No.'

'And when did it start?'

'This morning—just about an hour ago. It's just got worse and worse.'

'Right. Maisie, can you go out to my car and bring my bag from the boot, please?'

He flung her the keys, and she disappeared through the door and came back again instantly. 'Which car?' she said, and he realised that she'd probably never seen it.

'Dark blue BMW. It's in the far corner of the car park. Just press the remote and you'll see it flash.'

She disappeared again, and he turned his attention back to the vet lying very, very still on the floor.

'David, have you ever had anything like this before, or has anyone in your family suffered from vertigo?'

'No, don't think so.'

'Had a cold recently?'

'No—well, a bit of a sniffle last week. Hell, I feel grim. Is it my heart?'

James squeezed his shoulder reassuringly. 'No, I don't think so. I think you might have either a viral or bacterial infection of the inner ear. It affects the semi-circular canals which control our balance mechanism, hence the dizziness and nausea you're experiencing, and sometimes the cochlea, too, which can affect the hearing in the relevant ear.'

'I had my ears syringed yesterday because I was feeling a bit deaf in one ear,' David said heavily. 'Could that have caused it?'

'Possibly, but it's more likely the deafness was the first sign.'

'You're talking about labyrinthitis, aren't you?' David said, and James heard the dread in his voice.

'Possibly. I have to eliminate any cardiac or cerebral complications just to be certain, but so far that's looking the most likely diagnosis.'

'And it could make me feel this grim?'

'Oh, yes.'

The man swore, softly but succinctly, and James could only agree with him. Labyrinthitis was a horrible condition, the inflammation leading to dizziness and nausea that could last for weeks. Sometimes it could leave the sufferer permanently prone to attacks of dizziness brought on simply by turning the head sharply, but if David wasn't aware of that, there was no way James was going to tell him now. He had enough on his plate.

And grim as it was, it was probably preferable to the other things that could be going on, and which he wanted to rule out as a matter of urgency.

'Can someone call an ambulance, please?' he said, just as Maisie reappeared.

'Ambulance?' Maisie said, her voice full of alarm.

'Just as a precaution,' he said calmly as he opened his bag and took out the portable blood-pressure monitor. 'If it is labyrinthitis, David, you'll need IV antiemetics for a few days, and that means hospitalisation. Right, I want to check you over now to eliminate any other possibilities. I'll try not to move you too much, but I may have to ask you to do things that unsettle it.'

'Great,' he groaned, and retched again.

Maisie bit her lip, then looked at James. 'Do you need me for anything else?' she asked. 'I really should finish off this dog but I could get Pete to do it.'

James slipped the blood-pressure cuff round David's arm and pressed the start button on the little machine. 'No, you go ahead. I'll shout if I need anything. Oh—have you got ECG facilities?'

'Yes, here,' Kathy said. 'I don't suppose it's the same as yours, but it might work.'

'It should,' David groaned from the floor.

'We'll see.' James was conscious of Maisie moving to the operating table, but he could feel her eyes on him and sensed her concern for her colleague.

'I think I've finished, Maisie. All you need to do is close,' David said, his voice a little slurred.

James didn't like the sound of that. It might have been just plain misery, or it could have been a result of some kind of stroke. Without neurological tests it was impossible to tell, but David's blood pressure was elevated, and that could be significant.

'David, I'd like to test your pupils, but it means opening your eyes.'

'Damn,' he said unhappily, and his lids flickered open, then shut again. 'I can't.'

'Please. I need to do this. I know it's unpleasant.'

His eyes opened again, and he stared fixedly at the ceiling. Quickly, so as to disturb him as little as possible, James flicked the beam of light over his eyes and watched in relief as both pupils contracted equally and rapidly.

Unfortunately, the moving light was all that was needed to trigger another bout of helpless retching.

'Can't you give him an anti-emetic?' Maisie said from her position at the operating table.

'No—not until he's been thoroughly screened for

all other eventualities. Right, I'd like to do that ECG, if possible, please,' he said to Kathy, the vet nurse.

She handed him the leads instantly, and he raised his eyebrows at the little crocodile clips on the end.

'Ouch,' he murmured. 'This might pinch a bit.'

'Just do it,' David said grimly, so James put the leads on his patient's chest.

While he was waiting he found a butterfly and a swab so he could put in an IV line. A few moments later he scanned the ECG readout with relief.

'Well, that looks OK. No indications of any cardiac event or arrhythmia, but I'd need an eight-lead to be sure. David, I'm going to put a butterfly in your hand ready for IV access, OK?'

The man grunted consent, clearly too ill to care any longer what happened to him, and James slipped a band round his arm, flicked up the vein and inserted the needle.

'Anybody would think you'd done that before,' Maisie teased, and he realised she'd finished with the dog and was crouching beside him.

'Just once or twice.' He took advantage of the venous access to do a blood-glucose test, and he'd just ascertained that it was normal when he hear a siren approaching. 'Sounds like your taxi's here, David,' he said calmly, and hoped the journey would be uneventful and smooth. Even getting him into the ambulance was going to be well nigh intolerable, and James didn't envy David one little bit.

Poor bastard, he thought, and was suddenly terribly glad that he'd come in that morning with Tango and had been there when this had happened—not that he'd been able to give him anything to help, for fear of masking another condition, but at least he'd been able to set all their minds at rest about anything more sinister.

Then the paramedics were there, and James was handing over, filling them in and jotting notes hastily as they lifted David onto the trolley, retching violently with every slight movement, and wheeled him out through a side door to the waiting ambulance.

'Do you need to go with him?' Maisie asked, but James shook his head.

'I don't think so. He's in good hands.' He turned to the crew as they closed the doors. 'Thanks, guys,' he said, and then he put his bag into his car and turned back to Maisie, giving her a wry smile. 'I don't suppose you know what happened to my dog?'

Maisie chuckled. 'Yes. She's out the back, being de-flea'd.'

'Ah. Poor Tango.'

'She'll be fine. James, about David—'

'He'll be all right, Maisie. I'm virtually certain it's just labyrinthitis, though heaven knows that's bad enough, but it's better than a stroke or a potentially fatal heart condition. Nevertheless, I'm sorry, Maisie, your colleague's going to be out of action for weeks, if not months.'

'Oh, joy,' she said, rolling her eyes. 'All those extra surgeries and visits. I can hardly wait.'

As if it had suddenly dawned on her that he'd stepped in and taken over on his day off, she tipped her head back and smiled up at him, her eyes appreciative.

'Thank you for looking after him,' she said softly,

and at that moment he would have cheerfully given up the entire weekend just for that one smile.

'Any time. You would have done the same,' he reminded her, but she merely shrugged and gave a little dismissive laugh.

'Right, I do believe I've got a clinic going on,' she said. 'I'd better get back to it before they all give up and go home.'

They headed back inside, and as they walked through the door Kathy looked up from the phone. 'It's Lucy. She's got a horse in a ditch. Can you go over now, please?'

Maisie rolled her eyes. 'Sure, tell her I'll be twenty minutes. Has she called the fire brigade and any other big, strong men she can lay her hands on?'

Kathy relayed the message, laughed and put the phone down. 'She says if she could lay her hands on any big, strong men, she wouldn't be running a livery yard. Oh, and it's not a shire this time.'

Maisie chuckled. 'I'm sure it doesn't matter. Shire horse, Shetland—they're all darned heavy when they're stuck in the mud. Right, ask Pete if he can take the rest of my clients this morning, could you? I'd better get over there.'

She turned to James, cocked her head on one side and studied him with a mischievous little smile. 'How's your pulling power?'

He opened his mouth to make a smart retort, but then she wrapped her surprisingly strong little hand around his upper arm and squeezed, and his words died in his throat.

'Tense,' she ordered, and he obligingly flexed his arm. Her fingers tightened, testing his strength, and macho pride made him tense his biceps even harder to impress her.

'Very impressive,' she said, laughter bubbling in those sparkling caramel eyes. 'Are you busy?'

He looked at her for a second and then gave a rueful little huff of laughter. 'Apparently so. I think I'm pulling a horse out of a ditch.'

'Good man, right answer,' she said, patting him on the arm with a wicked grin and heading for the door. 'Kathy, can you hang onto Tango for us?'

'Sure. She's happy now—she's being cuddled.'

'What a surprise,' James said drily, and followed Maisie out of the door, his arm still tingling from the touch of her hand. He got into the passenger seat of her car, and she cut through the streets to the main road and the A12 intersection at a speed that made his blood pressure shoot up.

'You don't take any prisoners, do you?' he said faintly as she shot through a gap in the traffic and whipped round the roundabout, but she just threw him a grim smile.

'No time to hang about. I have no idea how long it's been there, but time is of the essence. They get exhausted, and if they get trapped around tree roots and sunken debris, they have to be put down on the spot. You can't pull them out. I've heard of horses having their limbs ripped off being towed out of rivers by inexperienced rescuers. I need to be there.'

'I can imagine you do,' James said, his voice full of horror. 'How did it get in the ditch?'

'Don't. They have to drink from it—well, it's a little branch of the Deben, really, not a ditch—but they go in at stupid places. They won't just use the gravel bit with a firm bottom, they get silly. Either the grass is lusher on the bank, or they go the wrong way to drink, but they end up in it sometimes.'

'Isn't that bad management?'

She laughed. 'Probably. It's happens in nature, though, very often, so I try not to judge. Horses can be very stupid.'

They arrived at the livery yard to find it deserted, but it seemed she knew where she'd find everyone. She drove down a track, following the ruts left by something large—a fire engine?

Yes. And it was stuck, right in a gateway. Terrific.

'That's handy,' he said.

'Tell me about it,' Maisie said. 'It means I'll have to run backwards and forwards across the field for everything I need, but hopefully I won't need anything yet. They're over there.'

They scrambled through the fence and ran to see what was going on. They found a knot of people clustered on the river bank, heaving on a rope and issuing instructions and yelling at the horse to encourage it. As they approached the crowd subsided into silence again, and the rope went slack. The horse had moved a fraction, but as soon as the struggling helpers eased off, it slipped back into the sucking maw of the river. Maisie squeezed her way to the front of the group and took in the scene at a glance.

The horse was buried in the mud up to its neck, the only visible part of it the head resting on Lucy's lap, and it was so plastered with mud it was impossible to tell what colour it was. Lucy didn't look much better herself, but she managed a rueful smile of welcome. 'Well, if it ain't the cavalry. Got any ideas?'

'Only the usual. It looks exhausted.'

'He is, poor old boy. Aren't you, Pharaoh?'

The horse was making no effort to free himself, but was simply lying with his head on Lucy's legs and struggling for air, his eyes rolling with fear and a tremor running through him from time to time.

'I brought muscles,' Maisie said, and Lucy ran an appreciative eye over James.

'Good,' she said, and struggled to her feet, holding the horse's head up as she did so. 'Right, let's have another go.'

The helpers took up the strain on the heavy lunge-line knotted through the noseband of the lunging cavesson. It was similar to a head collar, but because it was stronger it was less likely to break under the huge strain. This wasn't the first time they'd all done this, and it wouldn't be the last, Maisie was sure, but at least with experience they'd perfected the art of getting the horses out, and they hadn't lost one yet.

'Right,' Maisie said, grasping the rope, and found her hands being prised off it very firmly, finger by finger.

'I think not.'

'James, don't be silly, I don't have time to muck about.'

He returned her exasperated glare impassively. 'Time is exactly what you have. You're not pulling on this rope—or if you do, I won't, and I'm stronger than you, so which is it to be? You, or me?'

Their eyes locked, and she could see she wasn't going to win this argument before the horse died of hypothermia, and possibly not even then. But only yesterday she'd felt the baby move for the first time, a real solid kick that couldn't be confused with anything else, and she knew he was right.

She stepped out of the way, and they all took up the slack again.

'Right, on three. One, two, three!' Lucy said, scrambling out of the way and adding her weight to the lunge-line.

'This is hopeless,' a fireman gasped after the third fruitless attempt. 'We need a vehicle attached to this line so we don't lose what ground we gain. I don't suppose we can get one in here, though,' he added, giving the fire engine a speaking look.

One of the other firemen in his muddy yellow trousers looked acutely embarrassed.

Lucy sighed and rammed her muddy hand through her once-blonde hair. 'We'll just have to cut down the fence and drive my pick-up in here,' she said. 'Maisie's right, and the horse is exhausted. He can't take much more, we have to get him out now.'

'Can't we get a sling under it?' one of the firemen suggested, but his colleagues soon scoffed him into silence.

'We've tried before. That horse is enormous. Getting anything under it is impossible. The bottom of its ribcage is about three feet down, and I'm not going in head first!'

'Dig it out?'

'We could have used the winch on the engine, of course, only someone bogged it down in the gateway!'

More good-natured ribbing, but in the meantime Maisie was sitting with her legs under the horse's head, stroking him and checking him over as much as she could in the limited conditions while someone went to cut down the fence and bring back a vehicle.

'Poor old lad,' she murmured, feeling the base of his ears for cold. They were chilly and clammy, not surprisingly. He must be suffering from hypothermia. As she stroked him and spoke soothingly to him, another shudder ran through him. His heart was pounding, his breathing was laboured and she had a horrible feeling he had taken some water into his lungs.

Not good news. The horse was quite literally at the end of his tether.

'How is he?'

She turned her head at the sound of James's quiet voice in her ear. 'Not good. We have to get him out of here now,' she said firmly, just as Lucy drove up in her pick-up.

'I thought towing them out wasn't an option,' he said, still quietly.

'We aren't going to tow him. We're going to pull him ourselves, but then move the vehicle to take up the slack. It'll be as safe as we can make it.'

She scrambled out from under the horse's head, and Lucy took over the job of supporting it so he didn't drown.

'Right, tie the line onto the towhitch, but I don't want to pull him out with the truck if we can avoid it.'

It was a struggle, but in the end they managed—without Maisie's help, to her total frustration. She had to content herself with holding onto the head collar and encouraging the horse with her voice and her hands.

Slow, steady traction, lots of encouragement and

support for the horse from Maisie and Lucy, and finally his front legs were free and he flailed and struggled his way out onto the bank. They'd pulled him up onto a tarpaulin, and now this was hauled away from the river, horse and all, so that if he staggered when he got up, he didn't fall straight back in.

'Come on, Pharaoh, get up,' Lucy said, tugging on the line, and eventually the poor exhausted horse dragged himself to his feet to a great round of applause and cheering.

He was shivering, a sign Maisie found encouraging. If horses were too cold, they didn't even shiver, and that was much more significant. While Lucy walked him slowly forwards, she watched him for signs of lameness. It was so easy to damage limbs when dragging horses from mud, even if they weren't entangled on anything—in fact, not only limbs, but spine and neck, and Maisie knew that within a couple of days he would be checked over by the equine shiatsu practitioner Lucy used, to sort out any aftereffects of his escapade.

In the meantime she had to get him back up to the yard, hose him off a bit and check him over thoroughly for injuries. 'Can you drive my car back up to the yard, please?' she said to James.

He eyed her levelly. 'Only if you promise not to do anything stupid while my back's turned,' he murmured.

She managed to hold his gaze more or less steadily. 'Stupid? Of course I won't be stupid.'

'That's a matter of opinion,' he muttered, turning away, and she sighed with relief and turned back to the horse.

'Right, let's get Pharaoh back up to the yard,' she said to Lucy.

The woman was studying the horse worriedly. 'You reckon he's OK to walk? I could bring the lorry down. I don't want to cause any further problems, he's a valuable animal.'

No wonder she was looking worried. She'd have to answer to the owner, Maisie thought, who might have plenty to say about her horse being kept in a field with an unfenced river and no other water supply.

'Maybe you need to look at fencing off the muddier stretches of bank,' she said to Lucy as they walked. 'This is the third time—it's beginning to be a habit.'

'Tell me about it,' Lucy muttered. 'The trouble is, the landlord won't pay for the fencing and I can't afford to post and rail it—and, anyway, it's under water for weeks at a time if we get a lot of rain, and it would just wash it out. And I can't afford to waste the grazing, because it's wonderful down here.'

It *was* wonderful—the grass soft and thick and lush, the trees providing shelter from the heat and the flies and the rain, and it was as near as horses could get to being a natural environment.

'Maybe you need an alternative source of water and portable electric fencing,' Maisie suggested.

Lucy snorted. 'Tried that. They knock the water over and then trash the fencing and go in the river anyway.'

'So who do I bill?' Maisie asked, and Lucy sighed.

'Bill me. I'll discuss it with the owner when I talk to her. Just don't find anything awful wrong.'

She chuckled. 'Well, he's looking lucky so far.'

They were walking slowly back up the track, James following at a nice safe distance and watching her, Maisie was sure, like a hawk. No need. Pharaoh was too tired to do more than stumble up the track to the yard, and the most taxing thing Maisie was called upon to do was walk beside him.

In the end, they discovered he'd been lucky. Once he'd been hosed and checked, he had a few minor scrapes but nothing to worry about. The most significant factor was cold, and he was soon rugged up and drying off, with his nose in a bucket of warm mash.

She gave him a shot of an antispasmolytic in case he developed colic, an anti-inflammatory for the inevitable strains and pains and an antibiotic against the possibility of pneumonia, and she left Lucy with a course of antibiotics to inject daily for the next five days.

'I'm bound to be up here in the next few days, so I'll give him a look then unless you're worried. I'm sure you know what to look out for. You might need to hose his legs if they swell or heat, and you could try arnica and witch-hazel gel. In fact, I should put that on his poll where it took the strain of the head collar, and anywhere else that looks as if it's taken a knock.'

'Cheers. Thanks, both of you. I'll see you.'

Lucy went back into the box, her voice soft as she talked to the cold, weary horse, and Maisie and James headed towards her car. She knew Pharaoh would be well looked after now. It was just a shame it had had to happen.

They waved to the firemen, cleaning themselves up

and drinking welcome cups of tea, and climbed wearily into her car.

'Good job you've got seat covers, you're a bit on the muddy side,' James, frowning at her clothes, and she remembered she'd been sitting on the river bank.

'Why do you think I have them? Mud's an occupational hazard with large animals. I'll just take them off and wash them later.' Or not. Probably not. They seemed to shrug off the dirt pretty well and, despite not having been allowed to pull the horse, she was surprisingly weary. The seat covers, she decided, could wait.

'Thank you for your help,' she said, turning to James with a smile, and he gave a short, wry laugh.

'My pleasure. I didn't really want to do any unpacking this morning.'

Maisie thought of his house, probably still piled high with boxes, and felt a twinge of guilt. 'I'll give you a hand with your unpacking over the weekend, if you like,' she offered, and he chuckled.

'Feeling guilty, Maisie?' he teased gently, and she felt herself colour.

'You were a great help,' she told him, which was entirely the truth, even if it was designed to massage his ego, and he gave a soft chuckle and settled back in his seat, folding his arms over his chest and closing his eyes.

'It'll take more than that.'

'I'll buy you lunch.'

'No time. I've got a clinic at three, and it's already nearly two. Try again.'

'I'll cook you dinner,' she said without thinking,

and he cracked open one eye and studied her thought-fully for a second, then closed it again.

'Done,' he said softly. 'Tomorrow night—after you've helped with the unpacking.'

And Maisie, contemplating the thought of enter-taining her obviously wealthy neighbour in her own extremely modest little house, which was in dire need of her time and a significant cash injection, wondered why she hadn't just kept her mouth shut...

It was, James realised, the first time he'd been in her house. He'd brought Tango, on instructions, and the dogs greeted each other happily and went off, Tango with her nose to the ground, and left him alone in the entrance hall with Maisie.

'It's not as grand as yours, I'm afraid,' she was saying with a crooked little smile, and he had a sud-den overwhelming urge to wrap his arms around her and hug her. Instead, he shoved the chocolates he was carrying in her direction, and wafted the flowers under her nose.

Her eyes widened and she sniffed appreciatively. 'Flowers *and* chocolates? You must be feeling guilty for working me so hard this afternoon,' she teased, and he chuckled.

'I don't feel in the least bit guilty after dragging that damned horse out of the river.' He did his own bit of appreciative sniffing and grinned at her. 'Smells good. Hope that's for us and not the dogs.'

She laughed. 'My dogs have dry food, but it won't stop them hanging around hopefully,' she told him. 'It's beef stroganoff—I hope you eat beef?'

'I'll eat anything that smells that good,' he assured

her, following her through into a lovely, light and airy sitting room. It had wonderful views of the river over the low wall that divided it from his garden, and he suddenly understood the reason for the restrictive clause in his contract that prevented him planting anything tall in that position.

'I must take the secateurs to that lot and find the gate,' he said, looking at the ivy that all but swamped it.

'It would be useful with the dogs,' she agreed. 'Here, have a glass of wine.'

'Wine?'

He must have frowned, because she smiled at him knowingly. 'Yes, wine. Don't worry, I'm not drinking and once you've tasted it, no doubt you won't want very much. A grateful client gave it to me.'

He sniffed and sipped cautiously, and then sipped again, savouring the bouquet. Not the best he'd ever had, certainly, but quite passable. 'Thank your client for me,' he told her with a smile. 'Oh, I rang the hospital, by the way. David's improving. They're sure now that it's labyrinthitis.'

'So he'll be off for weeks. Great.'

'Can't you get a locum?'

'Probably. We'll certainly try.'

'Do. You shouldn't be taking on any more than you have to.' Which probably included cooking for him, he thought, his conscience pricking. 'Anything I can do?'

She shook her head. 'No, it's all done. The nice thing about beef strog is it's good and quick. I just put the rice on five minutes ago, so your timing's perfect.'

He tugged his forelock. 'Just obeying orders, ma'am.'

Her smile was disbelieving and very infectious. She went through to the kitchen, and he followed her, noting the tired units, the battered table and chairs and the hole in the vinyl flooring in front of the sink.

'It's my next job,' she told him, as if she'd read his mind. 'I was going to refit the kitchen this summer, but I don't suppose I'll be able to now I'm pregnant.'

'No.' Glancing down as she turned away, he could see that she'd started to show, the smooth round curve of her abdomen outlined by the soft jersey of her T-shirt. Damn. He swallowed the lump that the sight of a pregnant woman so often put in his throat, but it wouldn't go.

Maisie was beautiful. Fit, healthy, her skin glowing with an inner radiance, but he knew that just under the surface lurked a minefield of unresolved questions and health issues.

I feel—is violated too strong a word?

A cocktail of emotions washed over him again—anger, compassion and something he didn't want to look at too closely because, under the circumstances, it was entirely inappropriate.

Damn. James strolled out through the French doors into the garden and dragged in a lungful of the beautiful scented night air.

'What a gorgeous smell.'

'Nicotiana,' she said from behind him, and he turned and found her just there, inches away—close enough to reach out and draw her into his arms and kiss her...

'I'll have to learn something about gardening,' he said lightly, turning away again so he didn't have to look into those warm caramel eyes and be tempted by the soft, full lips below that surprisingly strong and slightly aquiline nose.

'Later. Supper's ready,' she told him, and reluctantly, because sitting over a meal *à deux* with her would inevitably be an exquisite form of torture, he turned and followed her back into the room.

'Thank you for your help today with the unpacking,' he said after they'd taken their places at her simple table and she'd piled his plate with rice and the delicious-smelling beef.

She laughed softly. 'My pleasure. I was dying to get a look at the house anyway,' she confessed, and he shook his head slowly.

'You should have said.'

'When? In between telling you off for leaving Tango alone and discovering I was pregnant?'

He laughed wryly. 'OK, I'll admit it's been a bit of an odd week. So, do you think Miss Keeble would approve?' he asked her, still curious about her benefactor, and Maisie smiled.

'Yes—definitely. Of you, and of the house.'

'And do you?' he asked, and she hesitated.

'Yes,' she said, and it was only later that he realised he hadn't known which of them she'd been talking about—him, or the house.

CHAPTER SIX

'I THINK I've found out where Tango got the chicken fleas.'

Maisie, in the act of weeding the little bed outside her sitting-room window, jumped a mile and stood up, hand on her heart.

'Are you trying to frighten me to death?'

James's crooked grin was appallingly sexy and made her stupid heart beat even faster. 'Sorry. Want to come and see?'

She scrambled over the low wall and followed him round the side of the house to the utility area behind the coach-house.

And there, tucked down in the woodshed behind a pile of logs, was Helga, fluffed up and indignant at their presence, sitting, if Maisie wasn't very much mistaken, on a clutch of eggs.

'You silly girl,' Maisie chided, and squirmed in through the narrow gap and grasped the little white chicken firmly. She was pecked for her pains, of course, but not hard, and there under the hen were nine little pale brown eggs, beautifully arranged in a circle, narrow end in. Maisie put her back on them and sighed. 'Well, at least she's still alive.'

'She's lucky not to have been eaten by a fox, I guess,' James suggested, and she nodded.

'She is lucky—but she's been missing about two to three weeks—which means those eggs are going to hatch any day now. I'll have to put her in the slammer and chuck the eggs—'

'But they're about to hatch, you said.' He sounded horrified, and she tipped back her head and looked up at him, a slightly hysterical laugh rising in her throat.

'Yes—and absolutely the last thing I need in my little garden is any more chickens, so given a grain of sense I'll put her in solitary confinement on a wire floor and throw away her babies. You, on the other hand,' she added, eyeing his garden meaningfully, 'have room for nine little chicks and their mummy, surely?'

He threw up his hands. 'Oh, no—no, Maisie, not me. I don't do chickens.'

She shrugged and reached for Helga again, ruthlessly calling his bluff. 'OK, I'll just chuck them, then.'

'All right!' His hands were up again, but this time in surrender. 'All right. I'll have the damn chickens. What do I do with them?'

She laughed and straightened up. 'Not a lot. You need a broody run, hay to make a nest, some chick crumbs, some flea treatment which I can give you, plenty of fresh water in a shallow container so they don't drown when they're tiny, and Helga will do the rest.'

He looked utterly bewildered, and Maisie took pity on him. 'I think there might be something round here you can keep them in, unless it's all been cleared out by the builders,' she said.

'No. I had enough on my plate with the house. I thought I'd worry about the garden when I got here, all bar the routine maintenance. I had that done, but nothing else, so whatever was here should be here still. I seem to remember something in the orchard.'

'Right, let's have a look,' she said, and under the apple trees at the far end of the garden she found a little ark almost buried in the long grass. 'Here we go. It's a bit mucky and if you kick it hard enough it'll probably fall to bits, but it'll do for now. It's got a nice little nest area, a wire run safe from the foxes and somewhere under cover for the food and water. Perfect. You just need to scrub it out—'

'Me?'

She turned her hands palms up and smiled at him innocently. 'Of course. They're your chickens now.'

His mouth tightened, and she suppressed a smile and dragged the heavy ark out of the long grass.

At least, she began to, but he prised her fingers off the carrying handle and glared at her.

'I don't think so,' he said firmly, and took hold of it. 'Right, where to?'

Chickens. Chickens, for goodness' sake!

James let his breath out on a sigh and gave the ungrateful Helga a baleful look. If she'd pecked him once, she'd pecked him a dozen times, but now she was de-flea'd and safely installed in her smart new run—because, of course, the other one had indeed fallen to pieces as he'd shifted it and he'd had to go out and buy another one at enormous expense—and the eggs were nestled underneath her on a bed of hay, warmed initially, as instructed by the resident vet and former owner of said chicken, with a hot-water bottle, and he was free to get on with his life.

Huh!

'You'd better be hatching hens, not cockerels,' he

told Helga sternly, 'because otherwise you're going to have to live about four hundred years to pay back the cost of that house.'

She returned his stare coldly, and he shut the end of the run and left her to it.

'All settled?'

He turned and glowered at his neighbour, who was looking fetching in a little pink vest top and shorts. Fetching and pregnant and very, very sexy. All this fecundity, he thought crossly, and rammed a hand through his hair.

'Do you have any idea what henhouses cost?' he said, still reeling from the bill.

She just smiled. 'Look on it as your contribution to animal welfare. Want a cup of tea?'

'I wouldn't mind a cold drink. This weather's getting hotter. I hope you've got sunscreen on those shoulders.' He swung one leg over the wall, then sat there astride it as Maisie went through the newly revealed gate. 'When did that happen?' he asked incredulously.

'Some of us have been busy while you've been messing around with your chickens,' she told him primly, and dragged the gate shut behind her.

'Those hinges need attention,' he informed her, but she just smiled and said, 'Be my guest,' and went on into the house.

'So, how can I tell when the chicks are ready to hatch?' he asked, following her through into the kitchen.

She laughed at him. 'They come out of the shells?' she teased, and he sighed.

'I must be mad.'

This time her smile was kinder. 'No, not mad. You're just a nice man.'

And suddenly it was all worth it.

The heat didn't let up all that week, and they were talking about it going on for the rest of the month. Terrific, James thought. The elderly patients would be struggling to cope, the little ones would be crabby and restless, and the pregnant women would all get high blood pressure.

Which reminded him...

'Jane, can I have a word?'

His colleague sat back at her desk and smiled at him. 'Sure. Come in.'

He shut the door and sat, stretching his legs out and wondering where to start.

'I saw one of your patients last week—Maisie McDowell.'

'Oh, yes, so I gather. She's pregnant.'

He shot her a curious look. 'Word travels fast.'

Jane laughed. 'Not at all. I looked at her notes—I thought I might have to call her in as I'd had to leave promptly, then Patsy told me you'd seen her the night before. She didn't sound very approving.'

James snorted. 'Patsy doesn't approve of anything the patients do. She's too protective of us. Anyway, she's my neighbour—'

'Patsy?'

'No—Maisie. So I don't feel happy to do her antenatal care. Can you do it?'

'Of course. Anything I should know about?'

He thought of Maisie's reluctance to reveal the circumstances of her baby's conception, and shook his head. 'No. She's fit and well—baby's due in November.

I ran a whole batch of bloods and so forth, because she'd been feeling off, but I really think it was just early pregnancy and she didn't recognise it.'

'A surprise, then. Is her partner pleased?'

'I wouldn't know,' he lied. 'She lives alone, as far as I'm aware.' He stood up. 'So, can I leave it up to you?'

'Of course. I'll contact her and invite her to the antenatal clinic. Thanks for looking after her.'

Jane's words gave him an odd tightness in his chest. 'Just doing my job,' he said lightly, and went back to his room. He had an emergency surgery starting in a moment, and calls to make afterwards, and he really didn't need to think about looking after Maisie.

'OK, Mrs Greer, take these three times a day, and remember to finish the course. That really is most important.' He tore the prescription off the printer, signed it and handed it to his patient, then was about to pack up his desk and go on his calls when the phone buzzed and he picked it up. 'Hello?'

'Dr Sutherland, I've got a Mrs Davies in here with her daughter Eleanor. She says she's still got earache and needs to see a doctor. I've told her you've finished, but she really is most insistent.'

He sighed. If only Patsy would stop protecting him.

'That's fine. I'll see her—I always see children, Patsy. Remember that. Can you please send her in?'

He frowned. Elly Davies was ten, and she'd been in earlier in the week with a middle ear infection. It should have been on the mend by now, unless the organism was resistant to the antibiotic he'd prescribed.

She came in with her mother, looking miserable, and he smiled reassuringly at her and indicated the chair. 'Take a seat, Elly. Mrs Davies, why don't you sit here?'

He drew up another chair for the woman, then sat down again and looked at Elly. 'Right, I gather you've still got earache.'

She nodded. 'It's awful. Normally it gets better after a few days, but this time it's still bad.'

'As bad?'

She shrugged. 'Not quite, but it's not better. It's still really sore.'

She sounded a little tearful, but she was obviously being brave and James got out the auriscope and checked her ear as gently as he could.

'Your eardrum's still very inflamed,' he said. 'Have you had a temperature?'

'Yes—it was thirty-eight last night,' Mrs Davies said.

He took it in the other ear—a simple and quick procedure these days, taking only seconds—and found it was still elevated.

'OK, Elly, I think I might have to change your antibiotics. I haven't got your notes in here—can you remember what it was?'

'Pen-something,' Elly said, and her mother produced the bottle.

'Here. I brought it with me.'

James took the bottle and glanced at it, then looked again. The label printed in the surgery dispensary said penicillin 250 mg in 5 ml, but the manufacturer's label on the bottle said 125 mg in 5 ml. Half the strength.

'Elly, I'm sorry, there seems to have been a dispensing error,' he said, frowning at the bottle. 'I wrote you up for the full strength, and you've been given the strength that would be appropriate for a much younger child.'

'Is that why it hasn't worked?' Elly asked, and he nodded.

'I think so. I'm really sorry. I'm almost certain that's what's happened, and I'm also pretty sure this is the right antibiotic for the job. Is it feeling *any* better?'

'A bit—just not as much better as it usually is by now.'

'Is that just carelessness?' Mrs Davies asked, an edge to her voice, and James shrugged slightly.

'I don't know, Mrs Davies, but rest assured I shall find out. It won't have done her any harm, though, thankfully, apart from the delay in her recovery which I'm really very sorry about. But it's an easy mistake to make.'

'There shouldn't be mistakes,' the woman said emphatically, a fact James heartily agreed with.

'Don't worry. It will be looked into. In the meantime, I'll take this, if I may, and get you a course of the right strength from the dispensary myself. You should notice a definite improvement in twenty-four hours, Elly. If you don't, I'd like to know.'

Mrs Davies stood up. 'Don't worry, Dr Sutherland, you will.'

He didn't doubt it for a minute.

James studied the rota, and found that Patsy had been on that night.

She worked not only as receptionist but also part-time as a relief dispenser, and he knew he'd have to talk to her, but it was one confrontation he wasn't looking forward to. The woman was difficult at the best of times.

He spoke to Jane, and they decided to talk to her together, since Jane knew her better.

Patsy, however, was anything but difficult. She was flustered, panicky and very upset, and they ended up comforting her.

'I can't believe I made such a stupid mix-up,' she said, wringing her hands. 'I mean, it could have been really important.'

'It *was* really important,' James pointed out. 'That child has been suffering unnecessarily for another three days because she had the wrong strength medication.'

'But at least nobody died,' Patsy said, the hand-wringing getting worse, and Jane intervened.

'No. Nobody died, but I wouldn't want you to underestimate this, Patsy. It could quite easily have been a fatal error had the drugs been different. You really must take more care.'

'I'm sorry,' she said, her eyes welling up again. 'I'll be very, very careful in future—if I have a future?'

Jane sighed quietly. 'Of course you have a future, Patsy. Everybody makes mistakes—but since you mention it, I've also been concerned about you vetting our patients at Reception and deciding for yourself whether or not they need to see us. Several people have mentioned it to me, and I think James has found the same thing.'

He nodded. 'This morning, for instance. If Mrs Davies hadn't been so insistent, I might not have seen Elly until tomorrow, and her ear by then might have been much worse,' he said, a little pointedly, and Patsy looked even more uncomfortable.

'But you're all so busy.'

'Patsy, that's what we're here for. We need to know if someone asks for us,' Jane said gently. 'You shouldn't be making clinical decisions. If there's a doctor in the building and someone says their visit is urgent, you need to take details and ask us when we want to see them. You aren't here to protect us from our patients.'

The woman nodded, still upset, and went back to her position at the desk, leaving Jane and James sitting in the office exchanging speaking glances. 'You know what'll happen now?' Jane said softly.

'Absolutely. We'll be consulted about every broken nail—but at least something important won't get missed, and with any luck she'll be a bit more careful in the dispensary. I wonder how many other mistakes there are out there going undetected?'

'Don't.' Jane shuddered and stood up. 'Oh, by the way, your Maisie's results are back. Everything's normal, you'll be glad to know.'

He was. He hadn't realised he was so wound up about it, but he felt the tension go out of him like air out of a balloon, and smiled at Jane. 'Thanks. I'll tell her.'

'Good. Right, I have to go. My husband's got clients coming for dinner, and I have to be there and look charming.'

'And cook?' James asked, worried about the lines of strain around her eyes, but she just laughed humourlessly.

'Hardly. I put my foot down about that and we get it catered. All I have to do is be there, but it's pretty frequent and frankly sometimes I could do without it. That's why I had to go when Maisie McDowell was late—we had a private view to attend. The wife of a client. Politics. I hate it.'

James laughed. 'You and me both. If I'm told something's politically correct, I'm almost tempted to do the other thing just for the hell of it.'

'If it was for me, I would,' Jane said, 'but it's for Michael, and I love him. So I do it—but sometimes it's really hard, juggling work and home commitments.'

James sat back, studying her openly. 'Have you had a well-woman check recently?' he asked.

'Worried about my blood pressure?' she said wryly. 'Don't worry, James, it's fine. I just feel a bit stretched two ways and thin in the middle, if you know what I mean. Anyway, must fly. See you tomorrow.'

'OK, but, Jane? Any time I can help by taking something over for you, let me know.'

She frowned. 'That isn't fair, James. I couldn't do that.'

'Yes, you could. I'd rather cover the odd surgery or clinic for you than have you burning out and deserting me altogether because you're trying to do too much. And anyway,' he added with a grin, 'I'm sure I'll get my own back at some time. I'll give you one of my heartsink patients. That should make you feel better about it.'

Her eyes softened, and she smiled back. 'Thank you,' she said quietly. 'I'll bear it in mind, just in case. Now I really must go.'

He glanced at his watch, surprised to see that it was nearly seven. Amazingly he had no calls to make as duty doctor, and any that came in after seven would be referred directly to the on-call co-operative that all the local practices were a part of.

Which meant he was off the hook.

He grabbed his bag and headed for the door. He had to see Maisie, to tell her about her results. If he hurried, he'd be in time to walk the dogs with her along the river. There'd be a nice cooling breeze at this time of the evening, and they could stroll along to the quay and maybe have a drink at the pub on the way back. It would be lovely there by the water.

His step lighter, he locked up the surgery, hurried towards his car and drove home, but to his surprise Maisie and the dogs were in his garden.

'Your chicks are hatching,' she told him with a smile. 'You've got three so far.'

The walk forgotten, he went with Maisie round to the little henhouse and peeped in through the end door. He could hear the high-pitched cheeping of the chicks, extraordinarily loud for such tiny things, and poking out from under one wing he saw a tiny yellow head, the little beady eyes watching him.

Absurdly, he realised he was excited.

They're just chickens, he told himself in disgust, but Maisie's eyes were bright and he gave up and let himself go with the flow.

'Aren't they cute?' She straightened up. 'Come on, we need to leave her in peace. We'll go for a walk and check her when we come back. It might take until tomorrow for them all to hatch, and then in the late morning she might bring them out into the run.'

As they walked along the river wall, the cooling breeze tugging at their clothes, James wondered at the easy way she'd included him in the walk, just assuming he'd be coming. As, of course, he would. They'd fallen into a routine with astonishing ease, and the dogs seemed perfectly content with the arrangement.

And not only the dogs, he thought, strolling contentedly beside Maisie as she talked about a cat she'd operated on earlier that day to remove a tumour.

'It was horribly complicated, and under any other circumstances I would have given up, but this little cat's been such a fighter, and her owner's all alone and would be devastated if she died now, after all that's gone before. So I went in and did what I could, and to my relief I managed to get it all without killing the cat or destroying any vital nerves. Amazing.'

She was. He smiled at her, a stupid lump in his throat, and for two pins he would have scooped her up in his arms and kissed her, but he couldn't.

Not now. Not yet. She was still so vulnerable. And he hadn't told her about her blood tests, he realised.

'Your results came back today,' he said without preamble, and she stopped dead and looked up at him, her eyes suddenly fearful.

'And?'

'And everything's fine. You're OK, Maisie. You're in the clear.'

Her shoulders dropped, and without warning she burst into tears and he found her in his arms.

'Shh,' he murmured, rubbing her back soothingly and rocking her gently against his chest. Lord, she was tiny, and he could feel the small, firm swell of her abdomen against his body. And then, without warning, he felt the baby kick, and the lump in his throat grew to the size of a grapefruit and threatened to choke him.

He abandoned his plans for walking to the quay,

and instead eased her out of his arms, slung one arm around her shoulders and turned her towards home.

'Come on,' he said gently. 'We'll go home and cook something nice to celebrate.'

He was only being kind, Maisie told herself. It didn't mean anything. He was just being James.

He plonked her down on the sofa in his kitchen, and while he cooked supper she sat there with Tango's head on her lap and Jodie and Scamp curled up on the other sofa as if they owned it, and they drank her health in freshly squeezed orange juice, and then toasted Helga and the chicks. And then after supper, because it was still light, they took another peek at Helga and Maisie pulled out four more shells from under her.

'That's seven,' she said, and James chewed his lip thoughtfully and asked if she could tell the sex.

She laughed and shook her head. 'No—not easily. It's incredibly difficult.'

'So how do commercial producers supply day-old chicks for the egg industry?' he asked.

'Sex-linking,' she said promptly. 'Certain hybrid crosses have different-coloured hens and cockerels, so it's virtually impossible to get it wrong. Otherwise you have to wait until you can see the difference. And they tend to get the egg colour from the father, so your hens should lay the most wonderful dark chocolate brown eggs.'

'Like the ones you've been giving me?'

She smiled. 'Exactly.'

He cocked his head on one side and studied her thoughtfully. 'Are you by any chance a chicken fancier?' he said, with only a trace of humour in his voice, and she laughed and stood up.

'No. I am not. I am, however, a vet, and I'm called upon to know such trivia.'

'Right.'

'Besides which,' she continued with a grin, 'the chickens are quite funny and they have very definite characters.'

'Mmm,' he said, sounding unconvinced.

'Why did you want to know about the sex of the chicks?' she asked, wondering if, when push came to shove, he'd be able to wring the necks of the boys.

'I was thinking of selling the eggs to cover the cost of the chicken house,' he told her, and she felt a bubble of laughter rising out of control in her chest.

'Not a chance,' she told him frankly. 'You'll barely break even with the food, and anyway they'll need a bigger house once they've grown up. You've got eight chickens now, James—and by tomorrow you might have ten.'

'Good grief,' he said, as if it was only just dawning on him what he'd taken on.

'Look on the bright side,' she said cheerfully. 'The other two might not hatch.'

But they did. Or sort of. The eighth struggled out of the shell in the morning, moments after Helga had left the nest, and James squatted down at the end of the house and studied the tiny wet chick cheeping furiously. Helga was ignoring it, so he helped it out into the run and it went to her and snuggled under her wing, and he smiled and looked forlornly at the last egg.

And it was cracking! There was a hole in it, but

without Helga to keep it warm he knew it would die. It was still alive, cheeping and struggling, and of course Maisie was nowhere to be found. 'Let me give you a hand,' he said, and chipped away a little of the shell, but to his horror the membrane inside the shell started to bleed, and he realised that chicks must have a mechanism to cut off the blood supply to the membrane, a bit like mammals cut off the blood to the umbilical cord once they take their first breath.

And the little chick hadn't cut off that blood supply, and now, because of his interference, it might die.

'I'm sorry, little chick,' he said softly, disgusted at himself for being so sentimental. He wasn't even a vegetarian! But the little chick was lying there in his hand, half in and half out of the shell, still cheeping. With a heavy heart, but realising that it was the chick's only chance, James freed it from the remains of the broken shell.

The membrane bled a little more, and the chick was freezing in his hand, but still quite definitely alive. He was standing staring at it and wondering what the hell to do now when Maisie appeared.

'What's up?'

'The last chick,' he said, and told her what he'd done.

She tsked at him and looked at it. 'Poor little mite. You need to warm it up or it'll die. It'll probably die anyway, but you've got more than enough.'

'Hey! This is my chick, I can't let it die,' he said, fiercely protective, and caught the laughing glint in her eye.

'So stick it in your boxers to warm it.'

'It'll fall out of the leg,' he said, not fancying the

thought of the chick in his underwear, but she still had that twinkle in her eye.

'Not if you're wearing the jersey ones,' she said.

He tipped his head on one side. 'Have you been spying on my washing line?' he said accusingly, and she chuckled.

'Hardly spying. It's outside my bedroom window. I can't miss it.' Maisie reached out her hands. 'Here, give it to me, I'll stick it in my bra.'

'What?' Damn, his voice sounded strangled to his ears, but he handed her the chick and watched in fascination and envy as she took the little chick and nestled it inside her vest top.

'Oh, it's cute! Look,' she said, leaning forwards, but all he could see were the smooth, pale globes of her breasts criss-crossed with faint blue veins, and he discovered he didn't give a damn about the chick. He just wanted to bury his face in there between her breasts, exactly where the chick was, and kiss her smooth, pale skin until she cried out.

'Don't suffocate it,' he advised, turning away before she could see his reaction.

'As if,' she snorted, and followed him back to the house. 'If you make a little bed from a box filled with shredded tissues, you could put it in the airing cupboard. Of course, if the Aga was going you could put it on that.'

'If the Aga was going we'd all be dead of heatstroke,' he said drily. 'Here's a box. Make what you like, I'm making tea. Want one?'

It lived. After all the angst and trauma, he tucked it into the little nest box under Helga before he went to bed, and in the morning he discovered it was alive and well, if a little shaky on its pins.

And so he had ten chickens, and he found he was curiously happy. Tango thought they were fascinating, and so did he, and they crouched there for ages watching the tiny little things scratching at their mother's side, and he thought about the tiny bleeding chick in Maisie's bra and wanted to kiss her for saving its life.

Well, he wanted to kiss her for all sorts of reasons, and very few of them were to do with the chick, but she needed a friend more than she needed him coming on to her like a sex-crazed adolescent, he told himself, and so dusting off his knees he found Tango's lead, put her in the car, drove to Rendlesham Forest and took her for a long walk in the woods.

There were two advantages to that. One, it was cooler.

And, two, he wouldn't run into Maisie.

He couldn't get back quick enough.

CHAPTER SEVEN

IT WAS a time for growing, Maisie decided.

The crops were growing in the fields, James's chicks were growing—even, amazingly, the one she'd helped him warm up after Helga had abandoned it—and perhaps most amazing of all, her baby was growing. She was now twenty-one weeks pregnant, and there was no way she could hide it any more.

On the last Friday in June, just under a month since she'd found out she was pregnant and three weeks since his dramatic collapse, she went to visit David. She hadn't seen him except for a brief visit more than a fortnight earlier while he'd still been in hospital and not really paying much attention, and when he saw her, his eyes widened.

'My God. It's true, then.'

She gave him a wry smile. 'Yes, it's true. I was going to tell you, but you conked out on me, and I thought you might have had rather more important things to think about for the last few weeks than a junior colleague.'

He started to shake his head, but thought better of it. 'Nonsense,' he said instead. 'Nothing comes before the health and welfare of my team.'

She laughed. 'You're a sweet liar. How are you?'

His own laugh was hollow. 'Oh, better than I was. Please thank your friend. He was very kind.' David looked pointedly at her bump. 'Is he...um...?'

He trailed off, obviously at a loss for words, and Maisie helped him out. 'Anything to do with this? No. He's my neighbour, and a friend. That's all.'

'Pity. Nice guy.'

'Yes, he is,' Maisie agreed, but she didn't want to think about it too much, because it was pointless.

James seemed to be avoiding her.

Ever since the chicks had hatched, he'd been a little more distant. Busy, slightly remote—nothing specific, really, but she just had that feeling. And yet she found things had been done as if by magic, little things that helped her.

Things like mucking out her chickens, and clearing out the dogs' run, and oiling the hinges on the gate, and sweeping up the petals from her drive when the wind had torn them off one of the rose bushes one blustery day.

James walked the dogs every other day at lunchtime, and took them out in the morning, and in return she walked them in the evening if she was home before him.

Gone, though, were the lovely, companionable walks they'd shared in the first week or so, and she realised she missed them. Ridiculously.

'Like that, is it?' David said softly, and she came back down to earth with a start.

'I'm sorry?'

'You and the good doctor—James, wasn't it?'

'James Sutherland—and, no, it's not like that. It's not like anything.'

'If you say so,' he murmured, and closed his eyes. 'I wish everything would stop sliding off the horizon.'

'Are you still giddy?'

He laughed. 'Just a bit. I can't walk on my own, I can't stand—I can't even go to the loo without help. That really is the pits.' He opened his eyes again and looked at her, and she could see the frustration and worry in his eyes. 'It's going to be weeks, Maisie. Are you coping all right without me?'

'Mmm. It's great, actually. We get to the chocolate biscuits before they're all finished, and there isn't anyone standing over us telling us he wouldn't have done it like that.'

'I don't!'

'Not often,' she relented, smiling. 'But you do eat all the chocolate biscuits.'

'Pete said you've got a locum starting on Monday.'

'We have. She's just qualified, and she wants to work for two months to earn some money before she goes travelling—she didn't have a gap year and she's going to have one now. That could fit in really well.'

'Pete seemed to think she was rather nice.'

Maisie blinked and stared at him. 'Really? That sort of nice?'

'Indeed.'

She laughed out loud. 'I thought he was immune.'

'So did he. Watch this space.'

'Absolutely,' she said. 'Of course, she might not be interested in him. It happens.'

Had there been something give-away in her voice? Maybe, or maybe David was just good at reading between the lines. Whatever, he reached out his hand and wrapped his fingers around hers in an uncharacteristically personal gesture, squeezing them briefly before releasing her. 'Don't despair of James,' he said gruffly. 'If the man isn't a complete fool, he'll realise what a treasure you are, Maisie.'

'David, I told you—'

'I know what you told me. And everything may be sliding off the edge of the world, but I can still see what's at the end of my nose.'

She sighed. 'David, he's not interested. Please, just leave it.'

She remembered the grapes she'd brought him, and produced them with a flourish to distract him. 'Here— they're washed, so you can eat them now.'

'Or you can.'

She grinned. 'We'll share. Is there a bowl any-where?'

'Try the kitchen, and if you can't find anything, ask Ann. She's pottering in the garden with the rab-bits. In fact, call her in and we'll have tea.'

'I can't stop that long,' Maisie said regretfully. 'I've got consults starting again at three, and we're up to our eyes. I thought I'd just come and tell you not to bother to hurry back.'

He snorted. 'Like I can.'

She hugged him because, all things considered, he was a wonderful boss and she was very fond of him, and he patted her back a little awkwardly.

'You take care of yourself and that baby, you hear?' he said a little fiercely. 'I don't want you doing anything dangerous. Anything too heavy or unpre-dictable—any large-animal stuff—get Pete to do it.'

'Pete hates the large-animal stuff, and he's terrified of horses,' Maisie reminded him. 'You'll just have to get better soon, and until then, if I feel it's too much for me, I'll send the locum.'

He laughed. 'Sounds like a good idea.'

She plucked a grape from the bunch and popped it in her mouth. 'Right, I'm off. You take care of yourself, and do what Ann tells you. It'll be good training. You might come back civilised.'

'Not a chance!'

They both turned to look at Ann in the doorway, and although she was laughing, Maisie could see the lines of strain around her face.

'Ann! Hello—how lovely to see you.'

'Hello, yourself. Got time for tea?'

She shook her head. 'No, but I'll come another time. We haven't had a chat for ages. How are all the rescued rabbits?'

'Multiplying. It's that time of year, isn't it? People go on holiday and they can't find anyone to look after them, and they know I won't turn them away. Come on, I'll walk you to your car.'

Maisie waggled her fingers at David and followed Ann out to the car, sensing that she wanted to talk.

'So, how is he, really?'

'Awful. So, so dizzy. They're sure it was definitely labyrinthitis, but until they'd run all the checks and done an MRI scan there was still an element of doubt, and I know he can be opinionated and difficult, but when I thought I might lose him…'

Her eyes filled, and she sniffed and gave a ragged laugh. 'It's strange how you realise you love them when you'd almost forgotten that you ever did. And then, just to punish me for loving him, he turns into the world's worst patient and I could kill him anyway!'

Maisie laughed and hugged her. 'Poor you. Is anybody giving you a break?'

'Oh, yes, my sister and his sister are being very kind, but I still feel guilty. Don't worry about me, I want to talk about you. What's this all about, Maisie?' she asked, looking pointedly at her growing bump. 'You are a dark horse. I didn't know there was anyone on the scene.'

Maisie lowered her eyes and shrugged. She hated lying to her friends and colleagues, but she just couldn't face telling them the whole truth.

'Just someone I used to know,' she compromised. 'It was a one-off.'

'And is there any possibility…?'

This one she could at least answer honestly. 'No. There's no possibility of us getting together. I'm having this baby on my own, and I'm really excited and happy about it, so don't feel sorry for me. It's the best thing to happen to me for a long, long time. Maybe ever.'

'Then I'm really glad for you, and if there's anything I can do, let me know.'

She grinned. 'There is. You can get your husband well and send him back to us, but only when he's really better. The last thing we need is him overdoing it too soon. Anyway, we've got a locum starting on Monday, someone Pete's found.'

'Yes, I've heard all about her. She's going to stay in the flat over the practice. If I can get away I'll give it a thorough clean before the weekend. Don't want to put her off before she even starts!'

As Maisie drove off, she watched Ann in the rear-view mirror. Ann lifted her hand to wave, then turned away, her shoulders drooping. Poor woman. Still, hopefully it wouldn't be too much longer before David was back on his feet and she got her life back. There were countless people in that situation all the time. How did they cope? Badly, she suspected, and wondered how she'd manage if she had a disabled child.

'You'll do your best, and love it anyway,' she told herself fiercely, and went back to the surgery, took her clinic and drove home, to find a note on her door from James.

'Got the dogs. Bit worried about Tango. Can you come round? J.'

She had been looking forward to crawling into a nice cold glass of something refreshing and lying on the sofa watching television for a few minutes while something instant was nuking in the microwave, but for James to mention his concern on the note sounded serious.

The tabbies were rubbing round her legs and clamouring for supper, so she let them in, threw some dry food into their dishes and went round to see James.

Through the beautifully painted and smooth-swinging gate. Amazing. He'd been busy again, she realised, looking at the paint on her fingers, and she glanced at the chicks on the way past and did a mild double-take. They were getting their feathers, and at almost two weeks old were at least three times the size they'd been.

'Helga, you're such a clever girl,' she said, and went to knock on the door just as it swung inwards to reveal James, a worried smile on his face.

'Hi. Thanks for coming round. I hope you didn't mind me asking you. I don't like to take advantage, but—'

'Any time. It's fine. What's wrong with her?' she asked, patting her own dogs absently and looking at Tango for any sign of a problem.

There was nothing immediately obvious. Tango was wagging her tail and greeting her as lovingly as usual, but there was perhaps a slight lack of her usual exuberance. Maisie crouched down and fondled her gently. 'What's up, Tango?' she murmured, checking her eyes for brightness.

The left one was a little weepy, but that wasn't what had worried James.

'She can't seem to eat anything hard,' he said. 'I gave her a biscuit and she cried out when she bit it, and dropped it and ran away.'

'Really? Tango, come here, let me look at your mouth,' she said, and tried to prise open the dog's jaws, but as soon as they were open about an inch, she yelped and ran away.

Maisie sat back on her heels and stared at the dog in consternation. 'I wonder what's wrong. Has she been chewing sticks?'

'She's always chewing sticks,' James said. 'I never throw them for her, but I think my sister did. Why? Do you think she might have hurt her mouth on one?'

'Possibly,' she said slowly. 'I don't know. It might be just a little sore, or she could have strained the jaw joint or pulled a muscle playing with the others, or there could be a bit of stick jammed across the roof of her mouth. There are all sorts of possibilities, but until I can get her mouth open I can't begin to tell.'

'She just won't open it,' he said. 'I've tried, and I got the same reaction you did, only I don't think I got as far as you.'

'Let me try again. Can you hold her? I need to make sure there isn't a stick wedged up there.'

He knelt down, restrained the trembling dog between his knees and held her still while Maisie talked gently to her and coaxed her to open her mouth. She only opened it a fraction of an inch, but it was enough to see that there was no stick jammed across her palate. She didn't push it any further, though, but released her and went back to the academic exercise of eliminating possibilities.

'Is she eating and drinking?'

'Soft food—I gave her some rice and chicken, and she managed that, and she's drinking all right.'

'And she's not drooling.' Maisie sat back and sighed. 'Oh, Tango, my love, what's wrong with you, babes?' she murmured, and the dog wagged her tail and nuzzled Maisie trustingly.

'So what now?'

'Now we watch her,' Maisie said. 'You might find by the morning she's fine.'

'I hope so. I've got a surgery at eight-thirty.'

'So have I. I could take her with me if you like.'

'Let's see,' he said, and then tipped his head on one side and smiled ruefully. 'I bet you haven't eaten.'

'How did you guess?'

He laughed and got to his feet, then held out his hand to pull her up. She had no choice but to put her hand in his, and the warmth and strength of his touch just served to underline how much she'd missed spending time with him in the last week or two.

Had he changed his mind? Realised what a treasure she was, in David's words?

Apparently not. As soon as she was on her feet, he released her and turned away, washing his hands before opening the fridge and rummaging through the contents as if his life depended on it.

'Bacon and eggs?' he suggested. 'I seem to have eggs coming out of my ears.'

She chuckled, putting away her disappointment and taking the moment at face value. 'Funny, that,' she said, drying her hands. 'Your fridge must look like mine. And, yes, bacon and eggs would be lovely. Thank you.'

'Here, put your feet up and drink this,' he said, handing her a glass beaded with condensation.

'Oh, that looks good.'

'Spring water with cranberry and orange juice.'

He was trimming the bacon with surgical precision, and she went and sat down so she didn't have to watch those long, strong fingers working. He had beautiful hands—powerful and yet capable of great tenderness. She'd seen him cradling the tiny chick, holding it safe. Was that how he'd hold her? How would those hands feel on her body?

Gentle. Gentle and persuasive, she thought, and closed her eyes, stifling the moan of need that rose in her throat. If only he was interested in her as anything other than a friend, but if he was, he would have made it clear by now.

No, there was nothing between them, as she'd told David, and that reminded her.

'I've got a message for you from my boss,' she said, deliberately keeping her voice light. 'He asked me to thank you.'

'Oh. My pleasure. How is he?'

'Grim. Still dizzy, can't walk unaided, driving his poor wife mad. I can't imagine he's an easy man to look after. He's fit and healthy and used to doing things his own way. He wouldn't take inactivity lying down, so to speak,' she said, and James chuckled.

'I can understand that. I'd go demented having to rely on someone else for everything.'

'I was wondering how I'd cope with a disabled child,' Maisie said suddenly, and he stopped in the act of lowering the bacon into the pan and looked at her keenly.

'Are you concerned that it might be?'

She shrugged. 'Not really. I haven't thought about it much, but it occurred to me after I saw how David's wife was struggling, and that's just short term. I'm certainly not dwelling on it, and if it happens, it happens. I'll deal with it then.'

'Would it make a difference if you knew? There's a new diagnostic test that assesses your risk factor for Down's and compares it to the norm for your age. Would you like to have the test? It's non-invasive and not conclusive, like amniocentesis, but there isn't any risk to the baby from it.'

She shook her head. 'Seems pointless, and anyway I'm young and fit. If it happens, it happens. One bridge at a time.'

He nodded. 'I agree. How many rashers?'

*   *   *

Tango was worse in the morning. Her eye had streamed all down her cheek, and when James looked down on the top of her head, her eyeball had been pushed forwards by almost a centimetre.

He took her straight round to Maisie, and she looked down at the dog and tutted softly.

'Poor baby. James, I think I need to take her in with me. I don't like the look of that eye at all, and I have to warn you, she might lose it. Whatever's going on needs urgent investigation.'

He nodded, the thought of Tango losing one of those beautiful brown eyes gutting him. 'Sure. Do whatever you need to do. Don't worry about the cost.'

'I'm glad you said that. If she needs to go to Newmarket for specialist surgery, it will run away with the money. I'll get an X-ray of the area and we'll see what we're dealing with, and then I'll go from there. Shall I ring you?'

'Can I come and observe?' he asked, suddenly very worried for Tango and realising that, his sister's dog or not, he'd become ridiculously attached to her. And anyway, he wanted to know what was going on as much as Maisie did.

'Of course, but I thought you had a surgery.'

'I do,' he said, wishing he could cancel it. 'I should be finished by eleven, though. What time will you look at her?'

'Probably around then. We've got a clinic all morning, and then we'll have a few emergencies to deal with. James, you can trust me,' she said, and he wondered if she felt that he didn't.

'I know that,' he said, hoping she believed him, and so he said it again for emphasis. 'I know I can trust you, but I'd still like to see what you find. It might make it easier to explain to my sister.'

Maisie nodded, then took Tango's lead. 'I'll take her now. Has she had anything to eat or drink?'

He shook his head. 'No. I took away the water last night, because I had a feeling this might happen. Is there anything I can do for you now before I go?'

'Walk the dogs and feed my chickens?' she said with a smile, and he felt his heart lurch.

Lord, she had a beautiful smile. If only…

'Fine. You go. I'll see you as soon as I can get away. Start without me if you have to.'

'OK.'

He watched them go, then quickly grabbed her dogs and went for a run along the river wall, then fed the chickens and arrived at the surgery with only two minutes to spare.

'Dr Sutherland, thank goodness you're here,' Patsy said. 'There's a man to see you. He's most insistent, and he wasn't very polite.' She lowered her voice. 'I think he might be an addict. He's in the waiting room—the one with the tattoos on his face. I've taken the liberty of putting him first on your list, because he's a little bit on the high side, if you get my drift.'

He did, the moment he entered the waiting room. The smell hit him like a brick wall, and he took the man through to the surgery, opened the window and sat him down.

Or tried to. He was twitchy, though, and produced a dog-eared prescription and a medical card so scruffy and defaced it was hard to read. 'I've got a letter from my last doctor,' he said, and pulled an envelope in only slightly better condition from his pocket and handed it to James.

Needless to say it had been opened, but he pulled the letter out and unfolded it, scanning it quickly. It stated that the man was an addict, that he was on methadone 30 ml daily, that he needed to be given it daily and supervised while he drank it.

It was from a GP in Essex who James had never heard of, so he buzzed through to Patsy and asked her to phone the surgery. Moments later he was put in touch with the GP who'd been dealing with the addict in the past.

'Oh, you've got Lenny. He's a bit wild. Watch him. He's not very trustworthy, and he'll take it all at once if you give him more than one day at a time. The only exception is the weekend, and he's normally screaming for it on Monday because he has both days in one hit and then gets desperate, according to the pharmacy who've been dispensing his methadone. Where will he get his supplies?'

'Here,' James said. 'It's a dispensing practice.'

'Then watch him, and make sure it's thoroughly secured. Good luck. I'm only too happy to get rid of him. Oh, and get him to sign a contract.'

'Right.'

James cradled the phone and looked at Lenny thoughtfully.

'So. You're Leonard Price, is that right?'

'Don't call me that. I hate it. Lenny,' he said, rubbing his hands up and down his arms. 'So, can I have some stuff?'

'I'll make sure you have enough for today and to-morrow, and then I want you to come back on

Monday morning and see me again, and I'll get you to sign a contract.'

'What, the no-swearing crap?'

'That's the one—and no abusive language or threatening behaviour. No doubt you've heard it all before. Right, come with me and I'll get you your methadone for today and tomorrow,' he said, and to be sure, he dispensed it himself.

There was only enough to last the man for a couple of weeks, so he'd have to order more. Not surprisingly there wasn't much demand for methadone in the sleepy little town of Butley Ford, and he imagined they kept a small supply for just this sort of contingency.

He went back into his room, gave it a quick squirt of air freshener and called in his first patient, apologising for holding her up. It was the last thing he needed today, of all days, he thought, but he didn't allow himself to think about Tango until all his patients were finished. Then he shut the surgery, making sure it was properly secured in view of their latest resident, and headed for the veterinary surgery.

Maisie was just leading Tango into the surgical prep room when he arrived. Kathy showed him in, and he gave Maisie a tight smile.

'Any change?' he asked, looking down at Tango searchingly.

'Unfortunately, yes. It's still swelling. I'll knock her out, X-ray it and then we can have a good look without hurting her.'

They lifted her onto the table, and Maisie was conscious of James's eyes on her and his almost silent huff of disapproval. Tough. She didn't have time to worry about James and his over-developed sense of protection where her baby was concerned. She was fine, and as long as she could do her job, she'd do it.

She gave him a level look, and he raised a brow and backed off, folding his arms and regarding her in grim-lipped silence.

Until they'd shaved Tango's foreleg.

'What anaesthetic will you use?' he asked.

'Thio—thiopentone—to knock her down, and then Isoflo mixed with oxygen to keep her under.' She hit the vein first time, to her relief, since James was standing over her breathing down her neck, and the first thing she did once Tango was out and Kathy was happy she was stable was move her jaw very carefully to test if there was any resistance from the joint itself to indicate a dislocation.

There wasn't, and so she inserted an airway and secured it, then took an X-ray of the dog's head. Well, to be exact, she retreated from the room and Kathy took the X-ray. She wasn't that stupid. It took only a few moments to develop, and it was frustratingly inconclusive.

'There are so many structures in the head it's difficult to make out one from another,' she explained to James. 'I think I can see something here, though— just a vague outline of something that might be an abscess. Right, Kathy, let's turn her on her back and have a look.'

They tied her limbs out onto the table to hold her steady, covered her with drapes and then opened her mouth wide, securing it.

'Oh, yes,' Maisie said. 'Look—here, on her palate,

on the left side, right up near the joint. And it's obviously tracked up towards the back of her eye. Right, I'll open it up, take out what I can and look for a foreign body, but I may well not find anything.'

'What sort of foreign body? A splinter?'

'Or a thorn. Anything like that which has caused a penetrating injury resulting in infection. There may be nothing there at all, just a septic puncture wound. Is she right out, Kathy?'

Kathy pinched Tango between her toes, and nodded. 'Yup. Nice and stable. She's looking fine.'

'Good.' Maisie sliced open the abscess, removing the pus and checking it for splinters and thorns, but there was nothing. 'Rats. I was hoping to find something. Right, I'm going to go a bit further in, to try and find out why it's affecting her eye.'

'Do you think the splinter might have gone up further?' James asked, and she shrugged.

'I have no idea. I hope not. If I open it up so it can drain, hopefully it'll start to mend and her eye will go down, but it's bound to swell further with all this poking about. I don't want to damage anything, but if I'm not thorough enough, it could just flare up all over again.'

And then, to her relief, she found a tiny shard of wood, almost rotted away, soggy and soft but obviously enough to have caused the damage.

'There you are,' she said, holding it up. 'Your splinter.'

She hadn't realised how tense he'd been until she saw his shoulders drop.

'Thank you, Maisie,' he said quietly, and she threw

him a smile and carried on. She wanted to rinse out the area with saline, then leave it to drain.

'I won't give her antibiotics for twenty-four hours, until we're sure all the pus is out and it's on the mend, because otherwise you get pockets of pus sealed in and it just comes back.'

James leant back against the wall and crossed his arms, and his smile was crooked. If she hadn't known better, she would have thought that his legs were shaking.

'No doubt you'll help me keep an eye on her.'

'Of course. Right, let's wake her up.'

Tango came home at three, still a bit wobbly on her pins, but James had never been so glad to see a dog in his life.

'You just didn't want to tell your sister you'd killed or blinded her dog,' Maisie teased, and he nodded agreement and wondered if she realised just what a pushover he was for a pair of light brown eyes.

Canine or human.

They tried to encourage her to lie in her bed, but she didn't want to know. She staggered over to the sofa, climbed on, leaving one back leg behind, and flopped down with a big sigh. Seconds later a soft snore drifted from her, and he laughed quietly.

'So much for the bed. I might have known it was a waste of time.'

'She should be fine now. She probably won't eat today, but you could offer her water, and if she keeps it down you might try her with some boiled rice and chicken, very sloppy and cut up tiny, and just a very small amount at first.'

He nodded, then looked at Maisie. She was tired, he realised, her lovely sparkle absent, and she should have been resting. Instead, she'd been operating on Tango, and probably saving her sight, if not her life.

A lump came to his throat, and he swallowed it. 'Thank you, Maisie,' he said, but the lump was still there and his voice was gruff.

And then, just because he couldn't help himself, he took her in his arms, dropped a light and fiercely controlled kiss on her soft, surprised mouth, and hugged her.

CHAPTER EIGHT

IT WAS only gratitude, Maisie told herself.

Maybe if she said it enough times, she'd end up believing it, but her stupid, hopeful heart wouldn't give up, and she spent the night in turmoil.

Because, of course, she'd realised in the brief seconds of that kiss that she loved James—truly loved him, in the lay-down-her-life-for-him sort of way that had never hit her before, but it had hit her then, with the force of an express train.

Did he love her? Was that why he'd kissed her? She didn't know. All she knew was he'd said something about her needing to rest, and hustled her out of the door with what had felt like undue haste but had probably been more to do with her reluctance to leave his side for even a minute.

So here she was, on Sunday morning, taking the dogs for a walk and wondering if she'd bump into him. Of course, she had the perfect excuse to go round there and check on Tango, but she didn't want to use it. She wanted him to come to her, perversely, but he didn't, and she didn't meet him on the river wall, and it was only when she thought to check her answering-machine that she found a message from him.

'Hi. Tango's looking a bit better. Thanks for everything you did. I imagine you're walking the dogs. Fancy coffee? I'll be in all morning.'

Except, of course, it was almost twelve by the time she found his message, and she'd been moping all morning.

Idiot. She went round, tapped on the door and opened it. 'James?'

His voice came from the depths of the house. 'Hi. Come in.'

She went through the scullery and kitchen and found him buried up to his armpits in a packing chest in the hall. 'Lost something?' she said, feasting her eyes on his long, straight legs and taut buttocks as he bent over the box. What she wouldn't give for the right to go up to him and lean over and slide her arms around his waist...

'Oh, just some stuff of my sister's. She rang me, asking about it.' He straightened up, ran his fingers through his rumpled hair and shot her a smile that nearly blew her socks off. 'Morning.'

'Good morning. I see Tango's eye's gone down.'

'Mmm.' He looked down at the dog, studying her as she stood between them, her tail waving and her eyes fixed devotedly on him. Maisie could understand that. He crouched down and stroked her gently, and she took a couple of steps towards him and licked his chin. 'So—are you happy with her?'

And, of course, Maisie had to go close to see Tango, and that meant being right beside him, their legs touching as she crouched and looked at the dog's eye more thoroughly.

'Yes, I'm happy,' she said, and met his eyes. 'She'll be fine, I think. I'm pretty confident the danger's passed and her eye's safe.'

He nodded. His gaze stayed locked on hers, and for

a moment she thought he was going to say something, but then he stood up and turned away.

'I'll look for Julia's stuff later. Come and have a coffee.'

And that was it, the opportunity for him to lean over and kiss her good morning gone, wasted.

So it had been just simple gratitude, she told herself, the kiss last night nothing more complicated than that.

Damn. She swallowed the bitter regret and followed him through to the kitchen. There was a jug of coffee on the go, and he poured them both a mug and handed hers to her. They sat at the end of the big refectory table, and not for the first time Maisie wondered what on earth a bachelor was doing with such a huge table. The bulk of the antiques she could understand, but the kitchen table?

'My great-grandfather won this table at cards,' he said suddenly, as if he'd read her mind. His finger was tracing a little spill of coffee, doodling in it on the polished surface, and a smile flickered at the corner of his mouth. 'It caused havoc when it was delivered to the house in London. My father remembered it arriving, and the cook was so incensed at the huge thing in her kitchen that she flounced off and they had to manage without her till she calmed down. It took a week or more, apparently.'

Maisie laughed. 'I love it, but if you put it in my kitchen I might flounce. I wouldn't be able to walk round it, especially now. I'm getting huge.'

'What are you? Twenty-one weeks? That's over halfway.'

She nodded. 'I feel good now, though. Much better.'

'Good.' His smile flickered again briefly and was gone, and he started fiddling with a card that was propped up between the salt and pepper in the middle of the table. For a moment he frowned at it, then he shot Maisie a thoughtful look. 'Fancy going to a wedding?'

'A wedding?'

'Mmm. A friend of mine in London's getting married in two weeks. I have to go, and I was going to take Jools—my sister—but she won't be here. I wondered if you fancied coming.'

There was something he wasn't telling her, she thought, so she asked him.

'Why me?'

'Why not?'

She shrugged. 'Because when you turn up with a pregnant woman in tow, tongues will wag.'

He stared at her, as if she'd just said something extraordinary, then grinned. 'They will, won't they? What a wonderful idea. So—will you?'

'Only if you tell me why,' she said, standing her ground, and his grin became wry.

'My ex is going,' he said simply, and her heart crashed against her ribs.

'Ex?' she echoed, and he nodded.

'We were together for five years. I was happy in general practice, she wanted to go and save the world. She thought I was pandering to a load of spoilt and pampered capitalists, and she wanted me to go and save the children of Africa.'

'What, all of them?' Maisie said, wondering why

he hadn't gone, because if she knew nothing else about him, she knew he had a soft heart.

He laughed, then his smile died. 'Pretty much. She couldn't see that helping a woman cope when her baby was crying all night and she was worried sick about money and her husband was drinking it all could in any way be valid. I disagreed. It may not be cutting edge save-the-world stuff, but it's no less important, and I know what I do can make a difference.'

'So she dumped you and went to Africa to save the children?'

He gave a short, bitter laugh. 'No. I left her, just over a year ago, around the time my father died, and she prostituted her principles for a merchant banker. Still, he's probably better in bed than me.'

I doubt it, she thought, and then coloured hotly when she thought she'd said it out loud. Not that she knew, of course, and that kiss had been nothing if not chaste, but even so…

'Sorry. I'm just a bit raw about it, but in fact she did me a favour, because otherwise we probably would have got married—'

'You weren't married?'

He shook his head. 'No.'

'Oh.' Relief coursed through her, for no good reason, and she smiled. 'I just thought, when you said ex…'

'Just a figure of speech. So—will you come?'

'As a human shield?'

His smile was wry. 'I don't want her feeling sorry for me, or thinking that the road's open to come back to me, because it isn't. I'm happier now than I've been for years, and I feel settled here. I could put down roots, Maisie, real roots. I spent the happiest days of my childhood in this little town, and I want to stay here. And Carla would hate it.'

Maisie thought of the looks she'd get, the whispered remarks, some maybe more direct, and then thought of having James to herself all the way, all day long and all the way back.

No contest, really. 'Yes, I'll go with you,' she said rashly, and wondered if she'd regret it. 'So long as you don't mind all the gossip from the other people.'

He cocked his head on one side and looked at her quizzically. 'Why should I mind?'

'Because they might think it's your baby?'

A strange expression flickered in his eyes and was gone. 'Let them think what they like. I'm not ashamed of you, Maisie—far from it—so provided you don't mind if people think it's mine, we could give the society mill something to grind. It might be fun.'

Fun. Suddenly it seemed like ages since she'd had fun. 'I've got nothing to wear, of course,' she said, and he laughed.

'Women always say that.'

'But under the circumstances I think you might believe me,' she pointed out fairly, looking down at her steadily growing bump, and he grinned.

'I believe you. You do have a decent excuse, I suppose.'

'Will I need a hat?'

'Probably. Does that make you happy?'

She laughed, realising that it did. 'I am a woman, you know,' she said lightly, and again that strange light flickered in his eyes.

'Of course,' he said. Dropping the card onto the table, he stood up and poured his coffee down the sink. 'Sorry, I have to find this thing for Jools. Thanks again for looking after Tango. Don't forget to bill me.'

And that was that.

Dismissed, she took herself back to her house, studied her wardrobe and realised that she quite literally didn't have a thing she could wear. She'd been wearing her jeans and work trousers with the top button undone, but that was beginning to be insufficient and her shirts were gaping now because of her slowly swelling breasts.

She needed everything from the skin out, she realised, and there was only one person who liked shopping enough to cope with that. She picked up the phone.

'So what brought this on?'

'Apart from the fact that bits of me have gone up two sizes? I've got to go to a wedding in London with James.'

'What? You jammy thing! When? How? Why?'

'Two weeks—just under—and apparently it's fairly dressy, so I'll need a hat.'

'Great,' Kirsten said, cutting them both another slice of fruit cake and curling up on her sofa, eyes alight. 'You really need to choose the dress first, I suppose, and you can't have a big brim or anything too clumpy, you'll look like a mushroom with a fat stalk.'

'I feel so much better for knowing that,' Maisie said drily. 'So when are we going to do this?'

Kirsten looked at her watch. 'It's two-thirty. The shops shut at four on Sundays. We've got an hour and a half—bit less. Come on. No time like the present.' And getting up, she took the cake away from Maisie before she could take so much as a bite, and dragged her to her feet.

In fact, it was easier than she'd imagined. They went to a large department store, looked in the maternity department and found a wonderful dress in a silk and linen mix. It was pale green, almost pistachio, and in the winter it wouldn't have suited her, but because she'd caught the sun it looked gorgeous.

'I'll need a strapless bra,' she said doubtfully, and Kirsten shrugged.

'I'll lend you mine. I'm bigger than you, but it'll probably fit you now. Right, hat.'

And there, perched on top of a hat stand in the millinery department, was a delicious little concoction of pale green feathers.

'How appropriate,' Kirsten said with a grin, and plonked it on Maisie's head. 'Fabulous. What do you think?'

She turned her head, the feathers shimmering artfully over one eye, and chuckled. 'It's crazy.'

'It's a summer wedding. It's perfect—the colour couldn't be better. Buy it.'

So she did, mourning the fact that it represented at least one kitchen unit, but she hardly ever went out anywhere smart and she just felt like being silly.

And, besides, she didn't want to let James down, and if people thought they were together...

'Shoes.'

'I've got shoes. I've got some strappy sandals that

will do,' she said, refusing to blow the whole of her kitchen budget, James or not, and anyway her legs were aching.

'Right. Let's go back and finish that cake,' Kirsten said with a grin.

'Right, I want your assurance that you're going to abide by the letter of this contract,' James said. 'Are you sure you've read it and understood it?' He'd gone over the contract with the addict anyway, just to be on the safe side and because he wasn't sure how good the man's understanding was, but it was Monday morning and, as predicted, Lenny's craving was making him twitchy. He was so desperate he would have signed anything.

'Yeah, yeah, I understand. Just give me the damn stuff.'

'First things first. Sign here,' James said, trying not to breathe in as he leant over towards Lenny and countersigned it in front of Jane.

The contract was the usual one they had in the practice, Jane had told him, and should prevent any abuse of privilege.

Should. However, James had his doubts. The man was definitely strange. Nobody in their right mind got their face tattooed, in his experience, and there was something about the wild eyes and nervous twitching that made him very, very uneasy.

'Right,' he said, and ushered Lenny through to the reception area for his daily dose of methadone. To his relief the usual dispenser, Elizabeth, was on duty, and he handed the prescription to her, and also a copy of the contract.

'He knows the rules. No abusive language or threatening behaviour, or we refuse to dispense the methadone—and that's not just to staff, but to other patients. Any trouble, I want to know straight away,' he said, as much for Lenny's benefit as Elizabeth's, and went back to his room, squirted the air freshener round it again and called in his next patient.

Over the next week and a half, Maisie's bump grew much more noticeable. She had an antenatal appointment with Jane Shearer on Friday afternoon, the day before the wedding, and of course they were busy at the veterinary surgery, but at least they had their locum now, a lovely girl called Jenny, and, as David had predicted, Pete had fallen heavily under her spell.

'Could you cover me so I can go to my antenatal?' she asked Jenny, and she'd been given a willing smile in return.

'Sure. How are things?'

'Fine,' she replied, and physically, of course, it was true. It was only emotionally she was a little at sea, and that was all her own stupid fault. She kept thinking about that kiss James had given her—the meaningless one that she couldn't seem to get out of her sad, desperate little mind—and she was wondering if the romantic atmosphere of the wedding the next day would help things along.

She was still thinking about the wedding as she parked in the car park of the doctors' surgery in Butley Ford, and so her mind wasn't really on what she was doing as she walked towards the entrance.

If it had been, she might have seen him coming, but as it was the knife was pressed against her throat before she had time to register his presence. All she could feel was an arm around her throat, the prick of the knife on her neck and a choking, vile smell of unwashed body jamming in her throat.

'What—?'

'Shut up! Just shut up and get inside!' he snarled, and propelled her none too gently towards the door. He kicked it open and it slammed back, bouncing off the wall and ricocheting into Maisie's arm and making her cry out.

Behind the desk she saw the elderly receptionist's eyes widen, and seconds later James was there.

'I want my stuff,' the man said, and James nodded.

'OK, Lenny. Let her go and we'll talk about it.'

'No. I want it now. You gave me some other crap this morning—it tasted funny. It wasn't the same—you're trying to trick me, but I know!'

'OK, Lenny. Just let her go, could you, and I'll get it for you. Just let her go first.'

'No. I want my stuff.'

'You have a contract,' James said, leaning idly against the wall and studying his fingers as if he didn't care one way or the other if the man got whatever it was he wanted. Drugs, Maisie realised, and felt the knife move away from her neck.

She started to sigh with relief, but then felt the prick of the knife lower down, against her abdomen, and her eyes widened with fear.

'Touch that child and I'll break your neck,' James said mildly, and she could see the steel in his eyes.

'I don't believe you. Get me the stuff.'

James straightened away from the wall. 'If you hurt her or the baby, you'll never get the drugs. Now, which is it to be, a long wait in a police cell on a murder charge, or let her go now and I'll give you your dose? Which is, after all, why you're here, isn't it?'

She felt his grip loosen. 'How do I know you aren't lying?'

'You don't,' James said. 'But you're getting nothing like that. What have you got to lose?'

And that was it. She was free, running towards James, thrust behind him into the safety of the office while he twisted the man's arm up behind his shoulder and the knife fell to the floor with a clatter.

'Ow, you're hurting me!' Lenny whined, but James just smiled grimly.

'Sorry,' he said, not looking in the least repentant, and his eyes scanned over Maisie briefly, their expression unreadable. 'You OK?'

She nodded, wondering if her legs would give way. 'Yes, I think so.'

'Right. Stay there. I'll just find out what happened this morning, and I'll be with you.' His grip tightened. 'Right, Mr Price. Come with me.'

James felt sick with relief. Lenny was gone, hauled off by the police after he'd had his methadone, and Jane had taken Maisie gently away and pronounced her unharmed. She was sitting in Jane's room drinking a cup of tea with her now as her antenatal clinic was over, and as he joined them he was trying to get the image of Lenny with the knife at Maisie's throat out of his mind.

Not that there weren't plenty of other things to think about. They were dealing with another dispensing error. It had been obvious to him the moment he'd clapped eyes on Lenny that he was suffering withdrawal symptoms. He was sweaty, shaking, agitated and probably even more unpredictable than usual, and he'd complained the stuff he'd had that morning had tasted funny.

And when James had unlocked the cupboard at the bottom where the methadone bottle was kept, he'd found it empty, and beside it, in an almost identical heavy amber glass bottle in the same stock size, was temazepam elixir. Similar green syrupy liquid, only instead of the heroin substitute, Lenny had been given a sleeping draught.

The normal dose was five to ten millilitres, and Lenny had been given thirty, enough to send the average person to sleep for days, but Lenny, of course, was not exactly an average person and, as he'd confessed cheerfully once he'd had his methadone, he'd had temazepam before so it was no big deal, and he hadn't had to pay for it this time.

'At least the bastard won't sue,' James said to Jane, but his main preoccupation wasn't relief that they'd escaped a major disaster with this latest dispensing error, but that Maisie was all right. When he'd seen Lenny hold the knife to her throat, he'd felt sick with fear for her, and when Lenny had moved it down to threaten the unborn baby, his rage had nearly overwhelmed him.

'Sue? He'd better not try, after that stunt,' Jane said fiercely.

'He seemed to think getting the Temazepam was a bit of a laugh—a freebie on the National Health,'

James told them heavily. 'When I think what might have happened...'

He was thinking of Maisie, but Jane was clearly still concentrating on the dispensing error and the repercussions it might have had. 'We'll have to submit a report and instigate an inquiry,' she said. 'And you know who was on this morning?'

'I can guess. Is she all right?'

'Not really. I've sent her home she was so distraught. I'm not sure if it was the knife or the knowledge of what might have happened if someone else had taken that which worried her so much. I'll drop in and see her on the way home, make sure she's OK.'

He nodded, then his eyes flicked to Maisie's. 'Are you really OK?'

She nodded. 'Yes. I was just a bit shaken. I'm fine now.'

He swallowed and looked away before he made a fool of himself. 'Good. I'll take you home.'

'I'm fine. You've got a surgery.'

'It'll keep for a while if necessary. Are you sure you're all right?'

'Yes—really. I'm sure.'

James wasn't. He wanted to undress her and run his hands over every inch of her body, checking it for cuts and bruises and signs of harm, and kiss better every one he found.

Just as well, then, that he did have a surgery. 'I'll see you later,' he said as he showed her out. 'And don't be afraid. He's in police custody, he can't harm you, and we don't have any other addicts on the books at the moment. I'll come and see you on my way home.'

'James, I'm fine,' she said softly, and, rising up on tiptoe, she pressed a fleeting kiss to his lips and left. He watched her go, then turned to find Jane's speculative eyes on him.

She nodded slightly, then with a little smile she turned back to her room. 'I've got to be off. Will you be all right this evening?' she asked.

He followed her back into her room and closed the door. 'I'll be fine. What about Patsy?'

'I've called Elizabeth and asked her to cover tonight and tomorrow morning, because I think until we can get to the bottom of this, we'll have to suspend Patsy. We can't let it happen again.'

'No, we can't. We'll lose our dispensing licence, not to mention our reputations. Will you have time to see her?'

'Yes, I— Oh, damn! Oh, no. James, we're out again tonight.'

'I'll see her,' he said, cursing the fact that he couldn't do what he wanted to do and go straight round to Maisie's house and take her in his arms. Perhaps it was just as well. 'Where does she live?'

'Just down the road from you—the little terrace on Rectory Road. It's one of the middle ones, the one with the porch.'

He nodded. 'I'll find her. You go. Are you sure you're all right for tomorrow?'

She smiled at him. 'I'm sure. You go to the wedding and have a lovely time with Maisie, and forget all about this. It'll do you both good.'

It was seven-thirty before he got to Patsy, and he found her tearful and still beside herself with anxiety.

He tutted gently at her and led her back into her living room, sitting down on the sofa with her and holding her hands as she wept and tried to explain, almost incoherent.

Almost. One word stood out, though. The word 'blind'.

He took her chin, tilted her face up to him and stared into her eyes, searching for the clouding of cataracts and finding nothing, then sighed softly and let her go. 'Patsy, how long ago did you notice that you couldn't see as clearly?' he asked gently.

Her shoulders lifted in a tragic gesture. 'I don't know. I realised about a month ago that I couldn't really see clearly enough to drive, so I stopped. It's only the middle bit of the picture, though, if you know what I mean. My left eye's been funny for a while in some lights, but just recently the right one's been sort of fuzzy, too. Usually it's all right, but there's something about the light in the dispensary—have I got cataracts?'

He shook his head. 'No. I think you might have a condition called macular degeneration, and if you have, that could explain why you're finding it hard to read labels, because it affects the centre of the visual field only.'

'And am I going to go blind?'

He shook his head. 'I don't think so—not if I'm right. And the progress of this thing can be halted with laser surgery, too, in certain cases, so there's more hope than there used to be for it. The first thing is to refer you to an ophthalmic surgeon for a thorough examination, and then some decisions can be made. But in the meantime, I don't think you should be working with medicines,' he said, gently but unmistakably firmly.

'But who will do it?' she said, wringing her hands. 'I knew I couldn't see that clearly, but I thought, so long as I didn't make a mistake, I could keep helping out. Then there was that young girl with her penicillin, and now this—and when I saw that horrible, horrible man threatening to stick a knife in Miss McDowell's baby and it was all my fault—'

'Don't,' James said, trying not to think about it himself. 'Don't torture yourself. She's all right, thank God, and so is Lenny, for which we all need to be profoundly grateful. Just now he's sleeping off all the excitement in a police cell, and Maisie's OK, so there's no harm done.'

Except to my blood pressure, he added to himself, and when he'd calmed Patsy down a little more, he left her with a firm instruction to come into the surgery on Monday morning and see him so he could examine her more thoroughly and refer her to the hospital specialist.

And then, without any further ado, he went round to Maisie's and found her curled up on her sofa with all three dogs surrounding her, fast asleep. He tapped on the window, and she woke with a start and sat up, eyes wide.

He saw the moment she realised it was him, and told himself he'd imagined the flash of joy on her face.

It was relief, that was all—relief that it was him and not some random axe-murderer or junkie come to cause havoc with her life.

She opened the door to him, and he folded her against his chest and hugged her.

'Are you really all right?' he asked, his lips pressed to her hair, and she nodded and snuggled closer.

'I was so scared,' she confessed, and he remembered, not that it was ever far from his mind, that it was the second time in five months that she'd been assaulted by a man. He got his emotions firmly under control and then lifted his head and searched her wide, guileless amber eyes for clues to her emotional state.

'Will you be all right to go to the wedding tomorrow?' he asked softly, and she smiled her heartbreakingly lovely smile and shook her head at him in reproof.

'Of course I'll be all right. I'm looking forward to it. Have you eaten? I've saved you some supper because I thought you'd probably work late. It's in the fridge—it's only quiche and salad, and there's some crusty bread.'

It sounded wonderful, he thought, not least because it meant he'd get to sit and eat it in her company—and tomorrow he'd have her to himself all day.

Suddenly things were looking up...

CHAPTER NINE

THE wedding was wonderful. It was held in the beautiful and very ornate upstairs function rooms of an old pub right on the Thames, and sitting beside James during the warm and informal marriage ceremony with the river as a backdrop to the bride and groom brought a huge lump to Maisie's throat.

If only, she thought, but put her sentimental thoughts on hold and concentrated on doing what she was supposed to be doing—being a human shield to protect him from the beautiful and elegant and infuriatingly slender Carla.

The meal was wonderful, the group of people at their table great fun, and to her surprise she found herself thoroughly enjoying it. It was hot, though, and towards the end of the evening they stood on the balcony over the water and sipped mineral water instead of champagne, because James was driving and she didn't want to drink because of the baby. They caught the slight breeze coming up the river and watched the lights come on in the trendy apartments opposite as the sun went down.

The breeze fluttered the feathers in her hat and they tickled her face, and James laughed at her, teasing her about it and saying he'd always known she was a bird fancier, but his eyes said something quite different.

At least, she thought they did, but she wasn't sure, and up to now he'd been nothing but polite and friendly, attentive to her every need and yet keeping that infuriating distance that she didn't know how to erode.

But now, with the meal and the speeches over, the jazz quartet who'd played throughout the wedding cleared away their things and a DJ took over, playing all the cheesy old songs that brought a lump to her throat or made her want to sing along, and everyone was moving onto the dance floor.

Would he dance with her? Probably not, she thought regretfully. Too intimate—although, of course, if they were to give the impression he'd moved on, he would have to—unless he used her pregnancy as an excuse.

Very likely. But even so, although she'd managed to convince herself he wouldn't dance with her, she found herself swaying unconsciously to the music and watching the other couples longingly.

James noticed it, of course, and raised a brow. 'Want to dance?' he asked, and she nodded.

'If you do.'

He sketched a little bow and held out his hand, his mouth quirking into that wonderful smile, and she placed her hand in his and let him lead her to the floor. He took her in his arms, not close, like the others, but holding her at a respectable distance, until she wanted to scream.

Then the music slowed, becoming unmistakably sexy and romantic, and someone bumped into her from behind, pushing her into him. She felt him sigh softly against her hair, fluttering the little feathers against her cheek as he drew her closer to him, one arm sliding down to rest gently in the small of her back, the other cradling her hand against his chest as he swayed slowly to the music.

She laid her head against his shoulder and closed her eyes. He was a wonderful dancer. His movements were smooth and sensual, his sense of timing impeccable, and she found herself wondering what he'd be like as a lover.

No. Crazy. She'd drive herself mad thinking about things like that. If she wasn't careful she'd forget that she was merely there as a decoy, to throw Carla off the scent and make her think James was moving on with his life.

Which he was, of course, but just not with her.

More's the pity.

James closed his eyes and rested his cheek against Maisie's hair, careful to avoid the crazy little hat, if you could call it such a thing, and wished things could be different.

Every now and again he felt the baby move, sometimes a kick, sometimes a wriggle, and it brought a huge surge of protectiveness washing over him. Every time he closed his eyes he saw Lenny holding a knife at Maisie's throat, and he had to stop himself crushing her against him. She'd been so brave about that, and she'd been wonderful today.

She'd smiled and laughed and talked to all his friends, and had avoided saying anything which gave away their true relationship, so that all of them were left guessing.

And all of them adored her.

All but one, he thought, and then there was a tap

on his shoulder and he lifted his head and met Carla's eyes.

'Can I borrow you for a moment?' she said, and Maisie looked from one to the other, smiled at him and moved out of his arms.

'I could do with sitting down again,' she said graciously, and left them to it.

And Carla, the woman he'd thought he loved, the woman he'd once thought he'd marry and have children with, moved into his arms and he couldn't believe how wrong she felt.

'So, this is really it for you, isn't it?' she said, and suddenly he realised he couldn't lie to her, of all people.

'Yes, it is,' he said, then added honestly, 'It's not my baby, though.'

'Doesn't matter, does it? Funny how love just broadsides you without warning,' she said, and smiled understandingly at him. 'I'm glad you came. I've got something to tell you. I'm getting married, James— to Will.'

Extraordinarily, he felt nothing. 'Your merchant banker?' he asked.

She nodded, then her smile faded. 'Don't be angry with me about the Africa thing. I suppose I just wasn't in love with you, and I wanted an emotional challenge. I'm sorry I said all those things to you. I didn't really mean them, you know. I am proud of you, and I know what you do is good and makes a difference to people's lives. I was just bored, and we were going nowhere. I just didn't realise it.'

He smiled down at her, understanding her absolutely. 'Don't worry. You did me a huge favour.'

She smiled back fondly. 'I can see. I've never seen you look as happy as you do tonight.'

Was he looking happy? How odd. He shouldn't. He was marking time, waiting for a time when he could say something to Maisie, and somehow it just didn't seem appropriate, not while she was carrying another man's child.

'Good luck,' Carla said, and taking his face in her hands she kissed him. 'For old times' sake,' she murmured, then moved out of his arms and out of his life, going back to her Will, and he could see the sparkle in her eyes when she looked at him, and he knew it was right for her, too.

He found Maisie on the balcony, not sitting, as she'd said, but standing staring out over the water, a far-away look on her face.

'Are you OK?' he asked softly, and she turned and smiled up at him, but the smile didn't really reach her eyes and he realised she was tired.

'I'm fine.'

'Are you ready to go?'

'If you are.'

He nodded, and they said their goodbyes, using the baby and their journey back to Suffolk as their excuse, and then he was driving through the still-busy city streets, cutting through the suburbs and then out into the dark velvet night.

Maisie was asleep beside him, her lashes dark against her cheeks, and he drove carefully, his protective instinct at full throttle. It took two hours to get back, and he pulled onto her drive and cut the engine. She didn't stir.

'We're back, sleepyhead,' he said softly, and her

lashes fluttered up and she looked up at him, all disorientated and unfocussed, and he had an unbearable urge to lean over and kiss that soft, expressive mouth. Instead, he forced himself to get out and go round and open the door for her, helping her to her feet.

'Ouch,' she said, getting out of the car without her shoes, because her feet were sore from teetering about in strappy bits of nonsense. Without hesitation he scooped her up in his arms and carried her, giggling, to the door, her shoes dangling from his fingers behind her back.

'Key,' he said, and she found her key and slipped it in the lock and opened the door, and he carried her over the threshold with a strange feeling of unreality.

Wasn't that what the groom was supposed to do to the bride? And yet it hadn't been their wedding, so why was he even thinking about it?

He set her down, sliding her slowly down his body, feeling the solid fullness of her pregnancy against his body as she found her feet at last.

The dogs were milling around their feet, having been fed and walked and spoilt by Kirsten, who was no doubt waiting in the sitting room for Maisie. It was probably just as well, James thought, because with Maisie's soft unfocussed eyes staring up at him he wasn't at all sure he'd trust himself alone with her.

'Thank you so much for such a lovely day,' she said with that beautiful smile, and his heart crashed against his ribs.

'Any time. Thank you for coming with me. I really hadn't been looking forward to it, and having you there made all the difference,' he said honestly, and then, because he just couldn't stop himself, he bent his head and touched his mouth to hers.

Her lips softened and parted, and the invitation was almost too much for him, but with a superhuman effort he pulled away and straightened up.

'Goodnight, Maisie,' he said firmly. Calling Tango, he handed Maisie her shoes, walked out of the door, put the dog in the car and drove round the corner to his house. Then he sat in the kitchen and downed a hefty slug of single malt before making his way upstairs.

He didn't put on his bedroom light, just crossed to the window in the dark and watched for her bedroom light to come on. It didn't, and he realised she was probably having a cup of tea with Kirsten downstairs.

Yes. He could see her crossing the room, a mug in her hand, curling up on the sofa.

'Hell, you're stalking her, you're as bad as Stevenson,' he said. Disgusted with himself and frustrated beyond belief, he shut the curtains firmly and went to bed, and dreamed that it had been their wedding and the baby was his, and when he woke to Hector's dawn fanfare and the dream faded, the sense of loss was like a crushing weight on his heart.

'Idiot,' he told himself, and vowed to keep a greater distance, for both their sakes. Starting right now with a run along the river wall, he thought, and, pulling on his shorts and trainers and a fresh T-shirt, he clipped on Tango's lead and headed down the drive.

At least at five in the morning he wasn't likely to bump into her!

*   *   *

James was glad to get back to work on Monday morning and have something else to think about.

Patsy came to see him, as instructed, a little more composed but still very frightened of the repercussions of her dispensing errors, and he realised she was more concerned about that than about the fact that she was going slowly and inexorably blind.

'Lenny Price is OK,' he was able to reassure her, 'and Elly's ear's better, so I don't think you need to worry. It's not incompetence or carelessness, it's a medical problem. Now, you were saying on Friday that you find it's worse in some lights than others,' he said, and she nodded.

'The cupboard at the bottom, with the methadone and temazepam, is very dark, and the methadone was virtually finished. There was only the tiniest dribble in it, so I used the next bottle. They seemed just the same—I can't believe I didn't check the label more closely, but the bottles were identical and I just assumed we'd got more than one on the go.'

'Perhaps we should look into positioning them differently,' he said, 'but don't worry. That's another matter. I'm only concerned now with your health.'

To start with, he looked into her eyes with an ophthalmoscope, but it wasn't really conclusive. 'I can't really see clearly enough to diagnose anything,' he said, 'so I want to refer you to a specialist who can have a closer look at your eyes and find out if it is macular degeneration or some other condition. If it is, it means that the part of your retina responsible for your central vision is starting to fail, for one reason or another. There are two types of macular degeneration, wet and dry, and he'll probably inject some dye—fluorescein—into your veins and look into your eye to see which sort it is. That will help him decide what form of treatment, if any, you can be given, but I have to warn you, Patsy, there may not be anything very much that can be done to improve it, although there are new treatments being developed all the time which may be more effective at halting the progress of the disease.'

'So will I go blind?'

'Probably not. If it is macular degeneration, and I'm fairly certain it is, you'll gradually lose more and more of your central vision, although it can be a very, very slow process, and you'll usually retain your peripheral vision so it's more frustrating than anything. I'm really sorry.'

She shook her head as if to clear it. 'I knew something was going on, but I can still read, in the right light. I suppose that will go.'

'Eventually, probably.'

'Oh, dear. I do so love to read.' She sighed and gave him a shaky smile. 'Still, it could have been so much worse. Are you going to press charges against me?'

'Press—? Absolutely not, Patsy, but we may have to consider what you can do in the surgery so no vital mistakes of any sort are made because you haven't been able to read something clearly.'

She shook her head. 'No. I can't see well enough to be safe, Dr Sutherland, not doing such important work. I couldn't bear another mix-up. I'll leave. I'm sixty-two. It's time I went. I'll just take up knitting. I can do that without looking, and there's always the radio and talking books when it comes to that. I'll manage, don't you worry about me.'

And she went out, leaving him frustrated because there was nothing he could do to help her. Or, at least, not enough. He'd hand her care over to the specialist and hope there was something he could do to slow or halt the progress of the condition.

His surgery finished, he tapped on Jane's door and filled her in on the consultation with Patsy.

'Poor woman. Still, it explains a lot—not least her short temper. She's obviously been worrying about this all alone for ages. I wish she'd said something, but at least there weren't any fatal consequences.' She looked up at him and smiled. 'So—how was the wedding?'

'Lovely,' he said, and didn't bother to tell her just how lonely and frustrated he'd been ever since. Still, he'd get over it. He'd have to.

July moved into August, and Maisie found things were getting harder. Standing to operate, struggling to lift a reluctant horse's hoof and staying bent over to do a flexion test in a lameness assessment—heavens, just reaching her own feet—all of them started to become irritatingly difficult.

And James was being even more difficult.

Well, he wasn't, but she realised she wanted more from him than he was giving her, and she was frustrated and discontented because of it and that annoyed her, because it should have been the happiest time of her life and it wasn't.

She felt increasingly alone as the time of the baby's birth drew slowly nearer, and although she was really looking forward to meeting her little one, she was growing more aware of how much of the experience she wanted to share with James.

Instead, she shared it with Kirsten, who was itching to get her hands on the nursery.

'I haven't got a nursery,' Maisie said, laughing, but Kirsten was adamant.

'You'll need a nursery.'

'Not until it's born and I know what sex it is,' Maisie said, but it was nothing to do with the sex, and everything to do with not tempting fate. Like she'd felt with the house, she was still waiting for someone to tell her it was all a mistake and she wasn't having a baby after all.

She got round the problems at work easily enough. She sat to operate, and Jenny took over the equine and other large-animal work, and Pete helped her when necessary.

'So I just get to do the teeth trimming on the guinea pigs and all the cat spays,' she grumbled good-naturedly, but in fact she was grateful, because she didn't want to take any risks with her precious cargo.

David was getting better slowly but surely, and would be back by the time she needed to go on maternity leave, hopefully, especially if she worked to quite near the end.

Then she went to her antenatal class for the first time, held by the midwife in the health centre premises, and it dawned on her that she was the only one there without a partner.

Not that it mattered for the first few weeks, but during the last two classes, they were told, their birth partners should be present.

She bumped into James on the way out, and he asked how it was going.

'OK. I don't have a birth partner, though, which could make it awkward next week,' she told him, and she wondered if she sounded as forlorn as she felt. 'I suppose I could always strong-arm you into it.'

'Except that you'll probably give birth when I'm the emergency doctor, just for maximum nuisance value,' he said with a wry grin.

He sounded so reluctant she shook her head. 'Don't worry. I'll ask Kirsten, although she faints if she cuts herself. At least I'd know you wouldn't faint or do anything stupid, but you're right, you'll probably be busy and it needs to be someone I can rely on.'

But Kirsten threw up her hands in horror. 'Hell, no! I don't even want to be there when *I* give birth! Sorry, kiddo, you'll have to find someone else.'

Kathy, the head vet nurse? They didn't really have that sort of relationship. Ann, David's wife? Ditto. In fact, she didn't have that sort of relationship with anyone, she realised.

Oh, well. She'd manage. She went to the class alone.

One by one, they introduced their husband or partner, except for one woman whose mother was going to be with her. Then Eileen looked at Maisie.

'Who's going to be with you when you give birth?'

She lifted her chin and was about to announce that she was doing it on her own when a voice behind her said, 'I am.' She turned, her eyes widening, just as James strolled towards her with a lazy grin and sat down cross-legged beside her on the floor mat. 'Sorry I'm late—I was held up in surgery.'

Eileen opened her mouth, shut it again and smiled a little vaguely.

'Right. Well, at least I'll know you understand the principle of childbirth, Dr Sutherland,' she said, and then started talking about pain control in labour and the role of the partner in helping to alleviate it. The other pregnant women, many of whom saw James for their routine antenatal care, gradually stopped staring at James and Maisie with speculative gleams in their eyes and paid attention to what Eileen was saying.

And then they had to practise it, and Maisie found herself lying down as James tried each technique on her in turn.

Effleurage. Light, stroking movements over the skin, his warm palm gliding over her abdomen, soothing and restful. Back massage, with the heel of his hand firmly rubbing in the small of her back, easing the ache that was always there these days. Acupressure points for pain relief, used in shiatsu—between the thumb and first finger, for instance—and all the time his hands on her, the strong, supple fingers finding tight spots and soothing them away.

It was wonderful, she thought, relishing the feel of his hands on her body. If she closed her eyes, she could almost imagine that she wasn't pregnant and he was just touching her, the gentle, subtle movements of his massage a prelude to love-making.

But it wasn't. It was a vital part of preparation for the birth of her baby, and she needed to concentrate on it so she was ready when the time came.

But what if he was only here for this class, and not for the real thing? Would she be able to cope without him? And why was he here? She'd asked him last week, and he'd seemed so reluctant. What had changed his mind?

'Are you OK with this, really?' she asked him softly as they put the mats away at the end, and he grinned at her.

'I wouldn't miss it for the world.'

'People are going to talk,' she warned him, but he just flashed that grin again and shrugged.

'I've told you before, I'm not ashamed of you, Maisie. If they want to talk about us, let them talk. It's nobody's business but our own.'

'What changed your mind?'

Something flickered in his eyes, but he blanked it out. 'I wondered what kind of a friend would let you go through it alone,' he said after a moment. 'I didn't like the answer. So here I am.'

She swallowed and turned away. So, just a friend, then. Funny how much that hurt. 'I'm very grateful,' she said, knowing that, whatever the reason, she needed his support as much as she needed air to breathe. 'Will you be OK for next week? Because if you're busy, I'll quite understand.'

'Of course. I said I'd be here for you, Maisie, and I meant it,' he said, and she felt silly and ungrateful because she wanted more than he was prepared to give her, and that was just unrealistic. She should content herself with his friendship and not try and reach for the stars.

Knowing her, she'd just fall flat on her face.

The following week, he was back, slipping in just after the start again and taking his place beside her.

'Hi. How's it going?' he whispered, and she smiled.

'Fine.'

'Your timing's perfect, Dr Sutherland,' Eileen said with a smile. 'I want to talk about alternative positions for giving birth, rather than lying down on your back, which closes the pelvis, and you'll need your partners for this. Right, could you all stand up, please, nice and slowly, and face each other?'

And the next thing Maisie knew, James was standing in front of her, and she had her arms around his neck and was squatting, hanging on his neck, opening her pelvis to allow the baby to pass through more easily, and his hands were on her sides, helping to support her.

How could she be hanging there on his body and yet feel so supported, so secure, so...safe?

They practised other positions, squatting, leaning, kneeling—all of them involving her in touching his body in some way, feeling the support of his arms around her, the solid comfort of his chest, the sheer power of his legs braced around hers.

It suddenly all seemed very real, and she tried to imagine what it would be like to face childbirth without him.

Awful. She needed him, in so many ways, and not just for the birth, and if he kept on holding her like this she was going to break down and cry.

Don't think about it, she told herself, and after what seemed like for ever the class was over. James seemed as glad to get away as she was.

'Right, well, good luck, everyone,' Eileen was saying. 'I'm sure I'll see you all soon in clinic, either before or after your deliveries, but, remember, what do you have to do?'

'Breathe through the contractions!' they all chorused, and laughed and filed out.

Maisie felt James's hand on her back, ushering her through the door and walking her to her car.

'I'll be round shortly to walk the dogs,' he said, and she nodded. She was finding walking harder than ever now, because the join at the front of her pelvis was softening and the see-sawing movement of walking made it ache.

Only three weeks to go, she thought as she got home, and it occurred to her that she hadn't yet packed her case or bought anything for the baby.

She was still at work every day, although it was mid-October now. So close, she thought, and felt a flutter of panic. Still, it was the weekend, she could rest and recharge her batteries a bit.

She went upstairs to the bathroom, and glanced out of the window. James had taken the dogs and was heading down the lane. She watched him for a moment. It was getting dark, and he would only be able to go a short way before the light failed completely, so he'd probably only take them on the roads. Still, at least the heat had passed, finally, the Indian summer coming to an end with a spell of much-needed rain.

She lingered at the window for a minute, then was about to turn away when she heard the unmistakable screaming of a panicking horse. She stared through the gloom but she couldn't see anything. She knew where it was coming from, though. Anna's ponies at the end of the lane—and unless she was very much mistaken, one of them was in serious trouble.

Without thinking, without hesitation, she ran downstairs, flung open the door and drove down the lane. It was quicker than walking in her condition, and there was no time to lose...

CHAPTER TEN

HE COULDN'T believe it.

James had been heading off with the dogs when he heard what sounded like a horse screaming. He'd gone back to investigate, and had nearly been run over by Maisie's car skidding to a halt outside the field.

'Put the dogs in the run and come and help me,' she yelled, clambering awkwardly over the fence and running across the field.

He did no such thing. He shut them in her car, followed her over the fence and reached the far side of the field just in time to see her grabbing a horse by the head collar and dragging it away from a gateway.

'Go on, go away!' she yelled, hitting it on the rump, and it cantered off, leaving his field of vision clear.

And what he saw made his blood run cold.

A horse had reared up and got its foreleg caught between the gate and post at the hinge end, and it was struggling violently to free itself. But that wasn't what disturbed him. The thing he found most shocking was the image of Maisie, eight and a half months pregnant, sitting on top of the gate and trying to calm the panic-stricken horse, attempting to pull the hoof up and free it all at the same time.

'What the hell are you doing?' he yelled as she

hauled up on the hoof once more, and she turned and glared at him.

'What does it look like? Don't just stand there, James, come and help.'

'No way! It's crazed with pain, Maisie. It'll kill us both!'

'Rubbish,' she said, sliding down off the gate into the other field and grabbing the horse's head collar again. 'Are you going to help, or are you just going to stand there and watch it tear its hoof off?'

'You're mad,' he said, but he realised there was nothing he could do to stop her. She was utterly focussed on the horse, trying to stop it making the injury even worse. 'How about a sedative?' he suggested, but she shook her head.

'It won't work in time. We have to free it. I want you to lift the gate off its hinges.'

He stared at her for a fraction of a second, but, realising the only way to get her out of there was to free the horse first, he grasped the gate and heaved. The horse screamed again and threw itself backwards, but with another massive wrench the gate came off its hinges and the horse was free.

Incapable of gratitude, it wheeled round and lashed out. James grabbed Maisie and dragged her through the gateway and up against his chest, shielding her with his body. 'Are you all right?' he asked, his heart hammering in his chest, but she gave him a scathing look and shrugged him off.

'Of course I'm all right. It missed me by miles.'

He let her go, searching her eyes in the gathering gloom, and she pushed him aside impatiently and went back into the field after the horse.

'Maisie, get out of there. That's an order,' he said, his fear for her making him forget, foolishly, about her independent streak. She threw him a black look over her shoulder and carried on walking.

He tried again. 'If that horse lashes out again it could kill you or the baby.'

'It won't lash out again.'

He didn't believe that for a moment, and he ploughed on relentlessly. 'If you don't care about yourself, at least have the common sense to look after your unborn child.'

She stopped then, but only to turn and glare at him once more. 'Yes, *my* unborn child,' she said, her voice coldly furious. 'Remember that. It's *my* baby, James, not yours. Just because you're going to be my birth partner doesn't give you any rights over me, so you might bear that in mind when you're throwing your weight around. I know what I'm doing, and if you've got nothing useful to offer, then back off and leave me alone. I'm not a complete idiot.'

'You could have fooled me,' he growled, stunned by the ferocity of her attack. 'Are you coming out of there, or do I have to come and get you?'

'Are you deaf? Watch my lips, James. I said back off. There's an injured horse in this field, and I intend to catch it and treat it. If you don't want to help me, feel free to leave.'

But he wasn't free. He couldn't leave her, because she'd get herself kicked and trampled and he'd never be able to live with himself. So he stayed, and helped her catch it and lead it, hobbling on three legs, over to the fence where the lights from her car would illuminate its foreleg well enough for her to see the injury. He passed her things through the fence in grim-lipped silence until she was satisfied that the limb wasn't broken and she'd done all she could.

And then a car pulled up and a woman leapt out. 'Maisie? My God, what's happened?'

'Oh, hello, Anna, I'm glad you're here. It's OK. Bruno got caught in the gate but I think he's all right.' She straightened up, wincing a little, and met James's eyes defiantly.

'We'll be all right now if you want to go.'

He didn't. He wanted to drag her away from the horse and put her into a warm bath and rub her back, and hold her close and tell her how his heart had nearly stopped when he'd seen the horse lash out, but he couldn't, because, as she'd been kind enough to point out, he had no rights over her.

'Feel free to leave,' she'd said. Well, now he was, so he took Tango from her car and walked the short distance to his home, his heart still pounding and her words echoing in his ears.

My baby, not yours.

'How about *our* baby, Maisie?' he whispered, and felt the sharp sting of tears in his eyes. Damn. He was an idiot to have expected anything else, after all she'd been through. He poured himself a small shot of single malt with hands that shook uncontrollably, and downed it in one.

She could have been killed. She, and the baby that wasn't his, snuffed out just like that by a pain-crazed horse out of control.

'Bloody little fool,' he muttered, the tears scalding his eyes, and he blinked them away angrily and went upstairs to his bedroom. He could see the field from there, and he watched her as she finished off and then drove slowly home up the lane.

He ought to go round and check on her, he thought, but she'd only bite his head off. What she probably needed more than anything now was rest. He'd leave her alone. That was what she'd asked for, and it was the least he could do.

Great theory. He kept it up for an hour, in which time he glowered at the bottle of malt but resisted it and had coffee instead, but then his concern for her overrode his reluctance to interfere where he was so obviously not wanted, and with a growl of self-disgust he yanked open the door, to find her there on the step, a soft bag in her hand and her eyes filled with pain.

'James? I'm sorry. Can you take me to hospital? I think I'm having the baby.'

And as she stepped inside, her eyes widened and she looked down at the spreading pool of amniotic fluid at her feet.

'I think you could be right,' he said gently. Putting aside his own pain, he drew her into the kitchen, took off her coat and sat her down at the table his great-grandfather had won at cards. He crouched in front of her and took her hands in his, and noticed they were trembling.

'I'm all wet,' she said, sounding astonished.

He felt his mouth twitch. 'You are,' he agreed, but he was relieved to see that the amniotic fluid was clear and there was no blood or meconium in it, and no odour.

He'd been reading up on his midwifery since she'd asked him to be her birth partner, and it had all come back to him. Not that it was ever very far away, but it didn't hurt to brush up.

'How frequent are your contractions?' he asked, and she looked puzzled.

'Frequent? I don't know. I thought they were Braxton-Hicks'. I've been having them for days—weeks.'

'And have they changed?'

'Yes,' she said wryly. 'They hurt now.'

Just then she gasped and her eyes widened, and he looked at his watch, then reminded her to breathe, slowly and steadily, then more lightly as the contraction strengthened, then deeply again as it faded.

'Wow,' she said, her eyes slightly glazed. 'That was amazing. The breathing worked.'

'Good.' He kept an eye on her face as he retrieved his shoe from behind the sofa cushion where Tango had hidden it earlier, then started hunting for the other, but before he could find it she had another contraction.

'That was two minutes,' he said, and as realisation dawned he abandoned his search for the shoe. There was no way Maisie was going anywhere tonight.

'What are you doing?'

'Phoning Eileen. I'm sorry, Maisie, you're having this baby here, whether you like it or not. There isn't time to move you. Your contractions are too close together and I daren't risk taking you.'

'Here?' She felt panic rise in her chest. 'But I have to get to hospital,' she said. 'The baby's not due yet. What if something goes wrong?'

His mouth tightened. 'We'll just have to make sure

it doesn't, and you're thirty-seven weeks. That's fine. It's perfectly viable without support by now.'

'Are you sure?'

He crouched down in front of her again, the phone in his hand, and looked steadily, reassuringly, into her eyes. 'I am a doctor, Maisie. I do know what I'm doing.'

She looked away, suddenly ashamed because of the way she'd spoken to him in the field, but it had only been because she'd been afraid, both for herself and for the baby, and she'd known he was right.

'I'm sorry I yelled at you,' she said, looking back at him, and hurt flickered in his eyes before he masked it with a smile.

'Forget it. Eileen? Hi, it's James Sutherland. Look, Maisie's gone into labour, and she's progressing fast.' He was silent for a moment, listening, then his eyes flicked to Maisie's and away again. 'No, I haven't examined her, but her contractions are two minutes apart and her membranes have ruptured. No, that's what I thought.'

Another silence punctuated by cryptic remarks, and then he put the phone down slowly and looked at her, his eyes assessing.

'Is she coming?'

'She can't. She's at another delivery—the woman from your class who wasn't there tonight. She's about to give birth, and Eileen can't leave her.'

'So what about me?' she asked, not liking the sound of that one bit. The panic escalated. 'Who's going to deliver me?'

'Apparently I am.' He gave her one of those quicksilver smiles of his, but it didn't quite reach his eyes. 'You've got me, Maisie—all to yourself.'

He was a doctor, for God's sake! He knew what he was doing. He just had to call on his professionalism and get on with it.

'Stay there,' he ordered, as if Maisie was going anywhere. He ran out to his car and brought in his bag and a delivery pack that he kept in the boot for emergencies.

'I've had another one,' she said, and he wondered if he had time to get her upstairs, never mind to hospital.

'Come on, I'm taking you up to bed,' he said.

'Finally,' she said, and for a moment he wondered what she meant. No. Crazy idea. She'd told him to go to hell not two hours ago.

He took her to his room and covered the bed with clean towels and another sheet, then covered it all with the plastic-backed paper sheet that was in the pack.

'Right. You need to get out of those clothes,' he said, shooing the dog out and closing the door. He could be professional, he told himself as he helped her undress, he could—but when the last garment came off and she stood in front of him, naked and very gloriously pregnant, a huge lump the size of a house jammed in his throat and he could hardly speak.

She was beautiful. Beautiful and ripe and—bruised, for heaven's sake.

There was a mark on her hip, blue and purple, just starting to come out, and she looked down at it in astonishment. 'What's that?'

'I don't know, but it's hoof-shaped,' he said meaningfully, and the urge to shake her was only marginally overwhelmed by the urge to take her in his arms and crush her to death.

He did neither. Instead, he led her to the bed and helped her climb up on it, then threw her a clean T-shirt from his drawer. 'Put that on so you don't get cold,' he ordered, and went and washed his hands. Out of habit he snapped on rubber gloves, then took a steadying breath.

'I have to examine you, Maisie—make sure everything's all right.'

'OK,' she said, but her voice was tight and she didn't meet his eyes.

That was fine. He didn't want to meet hers either, because if she saw what was in them she'd probably run a mile. She'd told him exactly where he stood earlier, and now was not the time to get into how he felt about her.

'You're almost fully dilated,' he said, and as he sat down on the bed beside her, her eyes widened and she grunted.

'I've got to push,' she said, her voice urgent, and she started to struggle up from her sitting position.

He held her still with firm, gentle hands. 'No. Not yet. You're nearly there, Maisie. Just hang on.'

'But I need to push.'

'No, you can't. Not yet. You'll damage your cervix and hurt the baby.'

'The baby, the baby, always the baby!' she yelled, kneeling up and glaring at him. 'What is it with you and this baby? You've spent my entire pregnancy telling me what I can and can't do because of the baby!

Don't pull the horse out of the river, don't lift the dog onto the table—what about me? What about not doing things because they'll hurt *me*?'

'But I said—'

'Oh, you say all sorts of things, but I'm sick of listening! I'm sick of hearing you being reasonable! Do you have any idea how frustrating and hurtful it is being in love with you and knowing that you just think of me as a pregnant *friend*?'

She spat the word as if it was poisonous, and he stood there, his mouth open in shock, staring at her in awe as she continued to harangue him.

'When I met you, I thought you were gorgeous. Then I realised you're wonderful as well, and I stupidly went and fell in love with you. But you never meant me to, did you? You were just being kind, looking after me, because that's all that's in your job description—looking after Maisie. Well, to hell with looking after me! I don't want you to look after me. I want you to love me, to want me, not have to put rubber gloves on before you can bring yourself to touch me!'

She ran out of breath and slowly, deliberately, James stripped off the latex gloves and dropped them on the floor.

'Marry me,' he said, and she stopped dead in the middle of another tirade and stared at him.

'What did you say?'

'I said marry me. I love you, Maisie. I've been in love with you since you yelled at me about Tango, or maybe even earlier, since you got lemonade all down your front and blushed when you realised your T-shirt had gone transparent. I don't have to wear gloves to bring myself to touch you. I've spent the last five months keeping myself firmly in check because I find you so beautiful and so desirable. I want you, Maisie, more than you could ever imagine—you and your baby. I want to marry you, and have a family with you, and grow old with you—if you'll let me.'

She sat down with a plop on the bed, her labour temporarily forgotten. 'You love me?' she said, her face stunned, and he reached out a fingertip and lifted her chin, closing her mouth.

'Yes,' he said softly. 'I love you.'

And because there didn't seem to be anything else as urgent to do, he drew her into his arms and kissed her.

Seconds later she broke away, her eyes widening.

'Can we talk about this later?' she panted. 'It's just— I really do need to push now.'

She gave birth twenty minutes later, to a lusty, squalling, healthy little girl, and James lowered Maisie to the old bed in which generations of his family had been born. Lifting the T-shirt out of the way, he laid the baby against her breast. Instantly she turned her head, rooting for the nipple, and found it, latching on without hesitation. It was the last straw for him.

'Congratulations, Maisie,' he said unsteadily. 'You've got a beautiful baby daughter.'

She stared down, her expression rapt, and he moved away, giving her room to meet her baby in private. The love on her face was more than he could take, and he turned away, staring blindly out of the window and across the dark, windswept marshes.

She hadn't answered his question, he realised. He still didn't know if she'd have him, if she'd marry him.

'James?'

He turned, meeting the amber eyes still filled with love, and she smiled and held out her hand to him. 'Come and say hello to her,' she said, and he walked back to her, his legs shaking like jelly, and sat down beside her before they gave way.

'Hello, baby,' he murmured, touching her palm with one finger and feeling that wonderful response as the tiny little fingers gripped his fiercely and hung on. Then he lifted his head and met Maisie's eyes again. 'Well done,' he murmured. 'You did really well.'

She was still smiling, her eyes shining with love and happiness. 'I think we make a pretty good team,' she replied, then he saw doubt flicker in her eyes. 'At least—I think we do. What you said earlier…'

'About marrying you?'

She nodded. 'Did you…' She swallowed. 'Did you mean that, or were you just cheerleading?'

He chuckled softly and, hitching himself up on the bed beside her, drew her into his arms. 'Cheerleading? No, Maisie, I wasn't cheerleading. I've never been more serious in my life.' His smile faded. 'I meant every word. I love you, my darling. I love you, and I can't imagine life without you, but the choice is entirely yours.'

Relief flooded her eyes. 'Then—yes, please,' she said, a smile blooming on those beautiful, kissable lips. 'I'd love to marry you. Besides, I think we should, don't you, for the sake of your professional reputation? Or do you intend to escort all your patients to childbirth classes? In which case I might have something to say about it.'

He laughed and hugged her carefully. 'I don't give a monkey's about my professional reputation, as far as you're concerned. There's nothing that having you in my life in any capacity will do but enhance it. I've told you over and over again I'm not ashamed to be associated with you. I'm proud of you, Maisie—proud and very, very much in love with you, despite your headstrong independence. And, no, I don't intend to escort all my patients to childbirth classes, so you can relax.'

She laughed, then her face creased slightly in concentration. 'I think I can feel another contraction,' she said, and he eased her out of his arms and stood up.

'In which case,' he said, 'I'd better finish this job.'

They looked up at Eileen as she walked in an hour later, bag in hand, and took in the scene at a glance.

'Better late than never,' James said with a lazy grin.

'Everything all right, Dr Sutherland?'

He smiled at Maisie, then looked back at the midwife. 'Yes. Everything's fine, thank you. Absolutely perfect.'

'And has he been looking after you all right, Maisie?'

Maisie returned his smile, her eyes still on her soon-to-be-husband. 'Absolutely. Looking after me is what he does best. In fact, he's so good at it, I'm going to let him do it for the rest of his life.'

And James, because he didn't want to be found derelict in his duty, bent over and kissed her again...

EPILOGUE

THEY were all clustered in the kitchen—her husband, his sister Julia and Julia's new fiancé, Ann with David, fully recovered now, Pete and Jenny, looking increasingly like an item, Jane and her husband Michael, Eileen, the midwife who'd arrived like the cavalry when it was all over—and Kirsten, sitting at the kitchen table with the baby in her arms, looking for all the world like a besotted godmother.

Funny, that, Maisie thought with a smile.

It had been a wonderful day. They'd decided to do it all at once, and so they'd had a double ceremony, their marriage and the baby's christening, because all the same people would be there and it seemed silly to have two ceremonies in quick succession.

There were others, too—Carla and Will, and a few of James's London friends, and old friends of hers from vet school—and it had been a wonderful day.

The dogs, of course, were loving it. They were wandering around under everybody's feet, vacuuming up the crumbs and looking hopeful, and Julia, absolved of any guilt for abandoning Tango and going to live in Australia with her new husband, was busy fussing over the dog and spoiling her rotten.

Suddenly an arm snaked round Maisie's shoulder and she found herself being steered out of the kitchen and into the old scullery.

'James!'

'Shh.' He pushed the door firmly shut behind him and drew her into his arms, and she went willingly, laughing up at him.

'What are you doing?' she asked, and gasped as he drew her harder up against his body.

'It's my wedding night. I've waited long enough to get you to myself.'

'James! It's only mid-afternoon and we're in the scullery!' she said with a little shriek, but he smothered it with his mouth, warm and coaxing, teasing at her senses until her body flowed against him.

Then he broke away. 'Come on,' he said, a wicked smile in his eyes, and she felt a bubble of laughter rising in her throat.

'Where?'

'The Lodge. We'll sneak round and go in the back way.'

'But I haven't got the key, and it'll be freezing!'

'No, it won't. I turned the heating up—and I've got the key.'

He dangled it under her nose, and together they crept out of the back door and ran round, scattering Helga and the now fully grown chicks as they dashed through the gate into the garden of the Lodge.

His fingers fumbled the key, and he swore softly and tried again, then stopped her as she went to go inside, scooping her into his arms and carrying her over the threshold. He lowered her to the ground, sliding her down his body so she could feel every intimate part of it.

'Do you remember when I did this after the wedding?' he said, his voice gruff, and she lifted her hand and cradled his cheek.

'Yes. I wished it had been our wedding, that it had been real. And you kissed me, but then you pulled away.'

His brow creased. 'I had to, Maisie. I wanted you so badly. Dancing with you—'

'Dance with me now,' she whispered, and led him through to the sitting room. She put on her favourite romantic CD, and then turned into his arms. 'Dance with me,' she said again, and with a ragged sigh he eased her closer, lowered his head and covered her mouth with his.

A lifetime, she thought dreamily. I've got him for a lifetime. And there was another life inside her, a life he didn't know about. She'd tell him later. Just now, there were other things to think about...

 **MILLS & BOON**

Pure reading pleasure

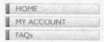 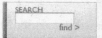

Visit millsandboon.co.uk and discover your one-stop shop for romance!

★ Choose and buy books from an extensive selection of Mills & Boon®, M&B™ and MIRA® titles.

★ Receive 25% off the cover price of all special releases and MIRA® books.

★ Sign up to our monthly newsletter to keep you up-to-date with all news and offers.

★ Take advantage of our amazing FREE book offers.

★ In our Authors area find titles currently available from all your favourite authors.

★ Get hooked on one of our fabulous online reads, with new chapters updated regularly.

Visit us online at www.millsandboon.co.uk

...you'll want to come back again and again!!

WEB/RS2

Romantic reads to
Need, Want

LOOK OUT...

...for this month's special product offer.
It can be found in the envelope containing
your invoice.

**Special offers are exclusively for
Reader Service™ members.**

You will benefit from:

- Free books & discounts
- Free gifts
- Free delivery to your door
- No purchase obligation – 14 day trial
- Free prize draws

THE LIST IS ENDLESS!!

*So what are you waiting for —
take a look* **NOW!**